CONTROL
SWITCH

CONTROL SWITCH

Leana Delle

iUniverse, Inc.
Bloomington

CONTROL SWITCH

This is a work of fiction. All of the characters, names, incidents, organizations, and dialogue in this novel are either the products of the author's imagination or are used fictitiously.

iUniverse books may be ordered through booksellers or by contacting:

iUniverse
1663 Liberty Drive
Bloomington, IN 47403
www.iuniverse.com
1-800-Authors (1-800-288-4677)

ISBN: 978-1-4759-7442-3 (sc)
ISBN: 978-1-4759-7450-8 (hc)
ISBN: 978-1-4759-7443-0 (ebk)

Library of Congress Control Number: 2013901974

Printed in the United States of America

iUniverse rev. date: 02/15/2013

For Jenesse for planting the seed of a dream

For my mother for always believing it would grow

xo

CHAPTER 1

"Presentation is everything. Look your best and achieve your best."

~Candace Bradford (from her new book, Total Mastery)

"So tell me, Candace. How would you describe yourself?" asked the budding reporter on the other end of the phone. I'd been weaving through traffic, sipping my latte, and praising Bluetooth technology when we neared the end of our interview. "Other than tall, dark and gorgeous that is." I rolled my eyes and glanced at my reflection in the rearview mirror.

"Well, I'd say strong-willed and always in control." The title of my book's *Total Mastery* for God's sake. Did she even read it? I heard her pause to jot down the obvious.

"And how do you think you'll feel when you're an international phenomenon?" she continued.

Okay, maybe I'd misjudged her. "Hard to say, but let's chat again a year from now and I'll let you know." A cocky response maybe, but I had no doubts about my pending boost in celebrity.

Calls from reporters, like this upstart from Portland, had doubled from out of State since the book release, and I embraced the idea of added exposure. I'd gained a significant following since my radio show had hit national syndication a year prior, but now I'd made my way into print. I could set my sights on the *New York Times* bestseller list.

"I love your attitude," she chirped. "And we love your show here in Oregon. I'm sure you're getting stopped in the streets now that you're becoming famous."

"Well, no more than usual here. You've got to remember that I've been on the Chicago airwaves for several years and a life coach for even longer. My face has been on a few billboards in my day, so Chicago's probably sick of me if anything."

"Oh, I highly doubt that," she teased. "One last question?"

"Shoot."

"Your dedication reads, 'To my greatest inspiration. I miss you.' Can you tell me who that's for?"

A small drop of coffee fell from my lip and plopped on the lapel of my white Armani jacket. "Shit!"

"Excuse me?"

"Oh, sorry," I said, peering into my purse for anything resembling a napkin.

I glanced up as the driver in front of me slammed on his brakes. I did the same and braced for an impact that never came. An orchestra of honks reached a crescendo from behind. "Traffic's insane," I added as a familiar shadow crept over me.

My mother. She'd been my greatest inspiration. She'd inspired me not to be like her—not to fail. Not to lose control and swan dive from the fifth floor balcony of a hotel room. Not to leave a seven-year-old kid behind to try and make sense of it all. And yes—despite it all—I missed her. I missed her like a lost limb.

"Well, I think I prefer to keep that name to myself," I said, adjusting my earpiece. "But I can honestly say that I wouldn't be who I am today without that influence."

The call ended, and I tossed the memory of my mother back where it belonged. Traffic warranted my full attention. I couldn't risk being late—not ever. I took side streets to avoid heavy traffic and left my latte tucked safely in the cup holder.

I drove up to Perkins Public Relations with five minutes to spare. I looked down again at the lapel and let out an audible sigh. With nothing but a flimsy camisole under my jacket, I'd have to make do. I yanked the bobby pins from my up-do, shook my hair out, and pulled it down over my shoulder to cover the offending stain. After a long deep breath, I strutted into the building with all the confidence of a full-fledged celebrity. When I reached the 14th floor office, the receptionist waved me through with a smile.

"Candace," said Geri Perkins from behind her desk. "Have a seat. I just need to wrap up this email."

I perched myself on the edge of her overstuffed chair and watched her pound the keys with authority. The glow of the computer screen reflected a pale blue in the lenses of her designer specs, and while her posture demanded attention, her suit guaranteed it. I'll bet she never spills coffee on her—

"Okay, done," she said, setting her laptop aside and adjusting her glasses. "You look great by the way. I've never seen your hair down like that. I think I like it." She didn't smile.

"Ah, yeah well. I like to have it down when I wear white. Shows off my chestnut coloring." I patted the ends of my hair over the lapel.

"Hmm. I've always wanted long hair myself," she said, fingering the bangs of her boyish auburn cut. "It gets any longer than two inches and I lose my professional edge." She smirked. "Now, let's get down to business, shall we?"

Geri moved her chair over beside mine and spread a calendar out on her desk. We eyeballed each other's heels and shared an approving nod.

"Now, before we get started, I just have to tell you how excited I am about this whole collaboration. If it wasn't for that little book of yours, I never would have left that wretched firm and gone out on my own. You gave me just the psychological boost I needed, and I'm thrilled that you agreed to come on as my first client."

"Hey listen. Working with someone who believes in the message? I'm the one that's thrilled."

She smiled and looked back at the calendar.

"So, I've brought you in here to share some good news. We're going to ramp up your exposure and really make you a household name. If I do say so myself, I'm working some marketing magic."

"Perfect," I said, inching my chair in closer. "Tell me more."

"National television spots, interviews, speaking engagements, you name it—and I've coordinated everything so that cities and dates correspond with your existing book tour."

"God," I said, peering down at her masterpiece. "You're amazing."

"Oh, and this is just the beginning. I'm going to work this whole thing into a frenzy, and we're going to kick it all off right here in Chi-town." She tapped her finger on the next day on the calendar.

"Tomorrow?" She must be kidding.

"Yes, tomorrow," she said. "I have a friend in the biz who owes me a favor, and I just found out that he has a small press gig set up in the morning for one of his clients who's launching a financial advice read. That shouldn't be hard to upstage." She raised her eyes toward the ceiling and back. "Anyway, I asked if we could get some time with the reporters. He made arrangements and we're down for the first 15 minutes. Short and sweet, but every interview counts, right?"

"They agreed to that?"

"Trust me. The favor I did for him pales in comparison," she said with an exaggerated wink. "Can you be there?"

"Ah, sure. I have a meeting scheduled, but . . ." My knee began to bounce at a steady pace. "I—I'm sure she won't mind rescheduling."

"Okay, good. It's going to take place in a small conference room at the Marriott on North Michigan: just a quick Q&A thing and some pictures. Mostly local reporters, but it's Chicago, right?" She smiled. "You can tell them all about the upcoming tour dates, talk about your life since syndication, and really plug the book."

I looked down at the schedule again. My finger ran down the list of cities and events: Seattle, Los Angeles, San Francisco, Dallas.

"Wait. Rockford? You've got me going to Rockford?"

"Sure do," she beamed. "You're speaking at the Rockford Social Club. I read in your bio that you were from there, so I made arrangements. Thought I'd sweeten the pot a little. Surprised?"

"Well, it's true my family's there, but . . ." My knee bounced a little faster and just a tad bit higher.

"Oh, come on. Don't you want to rub your success in a few hometown faces?" she asked. "Besides, if they know you, it's a pretty sure bet they'll buy the book. Think of it as a good business move." She patted my knee twice and pushed down hard to steady it.

Truth be told, I did want to rub my success in a few hometown faces, especially the ones who'd teased me when I'd started coaching fellow students in high school. They'd been merciless back then, and if any of them could afford my services now, I'd be shocked—but Rockford? I loathed Rockford.

Geri tapped her pen on the calendar to refocus my attention. "This will put you out of town longer than previously planned. Is hubby going to mind?"

"You mean Ross?" She'd met him twice and still couldn't remember his name. "I don't think so, but I'll go regardless. I'll do whatever it takes to make this book fly off the shelves. Besides, he's got a couple of high profile cases he's working on right now. He'll be plenty busy."

Would he mind? Considering our career obsessions, and meeting in bed over laptops most nights, why would he?

"And your producer at the station?"

"Karen? She definitely won't mind. We've already arranged the time off for the book tour, and I'm not scheduled to start taping live spots again for a few months. Besides, the exposure does nothing but boost ratings. She'll love this. We can work around it."

"Anything else that might stand in the way?" she asked, glancing at me over the top rim of her glasses.

"Well, I have my clients. I mean, I haven't taken on any new ones since I started in radio, but I still have my core group. They're supportive though, for the most part." I repositioned myself in the chair. "I'll video conference with them or make it up in other ways. It will be fine." I glanced back down at the schedule. "I'll make it fine."

"Okay good. So, tomorrow it is. You're on at ten in the morning, and bring a small stack of books for the photo-op. I'll be there too, so not to worry."

"I'm not worried. Actually, I can handle it on my own if you have other things to do." I've never liked co-pilots.

"What? My first client on her first interview? Wouldn't miss it."

"It's hardly my first."

"Well, you know what I mean. I'm just excited, so humor me," she smirked. "So I'll meet you there at 9:45 sharp?"

She folded the calendar and pushed her chair back.

"I'll be there," I assured her.

"Good." She rose and moved back behind the desk. "And I'll have my assistant email you all the details you'll need for the coming months: where you're going, what your schedule will be when you get there, who your contact people will be. You don't have to do a thing except get your game face on and pack your bags," she said. "Oh, and pick a few of your more powerful excerpts to spout off tomorrow. Maybe something from that chapter on health and wellbeing. One of my personal faves for what it's worth."

"Will do." Key paragraphs ran through my head vying for attention. I stood and extended a hand toward her.

"Oh," she squealed. "I almost forgot."

She opened her desk drawer and removed a small Tiffany box. Handing it to me, she added, "A celebratory gift."

"Geri, you didn't have to do that." I took the box from her outstretched hand.

"It's nothing, really. I just wanted to commemorate our partnership and show my gratitude. Perkins PR is counting on you as much as you're counting on us. We're in this together."

I removed the lid of the box to find an etched crystal globe on a red silk ribbon. Radiant beams of color shot from its North Pole as I lifted it toward the office lighting.

"Bright like your future, Candace Bradford," grinned Geri "See? You've got the world on a string."

I truly believed it, and that nothing—I mean nothing—could stand in my way. "I—I don't know what to say," I gushed.

Geri smiled and placed a hand on my shoulder. "You don't have to say anything. Just get out there and make us famous." She pulled her hand back, and her ring snagged on a piece of my hair. She grabbed the ends of it to untangle herself, and the brown stain on my lapel jumped out screaming for attention. I gasped and reached up with a jerk.

Geri shook loose. The globe slipped from my fingers and spun through the air between us. I lunged forward as it rotated out of reach. The North Pole headed south. The red ribbon swung out like the tail of a comet.

I threw a hand over my mouth and held my breath. The globe bounced three times on an area rug and rolled into the corner behind a plant. Without hesitation, I dropped to my knees and dove in to retrieve it. Grateful to find it intact, I held it high in the air for Geri to see.

"Jesus, Bradford," she remarked. "I hope for both our sakes that you handle your real world better than you just did that one."

CHAPTER 2

*"You can't control other people, but you can control
how they make you feel."*

I knew the perfect place to display my globe and keep it from further mishaps: from the rearview mirror of my red BMW Z4. Ross had given me the car for my thirty-fifth birthday that same year, and the ribbon matched the paint job like a bridesmaid's dress to shoes.

I opened the Tiffany box and lifted my symbol of success into place. I tapped the globe twice and watched it sway in the sunlight for a moment before starting the car and pulling into traffic. My future looked as clear to me now as my route home. I knew every turn to take in both cases, and I knew just who to share it all with. I commanded my Bluetooth to dial my favorite number.

"Y'ello."

"Hey, Aunt Josie. It's Candace."

"Baby girl. How's things in Pizzaville?" she asked, her thick Texas accent laced with sleep.

"Well, I guess you could say extra spicy. You working tonight?"

"Yep. Just finished my nap. Doin' an extra shift in the ER," she yawned. "Whatcha mean by 'extra spicy?' Do tell."

I headed north on St. Clair Street. "I've got national television and magazine interviews lined up like crazy, and they're all coordinated with the book tour," I announced. "My new PR girl is working out like a dream. It's exactly what I wanted."

"My Candace on national TV?" she squealed, banishing drowsy from the conversation. "My God, sweetheart, that's fantabulous!" Her dogs, Patches and Toby, barked in the background like little cheerleaders.

The sun caught my globe and made me smile. "I know, right? She pulled some strings to get me started in town tomorrow, but I'll be racking up air miles before you know it."

"Rockford on your list?" she asked. "I mean, I'll drive to Timbuktu to see my girl, but I'd love to exercise braggin' rights here, if you know what I mean."

"Yep. Rockford's on the list," I said, feigning enthusiasm. "I'm speaking at the Social Club."

Red taillights brightened in sequence ahead as traffic began to slow.

"Good God," she giggled. "Who in hell would have pictured me at one of those meetings? I'll go though, by damn. There's gotta be somebody at work who knows someone in that crowd, surely. Swear to God, I might just burst." Her voice began to crack.

"Don't start crying on me," I pleaded. Toby and Patches seconded the request.

"Okay, okay. I know control's the whole reason y'all got this in the first place. I'll play along," she remarked, gaining composure. I knew she didn't buy into my philosophy—always telling me not to get hurt when control meant avoiding that very thing. She just didn't get it.

"You think Dad will come out?"

Traffic hit a standstill.

"Well, you know your Daddy. Hates crowds—hates them worse than ever now that he's older, I suppose. Besides, you wouldn't get any time with him anyway. Not with all them people buzzin' around ya like flies on peach cobbler."

Men in orange vests converged on the intersection ahead.

"No, you're right. I just thought that since it's in town and everything . . ." A jackhammer pounded in the distance.

"I know Kiddles, but Bill at a social club? Think about it. He'd stick out like a tick on a hairless dog. Doesn't mean he won't be proud as punch though. You know that, right?"

"I suppose."

"You gonna call him and tell him the news?" she asked. "He'd be thrilled to hear from ya, all personal like."

"Well, I'm pretty swamped, and—"

"Uh-huh," she said. "Look, I know he bothers you, but people can't help how they are, and you can't let them get you down."

The orange vest brigade directed a gravel truck out of nowhere. "I know. I preach that in chapter four, remember?"

"Well, regardless."

A familiar silence filled the phone, the stalemate kind that meant the topic needed closing.

"Look. When I'm in town I'll drop by and see him, okay?"

"Okay, deal. And you're gonna spend the night with me while you're here too. No argument."

"No argument," I echoed. The gravel truck moved on, and a young man with a *Slow* sign stepped out to direct traffic like a chance of going fast had ever existed.

"In the meantime I'm struttin' like a peacock, baby girl. Couldn't be more proud if I tried. Have you told Ross?"

"No, not yet, but I'm calling him next," I said. "How's that make you feel, Queen Josie? You got the first call."

"Like a million bucks, Kiddles. Like a million bucks."

The call ended, and I inched my way past the construction and into a ray of sunlight. It peeked around a towering building and shot in through my front windshield. The globe and I basked in the warmth of it for a moment; then I gave a silent prayer of thanks. Thanks for my many opportunities and thanks for my supportive aunt. She'd always been my first call. She always would be. As I drove into the shadow of a neighboring building, I made the next one to my husband.

"Ross Simpson here."

"And Candace Bradford-Simpson here.

"Hey gorgeous. Miss me?"

"You know it. Where are you, sweetheart?"

"Stuck on I-90, and I have to meet my client in half an hour. Damned rush hour." His words sounded forced through clenched teeth.

I glanced down at the latte in the drink holder. "I know. I just drove out of construction myself. It sucks."

"There's an understatement."

The sky became laced with clouds. "Yeah, well . . . I have great news."

"What's that?"

"Geri's got me a whole list of interviews that correspond with my book tour. Television spots, magazines, you name it. Honestly, she's a whiz."

"Geri?" he replied, sounding distracted.

"My PR girl. Remember?" Honestly, what's with these two? "Oh—oh yeah. Sorry."

"So, that's cool, right?" I took a shortcut down Ontario Street. The sky grew a darker shade of gray.

"Where are you right now?" he asked.

"Did you hear what I just said?"

"Yes, I heard: totally cool. Now where are you?" he repeated.

A cyclist whizzed past my passenger side window causing me to jump.

"I'm downtown. Why?"

"I need the Peterson file before morning. Stop at the office and grab it for me? I thought I'd have time, but this . . . Hey! Watch where you're going," he hollered. "Damned drivers."

I paused to allow him a further rant. He refrained, so I continued. "I guess I could, but—"

"Oh, and my navy suit at the dry cleaners? I'll need that too. Please, baby?"

"Ross," I barked.

"What?"

"The promo tour."

"What about it?"

"I'm just excited, that's all. Aren't you excited for me?" I took a drink of the latte. The coldness of it somehow surprised me.

"Yes, Candace. I'm excited for you. Congratulations. Is that what you want to hear?" "More or less." More to be specific.

"Look, it's all great and I'm thrilled," he conceded. "Honestly. It's just been a rotten day and I have a lot on my mind right now, you know?"

"Yeah, yeah. I get it," I said, wondering why his rotten days seemed to be growing increasingly more frequent.

I stopped at a red light and watched a young couple cross the intersection holding hands. The young man's eyes seemed full of adoration, and I remembered that same look from Ross when we'd first started dating.

"Listen. Things will lighten up soon and we'll celebrate," he said. "Why don't we extend the fund-raiser trip to New York next month? We can stay over a few extra nights and do it up right."

"Shit," I muttered, "the fund-raiser."

"What do you mean by, 'shit, the fund-raiser?'" His teeth sounded clenched again.

"Well, it's just that I'll be out of town for longer than expected now. The whole schedule's mapped out, and—"

"Are you shitting me?" he asked. "Come on, Candace. Dad's entire firm is going to be at that thing. It's a networking free-for-all, and you're telling me I have to be the only stiff there without his wife?"

The clouds overhead banded together into one big blob.

"It's my life's dream, Ross. It's everything I've worked for."

"And what about what I've worked for, Candace? You ever think about that?"

Silence followed, and a soft rain began to fall. I glanced up at the crystal globe swinging from the rearview mirror. It had looked so much better in the sunlight.

CHAPTER 3

*"It is possible to balance careers and relationships. It just takes
creative scheduling and the practice of being mindful and present
when spending time with loved ones."*

The lamp in our bedroom shone down on the Peterson file.
Ross's navy suit hung like battle gear on the clotheshorse nearby.
I had just tucked myself into bed with my laptop when I heard
his key in the front door sometime after ten.

He stumbled a little, dropped his keys, and belched: tipsy
no doubt. He never met with clients without getting tipsy. He'd
switched from beer to scotch after college saying it gave him an
air of credibility, but I knew it had more to do with his father.
Dad owned the firm, so Ross drank what Dad drank. He'd have
funneled turpentine if he thought it would make the old man
happy.

He staggered up the stairs and tripped into the bedroom.
With his tie half undone, and his dark hair somewhat tousled,
he looked like a lethargic puppy after a play.

"Hey," he grinned, running his fingers through his hair.

"Hey back," I replied.

I began typing an email. He removed his jacket and turned to throw it on the clotheshorse. When he saw it occupied, he chose the floor instead. "Thanks for picking up the suit, baby."

He reached out to steady himself on the dresser. His hand brushed the Peterson file. "Jesus, Candace. You're a lifesaver."

"All in a day's work when you've got total mastery," I quipped, continuing to type.

He jumped toward me onto the bed, grabbed my laptop, and struggled to set it on his bedside table. I reached over him to take it back. "Hey wait. I just need to—"

He grabbed my waist to stop me. "You just need to lithen to me apologize is what you need to do," he slurred.

I pulled back to create a neutral space. The stench of happy hour hung between us like a sheet. "Okay, I'm *lithening*," I said. The imitation went unnoticed.

"Candace, I couldn't be happier for you, I really couldn't—and I admit to being a complete asshole on the phone today."

He took my hand in his. "Go on," I demanded. My foot rocked back and forth under the sheets.

"Well, I may be an asshole, but I (hiccup) I'm not an idiot. I see how hard you've worked for this. You make it look effortless, but I know that hasn't been the case. You deserve to have your book take off. I mean it."

He pulled me closer. Despite my impatience, the warm moisture of his lips on my cheek tingled to the tips of my pedicure.

"It's just that I had a really shit day (hiccup)."

And yet again, the conversation circled back to Ross. He rose to pace out the details, and my laptop beckoned.

"Dad's put a lot of pressure on me with this Peterson case, and so has Todd. He's the perfect lawyer after all, and he'd just love to see me fail."

His feet stood in one spot. His body swayed in circles around them. I folded my arms across my chest.

"Honey, you've got to quit comparing yourself to your brother. You'll drive yourself crazy."

The muscles in Ross's chiseled jawline tensed in rhythmic motion. He blinked like I'd gone out of focus. "Maybe if Dad didn't compare us all the time I wouldn't care. I've tried everything. I went to law school like he wanted; I married the perfect girl; I choke myself with this fucking tie every day." He yanked the thing off in a flurry and lost his balance pitching it across the room. He stumbled against the clotheshorse knocking it over. "Shit," he muttered, trying to steady himself.

The battle gear landed in a heap on the floor. He left it there. "What more does he want, for Christ's sake? I feel like Peter Lawford scurrying around after Frank and Dean."

A giggle escaped me. I cupped a hand over my mouth. "Go ahead—laugh. You're right to. I'm a joke (hiccup). What I wouldn't give to walk out of there for good and tell them to shove it."

I imagined a spotlight appearing out of nowhere with an accompanying drum roll. *Ladies and gentlemen—back for an unlimited engagement—Ross Simpson and Glenfiddich doing their same old routine.*

I sighed. "Well, maybe you can quit at some point. With Geri's help, I'm projecting huge sales on the book, and I've already got the contract for a second one. I'll be doing more speaking engagements too, so it's not out of the question. Maybe you could start work on that novel of yours."

His face grew weary. "What, and give them the thatith," he cleared his throat. "I—I mean *satisfaction* of calling me a quitter again? No siree."

He tripped a little removing trousers, then regained his balance. "They don't give a shit about me. All they care about is money—the godforsaken almighty greenback."

"Point taken." For the umpteenth time. "Now come to bed."

I patted the mattress beside me and forced a smile. I had to get those emails answered in the next hour or everything would fall behind.

He flopped back down on top of the covers still wearing his dress shirt and socks. "Can you wake me at six, pleathe?" he asked, burrowing into his pillow.

"Six it is." I kissed his forehead.

"I don't deserve you, Candace Bradford-Simpson." He looked sad somehow when he said it. "I really don't. You know that right?"

"Yes, dear," I placated. "Now get some sleep."

I retrieved my laptop as Ross faded off into Scotchdom.

*　　*　　*

My eyes popped open when the alarm went off at five. Ross didn't flinch. An hour later, with a few more emails under my belt, I brought him a cup of coffee and kissed his cheek. He rolled over and grinned.

"God, you're beautiful," he said. "Why don't you jump back in here for half an hour?"

I kissed him again—on the lips this time—and headed toward our walk-in closet to change. "Not this morning, sweetheart. I've got a big day ahead and I want to get a run in before it starts."

He stretched and let out a monstrous yawn. "Tonight maybe?"

I exited the closet in my workout gear. "Sure," I winked. "A definite maybe."

I grabbed my hairbrush from the dresser and made a quick ponytail at the back of my head.

"Hey babe, what about this fund-raiser thing we talked about? Can't you get them to reschedule or something?" he asked. "It's really important to me."

"Ross, I told you. The schedule's been extended and I've made a commitment. I just can't."

He threw his legs over the side of the bed, yawned again, and scratched his new growth of beard. I noticed some gray in it for the first time. "So, you're not even going to try?"

"It won't work. Between my clients and the promo stops, there's no place to reschedule it. If it were an emergency maybe, but—"

"Well fine," he said, standing to his feet still wearing his dress shirt and socks. "That's just fine."

"Don't be like that."

He walked toward the bathroom and turned before entering. "You know I can't go to this thing by myself, don't you? I can't be the only guy there alone."

"Can't you just explain to them that—"

"Candace, it wouldn't look right. It just wouldn't. You know what these things are like."

"Yes I do. They're painstaking and full of formal pleasantries. I really don't think anyone will mind if I'm not there."

Ross's face puckered. "Fine. I'll go. I have no choice but to go, but I'm not going alone." He walked into the bathroom and shut the door.

"Ross, I'm in no mood for this. I just said I can't be there."

"Oh, I heard that loud and clear," he hollered from behind the closed door. "But I'm still not going alone."

I knocked twice on the barrier between us. "Ross, please come out here, and let's discuss this like adults."

The door swung open, and he glared at me with all the warmth of an ice pick. "Look, if you can't be there, I'll take someone else."

"As if," I scoffed. A warm flush washed over my cheeks. "Like who?"

"Like Eunice Carrington from the office, that's who," he said storming past me. "She'd be *more* than happy to go."

He pushed past me and back into the bedroom.

My eyes followed him in disbelief. "Cleavage Carrington? You're going to take Cleavage Carrington to a fund-raiser? She's a complete idiot, Ross." I sighed. "I swear, sometimes you're certifiable. One minute you're Mr. Supportive, and then you're threatening to take an air-head to a social event to humiliate me." I turned and headed toward the stairs with him on my heels. "You think you're a joke now? Wait until she opens her mouth to that crowd and see where you stand. Honestly."

"Hey, I've seen people take friends to these things before if their spouses aren't available, and somehow I think the boys in New York would be more than happy to meet old Eunice."

I turned to face him on the stairwell. He reeked of smugness.

"Friends?" I asked. "Since when have you and Cleavage been friends? And besides, the old boys might *think* they're happy to meet her but the old wives won't be. And mark my words, Ross Simpson. If those high-society girls aren't happy, nobody's happy. If you're going there to network, I'd think very seriously about escorting Ms. Melons."

We continued our march to the main floor of the condo.

"Oh, like my reputation is what you're concerned about." He maneuvered his way in front of me. "Admit it. You're jealous."

"No, I'm not jealous, because she's an idiot." An extremely sexy idiot, and I didn't like it one bit. "Your reputation does concern me but so does mine. I don't need my husband flaunted all over the society pages with a bimbo on his arm; not with my book just taking off."

I twisted my way past him and into the kitchen to grab bottled water from the fridge.

"I know. You've got a whole new set of priorities now," he whined.

"Yes, I do. You knew this was going to happen, that I'd have to market this thing. That doesn't mean that you're not still a priority, Ross. I just have to focus my attention on this for a while. You understand that, don't you?"

I stared into his eyes as I twisted the lid from the water bottle and took a swig.

"You act as though you don't care if I take someone else."

"Look, last night you said you understood and that I deserved this. There's no reason in the world why you can't go to that thing alone. You're just bringing her up to annoy me."

He relaxed back. "Fine," he said. "You do what you need to do, and I'll do what I need to do. How's that sound?"

"It sounds unavoidable."

He turned and walked back up the stairs. I headed out the door and onto the elevator with the added annoyance of Eunice Carrington to fuel me on the treadmill.

He didn't mean any of it. I knew he didn't.

*   *   *

I called out Ross's name when I'd returned from my workout, to no reply. He'd left for the office, so I hit the shower trying to wash off regrets. We'd been struggling in our relationship for some time but we never questioned our love for each other. Busy lives, that's all: just caught up in busy lives. I vowed to make more of an effort regardless of our schedules, and with a renewed sense of commitment I prepared for the day ahead.

I arrived at the hotel at 9:45 sharp and waited in the lobby. Geri breezed in five minutes later with two cups of coffee in hand. She held one out toward me.

"Figured you'd take it black given that stain on your jacket the other day," she said winking. I cringed.

"I've had my one cup for the morning thanks, but—"

"Oh well then," she stated, shrugging her shoulders. "I guess I'll drink them both." She began surveying our surroundings. "I believe we're just down the hall here in the Lake Michigan room. Did you bring a few books?"

A box of hardcovers sat on the floor beside me. I tapped it with my foot. "Right here."

"Excellent," she said, taking a sip of one of the coffees. "Let's head that way and get set up."

I reached down and picked up the box. Geri strutted off down the hall like working a runway. I made an awkward attempt to catch up.

I followed her into a small conference room. No more than twenty reporters had gathered inside, and they all stood chatting on the periphery as the seats remained empty. A table with a single chair faced the crowd. A small microphone sat in the center of the table begging for attention. Geri moved toward it, set down the coffees and checked her phone.

"Okay, let's stack a few books up on here so that they can see the product," she remarked, patting the table's surface and gazing at the small group gathered nearby. "That is if they can keep their eyes off of you long enough to notice it." She nodded toward a young man to our left who gave me a once over. I shrugged.

"Where's the financial advisor?" I asked.

"I just got a text. They're prepping down the hall."

I lifted some shiny hardcovers out of the box and stacked them up beside the microphone. Geri took the top one and propped it up to face the reporters. She motioned for me to take my place in the chair then tapped the mike to check its readiness. When the successful taps had drawn everyone's attention, she began to speak.

"Ladies and gentlemen," her voice echoed over the loud speaker. "If you could please take your seats, we'll get started."

People started filling the chairs in front of me. I smiled and nodded as each made eye contact.

"Thank you so much for agreeing to spend a few minutes with my client today. Some of you are already familiar with Candace's work locally, both on the air and as a life coach, but her new book is now on the shelves nationally with a great initial response. I, for one, am a true believer in Candace's message, and I'm sure that the rest of the world will be too." She smiled down at me. "Please feel free to ask her a few questions," she said, before stepping aside.

"So, just to clarify: you're not Betty Hammond the financial advisor. Is that right?" asked a rather large, middle-aged woman from the back of the room.

"No, sorry," I said, bending in toward the microphone. "I'm Candace Bradford. The financial advisor will be here shortly, but I thought that . . ." I looked up at Geri with a dazed expression. She stepped back in.

"Ah, yes folks. I was under the impression that you knew of Candace being here today before interviewing Betty?" she asked.

The majority of heads nodded in understanding. "Yeah, we knew," said the young man, smiling again in my direction.

"Oh," replied the heavy set woman. "I guess I missed the memo."

Geri leaned back in toward the microphone. "Sorry for any confusion. Yes, Candace is available for a few minutes and then Betty will follow."

"So you're that radio billboard girl, then?" asked a young metro-sexual from the center row. "Married to that hot-shot lawyer in the society pages; am I right?"

"Well, I like to think of myself as much more than a radio billboard girl," I replied. "I consider myself a life coach above all, which is where the advice in the book comes from."

A young woman in the front row turned to face those in the back. "If you haven't heard her radio call-in show, you're really missing something. She's amazing."

"Well, I appreciate that," I said. "And at the risk of sounding immodest, there are some pretty powerful messages in the book."

"You don't look old enough to have the experience needed to help someone like me," added the larger woman followed by a chorus of laughter.

"Well, I'll take that as a compliment, but I started success coaching in high school. So really, I have about 20 years of experience. I've spent that time helping people control everything from careers and finances to health and relationships. I truly believe that it all comes down to the right attitude and focus."

A senior Mr. Skeptic raised his hand in the second row. I nodded to acknowledge him.

"Well, I lost my wife to cancer a year ago. You telling me that was her fault?" he asked.

"What I believe is if you control your environment, you can control your outcome. The results of my studies are all detailed in the book, and there are numerous testimonials. Once you've done a full inventory of every aspect of your life and can dissect the problem areas, you can—" My hands grabbed at my abdomen.

"You can what?" I heard the man ask.

"You can . . ." I whimpered. My words dropped away from me. A gripping pain tore through my insides like a serrated blade.

I reached out to steady myself knocking the microphone down with a thump. Copies of my book slid across the desk like dominos. My body shook. My heart pounded against my rib cage. Beads of sweat multiplied along my hairline. Numbness overtook my hands, and my legs went limp.

"Oh God," I gasped.

"What's happening?" screamed Geri.

I dropped to the floor conscious only of how the pain intensified with each picture a photographer snapped of me collapsing.

CHAPTER 4

*"Procrastination robs you of potential successes.
Control your time before it controls you."*

"You okay?" I could hear Geri pecking over me like a hawk on prey. "Candace, answer me."

Commotion dominated the background. Someone offered to call 911.

"No wait," added Geri. "Not until we know for sure she needs it. Candace!" she snapped, shaking my shoulders. "Are you all right?"

God, this can't be happening.

Another wave of pain steamrolled through me. I pulled my knees to my chest. Short, rhythmic breaths pulsed through my lungs, and my eyes squeezed shut. Then as fast as it hit me, the pain disappeared.

I took a stabilizing breath and tried to make sense of my surroundings. *Am* I okay? I felt around my abdomen. Severe pain to nothing: but why?

A mosaic of faces stared down at me as though in shock. I had to compose myself. I had to get control. "I—I think I'm okay," I said grabbing Geri's hand to help me up. "Just give me a minute." I wiped the sweat from my forehead.

Geri settled me back in the chair. "Okay, I think all is well folks," she announced. A glass of water appeared out of nowhere. She looked around the room at the ogling reporters then she leaned in toward my left ear. "Okay, we're going to get you out of here, then I'm going to do some serious damage control. You think you can stand up?"

I took a sip of water and blinked to focus. "Yes, I think I can."

Geri retrieved the toppled microphone to speak into it. For a brief moment my vision blurred, and I could see two of her. "Ladies and gentlemen, we apologize for this. I'm sure our girl will be just fine. I'm going to get her settled somewhere comfortable, and we'll get Betty out here for you."

Mr. Skeptic spoke above the crowd. "I wonder what chapter *that* control came out of." An uncomfortable silence followed. Geri appeared annoyed. She grabbed my arm. "Come on."

We headed toward the front lobby of the hotel. Geri's pace quickened with each step and I struggled to keep up. She led me to a plush chair by the window and plopped me down into it. "You going to live?"

"Of course I am." I placed a hand on my forehead and bent forward in the chair.

"Good. Now stay here and wait for me. I've got to talk to that damned photographer."

She headed off down the hallway. "Get my bag for me?" I called out. She waved a hand in the air to acknowledge my request.

I sat dumbfounded and stared down at the swirling greens and yellows in the lobby carpet. I decided that designers should design while nauseated to spare the queasy further suffering. I changed my mind when I imagined how bland the world would look if they did. Glancing up, I caught the concierge staring in my direction. He turned his gaze away from me, and I noticed the full length mirror to his right. A pale and bewildered version of me reflected back.

What the hell happened in there? I held my hands out in front of me with my palms down. A slight quiver rocked through them. I'd screwed it up. Thank God it had been a local interview with only a few people. Thank God it hadn't happened on television, but why had it happened at all?

Geri rounded the corner with books and bag in tow. She set everything on the floor and crouched down in front of me.

"Well, we wanted them to talk about you and they sure as hell are now."

"And the photographer?"

"He's promised not to post the pics if I pull some strings and get him and his sidekick an exclusive with an old client of mine."

"Can you do that?"

"Maybe, maybe not. We'll worry about that later."

I apologized until the words sounded empty. Geri conceded that I couldn't have helped it and said that she was just glad I was all right. I could sense her annoyance all the same. I'd let her down. I'd let myself down. Good Lord, I'd fallen down.

The flirting reporter sauntered around the corner and headed toward us. Geri stood and pulled me up with her. "Come on. Let's move before things get worse."

We made our way through the front door. When the fresh air hit us, I stopped and put a hand on the side of the building to steady myself.

"Now what?" snapped Geri, setting the box of books down on the sidewalk. She peered over my shoulder then scanned to her left and right.

"I just feel a bit shaken, that's all."

Her eyes came to rest on mine. She put her hands on her hips and let out a long sigh.

"I know you're annoyed," I said. "Just say it."

"Somewhat, yes: not exactly what I'd call a stellar start. The intent was to show your face, not fall on it."

"Look, I said I was sorry."

"And right after your spiel about controlling your wellbeing. Brilliant."

Thunder clapped in the distance, and I pulled my jacket collar up around my neck. Geri reached in her bag and pulled out a pack of Marlboros.

"Well, excuse me. If I'd planned the whole thing, I could understand why you're getting upset. As it stands, I'd appreciate it if you'd back off."

We maintained eye contact as Geri put a cigarette to her lips and lit it. Taking a long drag, she blew the smoke just over my head.

"Point taken," she said. Her expression softened. She placed a hand on my shoulder and inspected me like a crime scene. "Look, I know I can get pretty intense sometimes and I apologize for that. I just really need this, you know? I've busted my ass to get this company off the ground." She took another drag from her cigarette. "Seriously though, are you okay?"

The smoke made me more nauseous. "I think so. I mean the pain's gone, but it wasn't like anything I've ever felt before." I put a hand to my mouth and coughed.

"Was it stomach? Cramps? Bad bagel? What?"

"I don't know. It came in waves like excruciating cramps or something." I shuddered at the thought that it might return.

"You're not pregnant, are you?"

"No, definitely not. That's not it."

"Well, I suggest you get checked out. We can't afford to have you falling down—literally—during your speaking engagements. We're in too deep. If you screw this up, we'll both go down."

I swallowed hard.

She took one last drag from her cigarette and crushed the lipstick-stained butt into the sidewalk with her heel. "Well, what about a ride home?" she asked, putting the disaster behind her. "I can arrange a car, or call your hubby, or—"

"No, don't call Ross," I snapped. Geri raised a perfectly plucked eyebrow. "I—I mean, I'm fine to drive myself. He'd just get all bent out of shape. The pain's gone so why worry him?" She looked suspicious. "Really, I can handle this."

"Okay then. That's more like my little control freak." She lifted the box of books into her arms. "I'll take these back to the office for now and save you the lifting." She waved her hand at my middle and said, "Get all of this taken care of, will you?" She headed off down the street.

I made my way back to my car. The smell of smoke clung to me like a wet bathing suit. I got in and opened the windows.

My mind raced to make sense of the morning. Geri had a point though. I couldn't just ignore it, or could I? I mean it had come and gone. Maybe there was some minor explanation for it. If it wasn't for this damned schedule, I'd—

Chapter Four in Total Mastery: Putting off procrastination. The art of taking action.

I'd practice what I preached, that's what I'd do. Dial the number Candace.

*   *   *

I'd been going to my gynecologist, Dr. Jefferies, since I'd moved to Chicago for college. I'd never bothered getting a family doctor because I never got sick. And besides, I trusted him like family. When I called his office about the pain he agreed to fit me in at noon.

The receptionist (a new one) checked me in and asked me to take a seat in the waiting room. A half-dozen or so expectant mothers sat against the wall ready to bust. Every one of them took turns smiling at me with a seemingly knowing grin. My God, they think I'm pregnant.

My foot began tapping to the sound of magazine pages flipping in rhythm. Portraits of the doctors and their families lined the waiting room wall across from me. All perfect, all smiling, all in matching blue jeans and white starched shirts. I stood to get a closer look at them when Dr. Jefferies' nurse appeared through the doorway.

She smiled and nodded in my direction, then motioned me to follow her to an exam room. Once inside, she spared me the social chatter and went straight to checking my blood pressure. Perfect as usual: big shock. She then handed me a piece of paper with two arm holes in it and instructed me to leave it open at the back.

When she'd left the room I stood staring at the closed door for a moment sighing. One hell of a day so far, and now I'd have Sophie Blanchard to deal with. She'd been my client the longest and I'd had to reschedule our session for all of this nonsense. I changed into the paper gown and made a note on the hem—Flowers for Sophie. Maybe lunch at Vilbert's?

Dr. J. bounded into the room a few minutes later. "Candace. So good to see you." He washed his hands at the sink. "Now, what's this I hear about a pain you're having?"

"Well, I'm not having it anymore. I'm probably wasting everyone's time."

He walked toward the exam table and faced me. "You've never been a girl to waste time. Now, what happened?" he asked, motioning me to lie down.

"Felt like someone stuck their hand into me, grabbed at my insides, and yanked on them four or five times. It was horrible to be honest with you, but it went away completely after a few rounds."

He began pushing at every conceivable spot on my stomach. "Was it on one side more than the other?"

"More on the right side I guess, but it sort of spread across me like a wave. It came in waves."

"Does it hurt anywhere that I'm touching?" he asked.

"Nothing."

He called the nurse back into the room and positioned himself on a stool at the foot of the table. He donned gloves and performed an internal exam. The usual questions followed. Date of your last period? Anything unusual or out of the ordinary? Blah, blah, blah? The nurse left the room on completion.

"I think we should get an ultrasound to see if there's anything going on. It can't hurt." He ripped his gloves off and re-washed his hands.

"You think it might be something serious?" I asked, allowing my curiosity to get a word in edgewise.

He pulled a few paper towels down from their holder and turned to face me. "Could be a number of things, and it could be nothing at all but until I get some test results back, there's no point in speculating." He took my hand and helped me into a sitting position. "You of all people know not to waste energy on what-ifs." He grinned. Is he mocking me?

"When you say 'a number of things' what do you mean exactly?" The thought of an actual list hadn't crossed my mind.

"Could be a cyst, could be scar tissue. Again, it could be nothing at all."

"A cyst?"

"Like I said, let's not worry ourselves until we have the results back."

Could it really be a cyst?

"So, how's the book coming along?" he continued.

He's right. Worry never accomplished anything. "Great, actually. Promo tour scheduled."

"Good for you," he said, putting an end to the small talk. He handed me a piece of paper. "Give this slip to Brenda out front. She'll schedule your ultrasound, and we'll figure this all out. Don't you worry." He closed the door behind him leaving me to change out of my paper gown. I tore my note from the hem and stuffed it into my purse before heading to the front desk.

Brenda sat waiting to attack my day-planner. "We can fit you in at three o'clock this afternoon," she said.

"That won't work. I've already canceled one appointment today, and I can't—"

"Tomorrow morning then?" she asked, with her head cocked and eyebrows raised. She tapped her pen repeatedly on the surface of her keyboard.

"What time tomorrow morning?" I moaned.

"I can get you in as early as seven." Her pen stopped tapping. She snapped her gum at me instead. "That is if we're not inconveniencing you."

My iPhone beeped with an appointment reminder. "Shit, my one o'clock." I reached in my bag to silence it. "Seven's fine."

I turned to leave. "You're welcome," hollered Brenda, as the door shut behind me.

CHAPTER 5

"Panic doesn't accomplish anything. Remain calm and
focused when faced with difficult challenges."

Sunday mornings always inspired me, and this one had been no different. I'd already been up for several hours and had returned from a long, effortless run through the sleepy streets of Chicago. A peaceful day, by city standards, with a crisp see-your-breath kind of temperature in the air. Now I'd opened up every drape in the condo to let the light spill in.

Ross had long left to play golf with the boys, but not before we'd made love to the sound of birds awakening in the neighborhood. The argument had passed, and we'd vowed to be equally more supportive and not bring the stress of our daily lives home to each other. For me that included my recent episode of pain. There was no need to worry him over nothing. It had not returned, so I felt confident it had just been a minor glitch. An odd one, and poorly timed, but minor nonetheless.

I poured a cup of coffee and started planning my day. I'd spend it getting organized and rescheduling appointments. The extended time that Geri had added to my out-of-town dates had made things far more challenging, but I knew I could make it work. The excitement of the whole promo tour had begun to surface as I made my way up the stairs to the office. That's when the phone rang.

"Don't want to alarm you, Candace," said Dr. J.

"You're calling me on a Sunday?"

"Just in the office getting caught up." Feasible, I guess, since I'd been doing the same. "Whatever happened to weekends? Am I right?"

"A fine question." He replied. "You got a minute?"

"Sure. Good news I hope?" I asked, fully expecting to receive some.

"Well, good news in that there weren't any visible tumors on ultrasound."

I sat down in the office chair and smiled. "Good. I knew everything would be okay."

"But . . . there was a lot of free fluid in your abdomen."

"Fluid? You mean the umpteen gallons of water I drank before walking in there?" It seemed obvious to me.

"No, it's not *that* kind of fluid. It's *free* fluid in that it's freely floating throughout your abdomen where it doesn't belong."

I cradled the receiver on my shoulder and grabbed an elastic band from the top of the desk. I stretched it out between my thumbs. "I—I don't understand. Where did it come from?" I turned the chair to face the window.

"I'm not sure. Again, there's no obvious reason, so I think we should go in and find out what's causing it."

"Go in?" The elastic band slipped from my right thumb and snapped against my left hand. I pulled it back in pain.

"We need to do a laparoscopy," he announced.

Laparoscopy. Laparoscopy? What the hell's a laparoscopy? I spun the chair back around to face the door and stood in the middle of the office.

"Are you still there?" he asked.

"Yeah . . . yes, I'm here." I placed the elastic band around my left wrist and wandered down the hall toward the bedroom. "I'm just a little confused. What do you mean by laparoscopy?"

"It's an exploratory procedure; pretty routine, really." He cleared his throat. "Well . . . you'll need anesthesia, but I've done a million of them, and—"

"Oh. So, they're routine for *you* is what you're saying?"

He laughed. "Well yeah, routine for me. It's basically a way of me going in there to take a closer look around. A camera of sorts, but I can explain all of that to you later."

I entered the bedroom and sat down on the edge of the bed. "A camera?"

"Yes, a camera."

I glanced at our wedding picture on the bedside table. A young Ross and Candace smiled up at me full of hope. I ran my hand over the duvet cover and yearned for the safety of the arms that had held me only hours before.

"And this fluid: what *could* be causing it?"

"Actually, it looks more like the result of an inflammatory response of sorts. Like you had a peritonitis at some point that may have encapsulated itself. Could have actually happened when your appendix burst." The taste of bile rose in my throat. I caught myself holding my breath.

"I don't understand what you're saying. My appendix burst over 20 years ago."

Dr. J. sighed. "I know, I know. It's hard to explain, but these things can happen. Regardless, it looks like your fallopian tubes are dilated out as well. The only way I can know what's going on is to actually go in there and look."

My cell phone began ringing from the office down the hall.

"And Candace, we need to talk about potential problems."

"Problems? What kind of problems?" I snapped the elastic again against my wrist—harder this time, and on purpose.

"Okay. Worst case scenario, we'll need to do a hysterectomy."

I rose to my feet. "Excuse me?"

I shut the bedroom door on the incessant ringing of my cell phone from down the hall. I then plopped back down on the edge of the bed and caught my expression in the dresser mirror. I looked pale. I looked tired. I looked sick. I tore the elastic band off my wrist and shot it at my own reflection, missing it entirely.

"Listen, I may get in there and find more than we've bargained for, that's all I'm saying. It may all be perfectly straightforward, but if I find something suspicious I'd like your permission to remove it then and there. Otherwise I'd have to wake you up in the middle of it all and put you back to sleep to continue. Make sense?"

"No actually. None of this makes sense." I grabbed a pillow from the headboard and squeezed it hard against my gut. My body began a gentle rock, forward and back.

"I want you to take some time and process things, Candace. I know it's a lot. Talk to Ross, and in the meantime I'll get the scheduling girls busy finding us a date to do this thing."

Do this thing? He's moving too fast. I don't have time for this.

"Well, I just . . ." I swallowed. "A hysterectomy? Really?"

"Worst case scenario, like I said."

"Not to worry?" Breathe. Jesus, breathe. "You really think you might have to take things out?"

"That will all depend on what we find. We might though, yes. Hopefully we can keep your ovaries, and—"

"My ovaries? *If* we keep my ovaries?"

37

I fell back on the bed and put my forearm over my eyes. A sinking sensation overcame me, and I envisioned the bed swallowing me whole. I grabbed at the duvet and held tight.

"You're panicking, aren't you?" he asked with a tone of genuine concern.

"But my ovaries?" Volleying his words back to him seemed all I could muster.

"Look, I won't remove anything I don't need to. Trust me."

An almost visceral response kicked in—like my ovaries decided to spasm and scream for protection—my protection. "I don't understand."

"Hey, listen," he said. "Take your time. I'm sure you'll think of a ton of questions after we hang up and things have sunk in. Write them down, and I'll help you make sense of it all beforehand."

"Okay," I whimpered.

The receiver became a stone weight in my hand. My chest tightened. I squeezed my eyes shut and sat up. "I don't know what to say. This doesn't make any sense. I've done everything right. I workout, I eat right, I don't smoke. What did I do wrong?"

My thoughts and my heart rate competed for the fastest time. I bent forward and exhaled to the point of concave. I could hear my cell phone beeping down the hall with a message alert.

"Candace, listen to me. I've known you a long time, and I know that you make a living out of maintaining control, but this isn't anybody's fault. Our bodies have minds of their own sometimes, and sadly they're prone to malfunction. Things just happen."

Malfunction? I hung up the phone with that word reverberating in my head. It started bouncing around inside my skull until it created a driving rhythm, and I couldn't get it out.

Soon other words came in to accompany it. Broken. Defective. Imperfect. Infertile. They swirled around each other to avoid collision. I grabbed my head to try and mute the chatter. Ensuing nausea became my only distraction.

I stood and paced through the bedroom, and my cell phone beeped again.

This isn't fair. Not even remotely. I don't deserve this. And talk to Ross? I couldn't tell Ross—not yet anyway. And Aunt Josie? She'd lose her mind with worry.

I opened the bedroom door and shuffled back toward the office.

And I couldn't risk fallout from the press—not with my stance on physical control. Bad enough that I collapsed during that damned interview.

I reached my cell phone and checked the caller ID. *Fiona Fitzpatrick.*

Of course. I could confide in Fiona, my best friend since college, and the one person who could keep quiet without worrying to the point of having a stroke. I called her back without listening to the message. When the news spilled out of me like a broken faucet, she insisted I come to her right away.

*   *   *

Fiona had purchased a farmhouse after graduation—one that she thought would inspire her career. It worked. She'd made quite the name for herself as an artist, and Huntley, Illinois now claimed her for its own.

Getting there only took an hour from Chicago and the scenery never disappointed. Something about the way the wind brushed through the corn stalks calmed me. On that day, however, I didn't recall making the trip at all. I remembered getting in the car, but past that everything seemed a blur. Not until I stepped out onto her laneway and felt the whipping of leaves around my ankles, did I become the least bit conscious of anything; red and yellow maples leaves for the most part, all swirling around me as though I had the power to give them another season. I brushed through them and made my way to the front door.

Fiona met me on the porch wearing Birkenstocks and a paint-splattered apron over a pale green flowered dress. "It's dry," she said, pointing at the front of the apron and pulling me in for one of her signature hugs. She held me a little longer than usual that day, and I welcomed it.

"You painting?" I asked.

"Baking. It's a multi-purpose ensemble," she grinned and ushered me inside.

Slightly taller than I, she said that God gave her a little too much of everything—generous weight, wide hips, big breasts, and the wildest curly red hair I'd ever seen. Her eyes shone with the green hues of Ireland itself, and they danced with endless enthusiasm.

She took me straight to her kitchen and sat me down at the Formica table she'd decorated with blue paw prints. The scent of freshly-baked apples filled my nostrils, and the bright yellow room enveloped me. She put a hand on my shoulder, and I told her every detail of my conversation with Dr. J.

"Okay, so let's look at the positive. You might not have periods anymore," she said, pulling two hand-painted wine glasses down from her multi-colored cupboards. "Seriously, though. You sure you aren't blowing things out of proportion?" She disappeared into the pantry and re-emerged with a bottle of Châteauneuf-du-Pape. "Isn't there a chance it could be nothing at all?"

"He said that *before* the ultrasound, but now he apparently needs to go in and find a cause." I tapped my fingers on the table.

Fiona popped the cork and grabbed a remote control from the kitchen counter. She aimed it in the direction of the living room and took a seat across from me at the table. Edith Piaf began warbling from the stereo in the other room.

"I just don't have time for this . . . and it scares me," I confessed.

Fiona filled our glasses and raised hers for a toast. "Remember the Champs-Élysées? Our vow to weather any storm with a robust red and *The Little Sparrow?*" she grinned.

"Fiona, honestly; we were kids in Paris." I rose from the table and walked toward the window. "Pretending doesn't fix anything."

She raised her glass again and took a sip. "Well, it still works for me, but c'est la vie."

I looked out at the noonday sky full of clouds. "Well, it's childish and there's no silver lining. I don't want to go through this. I just don't."

"Jesus, Candy." She stood and walked toward me. "There are worse things, and there's always a silver lining." She brushed a piece of hair out of my eyes. "You're not dying."

"But what if I am?" I turned and crossed the room. "What if they get in there and find something horrible?" I shuddered at the thought.

"Did you not just say there weren't any obvious tumors?"

"Maybe not obvious, but—"

"Oh, for heaven's sake. I fail to see how envisioning a worst case scenario befits the queen of control," she said, sitting back down at the table.

Fiona's cat, Vincent, sauntered into the room and meowed. She reached down to scratch behind his one and only ear.

"I'm sorry. You're right. I know you're right. I just hate this."

"Of course you hate this. That's not the point. Life's full of things to hate, but you have to—"

"Don't." I raised the palm of my hand up toward her. "I don't want to hear any of your preaching on positive thinking. I think I do pretty well with that under normal circumstances."

"Normal circumstances aren't when it's needed." She took another sip.

I sighed, sat back down at the table and hid my face in my hands.

"Okay, let's consider this worst case scenario crap for a minute," she continued. "Say, for example, you have to have this hysterectomy."

I reached for the wine bottle with my glass half empty.

"Maybe your hormones will get out of whack, and you'll get the odd chin hair—or some actual belly fat like the rest of us. There may even be the occasional public outburst. Could be entertaining," she chuckled.

She'd become a master at teasing me out of a frump, but it would take a lot to make it work this time.

"Lovely. I hadn't thought about chin hair." I smiled in spite of myself but then my chin, hair or not, began to quiver.

Fiona reached out and squeezed my hand; then she rose and walked toward her stove with the cat on her heels. She pulled the oven door wide open, and I could see the golden crust of a pie. She poked it a few times with a fork and grinned back at me like a fifties housewife.

"You're too thin. You should have some of this when it's done." She shut the door on it.

I hated sweets. "Well, I might not be that thin if my hormones get—how did you put it—out of whack?" The back of my throat stung.

"Yeah, and let's not forget the loss of libido and a hyper-intolerance for stupidity—not like you don't secretly have that already. Oh, and the hot flashes." She giggled and sat back down across from me.

"Fiona, I—I . . ."

Vincent meowed again. She lifted him to her lap to quiet him.

"I know you're scared, hon, but you'll handle this like you do everything else. You'll get all the information you need, adjust your attitude, and focus." She leaned in and patted my arm. "It's all in that little book of yours. Read it if you get confused," she whispered.

Sometimes her sarcasm irked the shit out of me.

"Well, that's another point isn't it? I've been running around telling people that they're responsible for all aspects of their health and well-being; now this?"

"Candy, come on. You can't really believe that? Not deep down where you live?"

"Yes, damn it. I do. That's why I don't get it. I didn't allow 'free fluid' to start floating around inside me. It's ludicrous."

My cell phone rang; Geri's name displayed on the caller ID. I hit the silence button. "And if the press gets hold of this? They'll eat me alive."

"I'm not entirely convinced they'd care. Maybe you're—"

"Oh they'd care, believe you me. My whole persona's at stake here—everything I harp about—and they'd just love to see me fail." I reached up and pulled at my ponytail until my scalp hurt.

"Candy, I'm starting to wonder if you don't have delusions of grandeur."

My cell phone beeped with a message alert.

"Okay, so they write something about you in a few articles," continued Fiona. "At least you'd get some attention out of it. Any press is good press, isn't it?"

"Not in my book."

"No pun intended, I'm sure," she snorted.

My collapse in the Marriott conference room came to mind. I looked back at the caller ID on my phone and prayed that Geri could keep that photographer under control. They'd followed me once on my way home from school after my mother's death. I wasn't anybody then, just a brokenhearted kid wrapped up in drama. Merciless bastards.

Fiona continued. "I say let them find out about the tests. In fact, let's have Dr. J. take some pictures while he's in there. We can sell them online for a little extra dough."

"Oh, brilliant," I scoffed, "exactly why you'll never be my personal manager."

"Well, how exactly *do* you plan to keep this from the five o'clock news if they're so obsessed with ruining you?"

I didn't have a plan. For the first time in my life, I didn't have a plan. My eyes widened and I tapped my fingers on the sides of the wine bottle. "I don't know. Maybe Dr. J. could sneak me into his office on a weekend or something. Take care of it there without having to involve—"

"For a laparoscopy? I don't think so. Don't you have to be put out for something like that?"

"Apparently, but why couldn't he . . ." What am I saying?

"Well, let's consult Josie. She's a nurse, and—"

"No," I snapped. "Not Aunt Josie. She'd freak."

Fiona twirled the base of her wine glass directly over a paw print on the table and stared at me with a furrowed brow. "What did Ross say when you told him?" she asked. She put the wine glass to her lips.

"I haven't told him, and I don't plan to."

She lurched forward and gulped. "Excuse me?" She wiped the corners of her mouth with her index finger. "Have you lost your mind?"

"He won't take it well, and I can't admit that this is happening to me. Not yet."

"That's crazy talk."

"No, it's not. Don't say that."

My mind raced. I put my head down on the table. I needed a way to turn things around. I needed to undo it all. Shit.

"Look, you know I rarely side with the guy, but he's your husband for God's sake. I think he needs to know."

Another beep echoed. Damn phone. I sat back up. "You'll help me, right?"

"Candy, I—"

"Please Fiona. He couldn't handle this. I need to deal with it on my own. Please." My eyes pleaded with hers.

"On your own, but with my help?"

I nodded; she shook her head. "He's still your husband. It's not right."

"Have you heard anything I've said?" I asked, pushing my chair back and rising from the table. "What if they have to take everything out?" I walked back toward the window.

"Well, what if they do? What's that got to do with telling him or not telling him?"

I looked outside. A few random snowflakes floated through the air and threatened an early winter.

"Candy. What is it?"

I turned to face her, then slid down the cupboards and sat stone still on the linoleum. She came and squatted in front of me. The oven timer chimed.

"Children, Fiona." My eyes filled with tears. "He wants children."

CHAPTER 6

*"Don't second guess your instincts. Your gut
always knows what needs to be done."*

The corn stalks whipped in chaotic motion on my drive
home—nothing calm about them. I decided to work on my
questions that night and call Dr. J's office in the morning before
letting them schedule the procedure. Did I even need to have it
done? Maybe Fiona'd been right. Maybe I'd blown things out of
proportion. Maybe he'd blown things out of proportion.

A slight chill shuddered through me, and I reached down
to turn the car heater on. I pointed the air vents directly at my
chest and set the fans on high. How I wished at that moment
that I still had my mother, but would I have told her about
this if she were still living? Would I have tried to save her from
the worry as well? Would I even care about saving people from
anything if I hadn't lost her in the first place?

"Why did you have to leave me?" I whispered, straining to
fight back tears.

My cell phone rang again, and this time I welcomed the
distraction. I answered and turned the heater down so that

I could hear more clearly. Geri's voice filled the vehicle, and I began rattling off details about all that had happened since I'd seen her at the hotel. I spared nothing. After mentioning the laparoscopy, I heard her car door slam followed by the clicking sound of heels on pavement. She seemed to walk only a few feet before flicking her cigarette lighter a few times and exhaling like a north wind. The traffic on her end sounded louder than it did on mine.

"When?" she asked.

"When what?"

"When does he want to do the test?"

"Oh sorry, I'm not sure. He called this morning, but the scheduling girls aren't in until tomorrow."

A crow soared above traffic to the left of my driver's side window. It turned its head in my direction and appeared to look me in the eye. I blinked to focus convinced I must be imagining things.

"But these girls know you're leaving town in a week, right?"

Could she sound less concerned? "No, they don't know that, Geri. I haven't talked to them yet."

The crow positioned itself a little ahead of my vehicle and appeared to follow the bend in the highway. I felt led by it somehow, regardless of the singular asphalt path that lay before me.

"Okay, Bradford. So what are you saying exactly? Any chance this is going to interfere with our schedule?" The sound of her lungs filling with smoke made me half sick.

"No, not necessarily. To be honest, I'm not even entirely sure that I want to have it done." Did I want to have it done?

The crow dipped its wing and swooped to the right of my passenger side window. It set into a gliding pattern about 20 feet from the car. I stared at it long enough to drift into the adjacent lane. Geri coughed and jolted me back into paying attention.

"Valid point. Valid point. It probably isn't anything anyway. My sister had a similar thing once, and it turned out to be nothing."

"She did?" Why didn't she tell me this at the hotel?

I turned to look again at the crow. It returned my gaze for a few seconds and soared out of view. My spine tingled, and I turned the heater back on low.

"Yeah, almost exactly the same. She doubled over in agony during my niece's baptism. Everyone freaked. Mom wanted to rush her to the hospital: the whole drill."

"And?" Give me a positive outcome here. Please.

"Nothing. Absolutely nothing. They did a laparochaphy on her too."

"Laparoscopy."

"Whatever. Went in there and everything was fine. Basically left her with a couple of extra scars to add to her cesarean. Let's just say bikinis are out of the question."

"Scars?" I glanced out of every window and into the rearview mirror trying to locate the crow. Nothing. Gone.

"Oh yeah. Not pretty."

"And did they say she had fluid too?"

"Sure. That's exactly what they said. I mean, come on. We're women. Fluid? That's our middle name, am I right?" She giggled and took another drag from her cigarette. "These guys are just afraid of getting sued, that's all. They poke and jab at you with every little complaint."

"Well, I'd hardly say that my pain was a little—"

"No, no. That's not what I'm saying. But you've got to consider that they go too far to cover their asses these days."

A gust of wind pushed at my car, and I held tight to the steering wheel.

"Well, maybe. But I've been going to Dr. Jefferies for years, and I don't think he'd put me through something I didn't need."

Horns honked on Geri's end.

"Don't kid yourself. Have you had any more pain?"

"No, but—"

"There you have it. A onetime thing. Everybody has pain once in a while."

"Maybe, but surely not that intense."

"Well, my sister did. I'm just saying." She could actually be making sense. "Here's my advice, for what it's worth. Just forget it ever happened. You've got a big schedule ahead of you with little time to waste. It was probably just stress related anyway. You'll be fine once you get the ball rolling."

"Maybe you're right, but I still need to talk to him. Just get him to answer a few questions for me, you know?"

"Sure, sure."

I heard her get back in her car and start the engine. "Do what you need to do, but I'm going to continue on the assumption that all systems are go."

"Absolutely." And why shouldn't they be?

"Good. Now, we're still on for our lunch meeting on Wednesday?"

"We are."

"Super. Hang in there, and don't worry. Everything's going to be just fine. I can feel it." We hung up.

I could feel it too. I would be fine. I'd be just fine.

The corn stalks disappeared from view and leafless trees appeared sporadically in the distance. Signs of approaching city life began popping up along the side of the road as I zipped through an I-Pass toll booth and turned on the car radio. I hit the scan button looking for something inspiring. Michael Bublé? Not in the mood. Lady GaGa? Nope. AC/DC? Not in this lifetime. Cher? Ah, forget it. I turned it off again.

Could Dr. J. really be overreacting? I mean, I feel fine. I actually feel great. Why should I put my life on hold for one stupid incident?

A text message beeped through from Ross. *"Don't wait up. Will be late. Going somewhere noisy 4 beer. Might not hear the phone if u call. BTW—kicked Todd's ass on the back nine."*

I sighed, and my car hit a pothole. Ah well; an evening alone. I'd have a glass of wine and process the whole mess while I got some work done. And Fiona had a point. Why entertain a worst case scenario? No more panic until Dr. J. answered my questions and heard me out about Geri's sister. Maybe there's a way to avoid this whole—"Ach!"

The pain shot out of nowhere. "Oh, God!" I white knuckled the steering wheel. I fought to maintain control and not veer into traffic.

Stabbing, jarring waves of intensity overtook my body. My lungs struggled for enough air to fight back. My limbs shook with a mind of their own. I crossed the center line; once, twice. Another shot of pain. "Jesus, help me."

I held the steering wheel tighter and tighter. I checked the side mirrors; no one there. Stop shaking. Somehow I managed to pull onto the shoulder. I came to a dead stop. I opened the car door and swung my feet out onto the gravel. Wind whipped past me and into the vehicle. My teeth chattered. I gulped for air. I threw my head down between my knees and hugged my legs against my chest. Oh God, the pain. Not again. Please, not again.

CHAPTER 7

*"When you attempt to deceive others,
you're only deceiving yourself."*

Just as it had the first time, the pain left me like an angry lover. Why? My forehead dripped with sweat despite the cold wind that pounded against it. I could hear a faint caw in the distance. Loose gum wrappers danced around the inside of the car. They stopped when I pulled my feet back in and slammed the door. My shaking limbs then seemed exaggerated in the stillness. Calm down. You have to calm down.

Vehicles sped past and I turned the heater back to high. Can I drive? I looked up at the crystal globe hanging from the rearview mirror. No twirling, no swaying, no rays of light. My world stood still.

I reached down with both hands and felt my abdomen as though for the first time. I squeezed, poked, and prodded. What could be in there? My own body. I live in this skin every day, and I haven't a damn clue what's going on.

I pulled down the visor to look in the mirror. Pale as a ghost. I flipped it shut again and let out a monstrous sigh. I had little choice, but I wasn't sure I could face the unexpected.

I gave myself a gentle slap on my left cheek. Snap out of it, Candace Bradford. You can face anything. But not alone; I couldn't do it alone.

"Hello?" Fiona's voice sang on the other end of the phone when she picked up.

"It's back," I cried.

"What's back?"

"The pain. That's what's back. The fucking pain!" I gasped. "Well, it's not here now. It came and went just like last time."

"Oh shit, Candy. Are you okay?" An eighteen wheeler sped past me rocking the car. The globe swayed ever so slightly.

"I'm okay. I'm shaken and completely discouraged, but otherwise I think I'm fine. I don't know." I put a hand to my abdomen and bent forward against the steering wheel. My head pounded with the pressure of despair.

"Are you home already?"

"No. I'm sitting on the side of the road. It hit me when I was driving," I whimpered.

"Christ," she said. "You need me to come and get you?" Did I?

"N—No. I'll be okay." Will I? "I'm just going to sit here for a few minutes and then carry on. I'm only 20 minutes from home now, and the pain's gone." I wrapped my arms around the steering wheel and hugged it tight against my chest.

"You sure?"

"Yep, I'm sure." Am I? "Fiona?"

"Yeah?"

"What's happening? Why is this happening?" I sobbed.

"I don't know, sweetheart, but you have to get this thing checked out for sure. You know that right?"

"Yes damn it, but why now? My life's dream is finally taking off, and—" I sat back against the seat and put a hand over my mouth. Tears blurred my vision.

"No rhyme or reason, but it's not your fault. I don't want to hear any self-blame crap, you understand?"

I rubbed my eyes. "No one can know about this, Fiona. Promise me."

She sighed. "Well, I can't believe I'm even entertaining this stupidity, but I've been thinking about this obsession of yours with secrecy."

"And?" I took a deep breath and tried to compose myself. I looked in the visor mirror again. Mascara painted my cheekbones. I wet my thumb and started rubbing it off.

"Remember me telling you about my eccentric Uncle Leroy?"

"The one who died of AIDS?" I sniffled.

"That's the one. Quite the character," she said. "Well, he didn't want to have his reputation tarnished when he got diagnosed back in the day, so they'd always put him in the hospital under an assumed name. Mr. Les O'Dour or something of the like," she giggled.

"You mean, like an alias?" I pulled a tissue from my purse and blew my nose.

"Mind you, he was friends with the doctor, but they made it happen."

"Fiona, that's brilliant," I exclaimed. "But everybody knew eventually, didn't they?"

"Not until after he died. Up until then, it was all hush-hush. God rest his crazy Irish soul."

I reached up and touched my crystal globe. I twisted the ribbon on it and let it spin. "I wonder if Dr. J. could do that for me. I mean, he wouldn't if he thought I was hiding things from

Ross, but he might to protect me from the press." A glimmer of hope. I closed the mirror and flipped the visor shut again.

"Okay, let's get back to Ross—presuming Dr. Jefferies is fool enough to go along with this. Where is your husband supposed to think you are while you're pretending to be someone else?"

"I—I don't know yet. Maybe I'll add a fictitious day or two to the book tour. I'll think of something." It could work. In some crazy way, I really believed it could work.

*   *   *

"You'll need six weeks to recover if we need to do the hysterectomy, Candace," said Dr. Jefferies.

I'd been in my rescheduled meeting with Sophie Blanchard when he returned my call. I wanted privacy, so I stepped out onto the wrap-around porch of her ranch style bungalow. A crisp breeze met me head on.

"Well, I hardly think that's going to be necessary. Can't we just move forward and not talk about that?" I asked.

"No actually, we can't. You need to know what to expect." I pulled the collar of my jacket up around my neck.

"Well, how long without the hysterectomy then?" I began a quick pace back and forth on the porch to keep warm.

"A couple of days depending on how you do."

"That's more like it."

Sophie opened the front door. "Candace. Could we please?" she asked, pointing at her watch.

"One minute, Sophie," I said, raising my index finger in the air for her to see. She shook her head and went back in. I resumed pacing. "And the procedure itself? How's this camera thing work?"

"We make three small incisions. One goes through your belly button for an arm with a camera on it, and then there will be two lower down on either side of your abdomen that will act as my hands."

The wind picked up and a dozen or so leaves detached from a nearby tree and fluttered frantically in as many directions.

"So, they're small you said—these incisions?" I clung to the memory of my bikini.

"Yes, they're small. Nothing Frankensteinish, I promise. I'll make sure our little celebrity gets the star treatment."

Sophie peeked out through her front room curtains. I walked out of her range of view.

"Ah, speaking of celebrity," I said, lowering my voice and rounding the corner of the porch. "I don't want anyone to know about this."

"Why does that not surprise me?" he replied with a hint of fondness in his voice.

"I just can't risk it right now. The press will chew me up if they think I'm sick."

A squirrel peeked it's head over the edge of the eaves trough and disappeared again causing me to jump.

"Well, it's not like you can help it if you are, Candace."

"Maybe, maybe not. Regardless, I want to have this done under an alias. I've done some Googling, and—"

"Oh, you've done some Googling have you? You are resourceful, I'll give you that."

"So, you think it could be done?"

"Yes. A lot of paperwork, but it can be done," he sighed. "I'll have to speak to administration, and some people would have to know regardless; security for example, and the public relations department at the hospital for sure. They need to devise a plan of action if someone gets wind of your admission."

"And can we trust them?"

My jacket flew open. I grabbed it and wrapped it tight around me.

"We have little choice if this is what you want, but the process has been successful in the past for bigger names than yours. No offense of course."

"None taken." I wondered who else's insides he'd explored with cameras and why he hadn't suggested an alias himself.

"But you know we can't protect you entirely from people who might recognize you. Only a handful will know who you really are, but others might figure it out. I mean, everyone knows about the privacy act, but you can't stop people from whispering in the elevators if they can't contain themselves."

"I'll take the chance. We have to try. Please?"

"Fine," he sighed. "I'll make some phone calls to the hospital and see what I can arrange. In the meantime I'll have Brenda call you back to get you scheduled. You'll have to have pre-op blood work and paperwork completed ahead of time."

I felt wary of the new gum-snapping addition to his medical office. "Can we trust Brenda?"

The sound of footsteps echoed from the front of the house followed by Sophie's impatient voice. "Candace!"

"Coming," I replied, as her poodle rounded the corner and jumped up on my skirt.

"Yes, we can trust Brenda. But honestly, it's not like we're sneaking Marilyn into the White House. Most people are pretty disinterested."

I couldn't agree less. Paparazzi had been following Ross and me around for years on the Chicago social circuit, and I knew that they'd love to get their hands on this.

"I operate on Fridays, so we'll fit you in this week. If you have severe pain between now and then, you are to call me right away. You understand?" he asked.

Friday. Jesus.

* * *

I spent the next few days organizing details. Brenda called Tuesday afternoon with instructions. I'd be admitted under the name Catherine Newman, and I'd need to be there by 5:30AM. I wasn't to drive, and I'd have to have pre-op blood work done on Wednesday morning. The lack of empathy in her voice made it sound like we'd just booked a dental appointment.

Fiona agreed to be my designated driver and to let me stay with her for a week following the procedure. After the fund-raiser annoyance, Ross had seemed to resign himself to my schedule changes, so he bought the whole story about the added tour dates. And my clients, for the most part, were agreeable to having their appointments changed, so I felt confident that I had everything under control.

Geri, on the other hand, proved to be a challenge. We met for lunch on Wednesday afternoon as planned, and I told her about moving forward with the procedure. My PR girl appeared to need more reassurance than I.

"I still don't understand why you're having this done?"

"I told you; because the pain came back."

She took a long sip of her Cosmopolitan. A small bead of sweat appeared on her left temple.

"Look, nothing's going to change. The procedure's on Friday, and I'll have the weekend to recover. Really, there's no need to worry."

"Well, I don't like this. Any of it." She reached inside her purse and pulled out her Marlboros. She flipped the pack open and stared at her cigarettes with longing. She then shut the lid again, left the pack on the table, and rested her left hand on top of it. She stared at me for a moment as though pondering every conceivable bad outcome; then she leaned in toward me and whispered, "And what if people find out you might be sick? How well is that going to go over?" She sat back and regained her normal tone. "That would be like Dr. Phil being locked up in a mental institution."

What I wouldn't give to be that famous. "I've thought of that. They're admitting me under an alias."

She raised her eyebrows. "Okay," she said, with an approving nod. "Thinking ahead—I like that." She took another sip of her drink.

"Thought you might."

A waitress buzzed by and dropped a basket of bread in front of Geri with a thud, causing her to jump.

"And what if they find something in there?" She began twirling her cigarette pack around and around against the surface of the table and stared at me over the rim of her glasses.

"They won't. You just have to trust me on that. They won't."

"You sound pretty sure of yourself." She grabbed a piece of bread and took a huge bite out of it.

"I am sure of myself. In fact, I'm so sure of myself that I'm not even worrying my husband with this. No one is to know."

She cocked her head, shot me a deviant smirk, and swallowed her bread.

"Candace Bradford, I may have underestimated you," she said, draining her glass. "Okay then, mum's the word. I'll keep your little secret, but only if you promise to get this pain behind you and make us rich." She reached out to shake my hand. I reciprocated.

*   *   *

I didn't sleep Thursday night. Not one wink. I lay awake staring at the ceiling and listening to Ross's soft snore. I kept my hands on my abdomen like I wanted to shield it from the day ahead. Hard metal instruments waited somewhere in a cold sterile room. They waited to enter me.

I told myself I'd be fine. Nothing would go wrong.

I'd looked at the clock every 20 minutes for hours but still jumped when the alarm went off at 4:00AM. I'd packed a suitcase the night before and arranged an early taxi. Ross stumbled down the stairs with me to say goodbye. Everything would be just fine.

"Good luck baby," he said, giving me a hug. I dropped my bag and held him as tight as I could. "Hey now, what's with the grab? I thought you'd be excited to leave?"

Excited? Hardly.

"I know," I said, hanging on even tighter. "I—I'm just going to miss you, that's all."

Tears welled up in my eyes. The soft reassuring tick of my mother's antique mantel clock echoed through the condo.

He held me back at arms length to get a better look at my face, then he smiled. "I'm going to miss you too, but you'll get swept up in the adoration and forget I even exist. You actually may *want* to forget after the way I've behaved lately."

"Forget you exist? Like that could ever happen." I looked deep into his eyes and squeezed his biceps with both hands.

"It's going to be a great experience, baby. Just enjoy."

"You're right. It will be great. It will all be fine." How I loved that man. I kissed him long and hard as though leaving for battle.

He pulled me tight against him and ran his hand along the curve of my right hip. "Hey now, I'm not going to let you go if you keep that up."

Please don't. Don't let me leave. Make me stay. Make this all go away.

"Now, go on before you miss your flight," he added, tapping me on the ass.

"I love you Ross," I said, grabbing my suitcase.

"I love you too, sweetheart. Let me know when you get to Seattle, okay?"

"I will, I promise. But it will probably be pretty late with layovers and all." I looked away when I said it.

"No problem. Travel safe, and break a leg—if that's even an appropriate expression for a promo tour." He started toward the kitchen, but turned to blow me one last kiss.

I blew one back, shut the door behind me, and headed toward the elevator with a weighted knot in my gut.

When I reached the ground floor, our doorman met me and took my bags. "Good mornin' to ya, Ms. Bradford. Off on a little adventure, are we?" asked Seamus with his lilting Irish accent.

I got half way to the car and turned to look back up at our building. "More like a trip than an adventure. One that I'm hoping is entirely uneventful." I entered the back seat of the taxi.

"Well, may your travel be a safe one, and may you be leavin' nothin' of value behind."

He shut the door for me, and the taxi slinked into the darkness.

"O'Hare or Midway?" asked the driver.

"Neither," I said, passing him the address for the Women's Surgical Center.

CHAPTER 8

"How do you build self-esteem? Impress yourself, not others.
Follow through with the things you fear the most."

"You ready?" Fiona asked as I got out of the taxi. She'd been
standing at the hospital entrance when I arrived.

"Ready as I'll ever be. Let's get this thing over with."

We walked inside where I presented myself as Catherine
Newman and introduced Fiona by her first name only. The
paperwork had been prepared without a glitch. Thank God.
They led us back to a small cubicle where I changed into a
hospital gown and gave my belongings to Fiona as instructed.
I climbed onto the stretcher in the middle of the room and
covered myself with a sheet. Fiona parked herself in the chair
beside me. I began to fidget.

"You okay over there, Catherine?" she giggled.

I couldn't sit still. "No, no I'm not. I feel like a caged cat."

"It's that loss of control issue of yours. You're fine."

"Well, what the hell do you know?" I snapped. She stuck
her tongue out at me. "You should have an alias too. It's only
fair."

"Should I now? Hmm, let's see," she said, placing a finger to her chin. "It would need to be something exotic. We want to draw as much attention away from you as possible, after all." She looked toward the ceiling. "I know—Immafree Takeamenow," she laughed.

"You and your one-track mind. Would you find a man already? You're killing me," I said, only half kidding.

"Believe me, I'm trying," she smiled. "So, you don't like the name? I think it sounds kind of Yugoslavian—or Italian maybe?"

"Well, maybe a little. Go with it. See if I care."

The sheet that lay over me worked its way around my ankles. I kicked like a mule to loosen it. I looked back at Fiona. She continued grinning. "Look, I'm sorry. I don't mean to snap. I'm just scared, you know?" I said.

"I know, but everything's going to be fine." She moved her chair in closer to me and took my hand. "You trust Dr. Jefferies, right?"

"Of course. It's just weird, you know?" I pondered my state of mind. "I can't really put a finger on why I'm scared. I—I mean, I know I'll be okay. I guess it's just the thought of being knocked out. Does that make sense?"

"With you? Definitely," she responded. "Well, with anyone I guess, but you especially."

I put my hands over my face. "God, it was hard leaving Ross this morning." Deception burned at the center of my chest.

"I still think you should have told him. Actually, there's still time if you want to." She reached for my bag to get my phone out.

"No. I've made up my mind," I said sitting up on the stretcher. "He doesn't need to know until I'm ready to tell him."

"Uh-huh, whatever you say." Fiona leaned back in her chair. "And when he notices your scars?"

"Well, I've thought about that. I'll confess somewhat after the fact. I'll just tell him that I had a little scare and that Dr. Jefferies did some tests or something in his office. He won't know the difference, and as long as I'm fine he'll be fine."

"I hope so, Candy."

"Look, I know him, okay?" My foot started twitching. "Once he knows that everything's okay and that it's business as usual, he'll probably even thank me for leaving him out of it. He's useless when it comes to anything medical—absolutely, full-blown useless."

"I still think you're making a big—"

"Good morning ladies," Dr. Jefferies said, entering the room in pale green scrubs and a lab coat. I lay back down. "How's my patient doing? All set to put this behind you?"

"I am," I said. "I'd be happier if it wasn't necessary at all."

He grinned. "Feeling okay otherwise? Not plotting ways to do the procedure yourself, I hope?" He raised his eyebrows in Fiona's direction. She snorted. Smart asses.

"Don't kid yourself. If I could, I would."

"No doubt." He scanned the room. "So, where's Ross. Has he gone for coffee or something?"

Fiona cleared her throat. "I'll just step out for a minute," she said, glaring at me from behind Dr. J.'s shoulder on her way by.

"Ah, Ross is out of town for the next couple of days for work. It couldn't be avoided. I told him that this wasn't going to be any big deal and that Fiona wouldn't leave my side." Am I convincing enough? "He's grateful that we have her to step in, and I promised to call him as soon as we know something." Please don't ask any more questions.

"But it does have potential to be a pretty big deal, remember?"

I shrugged.

"Look, if you like I can call him myself when we're finished." He reached into his scrubs and pulled out his phone. "Just give me his number and I'll program it into this—"

"No, no. It's okay. He'll be expecting Fiona, and I'll call him myself when I'm fully awake." I fidgeted on the stretcher. "So, this big deal 'potential'?"

He cocked his head to one side and furrowed his brow. "We discussed this, Candace. You signed both consents when you came in the other day. One for the lap, and one for the possible hysterectomy. If you need the latter, it will be a major procedure."

"Y—Yes, but you said that would only be a worst case scenario."

A metal tray dropped somewhere down the hall, and my nerves rattled with it. I kicked at the sheet that half covered me.

"Worst case scenario, yes. You went over all of this with Ross as well, right?"

"Yes, yes. Of course I did." The burning in my chest climbed to the back of my throat. "It's just not feasible for him to cancel his business trip for a 'what if' scenario, and Fiona's more of a support at times like this anyway."

"Fine. Suit yourself," he said, seeming to tire of the issue. "Does this mean I can discuss your case in front of Fiona then? It's good to have someone there for the results who hasn't been heavily medicated."

"Absolutely. Anything you have to say to me you can say to her. She's my best friend, and I trust her with my life." I grabbed the bedrail and looked up at Dr. J. "I'm not happy about this."

He reached out and squeezed my hand. I wanted to put a stop to it all and just go home.

Fiona returned to the room with a cup of coffee; a welcome intrusion. I gave her my full attention.

"Oh, that's it. I was just telling Dr. J. what a good friend you are, and now you come in here tempting me with the smell of java?" I forced a grin.

"Sorry love, but I do want to be alert for the duration. Plug your nose." She moved toward the chair and sat down.

"Speaking of coffee," said Dr. Jefferies, "I'm going to have a few cups myself before we get started. Trust me. You don't want me coming at you with instruments before I've had my morning dose."

"No, no, by all means. Get as awake as necessary," I teased.

"So, you fully understand then, Candace?" he asked with a weary gaze. "No false perceptions about the procedure or what you've signed?"

"No, I'm fine," I said.

I'm fine. I'm fine. Everything's going to be fine.

Fiona looked back and forth between us with a puzzled expression.

"All right then." He started walking toward the door. "Oh," he said turning back. "If I haven't warned you already, you're going to wake up in an anesthetic haze of sorts, so don't freak out if you feel a bit out of control."

He nodded in Fiona's direction. She nodded back.

"It may take you a few minutes to figure out what's going on, maybe longer. This could prove frustrating for you and entertaining for your friend here, but it will pass."

"Oh, goody," replied Fiona, clapping her hands together. "Can she go home with some of that stuff? I could use a few laughs."

"Well, I doubt she's going to want much if I know her." He turned to face me. "I always say there are three types of post-op patients: the ones that need nothing, the ones that need Tylenol and a pat on the head, and the ones that need morphine and a room full of people. I'm betting that you're the Tylenol type. What do you think?"

"I prefer nothing," I snipped.

"Just testing," he grinned.

Fiona laughed from her seat beside me and I shot her a glare.

"Okay." He turned back toward the door. "I'll be in to discuss the results shortly after you wake up."

"How long after?"

"It won't be that long Candace, but you'll have little choice but to wait. I don't like my patients getting their results secondhand. I've had issues with that in the past and I won't allow it. Trust me: it's better to get it from the horse's mouth."

I crossed my arms across my chest in annoyance.

"Okay, so in a few minutes the anesthesiologist will be in to start your IV and give you some medication. He'll get you started on your day trip; then I'll meet you in the OR."

He turned to look at Fiona. "There's a waiting room on the fifth floor where you can—hopefully—make yourself comfortable. As soon as we're done, I'll send someone to let you know which room she's going to. I'll meet you both there to give you the news."

"The good news, you mean," I added.

"Always the optimist," chirped Fiona.

"Candace, I'll give you the news. Now relax and get ready for a nap," he demanded.

He shot me a paternal gaze and left the room.

"I like him," said Fiona.

"He's married," I snapped.

"Not as a potential lover, as a doctor. And he's my Dad's age, for God's sake. I know I'm man crazy, but . . ." She rolled her eyes at me and slurped her coffee. "So, what did he mean by 'no false perceptions?'"

"Nothing," I barked.

Fiona rolled her eyes again and crossed her legs toward the opposite wall.

"Again," I sighed. "I'm sorry. I'm not myself. He was just recapping all the shit we talked about before. It's his job to go over everything ad nauseam."

"Uh-huh."

"Why is it that you always sound like you don't believe me? Can you answer me that?"

"Because you're full of crap, maybe?" she asked.

I glowered at her, and she stuck her damn tongue out at me again, this time with her eyes crossed. A spontaneous laugh escaped me. My dear friend. "Hey, thanks for being here, Fiona. I do mean it."

"Now, now, Catherine," she teased. "I wouldn't have let you go through this alone. Not in a million years."

"Ms. Newman?" asked a young, attractive man in blue scrubs as he entered the room. Fiona sat straight upright in her chair and fussed with her hair.

"Yes, that's me," I said.

"Dr. Rivas. Anesthesiology."

"Ah, yes. How are you?"

"Good, good," he said, setting a metal tray down on my bedside table. "Just going to start your IV and get you ready for the OR."

"Okay," I said with some hesitation.

"She's not fond of needles," remarked Fiona.

"Few people are," he said in her direction. Then he turned back toward me. "But I promise to make this as painless as possible." He smiled down at me and began inspecting my veins.

Fiona fanned herself with a magazine and smirked at me from behind him. I shook my head.

Dr. Rivas applied a tight rubber band around my upper arm. My foot started twitching again, although he did have the ability to distract. Strong arms, square shoulders, and beautiful brown eyes. I decided that every woman should fall asleep—at least once in her lifetime—with a view like that.

"Okay, just a little poke," he said. Fiona collapsed back in her chair. I fought back laughter in spite of myself.

"Ouch."

"Sorry, but the worst is over for a few hours," he said, removing the rubber band and taping me up like a present. "Now I'm going to put some medication in your IV. It's called Versed and it's going to relax you a great deal. Are you okay with that?"

"She could stand to relax," said Fiona from the sidelines. He smiled back at her and then at me. Fiona put the back of her hand against her forehead and threw her head back to feign fainting. Good God—the drama.

Dr. Rivas injected the medication and put the needle in a box on the wall. I waited, but nothing seemed different.

"It will only take a minute, but you'll feel pretty chilled out. When we get into the operating room, I'll give you a bit more. You're guaranteed to have a great sleep."

Did he just wink at me? A wave of calm washed over my body. My God, the man's stunning. A floating sensation lifted me just off the stretcher.

"You feel anything different yet, Ms. Newman?"

Where did he get that smile?

"Call me Cathy," I giggled.

"Okay, Cathy. How are you feeling?"

"I—I'm—wow." My eyes closed. I could hear Fiona laughing in the background. The doctor put his face directly above mine. I wanted to kiss him. Did I just lift my head to kiss him?

"Wow's good," he grinned. "We'll be in to take you down the hall in just a few minutes. You okay to keep an eye on her until then?" he asked Fiona.

"You betcha," she replied, and he slipped out the door. "You betcha. I can't believe I just said that. I'm such a dork."

"Dorkie, schmorkie," I said, with the words echoing against the walls around me. I let out a loud guffaw.

"Well look at you, Catherine Newman. Gone all cutesy wootsy on me," teased Fiona. "I suggest you get a to-go order of that stuff for us to share at home."

I tried to stick my tongue out at her, but the thing felt rubbery and huge in my mouth. A young woman entered wearing matching pajamas and nightcap.

"I'm here to take you to the OR, Ms. Newman. All set?" she asked, peeking at my hospital bracelet.

"Setsy, wetsy," I giggled again. "I love your PJs." I reached out to touch the sleeve of her jacket.

"God, I'd love to film this," Fiona remarked with a snort.

"Thank you," said the nurse, "But they'd never do as PJs. They've seen too many nightmares."

She kicked the brakes off the stretcher and started wheeling me into the hall. She paused to address Fiona. "Did they tell you about the waiting room?"

"Yep. Fifth floor," said Fiona, approaching my stretcher. She grabbed my hand and squeezed it tight. "Everything's going to be just fine. You know that, right?"

I looked up at her and laughed. "You're such a dork."

She smiled down at me. Her red curls lit up like the aura of an angel.

"Uh-huh. Love you too Cathy Wathy." She kissed me on the cheek.

Fiona let go of my hand, and the stretcher began to roll. Little blue Disney-like birds appeared to hover over my stretcher. At least, I think they were birds. They began chirping as we neared a wide doorway at the end of the hall. I pointed upward.

The nurse parked the stretcher beside a metal table and helped me shimmy onto it. "Oh, it's cold in this forest," I blurted out.

"Forest?" laughed Dr. Rivas. "Ah yes, the forest. It can be cold but only until the dew wears off." He smiled down on me; my handsome prince. "But fear not young maiden. The sun will soon peak over the horizon, and we'll all be warm and toasty."

The birds began to giggle, or maybe the nurses. Someone's giggling. Oh, it's me. Ha!

"I love this place," I grinned.

"Good, we want you to. Now Ms. Newman, we're going to give you a little more medication and I want you to do me a favor, okay?"

"Dance?" I asked.

They're giggling again. Stop giggling.

"No not right now. What I want you to do is count backward from one hundred. You think you can do that for me?"

"Uh-huh."

I closed my eyes and started floating above a grove of trees. Am I being carried by the birds? Am I flying?

"How about now?" he asked.

"Now, what?" I tried to focus, but his face had gone all blurry.

"Start counting backward?"

"Oh, okay. Can I start with the trees?"

"Whatever works," said Dr. Rivas.

"Will you count with me?"

One of the birds winked in my direction.

"Oh sure. What the heck."

Look at that smile.

"One hundred," we said.

A male voice echoed through the trees. "How is she?" Dr. J.?

"Ninety-nine . . ."

"She's counting trees in the forest," someone said. They're laughing again. What's so funny?

"Ninety-eight . . ." I don't know how long I can float like this. My arms feel too heavy. The sun's going down, and . . .

"Ninety-theven . . ." Where did the happy laugh go? Someone's crying. "Ninety-sith . . ." I can't move at all. It's too dark. I don't like this. Who's crying? Am I crying?

I began writhing on the metal table. "Ninety-five . . ." I've changed my mind. Make it stop. Please, stop it. I don't want to . . .

CHAPTER 9

"Exercise patience and it will grow stronger."

The hard surface under my back seemed the only thing solid. I forced my eyes open, but a mist clouded my vision. The ceiling spun in a slow, steady circle. I struggled to push my body up. "Where am I?" My voice seemed to echo down a long tunnel.

"Relax, sweet cheeks. You're in Versailles. Your dream of spending a night in the Petit Trianon has finally come true."

I turned in the direction of the voice. "Fiona?"

"One and the same. How you feeling, Candy girl?"

"Feeling? I—I'm not . . ." The haze persisted despite marathon blinking. "Stoned, I feel stoned." My hand reached out for nothing. "Where are my birds?"

"Birds?" She asked with a grin. "What birds?"

I shook my head. I touched the bed rail and tried to pull myself up. A deep ache rocked through my middle. "Please, where am I? What's going on?" I begged. I tried to roll onto my side. "I want to sit up."

"You're just waking up from surgery," she said, easing me back onto the bed. "Remember? The hospital?"

"Oh God." I relaxed into her coaxing voice.

My heartbeat vibrated through the mattress. "What did they find?" I half whispered. "Were there trees in the way?"

"They didn't say anything, and there were no trees. My, but you are entertaining," she teased.

"But he's supposed to save me from them, right?" The fog around me danced in a swirling two-step.

"Dr. Jefferies? Oh, I'm loving this conversation," Fiona giggled. "He'll be in shortly to discuss everything. Remember? He likes to be the one to announce the results?"

"From the forest?" Focus. Focus.

"Yeah, that's right. From the forest," she conceded.

"I thought I was in a . . . Dr. Jefferies? Did you say Dr. Jefferies?" I sputtered.

"Yes. Your surgeon. He'll be here soon. Everything's okay, hon," she said, patting my hand.

My foot got caught on something. The pain got worse. "What is that?" I asked, putting a hand down between my legs.

"That's your catheter," she said, standing to straighten out tubes. "And don't go doing more damage to yourself."

"Well, where is he then? I don't understand." The ache inside me intensified.

"He'll be here shortly. Just stay stoned for now. It becomes you."

"No, I don't like it." I tried to sit up again but couldn't. I flopped my head back down on the pillow. "Help me, Fiona."

"Candy," Fiona stood over me and took my hand. "You're fine, and I'm right here to make sure you stay that way."

I blew out a long exhale and tried to orient myself. The starkness of the decor did little to comfort me. Where did all the green go?

"How long was I lost?" I asked.

"Well, if you mean in surgery you were lost for quite a while," she said.

"Like what kind of while?" Had we had this conversation before? I couldn't think straight or concentrate.

"About five hours, but they said they had trouble getting your pain under control or something, so don't freak out just because—"

"Five hours?" I pulled my hand away from hers. "Just to look around? Christ." I put my hands over my face. "They must have found someone in there." Short, shallow breaths struggled to deliver air against the heaviness in my chest. "I—I mean, some-thing, not some-one. Did they find something?" Think. I must think.

"Okay, look at me." Fiona sat down on the edge of the bed and pulled my hands down from my face. "There is no forest. You're in your hospital room and you need to calm down. When Dr. Jefferies gets here we'll find out everything we need to know."

"I know, but—"

"No buts about it. Just lie here and behave yourself for me, will you?"

A nurse entered and Fiona stood to get out of her way. "Ms. Newman?" she asked.

"No. Leave me alone," I whimpered.

"Uh, yes she is Ms. Newman," said Fiona, shooting me a look of impending danger.

"I am?" I asked Fiona. "Oh, Oh yes. I am."

My vision began to clear a bit, which seemed to cause my pain to worsen.

"Okay good," continued the nurse. "My name's Angela, and I'll be taking care of you for the next few hours. Can you please tell me your birth date?" she asked.

She lifted my wrist to inspect my paper bracelet.

"Why?" I asked. Why does nothing make sense?

"It's okay," she smiled. "We just double check the information on your wristband with what you tell us. It's one of the ways we ensure that we're giving medications to the right person."

"Oh." I squeezed my eyes tight and opened them fast hoping it would clear my confusion. Focus. Did I fake a birth date as well? I couldn't remember. "March 28, 1977?"

"Super."

She proceeded to wrap a blood pressure cuff around my left arm. The slow, agonizing squeeze made me more alert.

"I'll just finish checking your vital signs, then I'm going to hook up a medication in your IV here." She pointed at a small port-type contraption in my left arm, and then stuck a plastic probe into my ear. Star Trek: I'm in a Star Trek episode.

"What kind of medication," asked Fiona. "She doesn't like drugs."

"Is it that blue bird drug again?" The plastic probey thing beeped, and she removed it.

"Oh my," Fiona said grinning from the back of the room.

"You'll like this one. It's Dilaudid for pain," said Angela. She removed the cuff from my arm and looked me in the eye. "It will be set up so that you can give yourself a bit at a time. Are you having pain now?"

"Yes . . . yes I am," I replied, suddenly aware of my constant grimace.

"On a scale of zero to ten, where would you say your pain's at right this minute?" she asked. Scales? I hate scales.

"I don't know." I rubbed my forehead. "Maybe a seven and three quarters?"

Fiona laughed from the corner of the room. "Can you be more specific, hon?" she asked.

"That's okay," the nurse responded, shooting a glance in Fiona's direction. "Specific is a good thing."

Fiona rolled her eyes toward the ceiling and turned to face the window. Angela smiled down on me. The memory of my mother entered the room. I bathed in it.

"Here. I want you to take this," said Angela. She passed me a cord with a button on the end of it.

"What's this?" I asked. "A detonator?"

She smiled. "This is the button you're going to push to give yourself pain medication. It's patient controlled, but it's got a timed setting so that you can't give yourself too much. Because of that, there may be times when you push it and nothing happens. When you hear a soft beep it means it worked."

I turned the little button over and over in my hand. "I like this. Having control I mean."

"No doubt," scoffed Fiona.

"If you don't have any further questions, I'll just check your incisions and let you rest."

"Incisions? Th—There's incisions?" I started a fast move forward. Every part of my body told me to stop. Moaning, I grabbed the side rail on the bed. "But I . . . how many?"

Angela took the button from my hand and pushed it. A soft beep came from the direction of the IV pole. She continued. "You have three small puncture marks on your abdomen." She lifted my gown, and I strained to look.

Three small bandages, the size of saltine crackers, decorated my stomach. "They look fine," she said.

A cart rattled past the doorway. My surroundings grew clearer. I started remembering what Dr. J. had told me about the cameras and incisions.

"They're not so bad," Fiona added. "Could be worse, right?"

Angela pulled my gown back down. "You're all set. Your call light is here, so ring it if you need something. And don't try getting up on your own, okay?"

"Before you go, can you please tell me what they found?" I asked. "I know Dr. Jefferies is coming but he hasn't been in yet, and I . . ." My voice cracked. I put a hand over my mouth. Fiona came to my side.

"I'm sorry, Ms. Newman, but it's Dr. Jefferies' preference that he talk to his patients himself about results."

"Fine," I barked. I pushed the magic button—nothing. "What's wrong with this thing?" I pushed again.

"Timed out still, Ms. Newman; it's too soon." Angela smiled and left the room.

Fiona sat down in the chair beside me. "Well, Nurse Ratched was lovely, wasn't she?"

I tried to lie still, but I couldn't stop fidgeting. I couldn't get comfortable. "She was lovely."

"Well, maybe to you but you should have seen the look she shot me—like I was some kind of threat or something."

"Well, this isn't exactly about you now, is it?" I barked.

"True enough," she responded. "I do tend toward den mother mode in situations like this." My limbs grew heavy. "Peter used to say that," she grinned. "Remember Peter?"

"If you mean the guy that lived in your mattress all through college, yes."

Fiona shrugged with a smirk on her face.

"Oh God Fiona, I'm worried." She leaned in toward me. "I hate this."

I tried the button again, still nothing.

"I know, Candy. This has to be awful for someone like you—for anybody for that matter, but we have to wait for the good doctor."

"You're not helping."

She grinned and made a false start to get out of her chair. "Well, I could just go and let you—"

She knew full well that I'd stop her. "No wait. Of course you're helping. I need a distraction." I needed answers.

My nose starting itching, and the more the anesthetic fog lifted, the more I wanted it back.

"Maybe you should try to sleep until the he gets here."

"Sleep? Yeah right."

The bed encased me. I struggled to move in it.

"TV?" she asked, reaching for the remote.

"I hate TV. Just talk to me."

Where in the hell could he be? I pulled at the sheets to free my feet from bondage.

"About what in particular?" she asked.

"The weather; your sex life—I don't care—anything to take my mind off this. I'm going crazy."

I threw my legs over the side of the bed. My abdomen protested.

"Candy, you need to—" Fiona pushed my legs back in.

"I know what I need to do. Just talk to me. Please." God, make this stop.

She handed me an extra pillow from the chair. I embraced it.

"I thought you were sick of my sex life?"

"I lied."

"Well I'm sick of it, but here goes," she said. "If this doesn't distract you nothing will." She paused. "You're sure you want me to—?"

"Thanks, Fiona," I whispered. A tear rolled across my right cheek.

"Okay. Well, his name was Hugh. Not bad looking: receding hairline, slight paunch, kind of charming in a curious sort of way; but not my type at all. How they match people up on those websites is beyond me. This one was a freak."

"How so?" I asked, turning the button over and over in my hands.

I glanced at the door. He's making me wait on purpose, I know it. My whole face itched.

"We met for dinner, during which he leans toward me and I notice this big tattoo peeking out from under his shirt sleeve. So I mention it. He pulls up the sleeve to show me a dragon and tells me it's only one of many."

"One of many what?"

"Tattoos."

"Oh."

A constant beeping echoed from the hallway and added to my annoyance.

"Apparently there's a naked woman that runs down his right leg, and a tree that starts at the small of his back that branches out to both shoulders."

"Really?" I turned toward her. My vision took a minute to catch up. The room did a half spin.

"Oh, wait: there's more. Then he says to me, 'I've got piercings too.' Well, I didn't ask but he offered up that they're in both nipples, and 'other places as well.'"

"You don't mean . . ."

"I'm assuming so, but why would someone do something like that?" She squirmed her bottom in the chair. "So he's basically thinking I'm getting turned on by all this talk, when I'm totally repulsed. I tell him he's quite the little collector of body art, and he says that he collects other things too: acoustic guitars, antique pens, tricycles."

"Tricycles?"

A flash of pain shot through my pelvis. Fiona started to stand up. I held my breath, rolled back on my back, and motioned with my left hand for her to continue. She sat back down.

I tried the button again. A soft beep rose in the air like an angel of mercy.

"You sure you want me to continue?" she asked.

I forced a grin and nodded. "Come on: tattoos, piercings, and a tricycle collection? Don't stop now."

I watched the IV line. Nothing looked different. Is that damn Di . . . whatsit medication working?

"Okay, you asked for it," said Fiona. "He says to me, 'You want to know what my favorite thing to collect is?' so I played along." Fiona leaned in to whisper to me. "'Sexual experiences with women.'"

"What? He said that?" A laugh burst out of me unexpected. The muscles of my abdomen cringed. "Are you kidding me?" I squeezed my pillow hard against my torso.

"I swear to God."

"Oh Fiona, it hurts."

She kept going. "So, I'm sitting across from this guy with my jaw agape. I think he got off on the shock value."

The medication finally seemed to pulse through my brain. My thoughts became lighter. Giggles overtook me.

"Oh God," I gasped. "Stop."

"That's what I said to him," she laughed. "There's not enough latex on the planet."

I wiped a tear from my cheek. "Oh, you poor thing. I don't know how you do it."

"Well, I'm determined to find Mr. Right if it kills me," she sighed.

I wiped my eyes and ran my hands through my hair. "How did the night end?" I became weary. My feet got cold and I kicked the sheets down over them.

"I did the only thing I could think of: I put on my best Irish Catholic face and told him I was saving myself for marriage."

"You did not?" I giggled as my eyelids grew heavy.

"I know, I'm evil. And he wanted nothing to do with me after that. Imagine me a virgin," she scoffed. "And at my age? Never a dull moment."

My mind and body relaxed back like a swaddled babe.

"Well, I could use a few dull moments," she added. "A nice, normal, dull-moment kind of guy would be right up my alley."

"You need anything but dull, Fiona." I wiggled to a slight sideways position to watch the door more closely.

"You're probably right," she sighed.

"Hugh what, by the way? Maybe we know him."

"Bastard. Hugh Bastard," she said. "At least, that's what I called him under my breath on the way to the car."

We burst out laughing again just as Dr. J. entered the room. "Well, it sounds like I should have gotten here a few minutes earlier," he grinned.

Fiona retreated back to the shadows.

Dr. Jefferies approached me and lifted my gown. "Dressings look good." He covered me again and sat down on the edge of the bed. I rubbed my face with my hands.

"That's the Dilaudid. Makes you itchy," he said.

"Well? What happened? I can't stand it any longer." I shut my eyes tight and held my breath.

"Nothing life threatening." He took my hand.

I opened my eyes again and exhaled in a sea of relief. I'm going to be okay.

"Thank God," Fiona whispered from behind him. He turned to acknowledge her presence.

"Okay, so why all the pain then? Fiona said they had trouble controlling it or something."

"Candace, your uterus and ovaries were a mess. There was so much scar tissue in there—I'm assuming from that burst appendix several years back—it looked like everything was wrapped in binder twine. I'm really surprised that you weren't having more pain long before this." He paused, his voice dropping to a low, conciliatory tone. "I had to take it all out."

"Wh . . . what?" He's lying. He's making it up. It's all a mistake.

"Shit," mumbled Fiona.

"I had no choice."

This isn't funny. I'm hearing him wrong; I have to be. I fought to sit up, but my chest tightened.

"What are you saying?"

I stared at him in disbelief. He must mean the binder twine: that's what he took out. Not me . . . not my . . .

"I had to do a total hysterectomy, Candace." He squeezed my hand. "There was no other option."

CHAPTER 10

"Value true friendship, and accept nothing less."

Fiona approached my hospital bed and put a hand on my shoulder.

"I don't understand this," I said. "I was sure everything would be—oh my God," I cried. I felt for my bandages. The ache beneath them warned me not to sob—warned that it would only make things worse.

"Where's my button?" I pulled my hand from Dr. Jefferies and dug in the sheets for it. "I need my button."

Fiona and Dr. Jefferies glanced across the bed at each other. "What? What are you two looking at?"

"Okay now. Calm down," said Dr. Jefferies.

My hand found the detonator. I pushed on it with all my might. Air rushed in and out of my lungs. A soft beep blessed my ears.

"Calm down? Why did you do this to me? You told me that—"

"What? What did I tell you, exactly? Do you remember?" He'd won the hand. He'd warned me. He'd said all along that this could happen. I didn't believe him.

"B . . . but there was no other choice?"

I rubbed my face until I thought the skin would wear off.

"None," he said point blank.

"And my ovaries?"

"Everything, Candace. I had to take everything. They were unrecognizable."

Everything? My God, he's taken everything. But I didn't feel empty. How could I be empty?

"What am I supposed to do now? I don't know what to do." The caged feeling came back, and I wanted to claw my way free. My eyes darted around the room. I grabbed at the side rails on the bed.

"They were talking about having kids," Fiona said to Dr. Jefferies in a hushed tone.

Rage scratched at my incisions from the inside. "I'm right here, Fiona. Don't talk over me like that."

"Well, this doesn't mean you can't have kids, Candace. There are plenty of options available for you to be a mother, just not the old-fashioned one. When you're ready, I can get you in touch with—"

"Ready? Oh my God."

I began sobbing despite the pain it caused. Fiona disappeared and came back with a box of tissues.

The room spun. Dr. Jefferies stood silent for a few moments, and then his restlessness became palpable.

"Candace, I have another patient I need to check on, but I'm going to order something to help calm your nerves."

"I don't want to see birds again. I won't," I snapped.

"Birds?" he asked.

"I started seeing things before the surgery, and I don't want to again. I don't like feeling messed up. I'm all messed up."

The tears multiplied.

"Birds aren't one of the side effects. It's just a little Valium. If anything you'll sleep, and you need to."

Exhaustion weighed on me. My emotional state pushed it down further.

Dr. J. turned toward Fiona. "Are you going to be here with her tonight?"

"We have to stay the night?" I asked. "Why?"

He turned back toward me. "Because this was major surgery. I need to monitor you overnight in case of bleeding."

"But Fiona can watch me at—"

"Oh, no I can't," she replied. "I'm no nurse Angela. I would like to stay here with her though," she added nodding in Dr. Jefferies' direction.

"I'll tell them it's doctor's orders," he said. "Do you need me to talk to Ross?"

"No," I barked. "N . . . no, thank you. I—I'll talk to him. He needs to hear this from me." I put my hands to my mouth. "Sweet Jesus," I whispered into them.

"You sure? Because I don't mind and—"

I put my hands down and shook my head. "No, really; I'll take care of it."

Ross: my poor Ross. How do I tell him?

"Okay then. I'll be in first thing in the morning to check on you. I'm going to order the Valium every four to six hours in case you need it, so rest and worry about the details later. You need to heal."

Heal. Yes, heal. "You're right, of course. I need to heal and fast. I have this promo tour coming up and—"

"You don't have anything for at least six weeks, young lady," said Dr. Jefferies.

"Six weeks?" He's got to be kidding. "You said a day or two." I scratched at my face with both hands.

"When we were doing a simple exploratory, yes. Not for a hysterectomy, remember? I told you all of this. And no driving for two weeks either." I shook my head in defiance. My thoughts scrambled. "Flying's out of the question too until I give you permission."

"That won't work. It just won't work," I said.

"It will work, and you won't. End of story."

"But I can't just . . ." I sputtered. "I have dates set up, and I . . . They're all expecting me, and we've . . ."

I looked up at Fiona. My eyes pleaded with hers for answers. She grabbed my hand and squeezed it tight.

"You're just going to have to rearrange things, Candace," he said.

"But I've already rearranged so much, and I promised . . ."

I pushed the button again and again: no sweet sound to comfort me.

"Look, you can't help this, and I want you to look on the bright side. I didn't come in here and tell you I found a terminal disease, did I?"

Shame lurked in the shadows but I wouldn't allow it closer.

"No. No, you didn't."

"So, you can go about your book business and lead a happy and productive life when you feel better. Isn't that right?"

But I needed to lead it right then. I had obligations.

Fiona handed me a tissue.

"Yes, that's right." I wiped my nose. I'd had it with him. I wanted him to go away.

"Okay then," he said, seeming to doubt my conviction. "Now, get some rest, and I'll see you in the morning."

He motioned for Fiona to follow him out into the hall.

"I'll be right back, hon," she said, ducking out of the room.

What's that all about? They're conspiring. They have to be. I looked out the window at a nondescript sky. Nothingness, just like my insides: nothing but nothingness.

"What did he say to you," I snapped, as Fiona reentered the room. "Has someone recognized me?"

I tried to shake the bedrail loose. "They can't know I'm—"

"Relax," she said. "He just said that he wants you to rest and for me to make sure you do. I'm to ring for the nurse myself if I think you need Valium through the night. He's having her bring some now."

"Put this rail down," I demanded.

Fiona sighed. "Okay, but don't try any funny business. I'm right here."

She put the rail down and sat on the edge of the bed.

"Rub my feet."

I threw my left foot onto her lap. My right one tapped against the footboard. Fiona glanced at it.

"I'll rub your feet if you promise to calm down."

"I don't want to calm down," I whined.

"Well, do it for me. You don't want me suffering from your outbursts all night, do you?"

I pulled my right foot up under my left thigh to steady it.

"Fiona, I—I . . ." I began crying again. "I—I can't have babies. Can you believe that? I mean, I don't even know if I wanted them. I've been so busy, and I just thought it would all come together in time, you know?" I sniffed. "I—I can't have babies." The sentence echoed through my brain.

She moved up closer to me on the bed and put my head against her chest. I squeezed her arm with one hand and hugged my pillow with the other. She gave me a gentle rocking and stroked my hair.

I'm not whole. I'm no longer me. I'm empty.

"Well, if I ever find a man, I'll have a hoard of kids and we can share," she whispered.

Angela tiptoed into the room with a syringe.

I wiped my eyes. "I don't want a needle," I protested.

"No, no. It's okay," said Angela. "This is going in your IV."

I buried my face deep into Fiona and ignored the nurse.

"Ross," I said trying to sit up. The dull ache pushed me back. "What time is it?"

I wiped my eyes.

"Let me know if you need anything else," Angela whispered on her way out of the room.

"Three-ish. Why?" asked Fiona.

"He needs to know I made it okay," I said.

I need to concentrate. Think, damn it. Think.

"And where exactly did you say you were going?" she asked.

"Seattle. Can you text him for me from my phone? I can't see straight."

"I suppose," she sighed.

Fiona walked toward my bag in the corner of the room and pulled out my cell phone. She hit the power button to turn it on causing it to beep several times with messages. My heart fluttered with each one.

"Who are they from?" I asked.

"Hang on," she said, fumbling. "I hate these things."

"Here, give it to me," I barked. She handed me the phone and sat back down in the chair beside me. I tried to focus on the screen. Tiny little apps danced before my eyes like lightening bugs. I blinked to no avail. "I can't focus. Try again," I said, shoving the phone back at her.

She rolled her eyes and poked around at the screen. "Five text messages."

"From who?" Jesus, help me.

"All from Geri."

"Good God, Geri," I whimpered. "What in the hell am I going to tell her?"

"The truth. She'll just have to adjust," said Fiona. "That woman sounds like a total freak."

"She's not a freak. She's a businesswoman," I snapped.

"Same diff."

My body seemed to morph into a giant sponge. Could Valium make me spongy?

"Why does everything have control over my body except me?" I cried.

"What now?" she asked, still frowning at the phone.

"Nothing," I whimpered.

I found the medication button and pushed it. Thank God—a soft, sweet beep. "I can't talk to Geri right now," I sighed.

"No you can't, but I can if you want."

"No, just text her," I sniffled. "Just tell her that I'm resting and I'll call her later."

"You'll call her tomorrow, not later. I say so," she demanded. "And by the way," she said, holding the phone aside and staring at me with her head on a slight tilt. "Did the good doctor take out all your manners during the surgery as well? What happened to please and thank you?"

"Well, excuse me. I'm just a little too preoccupied for cordialities," I snapped.

She winked at me, and I relaxed into the mattress. Thank-God she's here.

My mind wanted to keep processing, but concentration grew more and more difficult. I have to think. I have to come up with a plan. I have to make everything okay. I have to . . . "I can't."

"You can't what?" asked Fiona. Her thumbs tapped the screen of my phone.

"Nothing." Sleep beckoned me, and my eyes fell shut.

"Okay, done," said Fiona. "I told her that we'd talk to her tomorrow, and that you're resting."

She set the phone down on the bedside table.

"Good," I said, without moving my lips. I marveled at the sound of my own voice. My right calf itched, but I was too tired to scratch it.

"You okay?" asked Fiona.

"I'm better I think."

"Ah, sweet, sweet Valium," she giggled.

She came to me and stroked the hair back from my eyes. "You rest now."

"No," I barked, opening them again. "Ross. We have to text Ross."

"Okay, okay. I'll text Ross." She sat back down and picked up my phone again. "What am I saying to the poor sap?"

"Text exactly what I tell you," I instructed. She nodded.

I closed my eyes again. Concentration is so spongy. "Hi honey. Made it fine. At the hotel."

"Candace, I—"

My eyes popped open. "Just type it, Fiona. Please?" She grimaced and began tapping on the screen of the phone. I shut my eyes again. "And there's more when you have that done."

"Fine," she sighed. "Why in hell I'm going along with this I'll never know."

"Ready?"

"Ready."

"Quick nap then meeting contacts for dinner. Will call later. Miss you," I dictated. "And don't forget a couple of Xs and Os at the end. I always put Xs and Os at the end."

"Gag me," she snorted.

I shut my eyes and waited for her to finish.

"Okay, done."

I heard her set the phone back down. My own breathing sounded like waves on an ocean. It calmed me. My mind wandered. Noises seeped in from the hallway. People talking, metal carts clanging, phones ringing. I didn't care.

"It's ringing," said Fiona.

I forced my eyes open again. Everything blurred. "Oh, that's *my* phone."

She looked at the caller ID. "It's him."

"Don't answer it," I said. "He'll think I turned it off to nap." My eyes dropped back shut.

"But I—"

"Trust me. Just wait."

It stopped ringing. I have to sleep. It's time to sleep.

"He gave up," she said.

"He always does," I slurred. "He'll leave me a text for later." My breaths grew softer.

"Sure enough," Fiona said, as the phone beeped.

I continued listening to my breathing: so peaceful.

"Read it for me?" I wanted his Xs and Os. I wanted him.

"Shit."

"What," I asked, opening my eyes again. I blinked to focus.

Fiona stared at my phone like she'd seen a ghost. "He says they settled out of court."

"How does that warrant a *shit?*" I asked.

"He's wants to meet you in Seattle for a few days."

CHAPTER 11

"Denial does nothing but intensify the impact of shock."

A soft snore cradled me. I smiled without opening my eyes. I loved that reassuring sound that my husband made when he slept. Not too loud, just loud enough. I rolled onto my side to get closer to him.

"Oh," I moaned. "Shit, that hurt."

The pain shocked me fully awake. The sun had disappeared from the sky. Fiona jerked awake in the chair beside me.

"You okay?" she asked, rubbing her eyes.

"I don't know," I answered. I felt my abdomen. Three little bandages clung in place. I reached for my button. I pushed it. It beeped. I hadn't been dreaming. It really had all happened. I pulled my blanket tight around my shoulders.

"What time is it?" I asked.

Fiona looked at her watch. "It's late," she said, standing to turn the light on over my bed. "You were out for a while. Nodded off myself, apparently."

"And you've been here this whole time?" I looked up at her, knowing full well she had.

"What do you think?" She reached her arms over her head in a long stretch. "You need anything?"

I ran my tongue around the inside of my mouth in search of moisture. "I'm bone dry."

"Let me ask the nurse if you're allowed to drink. You weren't earlier, but it's worth a shot." She left the room.

I glanced around the stark, gray hospital room and thought back to that colorful lobby in the Marriott—the place where this whole mess had started. Now I knew how the world would look if designed without color. I knew in more ways than one.

The memory of Ross wanting to join me in Seattle gave me a jolt. Where do I start? What do I do next? What have I done?

"Ice chips for now," Fiona said on her return.

She plopped a plastic spoonful of frozen water into my mouth; a small taste of heaven. I closed my eyes and sucked until the last one had melted down the back of my throat.

"What time is it in Seattle?" I asked.

She sat down on the edge of the mattress. "Earlier. Look, I've been thinking about this mess all afternoon, and I think there's only one way to handle it."

"How?"

"You've got to tell him the truth."

"Well, obviously. I don't have much choice, do I?" I put a hand to my forehead. "Once I've had some time at your place to rest, I'll—"

"No. Now."

"Now? You mean right now?" I asked. "But I . . ." She put more ice in my mouth.

"As soon as possible. You're in too deep as it is with this bullshit. Bad enough he didn't know about today, but now that you've had a hysterectomy you'll only make matters worse by dragging it out."

Another wave of pain washed through me. I closed my eyes and held my breath. "Jesus." I pushed the button with no results and chomped down on the ice with the full force of my jaw.

"I mean it, Candy. As your best friend, I now refuse to let you stay with me when you leave this hospital. I'll spend the night here with you, and I'll drive you home tomorrow, but you have to face the music."

I let out a long sigh. Such an idiot: how did I think any of this would work?

I rolled onto my side and pulled my knees up into a fetal position. "Fine, but I'm not telling him tonight. I'm sick. I'm not myself. I need time to think."

I rubbed my face. Damned itch.

"So, how do you plan to answer his text? You've got to tell him something."

"Damn it, Fiona. Lighten up for one minute, will you? I can't think."

She threw her hands in the air and moved from the mattress to the chair. A young man came in and emptied the trash. She smiled up at him and batted her eyelashes.

"Jesus. Do you ever quit?" I asked when he'd left the room.

"What?" She picked up an art supply magazine in a huff and started flipping through the pages. "Why don't *you* lighten up for a minute."

How am I going to answer Ross? What am I going to say? I hate this.

The page flipping grew louder.

"Look, I'm sorry," I said, lifting my head off the bed. "I screwed up, okay? I admit it. I was sure everything would turn out fine. I swear."

My head fell back onto the pillow, and I began to cry without warning. She put down her magazine and leaned in toward me.

94

"Look. You made a decision and it was the wrong one. Welcome to the human race."

"Don't be a smart ass." I reached for a tissue from the box of Kleenex that lay on the bed beside me.

She grinned. "I'm just saying. You always build these little scenarios in your head and then practically kill yourself trying to control them. Granted, you've had good luck with them for the most part, but that's all it's been—pure luck."

How dare she. "It's not just luck. It isn't. I've busted my ass to get where I am today, and luck had nothing to do with it."

I tensed my back muscles. My face flushed warm.

"If by where you are today you mean waist deep in shit, then great job."

"You're pissing me off, Fiona. I thought you were here for support. What the hell?" I tried to reach for the cup of ice on the bedside table.

"I am here for support, and I've actually let you down. I never should have gone along with this harebrained scheme in the first place."

She passed me the ice then stood and walked toward the window. "Hiding this from the world—and Ross. Honestly. People go through shit like this all the time. It doesn't mean you're a failure or that you're weak."

I closed my eyes and lowered my head. "I am a failure," I mumbled, with a mouthful of ice.

"See? Now you're pissing *me* off. You had a hysterectomy. It couldn't be helped. You're not a failure." She moved toward the end of the bed to face me. "Look at me," she demanded. I raised my eyes. "You can make healthy choices, but you can't control every aspect of your body. You couldn't do anything to stop this from happening. And failure is all in your head. It's in everybody's head. You try something; it doesn't work out; you change direction. Simple as that."

I turned my head in the direction of the window. I didn't want to hear it.

"I know you don't want to hear this Candy, but you have to abandon this fear of failing. It's absurd."

"Well, regardless of what you think. I've made a total mess of things."

I leaned the cup of ice against my pillow and put my face in my hands.

"So, what does that book of yours say? Wallow in self-pity instead of doing something about it? Did I miss that chapter?"

She sat back down in the chair, pulled out my phone, and hit the power button. "Call him."

"I can't, Fiona," I said. "Not tonight."

"You have to say something so that he doesn't catch a standby flight. That is, if he hasn't already. You've let it go long enough."

I tried to run my fingers through my hair, but they got stuck on tats. "It's too much. I can't handle this."

"Excuse me, you? Can't handle something?" she mocked.

Determination began a slow simmer deep inside me and rose to meet my pain head on. "You're right," I conceded. "You're absolutely right. Give me that phone."

Fiona gave a proud nod and handed it to me. "What are you going to say?"

"That I can't talk, but I'm coming home early; that I'll be back tomorrow and will explain everything when I see him. It's the best I can do right now." I typed the text message into my phone and shut it off.

*   *   *

The sun hadn't risen yet when a nurse tiptoed into the room the next morning to empty my catheter. She woke us both.

Fiona had spent the night in the recliner beside me. She looked exhausted but didn't complain, and went straight to fussing about the room to gather my things. Gratitude filled my heart. My rocks: her and Aunt Josie.

Shit, Aunt Josie. She'll kill me for not calling her sooner.

"G'morning ladies." Dr. Jefferies sauntered into the room. At least someone looked rested. "How are we doing?" he asked, making a beeline for my abdomen. He lifted my gown, peeked at my bandages, and put it back down again. Apparently dignity and modesty left with my ovaries. "Looks good."

"I'll just step out," said Fiona. "I'll get us *both* some coffee this morning." She winked at me on her way out the door.

"Good friend you've got there," said Dr. Jefferies. I nodded. "And? How are you feeling?"

"Exhausted. Hurting. Dizzy. Itchy. Angry. Humiliated. Empty—"

"Whoa, slow down," he said, putting his palms up to stop me. "Not angry with me I hope."

"No, the situation. Myself mainly," I added. "I really didn't expect this to happen. Honest."

"Yeah, I got that impression. I tried to make the possibility clear to you beforehand, but denial's a powerful drug."

"I know, I know. I didn't want to hear it." I pushed a button on the side rail to raise the head of the bed.

"Well, the good news is that your blood work looks fine this morning. No signs of bleeding and your vitals signs have remained stable. You can definitely go home today."

"Do I have to?"

"Don't tell me you prefer it here?" he joked, oblivious to my sincerity.

In some ways, I did.

"Okay," he said, taking Fiona's spot in the recliner. "Let's get the discharge chat out of the way, shall we?"

"Fine." I angled myself better to face him.

"I'm going to send you home with enough pain medication to get you through until our next visit for one thing, but I want to see you in the office in a week. Brenda will be contacting you to arrange a time. Someone will need to drive you."

I closed my eyes and nodded.

"And nothing in your vagina for two weeks. That means no sex—not that you'll feel like it anyway—but no tampons either. If you have spotting, I'll need to know about it."

I opened my eyes and nodded again.

"And something we'll need to discuss later is whether or not you'll want hormone replacement therapy."

"Hormone replacement? What do you mean?" Horror stories of side effects flashed through my head. I grabbed a handful of bed sheets and squeezed.

"No ovaries, no estrogen. Sorry."

"Jesus," I said, pulling the covers up over my head. "Am I going to lose my mind now too?"

He chuckled.

I dropped the sheet in a flurry and snapped at him. "I'm serious."

"I'm sorry. I know you are. And no, you're not going to lose your mind. Ross might, but—"

"Stop it. This isn't funny." My throat burned from unspoken truths.

"Look, I know. That's why I want you to start thinking about this replacement therapy. We'll assess how you're doing when I see you, but we can put you on estrogen to compensate for the loss. Google while you're at home and get your questions ready." He smiled. "We don't have to talk about this today."

God. No more estrogen? "I—I don't even know what to say."

I looked at him hoping he'd confess to the joke—tell me that nothing had happened at all—call my pain imaginary.

Fiona breezed back into the room with two cups of coffee. "Did you get your walking papers, Ms. Newman?" she asked.

"Yes, she did. Our little alias is free to go. I'll have the nurse come in and get rid of that catheter of yours," he said in my direction. "She'll also bring your script with the discharge instructions, and she'll take out your IV, so you might want to give yourself another shot of that Dilaudid before she does."

I reached for the button and pushed down hard. My last soft beep. I gave my face a reminiscent scratch.

"You okay?" asked Fiona. She moved in closer to me. "You look more frazzled if that's even possible."

"We talked about the fact that she won't be producing estrogen anymore," Dr. Jefferies said to Fiona. "I've told her to get a list of questions together before we decide on replacement therapy."

Fiona nodded. They both turned to stare at me.

"Jesus. There you go again. I'm right here," I said.

Dr. Jefferies smiled and reached out to take my hand. "You did well, Candace. You're a strong girl and you're going to do just fine. You know that, right?"

"Yes, I know that." Deep down, I needed convincing.

"All right then. I'll see you in a week." He turned to leave. "And call the office number if you have any issues between now and then; any bleeding in particular, or if you can't control your pain. Someone will be on call 24/7 so don't hesitate, okay?"

"Fine," I said. He nodded at Fiona and walked out.

I lay still in the bed for a moment trying to sense the physical changes. Was I feeling the lack of estrogen already? Had I become different somehow but oblivious to it? Could people tell?

"Okay, I saw the nurse in the hall, and she said I could help you take a shower before we leave. I won't take no for an answer," said Fiona.

She walked into the restroom to look for supplies. "Oh, and I hate to tell you this, but I turned your phone on while I was waiting for the coffee."

"And?"

"A couple of text messages from Ross last night, and umpteen from Geri. She's a bit much, don't you think?"

CHAPTER 12

"Always fight your own battles.
Sitting ringside is a guaranteed knockout."

My body slumped in the front passenger seat of Fiona's Jeep. "My God. How can anyone be this tired?" I asked.

The temperature outside had dropped into the low 30s, and a chill had settled into my bones that I couldn't shake. The sun hung low in the sky making emissions visible; car exhaust, vent steam, and the breath of passersby created a fog-like appearance that cloaked the city in monotony.

"You've had major surgery, kiddo. Dr. Jefferies told me to keep reminding you of that. He said you'd be hard on yourself, and you're not to be."

I shot her a disciplining glare. "And when did this conversation take place? During your little conspiracy session in the hallway?"

"Yes, as a matter of fact. Now, are you going to call that woman back? You said you wanted me to be there when you did, so now's as good a time as any."

She merged into traffic. I pulled the visor mirror down and watched the surgical center disappear from view behind us. I placed one hand on my abdomen, while the other cradled my cell phone: Geri and Ross to deal with in one day. I caught the reflection of my eyes in the mirror before shutting it again; dark circles framed a baffled look of fear.

Fiona spoke. "I can do it for you if—"

"No. I'll do it. She's my responsibility," I said, taking a deep breath.

I dialed and the phone began ringing. I prayed for voicemail, but no luck. I put the call on speakerphone and Geri's voice filled the vehicle.

"Bradford? Is that you?"

"Yes. It's me."

"Well, well. I've been trying to get a hold of you forever. What's the deal?"

Fiona slowed to a stop as a light turned red. She glanced over at me with a look of genuine concern.

"Sorry, it's been a bit crazy at my end. I just left the hospital. I was on heavy medication last night, and—"

"You just left the hospital now? You said you were only going to be in for a few hours?"

"Because I thought that would be the case, but things didn't turn out that way."

I rubbed my forehead. Fiona put a hand on my knee.

"What do you mean? You okay?" she asked.

"I'm okay, but I ended up having major surgery," I said, milking Fiona's expression. "They had to do a hysterectomy."

Silence followed. Geri didn't say a word.

"Geri? You still there?" Had she hung up?

"I'm here. I don't understand."

"Extensive scar tissue damage; I can explain more later. No diseases though, it just all had to come out." It sounded like a bad tooth—like it meant nothing at all.

"You're okay then?" she asked again.

"Yes, I'm okay. I'm exhausted and hurting, but I'm okay." More silence. I waited. "Geri?"

"So, will you be able to travel next week?" she asked. Fiona rolled her eyes and the light turned green.

"No. No, Geri, I can't."

"Shit," she muttered, under her breath.

"I'm sorry," I whimpered. Failure began a victory dance.

"When then?"

"I can't drive for two weeks, and he won't let me fly without his okay, but he says I'll need at least six weeks for recovery." I hate this. I don't want this conversation. I don't want any of this. I want it all back. I don't care about the stupid scar tissue.

"Six weeks? Bradford, are you kidding me?"

"Six weeks," I repeated.

Her voice hit an unfamiliar octave. "I don't know what to say. This is a nightmare."

"Yeah, pretty much a big one from this end too," I reminded her. I glanced at Fiona. She shook her head in disgust.

"Like the interview incident wasn't enough? Jesus."

Her cigarette lighter flicked three times in my ear. "God, the whole thing's mapped out. I can't even begin to—"

"Geri."

"Getting these people to reschedule you will be like—"

"Geri!"

"What?"

"Look, I just called to let you know because you need to." My voice cracked. "I'm sorry, but what's done is done. There's nothing I can do about it except take the time to get better. Nobody hates this situation more than I do, believe me."

"But I still don't know how in hell we're going to—"

"I can't think about that right now. I just can't. It's taking every ounce of energy I have to try and make sense of this myself. I didn't expect this to happen—not any of it." I swallowed hard. "I'll be okay, I just need . . . time."

"Well, when can we meet to discuss this further? I need to have some idea about—"

"I don't know. Please." I sniffled and fought back tears. Fiona reached across me and pulled a small package of tissues from the glove box. She placed them on my lap.

"Fine. We'll think of something. Damned stupid timing," she said, followed by a long exhale of smoke. "I'll start formulating some ideas, and I'll check in with you tomorrow. But do me a favor and answer your phone when I call. This is important, Bradford."

"I know it is," I said. "But I have to get some rest. I can't think right now. You don't understand."

"Tomorrow."

She hung up. I tossed my phone into my purse, closed my eyes, and flopped my head back on the headrest.

"Well, that went as well as expected," said Fiona. "Lovely woman, that one."

I turned my face to the passenger side window. A group of women strolled past all laughing in unison. One of them looked pregnant. My pain intensified.

We pulled up in front of my building, and Fiona got me safely inside. She fussed about me like a mother hen, then tucked me into bed with a glass of water, a bottle of pain killers, and my cell phone. She wanted to stay, but I wouldn't hear of it. I needed to be alone to gather my thoughts before Ross got home.

I promised to rest until he arrived, but once I heard her shut the door behind her, I dragged myself to a mirror to try and ease the shock of it for him. Maybe if I looked okay, added a bit more rouge, he wouldn't feel the sting of it so badly. When I looked at my reflection, I put the make-up brush down and braced myself against the bathroom counter. No amount of paint could hide my pallor. I feared his reaction.

I crawled back into bed and under our duvet. Sadness weaved itself through every fiber of the thing, and I wallowed in it. I ached for the comfort of my mother, and I mourned for the children I'd never have.

*   *   *

"Candace?" Ross's voice echoed from downstairs rousing me awake. The sun had gone down. I turned the bedside lamp on and tried to get my bearings.

"Yeah. I—I'm here." I struggled against the pain and dragged myself to a seated position on the side of the bed. I could hear him taking the stairs two at a time. I braced myself.

He ran in the room and stood staring at me from the doorway. "What's going on?" he asked.

"Hey baby," I whimpered.

He walked in my direction. "Why are you home?" A twinge of pain jarred me. I lay back down on the bed. "You look like shit. Did something happen?" He moved in closer and stood directly above me.

"Thanks a lot." I forced a grin. "Yes." I paused, "Ah, no. I—I mean, I just—" Tears stung the backs of my eyes. Please God, let him understand all of this. "Give me a minute will you?" I reached for a tissue from the box on the bedside table. "Please, sweetheart?"

"What the hell, Candace? You leave for the west coast one day and come back the next looking like shit?" His cheeks reddened. "And sporadic text replies? What gives?"

"I can explain everything, but can you just do me a favor first?" I begged.

"Maybe, after you answer my questions."

"Please, Ross. Can you go downstairs and pour yourself a glass of wine?" I raised my index finger for a time-out. "I just need a minute."

He stood staring at me like he would a stranger. "Please?" I asked again. He turned and paused, then left the room at a slow pace. I could hear him taking one hesitant step at a time back to the main floor.

I stretched out flat and reached with both hands to pull our down-filled duvet around me. I squeezed my eyes shut and prayed for the strength to confess.

The sound of a wine bottle being uncorked shot through me like a starting gun. I had to be brave. I had to do this. I sat back up and reached for my painkillers. I removed two of them from the bottle and swallowed them without water, then I made my way down the stairs to find Ross pacing in the living room. Two full wine glasses beckoned from our coffee table. The sofa gave me little comfort as I eased down onto it.

"I'd love a glass," I nodded toward the wine. "Really I would—but I can't."

"All right, that's enough," he said, picking up one of the glasses for himself. "You're really worrying me here. What exactly is going on? Were you in an accident or something?"

He stopped in front of the fireplace and stared at me. I found myself longing for the days when we'd curled up in front of it cooing over our future.

I rocked in a slight back-and-forth motion while holding my abdomen. "Could you sit down please? You're making me nervous."

"I'm making *you* nervous?" he asked.

He paced two more steps and stopped. "Look, I'm sorry," he said, making his way to the sofa beside me. "I'm just confused. I need an explanation."

I put my hand on the side of his face. He placed his over mine and leaned into it. "Okay, fine. I'm just going to say it." I removed my hand and took a deep breath. "I didn't fly to Seattle." He cocked his head to one side and furrowed his brow. "I haven't been out of town at all."

"I don't understand."

"I wanted to protect you from all of this. It just all got so complicated." I reached for a nearby cushion and hugged it against my chest. "I was in the hospital. I had surgery."

His jaw dropped open. "You're dying, aren't you?" The color drained from his face. "No, I'm not dying, sweetheart," I said. "I'm going to be fine. Everything's going to be just fine."

I reached out and took his hand in mine.

"Jesus," he sighed. "Thank God." He wrapped his arms around me to hug.

"Careful," I pleaded. "Not too tight."

"Oh, sorry." He pulled back and looked me over for damages. "Sorry," he repeated in a whisper. He reached for his wine glass and drained it. "Okay then, good. You're fine." He ran his fingers through his hair. "Christ, you had me scared half to death."

"I'm sorry."

"No, no. It's okay."

We sat silent for a moment. Ross stared down at the coffee table. I watched his expression shift from relief back to utter confusion. "So, help me out here," he began. "What surgery? You're fine—I get that—but what exactly happened?"

"Well, I had this really weird pain a week or so ago, so Dr. Jefferies wanted to do some tests."

"Pain. What pain?"

He picked up the second wine glass that had been meant for me.

"Pain here," I pointed to my emptiness. "It was quite severe. Scary actually."

"But why didn't you tell me about it?" he asked. "I don't get it."

"I didn't want to worry you. I—It came and went, and I called Dr. Jefferies just to be safe, you know?"

"No, I don't know, but continue." His tone grew impatient.

"Well, they found all this fluid inside me that wasn't supposed to be there, and he wanted to do a laparoscopy." A pounding throb pulsed through my skull.

"*He* being Dr. Jefferies?"

"Yes, Dr. Jefferies."

"And he did this lapa—whatsit? That's the surgery you had done?"

"Well, sort of."

"Sort of," he said, followed by a large guzzle of wine. "Sort of?" He wiped his mouth with the back of his hand. "Any chance of getting the whole story here, Candace?"

I closed my eyes tight to summon the strength to continue. I thought of everything I stood for—everything I believed in. I had to be strong. I had to do the right thing.

"Apparently I had all this scar tissue in there from my appendix bursting years ago. Things were all twisted up, and . . . and . . . I had to have a hysterectomy."

There. I'd said it. It was out. My eyes remained shut. I waited for a response. Nothing. Time seemed to stand still, but the sound of my mother's mantel clock begged to differ. *Tick—tick—tick.*

I opened my eyes. He hadn't moved—hadn't changed expression. "Say something," I blurted. "Please."

Ross drained the second wine glass without taking his eyes off me. The clock ticked louder and louder in the background. My nerves jangled beneath my skin. He rose, refilled the glass with wine, and carried it across the room. He stopped at the fireplace with his back to me.

"You're angry," I said.

He turned around again with his eyes ablaze. "You think? You went in for a hysterectomy and didn't tell me until now? What the hell, Candace?"

"I didn't go in for a hysterectomy. I went in for a laparoscopy. The hysterectomy was the worst case scenario, and I never thought it would come to that. I honestly didn't."

I'd heard that a weight lifted after a confession. In my case, one had dropped on me like an anvil. I placed the cushion onto the arm of the couch and leaned hard into it.

"Oh, well then," he said, throwing his free hand in the air. "That's entirely different." His hand came back down hard on his thigh. "It all makes perfect sense to me now. I mean, a simple lapa-doodad with an off chance of altering our plans for a family? What woman wouldn't tell her husband about something like that?"

"Please Ross, I—I—"

"Don't 'please Ross,' me," he said, teeth clenched. "So that whole trip to Seattle was a lie?" I couldn't reply. "And those one or two pathetic text messages while you were away? And you think I'm certifiable? That's rich."

He reached back and rested his hand on the fireplace mantel close to the clock. The back of his head reflected in the angled mirror over our fireplace. His hair had started thinning. I wanted my young man back—the one that adored me.

"I didn't think it would come to this—honestly. I thought everything would be fine." I cast my eyes downward. Please make him understand. Please help me through this.

"So, was there ever a promo tour, Candace?"

"Yes, of course there was." I raised my eyes back toward him.

"And when was that supposed to take place?"

"It was to start next week." I looked back down at my lap. "Before that I was going to recover at Fiona's and then head to Seattle from there." It all sounds wrong. It's coming out wrong.

"Oh, I see. So you devised this master plan with Fiona Fitzpatrick. Mother of God, why am I not surprised?" He scouted the room like he wanted something to throw. I pulled the cushion back against me.

"She's my best friend, Ross. I needed someone there, and she—"

"You needed someone there? Oh, did you now? And did anyone question why that someone wasn't your asshole husband? Huh?" The veins in his neck protruded.

"I said you were out of town," I whispered.

He moved across the room toward me and leaned in close. "Excuse me?"

"I said you were out of town," I repeated, looking back up at him. Shame sat down on the sofa beside me, and Ross leered down at the both of us.

"Beautiful, just beautiful." He began pacing back and forth from the window to the fireplace. Back and forth. Back and forth. I couldn't move—the clock ticking and ticking like a bomb on the verge of an explosion.

"Ross, I—"

"I'm your husband, Candace. I should have been there. Not Fiona Fucking Fitzpatrick." He took another drink of wine.

"I was sure everything would be fine. I just didn't want to worry you. You've had so much on your mind, and—"

"Oh, but you could worry Fiona?" he asked. "This was her idea, wasn't it? All this not worrying me business?"

"No, she actually thought I should tell you. It was my idea; all my idea." I lowered my eyes again.

"Jesus Christ," he muttered, storming out of the room.

"Ross, don't be—"

"Give me a goddamned minute," he called from the kitchen.

A drawer opened and slammed. Indiscernible cursing filled the air. The clock's ticking bore into my gray matter. He returned with our cork screw and a second bottle of wine.

"You know what this is all about, Candace?" he asked. "Huh? Do you?"

"I just didn't want to—"

"No, you just *did* want to. You wanted to control the situation like you do everything else. Admit it."

He uncorked the wine. I shook my head.

"I'm so sick of you and your bullshit," he continued. "You knew you could control that damned friend of yours, didn't you? You could easily get her to go along with this asinine scheme. Just one more marionette in your relentless little puppet show."

"That's not it at all. What puppet show? I was trying to protect you."

Tears welled in my eyes. My throat squeezed tight around the air that fought to pass through it.

"Protect me, my ass. You wanted to control me. You've always wanted to control me; you and everybody else on the planet. Well, I've had it, I tell you. I've had it with everyone." He kicked the ottoman that sat near my feet. "Shit," he said, limping back to the fireplace.

I tried to speak again, but my words got stuck. I eased my body into a lying position on the sofa. Sobs heaved through my chest. I didn't do this to control anyone. I never meant to . . . Did I?

My abdominal muscles spasmed. I wanted him to come to me—hold me. I sniffled and held my breath, then raised my eyes toward him. He just stood there. A menacing grin stared back at me. Why is he looking at me like that? "Baby, I—"

"No," he said, holding up a hand to make me stop. "I'm doing the talking." He glared across the room at me. "You've betrayed me, Candace. *You* . . . have betrayed *me*."

"I'm sorry. I really am. I—" He raised his hand again.

"You and that bohemian bitch, Fiona."

"She was just trying to protect me, Ross. It was my idea. I told you that."

My head swam in confusion. The clock grew louder—louder—louder.

"Protect you from what? Me?" He stomped back toward the fireplace. "You're both nuts."

Don't hate me. Please, don't hate me.

He spun back on his heels to face me, and his expression chilled me to the core: his signature courtroom glare. He wanted me proven guilty; he wanted me punished.

I pushed myself up onto my feet and walked toward him in a move of desperation. We stared into each other's eyes. Mine pleading for forgiveness; his wanting to grab my throat and strangle me.

The floor felt like quicksand under my feet. I sank further and further down in it, and—for the first time ever—I felt he wouldn't reach out to save me. "Look, it's not the end of the world. I'll make it up to you, I promise."

"Oh? And how do you intend to do that?" My mind raced for an answer. "I sat back and let you pursue this foo-foo career of yours. I watched you staring into your computer screen writing that bullshit book for months on end. And what's the one and only true thing I've asked from you?"

"Ross, don't," I begged.

"No, humor me here. What's the one thing I have always said I wanted?" I couldn't speak. "Answer me."

"Children," I whimpered. A pulling sensation yanked at my gut causing me to bend forward.

"Yes, children. To carry on the blessed Simpson name. It's the one thing I could have beat Todd at, but now he's engaged to Marla, and you can't have kids. Isn't that right, Candace? You can't have kids?"

"Ross, please. We can adopt. Bill and Lindsay adopted, and they couldn't be happier."

He shook his head from side-to-side. "I don't want someone else's kids, Candace. I want my own kids."

"There are options, Ross. There are methods." I paused and grabbed my head to steady my thoughts. "What exactly did you mean by that 'bullshit book' of mine?" I asked. Did I hear him right?

There's that smirk again. Why is he looking at me like that? What does it mean?

"I can't talk to you about this anymore," he snapped. "I don't *want* to talk to you about this anymore." He set his wine glass down and walked toward the front door.

"God, Ross. Where are you going?" I begged. "Please don't leave me here alone. I need you to listen to me. Please."

"You need me? Is that right?" he asked. "Like you needed me yesterday?" He swiped his keys up off the hall table at the front door. "What's the matter, Miss Perfect? You losing control?"

"What? Why are you—?"

"Why don't you give old Fitzy a call. I'm sure she'd be more than happy to help you devise some way to handle all of this. Maybe the two of you can sit by the fire and read that bullshit book of yours. You know, that one that took up all of your free time for the past two years and left me fending for myself."

"Fending for yourself? What are you talking about?" My incisions burned. My head swam in confusion.

"You know very well what I'm talking about." He picked up his briefcase.

"Ross, please!"

My breathing became labored. My head pounded with the ticking of the clock from the mantel. My feet skated on the hardwood to reach the door. I tried to block him from leaving. He stood a few inches from my face and bore into me with his piercing eyes.

"You lied to me, Candace. You intentionally deceived me."

"Ross," I sobbed, sliding down to the floor in a heap. "How can you say that? How can you do this to me?"

"*You* did this to us, Candace," he said. "Remember that."

The slamming door reverberated through the emptiness in my core.

CHAPTER 13

"If you're too involved in a project to see the big picture, seek a trusted, objective opinion."

He didn't just leave. He wouldn't leave . . . And why did he look at me that way?

I began pacing through the living room replaying the conversation in my mind. He should be angry, sure—but malicious? My ribcage tightened around my lungs leaving little room for expansion. The pounding of my heart seemed as loud to me as the mantel clock, and my thoughts drove me to near panic. What if he had wanted to leave all along? What if he never came back? I couldn't face it if he . . .

I grabbed my cell phone and dialed his number. I stood with my hand over my mouth while it rang several times. The call went to voicemail. "Ross, please. Come back and let's talk this out. Please," I begged. "I love you, and I'm sorry."

The mantel clock continued to taunt me, counting every second since he'd slammed the door. *Tick—tick—tick.*

He's not calling me back. Why? "A text. I'll send a text," I muttered. My fingers tapped desperately on the screen of my phone. *Please call me. We can work this out.*

I sat down on the sofa with the phone on the table in front of me. I stared at the thing and waited. Pain and weakness begged me to end the vigil.

Tick—tick—tick.

Please, call me.

Nothing.

I picked up my phone to make sure it still worked. It did. "Oh God," I cried.

In desperation, I dialed Fiona's number. I knew I shouldn't. She'd done too much for me already. She'd be exhausted, and . . .

"Hello," she answered. I could hear a large crowd in the background.

"Fiona?" I cried.

"Candy? Is that you?" she hollered.

I raised my voice to be heard. "Fiona? Y—Yes, it's me. Where are you?" I stumbled to the main floor bathroom. Pain pills. Where did I put my damned pain pills?

"Just a minute. Hang on," she said, and then her voice became distant. "I'm just going to step outside and talk to a friend," she muttered to someone else. "She had surgery yesterday, and I told her to call if she needed me. Be right back."

"Fiona?" I flipped the toilet seat down and sat on the lid.

"I'll have to step outside, Candy. Hold on." Commotion followed. I grabbed a handful of toilet paper and blew my nose.

"Okay, I made it. Christ, it's cold out here."

"Where are you?" I asked.

"A little wine bar downtown. Blind date."

"Another one?" I sniffled.

"Yeah, I know. I'm a sucker for punishment. This one invited me for an evening of pairings, and trust me. Wine and food are the only things getting paired tonight."

"You didn't tell me you had a—"

"I know. I didn't want you to feel guilty about keeping me at the hospital all night."

"Fiona. I'm so sorry," I winced. My incisions ached in unison.

"No, no. Don't be sorry. I told you to call me. Besides, the interruption is welcome. He's not my type," she said. "So? What happened? Did you tell him?"

"Fiona, he walked out." My voice echoed off the tiled walls of the bathroom.

"What? He what?"

"He left me." I gulped air and bent forward with my head to my knees. "He got angry and walked out."

"Holy shit," she replied. "I don't believe it."

"I don't know what to do," I cried. "What do I do?" My limbs became flaccid. All of my energy had walked out with Ross.

"Listen. Give me half an hour. I can be there in half an hour."

"I can't pull you away from your date. You've already done so much. I just didn't know where to turn—what to do. I—I . . ."

"Trust me. This guy is a total waste of my time. Another stellar suggestion from Mismatch-dot-bomb," she quipped. "My God, I'm actually going to use the old, 'My friend is having an emergency, and I have to leave' excuse, and he's never going to believe it's for real. This is classic."

"Are you sure, Fiona?"

"I'm sure." I could hear her pause before going back into the restaurant. "Does Ross know I was with you at the hospital?"

"Yes, he knows, and he's livid," I cried. "I told him it wasn't your idea. I told him what you said." I squeezed my eyes shut as tight as possible.

"I don't care if he's livid, but he may have left just to blow off some steam. He could come back tonight, and I don't want to make matters worse by being there."

I shook my head. "No, his face. You should have seen his face. He's not coming back. He hates me," I moaned. "He won't even answer my calls."

I stood and caught my reflection in the bathroom mirror. Make-up ran down my face in streaks. I reached up and smeared the mascara around my eyes. I wanted to look awful. I felt awful. Everything about me reeked of awful.

"Well, I doubt he hates you," she replied.

I glanced over at the towel rack where two spotless Egyptian cotton hand towels hung at the perfect length. I grabbed one of them and rubbed it across my face, smearing it with make-up.

"You didn't see him. It was horrible." I tossed the hand towel onto the floor.

"Just calm yourself down, and I'll get there as soon as I can."

I hung the phone up and made my way toward the stairwell. My pills, I remembered where they were: upstairs beside the bed.

My gaze headed up toward the landing, but my body couldn't follow. Each step appeared insurmountable, as did losing the life I'd built with Ross. I sat on the bottom step and braced myself as a black cloud of despair approached.

Nothing made sense. Everything I'd spent my life planning sifted through my fingertips like fine sand. The empty pit in my gut had churned into an indigestible lump. The room embarked on a slow, steady spin.

What in God's name is happening? It can't be over. How could everything change so fast?

I'm not sure how long I waited, but the sound of the condo buzzer from outside jarred me out of my stupor; a stupor which had somehow made its way to the sofa where I found myself hugging a pillow and rocking back and forth like a metronome. The second bottle of wine that Ross had opened looked close to empty, and I had obviously made it that way as the dry taste of Merlot lingered on my tongue.

I continued to sit there in a stunned state until a knock came at the door. They'd bypassed the buzzer.

Maybe it's Ross? Maybe he's back? He's changed his mind.

My heart raced. I made a quick dash toward the door and got short of breath. Puffing, I flung the door open in anticipation.

Fiona stood before me wrapped in her embroidered green cape. She held a bottle of red wine in her hand. My shoulders slumped.

"This is for me," she said, lifting the wine in the air. "You're on medication." She pushed past me.

"Too late," I stammered. "The wine was closer than the pain killers." Dizziness filled my brain. I grimaced and grabbed her arm. "Shit, it hurts."

"And obviously you chose the wrong drug," she scolded, helping me back onto the sofa. She removed her cape and threw it across my knees. "No more wine for you, Miss Garland. I, on the other hand, can drink for you," she said, putting my glass to her lips and emptying it.

"How did you get past the buzzer?" I asked.

"Old Seamus likes my smile. Now, where's the corkscrew?"

"On the counter I think." I nodded toward the kitchen. "I'm sorry about your date," I called out after her.

"I told you. I wasn't interested in him." She returned with wine for her and water for me. "The sommelier at the wine bar, on the other hand? Yowza!"

I grimaced as a wave of pain begged for narcotics. Fiona's expression turned to one of empathy.

"Are your pain pills still upstairs beside the bed?"

"I believe so," I sighed. "I couldn't face dragging myself up there earlier. I'm so damned weak."

I threw my head back and closed my eyes.

"I'll get them for you." She left the room, and I listened as she climbed the stairs with ease.

Godforsaken stairs: why do people have stairs? Why can't we all live sprawled out on one level? Why does everything have to be so difficult?

Fiona returned with two pills. I swallowed them with some water.

"Thanks," I whispered. "I miss my button."

"Here, lie down," she instructed, and I stretched out. She put a pillow behind my head and covered me with her cape. "Jesus, Candace. You look dreadful."

"Well, make me feel better why don't you?"

She went back in the kitchen and returned with a damp cloth for me to wipe my face.

"I'm too tired," I said. "And I don't care."

"Well I care. I have to sit here and look at you. If I wanted to see Heath Ledger in <u>The Dark Knight</u> again, I'd have rented the movie." She grinned down at me.

"Well holy bitch-from-hell, Batman," I snapped, grabbing the cloth. I scrubbed my face hard to wash the day and the mascara off of it. Scrubbed and scrubbed and scrubbed.

"Whoa," she said. "Leave some skin on there." She took the cloth back from me. "You look better. Not great, but better," she grinned. "I'll rinse this out and be right back."

A slight wave of nausea gurgled inside me. Fiona returned with the wet cloth. "My grandmother used to do this for me when I was upset. It helps you relax."

She folded the damp cloth and placed it over my eyes. The coolness of it soaked into my tired lids. She sat at the end of the sofa and put my feet up on her knee.

"Okay," she said. "First thing's first. Your body has been through hell, and you won't be able to think straight if you don't get some rest. Besides, maybe things aren't as bad as you think." She began rubbing my feet.

"You always say that. Are you kidding me? Everything's crazy, completely out of control. Do you know what that means for someone like me?" The clock berated me in the background. *Tick—tick—tick*.

"I can't even imagine," Fiona replied.

"It's like some kind of nightmare. I mean, I never intended to hurt him. I never intended to hurt anyone. I just wanted everything to be okay, you know?"

"I know, Candy. I get it," she said, pulling on each toe until they snapped.

"Well, why doesn't Ross get it?" I asked. I took the facecloth off my eyes and lifted my head to look her in the face. "I thought he loved me. I thought this was for better or worse."

"Candy. You lied to him."

"So? Now we're in the worse instead of better. Besides, I didn't lie. I hid the truth. There's a difference," I snapped, throwing my head back down.

"Uh-huh," she chimed. "So, going to Seattle was hiding the truth?"

I ignored her. "He said specifically that *I* did this to us, and then he slammed the door on me. And he's never ignored my calls or text messages. Never."

Fiona stared down at the carpet as though deep in thought. I watched her in hopes that she'd uncover some great insight that would give me peace. "Well, I figured he'd be upset, but what I don't get is him wanting to meet you in Seattle."

"I know. Why did he pick now to be spontaneous? He's never spontaneous."

She moved her gaze to the fireplace mantel.

Tick—tick—tick. I looked up at the source of the sound and wanted to shoot it. "Can you do a favor for me and move that damned clock somewhere? Please?"

Fiona moved my feet and rose to hers. She walked toward the clock and took it down from the mantel with care. My eyes followed her as she disappeared into the kitchen and shut it in a cupboard. Silence stepped in where ticking left off. I felt guilty for wanting a piece of my mother hidden away.

Fiona returned to her spot beside me on the sofa. "What did he say to you exactly? When he left, I mean?" she asked.

"That I deceived him. That he was sick of me and everyone around him trying to control his life. That I took away the one thing he had over his brother." The true absurdity of the last statement didn't hit me until I'd said it out loud. "He actually wanted to beat Todd at having a child. Can you believe that? He's totally pissed that I took that away from him."

"I'm shocked. Ross Simpson? Competitive? Ego driven? Not possible," she sneered.

"No thought at all about how I might feel after losing my uterus. He's mad that he can't be the first one to provide his pompous ass of a father with the first Simpson grandchild—specifically, one from his own loins. God forbid we adopt." A spark of anger threatened to ignite within me.

"Go on."

Fiona stopped rubbing my feet and listened.

"He called my career 'foo-foo' and said that he's had to fend for himself the whole time I was writing that 'bullshit book' of mine." My face flushed warm. "Bullshit book?"

At that moment the book, the promo tour, and Geri's face all flashed in my mind's eye. I shook my head hard. I couldn't think about that now.

"And the look on his face, Fiona." I propped myself up on my elbows.

"What look?"

"Cold. Smug. Hateful even. Almost like he loved watching me suffer." I flopped back down. "I've never seen him like that in my life. It unnerved me." My body shuddered. "He hates me."

"Well, I don't know that he hates you, but I still . . ." She looked away. "Ah, forget it."

"What? What were you going to say?"

"I don't know. It's just a feeling I have." She stared into the corner of the room for a moment, and then turned back to face me. "Has he been acting strange in any way lately?"

"No, I don't think so," I said. "Wait. Maybe. A little moodier than usual, I guess. And he threatened to take someone else to a fund-raiser when I said I'd be out of town, but—"

"Someone else? Seriously?"

"He was just trying to get my goat. He wouldn't dare."

"I don't know, Candy. Something's fishy about all of this."

I propped back up on my elbows. "Jesus, Fiona. What are you driving at?"

"I'm not sure. I just find it odd that he wants to throw all of this away without more discussion. Actually, I'm surprised that he didn't stick around to argue everything into submission. Ross Simpson? Attorney at Law? That man never walks away from anything that has two sides to it."

CHAPTER 14

"Delegate and micromanage if necessary,
but never relinquish complete control."

Voices, did I hear voices? I wiped the sleep from my eyes and looked around the bedroom. No one else there. The morning sun blazed outside my window. It shot through the thin slit in the curtains and created a line across our burgundy duvet that made me look cut in half at the waist.

Memories of the night before flooded my mind and dizzied me. I reached for my cell phone. Nothing in my inbox—no voicemail—not a word.

I moved to sit up but my incisions balked. The voices returned in the distance.

"Fiona?" I called out. "Is that you?"

"Yes, it's me. Be right there," she hollered up the stairs.

My pill bottle beckoned from the bedside table. How long had I been sleeping? Footsteps approached—more than one set of them.

"Don't be mad," she said, entering the bedroom with my aunt hot on her heels. I couldn't have been happier.

"Aunt Josie," I said, throwing my arms out. She ran to me and pulled my face against her signature denim shirt. Her broad chest and strong arms brought me an instant sense of safety.

"My baby girl," she said, rocking me in her arms. "Fiona told me the whole story." She smelled like wet dogs, and I welcomed it.

She took my face in her hands. Her brown eyes searched deep into mine as though reading my unborn thoughts. She smiled, then wet her thumb with her tongue and wiped the evidence of tears from below my eyes.

"This is why I don't wear make-up," she teased in her thick Texas drawl. "And I ain't gonna pretend I'm not upset, because I am. You should of told me. I'm a nurse, for God's sake. I could of helped."

"I didn't want to worry anyone," I whimpered. "You know what you can be like when it comes to me. You get all bent out of shape."

She smiled and patted me on the head. "Point taken, but I'm still upset."

She reached behind me to fluff my pillow then leaned my head back down onto it. "Well," she said, slapping her hands down on her thighs. "I'm here now, and I ain't leavin'."

"But your job?" I said.

"Just finished a stretch of night shifts. As it so happens, I don't have to be back until later in the week, and I can probably switch a shift or two at that point if need be."

"And the dogs?"

"Eileen's gonna stay with them. She's still got a key." She smiled and brushed the hair back out of my eyes. "Joint custody, remember?"

Fiona made her way across the room and opened the curtains. The sun made a grand entrance and seemed to illuminate just those things that belonged to Ross. The brass on the clotheshorse glistened, the cover of his latest John Grisham novel shone up from his bedside table, and his collection of watches reflected tiny spots of light onto the ceiling. I grabbed Josie's hand and squeezed it.

"I'm glad you're here," I admitted. "So glad."

"So, you're not going to kill me for telling her?" asked Fiona from the doorway.

I looked in her direction. "No, hardly."

"Well, from the sounds of things, this young lady has been doin' overtime in the Bradford camp, so we're gonna let her go home now," said Aunt Josie, getting up from the bed. "She probably has a masterpiece she's fixin' to paint, am I right?"

"Yeah, well. I'm not sure about masterpiece, but I do have a commissioned painting I need to start on: a real estate magnate who wants angry colors for his downtown office." She shrugged her shoulders and walked over to the edge of the bed. "He says they inspire him."

"He sounds dreamy," I said.

The two women hovered over me smiling. The sunlight encircled their heads like halos.

"Listen, I'll be checking in regularly, but call me if you need anything," said Fiona. She looked back and forth between Josie and I. "Either of you, that is. Okay?"

"Will do," answered Josie. "I'll just walk ya out." She took Fiona by the arm. "Be right back, baby girl." They turned to leave the room.

"Fiona?"

They both stopped and looked back in my direction. "Thanks for everything. I mean . . . I don't know what I would have done without . . ." I couldn't continue. I reached for a tissue.

"Don't mention it." She winked and they left the bedroom.

I wiped my nose and dabbed at my eyes with the tissue. Such overwhelming support from these women, but as much as I loved them and felt grateful, I ached to have Ross there instead. I glanced over at our wedding picture and wondered where it had all gone—the passion, the excitement, the laughter. Where had those kids disappeared to who could weather any storm together? What had happened to the promise? Where had my husband gone?

I picked up my phone again and turned it over and over in my hands. I had to keep trying. I touched the message screen and began texting. *Please call me. I love u, and I'm truly, truly sorry.*

Aunt Josie came back in the room. "I've said it before, and I'll say it again. They don't come much better than that girl." She nodded in the direction of Fiona's exit.

I slid the phone under the duvet. "I know it," I sighed. "I owe her big time."

Aunt Josie smiled. "Well, I'm here for the duration, so I'm gonna whip us up somethin' to eat. Want anything in particular?" she asked. "One of your faves?"

"I'm not hungry." I gave the phone a tight squeeze beneath the sheets.

"You don't have to be hungry, Kiddles, but you're gonna eat." She headed down the stairs.

*   *   *

"Is that my cell phone ringing?" I hollered from the master bath. Josie had plopped me onto a plastic chair in the stand-up shower and had gone to change my sheets. "Damn it," I snapped. My eyes burned from the shampoo that dripped down my forehead. I left a film of it in my hair and turned off the water. Why now?

"Aunt Josie? You out there?" Stupid damned phone. I stood too fast and my insides spasmed. "Shit." The phone rang one last time as I stepped out of the glass enclosure. "Goddamn it," I barked.

The sound of her whistling a tune came into earshot.

"Josie?"

"What's up, sweet girl?" she asked, popping her head in through the bathroom door. "And did I not tell you to wait for me before gettin' out of that shower?"

"Was that my phone?" I reached for the towel that lay across the garden tub to my right.

"Was what your phone?"

"Just now. My phone; I thought I heard it ring."

Goose bumps covered my body, and I began to shiver. Wet, soapy water dripped onto the bath mat under my feet.

"Sorry, Kiddles. I was downstairs throwin' a load in. You want me to check it?"

"No. Can you just come here and help me please?"

I tried to hurry, but my limbs jerked and lunged like the Tin Man in need of oil. Aunt Josie took the towel from me to dry my back. I leaned on the granite countertop and caught a glimpse of my bandages in the mirror. The vision of them disturbed me. She handed me my bathrobe, and I tied it tight around my waist.

"What's the big damned rush anyway? The thing's not goin' anywhere," she said.

I made my way back into the bedroom and over to the dresser where the phone now lay silent. I grabbed at it to check the Caller ID and saw that Geri had been the one who called. Shit. I turned and faced the unmade bed.

"I take it that wasn't Mr. Wonderful," said Josie. She shook out a flannel fitted sheet and began wrapping the corners of it around the king size mattress.

"My publicist," I replied, setting the cell phone down.

I shouldn't have allowed her to change the sheets, not with his scent still on them. Why had I let her do that? I made my way to the wingback chair in the corner and sat down hard. My shoulders slumped forward; my hair dripped disappointment onto the taupe colored carpet.

"Why isn't he calling me?" I waited for a response. Josie threw the duvet on the bed and fluffed the pillows. "Well?"

"Oh, sorry. I thought the question was rhetorical," she shrugged her shoulders. "I'm the last person to ask about the workings of the male mind, but I would assume he's not calling until he's damned good and ready."

"When will that be? I can't stand this. He's killing me," I cried. I wrapped my arms around my waist and bent forward in the chair.

"He's not doing anything of the sort," she barked. "That's crazy talk."

What did she know? I'd built a life with this man. I had a reputation to uphold. I couldn't lose my husband. Not me; not Candace Bradford. I just couldn't.

I watched as she placed a clean, dry towel over my pillow and pulled the sheets back. She turned in my direction.

"You gonna call that woman now or take a nap? Those are your choices."

I shook my head. "I can't talk to her. She's just going to flip out on me." Exhaustion pulled me deeper and deeper into the chair. "I don't have the energy for her right now. I just don't."

"Good choice. Now get into bed."

She started toward me as though to help me up. The land line started ringing. I stumbled out of the chair without her and grabbed the receiver from its base on the bedside table. *Private number.* "Shit. It's probably her again." The phone continued ringing. I wanted to scream. I threw the receiver onto the bed and placed a hand on either side of my head. "She'll never leave me alone."

"Oh, she'll leave ya alone, all right." Josie picked up the source of my annoyance and hit the button. "Y'ello?" she said.

"No," I whispered, trying to grab it from her.

She pulled away and walked out of the bedroom. "Sorry. She can't come to the phone right now, but I'll be happy to take a message."

"Josie, please. Come back here." I followed after her with a hand pressed firmly against my abdomen to brace against the pain. My heart pounded at the thought of what she might say—what either of them might say.

"I understand your concern but that conversation is gonna have to wait."

I lagged too far behind. I couldn't catch up. My legs grew heavier with each move I made. I reached the stairwell and grabbed the banister for support.

"I'm her Aunt, that's who, and I'm here to take care of her. She's just had major surgery and—" I heard her pause as I struggled down the steps. Her tone became curt. "What's that ya say?"

Shit. Shit. Shit.

I made it to the bottom and followed the sound of her voice.

"Look, I don't care if y'all are the goddamned president of the United States. My girl ain't in need of any more stress right now, and it's pretty obvious that you plan to give her some."

"Josie, give me that phone," I said, rounding the corner to the kitchen. She circled the glass trestle table and darted past me to head back upstairs.

Damn it.

"I don't care what you've got booked," she continued.

I remembered the phone in the living room and headed that way until jabbing pains made me pause. I leaned on the back of a kitchen chair and gritted my teeth. My knees gave a slight unanticipated bend.

Josie's voice grew louder and angrier in the distance. "I'm sorry Missy, but that's not my concern. Y'all have to decide that for yourself. All's I know is that she ain't goin' anywhere, and she needs to be left alone right now. Period."

I gained a second wind and moved toward the living room. My feet skated across the hardwood floor until I could see the second land line at the far end of the sofa. The red *in use* light flashed at me like a landing strip. A few more steps, and . . . "Jesus." Another jab of pain slowed me down. I clenched my jaw and forced my body to push through it. Almost there.

"I'll tell her to call you, but not until she's feelin' better. And speakin' of Candace's book, there's a whole chapter in there on formulating back-up plans. I suggest you read it."

I reached the phone and grabbed the receiver. "Hello? Geri? You still there?" Gone. Shit. I fumbled with the menu on the phone. Call log, where's the damned call log? *Private number.* Damn it. I'd *have* to call her back now, and I'd need my cell for the number.

I held the back of the sofa for a moment to catch my breath. Everything from my waist down throbbed with pain. Everything from my waist up pulsed with anger. I took a deep breath and headed in the direction of the stairs. Josie met me head-on as she made her way back down.

"How dare you," I said. I squeezed the banister until my knuckles whitened. Heaving breaths forced my nostrils to flare. My body shivered and my face flushed warm.

"How dare I what?" she asked. "Stop that crazy bitch from causin' you more grief? I don't know, Candace. Call me impulsive," she said, taking my arm. I pulled back.

131

"I don't need your help," I barked. Rage fueled my legs as I climbed the stairs. "She'll be unbearable now."

Josie followed close behind. "She's already unbearable if you ask me."

I reached the top landing and turned to face her. "Great. Just great. You think you can waltz in here and . . . Ow!" I bent forward. I couldn't move. "Damn it," I groaned.

"Okay, okay. Easy does it," said Josie. She took my arm again, and I let her. "Let's get you into that bed."

We walked arm in arm back to the bedroom, and I leaned on her harder as we neared the doorway. The bed looked both inviting and desperate as we entered. Just the thought of not sharing it anymore made my pain worsen. I put my head on Josie's shoulder.

"Come on," she said, getting me seated on the edge of the mattress. She opened the pill bottle and removed two tablets. "Take these." I swallowed them down with a sip of water from the glass on the nightstand. She reached up to stroke my damp hair. I pushed her hand back.

"Don't be nice to me," I snapped.

"Too late. I can't help myself." She grinned, and I let out a surrendering sigh. With the soft touch of her profession she eased me back onto the pillow.

"I need to call Geri back. Hand me my cell?"

"No can do." She walked to the dresser and picked up my iPhone.

"Aunt Josie, I have to . . ." A wave of pain scolded me.

"You don't have to do a damned thing," she said, slipping the phone into the back pocket of her Wranglers. "She can wait. She has to wait. You've gotta rest."

Every fiber in my body echoed her instructions as she returned to my side. She pulled the duvet up over me and more fatigue came with it. I melted into the mattress like wax in a heated mold.

"Okay fine. I won't call her back right away I promise, but let me have the phone anyway?"

She patted the ass of her jeans. "I'll take good care of it for you."

I tried to lift my head from the pillow but gave up. "I need it in case Ross calls. Please."

"If it rings, I'll answer it. And if it's Prince Charming, I'll wake ya up. Deal?"

"You promise?"

"Cross my heart," she said, placing a hand on her chest.

I had my doubts.

"That includes text messages," I demanded. "And you're not to yell at him like you did Geri."

"Not unless he cops an attitude with me, which he won't. And by the way, she started it."

I closed my eyes against my will. "Well, I don't doubt that for a minute, but you never need much of a nudge."

My limbs grew heavy. Sleep beckoned to me. "I can't think straight," I whimpered. "I just can't." I heard Josie pull the curtains shut.

"You don't have to think straight, crooked, or otherwise. All you need to do is rest like I said."

The room fell silent, and I feared it would stay that way forever. When I opened my eyes again, I caught Josie staring at me from the foot of the bed. Her smile made a weak veil for concern.

"It's all beyond horrible, isn't it?" I asked. "Everything's fallen apart."

I sniffled, and she moved a box of tissues from the dresser onto the bed beside me. "Believe it or not, it ain't the end of the world, Kiddles."

"How can you even say that?" I asked. "I've lost complete control of everything. Things couldn't possibly get any worse than they are right now, not in a million years."

"Candace Bradford," she snapped, with a sternness I hadn't heard since childhood. "You know better. Things can always get worse. Y'all are just askin' for more trouble talkin' like that."

CHAPTER 15

"There is nothing to gain by losing your temper."

The weekend dragged like the tail of a dog in trouble, and everything reminded me of my recent failures. Commercial after commercial on TV advertised sanitary napkins and baby food. Magazines I flipped through showed pictures of happy couples and spewed relationship advice. And not a word from Ross. Not even a whisper.

Aunt Josie continued to guard my cell phone in her back pocket. She'd put it on vibrate and only answered it once in my presence when Fiona had called to check in.

Sleep became my only effective escape from it all, so I did a lot of it. Josie seemed to understand my need for isolation but would occasionally wake me to insist I eat. Twice when I'd awoken, I'd caught her sitting in the wingback chair staring at me. She'd looked pained and worried both times, but I'd rolled over and turned my back to her.

When Monday morning found me, I'd hoped it brought reinforcements. Wallowing had weakened my energy and resolve—the two things I'd need to find my husband. I had to talk to him and make some effort to explain my stupidity.

"Simpson, Abercrombie and Blythe. How may I direct your call?" answered the receptionist.

"Ross Simpson's office please," I said, fumbling with the bedroom phone while stuffing pillows between myself and the headboard.

"One moment please."

She put me on hold. Celine Dion's voice slammed into my eardrum. *All by myself. Don't want to be, all by . . .*

"Ross Simpson's office. Bethany speaking. How can I help you?" A familiar voice.

"Bethany? Candace." I could hear Aunt Josie climbing the stairs toward me. "Is Ross available?"

"Candace? Oh, ah . . ." stammered Bethany. "Can you hold a moment, hon?"

Celine came back before I could answer: *All by myself . . .*

"Who you callin'?" asked Aunt Josie, walking into the bedroom.

Sometimes I feel so insecure . . .

"Shh," I said, waving a hand at her to stay back.

And love's so distant and obscure.

"Candace?" said Bethany.

"I'm here."

"Just wanted to double-check, but he's definitely not in today. We thought he was with you."

"Oh, I . . . Well, he was but . . ." I braced a pillow against my abdomen for support and swung my legs over the side of the bed to sit up.

"The message we got was that you had some emergency surgery over the weekend, and he'd need to take the week off. So, he's not with you?"

Took the week off?

"N—No, well yes . . ." I stalled. "He was, but he had to run some errands. I—I thought he said he'd be stopping by the office, and I couldn't get him on his cell, so I . . ."

Aunt Josie sat down on the edge of the bed beside me and raised an eyebrow.

"I'm sorry Bethany," I continued. "I just thought I might catch him, that's all."

Why the lying? Had Fiona been right? Could there be more to his decision to leave than just the surgery?

"No problem, really," she replied. "You okay, Candace? I mean did everything go okay? He didn't give any details. Just left the message early this morning, and we've been worried half sick."

"No, no. I'm fine. I'll be fine. Just a little exploratory thing is all. We'll manage, but thanks for asking."

"Well, thank the Lord. Now's not the time for you to be getting sick. And I bought your book on Saturday, so next time you're in I'm going to insist you sign it," she gushed.

"Sure. No problem. And Bethany?"

"Yes, hon?"

"About the book: don't let anyone leak it out of the office that I'm under the weather, will you? I don't want my readers getting the wrong impression."

"Oh, don't you worry. We're a law office, remember? You have a secret, and our lips are sealed." She giggled at her own apparent cleverness. "Now, take care of yourself, and I promise that if he peeks in, I'll have him call you right away."

I tossed the receiver back on the base and stared at it. None of it made any sense.

"Just went out to run some errands, did he?" asked Aunt Josie as she rose to open the curtains.

"What was I supposed to say?"

She shrugged and began picking up stray pieces of clothing that I'd left on the floor.

"He told them he won't be in for a week. Apparently I need him at home. Can you believe that?"

She shrugged again. "Well, at least we know he's not dead," she quipped. "Damned shame if you ask me."

"Don't talk like that."

Every nerve in my body twitched.

"Email," I blurted. A glimmer of hope. "Where's my laptop? He's emailed me with an explanation. I just know he has."

"Okay, okay. Hold your horses," said Aunt Josie, glancing around the room. "Where'd you put it?"

"Um . . ." Think, damn it. Think. "Downstairs maybe? In the front hall?"

"I'll go get it." She tossed the clothes on the wingback chair "You want anything else while I'm down there?"

"No, no. Just hurry, please."

Urgency dominated my thoughts. Why hadn't I thought of this before? What if he'd been waiting for an answer? What if he thought I didn't care? What if . . .

"Do you see it?" I called out.

"Would it be in this fancy schmancy red bag of yours?" she hollered in response.

"Yes, that's it. Bring the whole thing, will you?" Why can't she just look in it and see for herself? Why does she take so long to do everything?

I could hear her lumber up the stairs. Could she move any slower? Christ.

"Y'all are in for a bad back if you keep carryin' this thing around on one shoulder," she warned, entering the room.

I held my arms out toward her and waved my fingers at a frantic pace. "Whatever. Just give me the bag," I demanded.

"Where's the plug," she asked, scanning the walls for one.

"To hell with the plug," I barked. "The bag. The bag."

She handed it to me and threw her hands on her hips. "I ain't takin' any of this personally because of the circumstances," she stated.

"Good. Fine." I flipped open the lid of my laptop.

"But you'd best tone down the tone if you get my drift."

I hit the power button—twice. Waiting. Waiting. My foot tapped feverishly against the edge of the bedside table. "Come on. Come on."

"Maybe we should take a little stroll today. Just a block or two to get ya limbered up." She scooped up the clothes from the chair and headed into the walk-in closet.

Why does she have to talk to me right now? Go away. I began twirling my wedding band around and around on my finger.

"Y'all can't stay in bed forever, and the fresh air will do ya good."

Sweet Jesus, shut up.

Desktop. Finally.

She emerged from the closet. "You could take a couple of pain pills before we go, and—"

"Please, Aunt Josie. Not now," I barked.

"Fine," she said, throwing her hands up in full surrender. "Have it your way." She walked out of the room.

Okay. There's my Internet icon. Head for it . . . and click. Come to mama.

I waited. Shit. Seriously? The dreaded hourglass appeared on my screen and flipped itself over repeatedly. "What is this? Some kind of conspiracy?" Frustration rose inside me like a volcano.

I twirled my wedding band back in the other direction until my email sign-in screen appeared. My fingers caressed the mouse pad and I tapped to enter my password. The hourglass popped up again.

"Dear God." Breathe. Five seconds isn't going to make that big a difference. Breathe.

It finally disappeared for good, and my inbox sprang to life. At last.

Sixty-two new messages. I typed Ross's email address in at the top of the screen and clicked on "search mail." *No messages matched your search.* Nothing. Nine from Geri, fifty-three from clients, and not a word from the man who took a week off to care for his ailing wife.

The volcano erupted. Full-fledged anger spewed out of me and filled the room. How dare he leave me hanging like this. How dare he . . . I clicked on "Compose mail," and began pounding on the keys.

Called your office today. Apparently you've taken the week off because I'm sick. I can't even begin to tell you how much that means to me. You're so thoughtful, I could vomit. Thanks for putting me first and not making me feel any worse after having my insides ripped out—you selfish, ignorant prick. Go to hell!

I hesitated for a split second and then clicked *Send*. The laptop lid slammed shut under the weight of my hand.

I reached back and grabbed the pillows from the head of the bed. One by one I threw them across the room and against the window.

"That no good son-of-a . . ."

My eyes scanned the room. My lungs filled and emptied with deep, heaving breaths. I needed more things to throw. I needed to break something.

I picked up my box of tissues. *Wham*—against the dresser it went.

"That bastard!"

Paperback novel. *Thud*—against the wall beside the lamp.

Blood pulsed through my veins and headed for my incisions. The burn of them fueled my anger even further.

Telephone. *Bang*—against the clotheshorse, knocking it over.

Footsteps pounded up the stairs. So, she can move fast if she wants to.

Fancy schmancy red bag. *Whack*—hard onto the floor.

"Okay, okay," said Aunt Josie, entering the room. "Whoa up there." She rushed to my side and pulled the laptop from my grip before it sprouted wings.

"Nothing," I screamed. "Not a goddamned word. How could he do this to me?" I begged.

"I don't know that, sugar, but he's probably somewhere right now askin' how you could do what you did to him."

* * *

It got physically easier to move as the days passed, but impossible to think—like my body's hard-drive had been removed. They'd taken my motherboard. I'd have to rewire, reboot and reprogram. It would all take time—valuable time—and I hated it.

"Y'all's appointment with Dr. Jefferies is in an hour, so I suggest we get movin'," Aunt Josie hollered up the stairs.

I didn't answer.

"Candace? You hear me?" she continued. "Sun's up. Cold out though. We'll need to bundle up."

A week had passed since I'd called Ross's office, and still no word. No text messages, no email, nothing; but his family? A massive bouquet of flowers had arrived—after my chat with Bethany—with a card that read: *Hope you're back on your feet soon and that we see you at the fund-raiser. Love Dad & Mom, Todd & Marla, & all the staff at Simpson, Abercrombe and Blythe.* I'd made Josie throw them out at once.

Josie climbed the stairs and stopped at the foot of my bed with her hands on her hips.

"Why were house calls such a bad idea?" I asked.

"No money in 'em. Drive around and see five patients, or sit on your fat ass and have thirty come to you. What would you choose? And why aren't you dressed? Good Lord, girl."

She had stayed with me as promised and had continued to handle all my calls. She'd even fielded emails from clients when I couldn't face the computer, making generic excuses and saying I'd be in touch soon. She headed into my closet to pick out some clothes for my appointment.

"Oh, no you don't," I said. "I'll do that."

"Good. You still give a damn." I do? I rose to choose my outfit. My incisions requested jogging pants and a roomy sweater. I got dressed and forced some rouge onto my cheeks. I looked like shit. I looked like my mother.

Aunt Josie rallied me out the door and into the cold November air. Bundled or not, Chicago winters had always chilled me to the core. My teeth chattered as I climbed into her pick-up truck. I blew air through my woolen gloves to warm my hands.

Aunt Josie climbed into the driver's seat. "You need more meat on your bones."

I donned my sunglasses despite gray skies. "What I need is the heater turned up."

"Well, it's only a few blocks. You'll live. In fact, you should be walking with all the distance it is." She turned the key in the ignition and pulled into traffic. I flipped the heater on high in a huff.

My head flopped back on the headrest, and I glanced out the passenger side window. City blocks paraded past me, all looking the same. Trees struggling to shake off dead leaves, concrete competing for the most menacing look, every conceivable person dressed in black. Oh joy, a day out.

Aunt Josie cleared her throat. "You think you'll feel up to a Thanksgiving—"

"Don't even," I snapped, still staring out the window.

Early signs of Christmas had begun to spring up in small pockets of the city: wreaths, bows, and the occasional string of lights. My stomach churned. Surely we'd have this all straightened out by Christmas.

A young mother in a bright red coat stood out from the crowd dressed in gray/black. She had crouched down beside her toddler—also in red—to point through a storefront window at a stuffed dog. They giggled, and I watched as she tugged down on her daughter's woolen cap to ensure full ear coverage. She then kissed her on the nose. The love between them exacerbated my loss.

"And here we are," said Aunt Josie, rounding the corner to the medical office entrance. She helped me out of the truck and into the waiting room. The same pregnant women from last time seemed to fill all of the chairs but one. They all grinned and nodded in my direction when I placed a hand on my abdomen. I rolled my eyes behind my dark sunglasses.

I took the empty chair, and Josie leaned on the wall across from me where the portraits of the doctors and their families hung. The smiles in the pictures looked almost menacing to me now. Pretty young mothers holding pretty little babies, all sneering at me in their blue jeans stuffed with the promise of more.

The woman to my right leaned toward me and smiled. "When are you due?" she asked.

"She ain't due, so mind your own damned business," snapped Josie from across the room.

"Jesus, Josie. Do you mind?" I turned back to the woman. "I'm sorry. She can be a bit—"

"Ms. Bradford?" Brenda had popped her head into the waiting room. Two of the pregnant women began to whisper. I put a hand up to shield my sunglasses and stood from my chair. Aunt Josie began to follow me.

"Oh, no you don't," I said.

"Kiddles, I just want to—"

I dropped my voice to a whisper. "Could you draw just a bit more attention to me in here?" I asked. "Honestly." She moved toward the seat I'd vacated and sat down.

I tagged behind Brenda into an exam room. She shut the door and left me alone with a new paper gown. By the sink sat a plastic model of a uterus cut in half with one ovary suspended above it; on the wall hung a poster of fetal development stages. I removed my sunglasses and examined the trimesters. Each one brought a new level of sorrow.

I took off everything except my socks and bra. I donned the gown, leaving it open in the back, and climbed up onto the exam table. The paper felt coarse against my skin. I began making small tears in the hem of it to create a fringe, and I thought about the note I'd written on my last gown about taking Sophie to lunch. How oblivious I'd been that day, so obsessed with my schedule while my entire world teetered on the edge of disaster.

Dr. Jefferies entered the room. "Well, how's our patient?" The same young nurse from my last visit accompanied him. She smiled and stood out of the way.

"Tired," I said. "Really, really tired." He went straight to the sink to wash his hands.

"To be expected. I know you only have three small incisions, but it was major surgery nonetheless, and it's going to take time for you to get back to your old self. I had elbow surgery once and it took months to get better. Body's need time."

Elbow surgery? He's got to be kidding me.

He dried his hands and turned to face me.

"Other than tired, you okay? Any bleeding, severe pain, anything like that?" he asked, assisting me onto my back and into the stirrups.

"No bleeding and moderate pain."

"Well, I do have some good news for you, if that helps. Biopsy came back negative."

"Biopsy? You didn't say anything about a biopsy."

"Routine. We always send a tissue sample off just in case. Okay, let's take a look." I closed my eyes and took slow deep breaths. "Relax your legs, Candace."

Easy for you to say. Relax your stupid elbow.

Cold metal entered me and I winced. A tear fell from my left eye and rolled across my temple into my ear.

"Everything looks good," he said, removing the instrument and pulling off his gloves. "We're going to do some blood work today as well. Just routine stuff."

The nurse bowed out of the room, and Dr. J. headed back to the sink. I sat back up on the edge of the table.

He turned and stared for a moment while drying his hands on some paper towels from the dispenser.

"Okay, what's going on?" he asked.

"What do you mean?"

He grabbed his rolling stool and plopped himself down in front of where I sat. "You're not yourself. Talk to me."

"I'm fine." I looked down at my lap and began tearing again at the hem of the gown.

"Candace, listen. It's not uncommon to mourn after this type of surgery. It's a loss, no question about it. Are you okay?"

I couldn't answer. "Hey," he said, lifting my chin with his finger. "Spill."

My lip began to quiver. My eyes welled up with tears. He reached for a tissue and handed it to me. "Are you having trouble dealing with all of this? Be honest."

"I—I can't . . ." I put the tissue up to my face and sobbed into it. Visions of all those pregnant women in the waiting room, the plastic uterus, the poster—all that potential, gone.

"You can't what? Tell me."

"It's Ross," I sniffled.

"What about Ross?"

I made eye contact. "He left me." My shoulders slumped forward, and the sobbing intensified.

"Excuse me?" He sounded shocked. "He left you?"

"He left."

"Surely not because of the surgery?" he asked. "When did this happen?"

"Last week."

"Whoa up." He stood and pushed the stool back into the corner. "You're telling me that he left you because you had a hysterectomy?"

"Does it matter why?" I sputtered. "Does it? The fact is he's gone."

I put my hand out for more tissues. He gave me the box.

"Good Lord," he said, rubbing his head. "I mean, I've had couples who had difficulty coping with this type of thing, but he left you right after surgery?"

I didn't answer. I just sat there. Watching him try to absorb the news made me feel less isolated, validated almost.

He reached out and put a hand on my shoulder. "Look, I'm no counselor, but this is too much."

I nodded.

"Okay, I think there are a couple of things I can do to help."

He turned and pulled a prescription pad out of the drawer by the sink.

"For one thing, I was going to discuss whether or not you should go the route of hormone replacement therapy, but I think you should." He began writing. "Given the circumstances, you're going to need every ounce of emotional stability you can muster." He ripped the prescription from the pad and handed it to me. "It's a patch. You change it twice a week. You'll get a steady absorption of estrogen through your skin this way."

"I didn't get around to Googling anything," I said, staring at the prescription.

"Doesn't matter. You'll be fine. I just figured, knowing you that you'd want to research every detail, but you can trust me. This is the right thing to do right now."

"And the other thing?" I asked, wiping my nose with my tissue.

"I think you should talk to somebody about this."

"Somebody, like who?" Fatigue made it hard to hold my head up. I leaned back against the wall behind me.

"Like a therapist."

I sat straight up and stared at him with my jaw open. He didn't just—

"I know, I know," he said. "You of all people."

"I'm not crazy, for Christ's sake," I snapped. The nerve of this guy.

"No one's saying you are, Candace. And what's with the stigma?"

I could see them in my mind—all of my mother's appointment cards stacked on her bedside table. I'd had to beg her to go half the time, and what good did it do?

"I often suggest counseling after this type of surgery, and you appear to have enough other things going on to warrant it," he continued.

"A therapist? Ross is the one who needs a flipping therapist." My entire face began to burn.

"Be that as it may, I think you should—"

"When can I fly?" I barked.

"Excuse me?"

"When can I fly?" My eyes bore into his.

"You're not to get on a plane for four to six weeks like I said, and I want to see you before you do."

"Fine. Are we finished here?" I asked.

"Candace, listen to me."

"I'm finished listening. If you want blood, have them come in here and take it, but I'm not hearing one more word about therapy. Not now, not ever."

CHAPTER 16

"Life is full of disappointments, but a positive attitude can re-frame almost any unsavory picture."

"It's about time, Bradford. That aunt of yours is too much," said Geri when I called her office.

I'd convinced Aunt Josie to give me my phone when we got back to the condo. I told her I had a few things to settle and that I couldn't rest until they got out of the way. She didn't like it, but she gave in. My chat with Dr. J. had snapped me back to reality.

"We need to meet and discuss moving forward," I said from the office upstairs.

"You think?" Geri's voice dripped with sarcasm. "Do you have any idea how much hassle I've had with these cancellations?"

I sighed. "Can you come by my place? Tomorrow sometime?" The smell of Aunt Josie's homemade soup wafted up from the kitchen and tickled my nostrils.

"First thing in the morning. Make sure Auntilla the Hun lets me in."

Geri could exhaust me on the best of days, but since the surgery her conversations left me in full collapse mode. I had work to do, however, and I now had my cell phone with which to do it. I couldn't allow time for rest. Not any longer.

First on the list? Tracking down Ross. Someone had to put an end to the silence, and that someone would obviously have to be me. I started and ended with his best friend, Jim.

"Hello?"

"Jim? It's Candace."

"How you doin', Miss Celeb? Racking up the book sales?"

"Doing what I can," I chirped.

I began fidgeting in my wooden desk chair. The seat springs squeaked.

"Listen, have you talked to Ross?" I asked, afraid of raising suspicion. "I missed him this morning, and I keep getting his voicemail."

"Missed him this morning? Aren't you two in New York together?"

The fund-raiser, of course. And he'd said he couldn't go alone.

*　　*　　*

I rose the next morning and applied a coat of optimism along with my make-up. I had to put my new-found determination into action and repair damages, or at least look the part. Aunt Josie served me a huge breakfast of scrambled eggs, and I ate every morsel. I'd meet with Geri and then find a way to talk to Ross once he'd returned from New York. I knew I could get things back on track.

"Jesus, Bradford. You look awful," remarked Geri when I greeted her at the door. Too much optimism; not enough make-up.

"Well gee, thanks."

"I'll just be upstairs if y'all need me," growled Aunt Josie. She gave Geri a warning glare as she left the room.

"They're hiring security guards at our office building. She should apply," whispered Geri, nodding toward the staircase.

"She's got my best interests at heart. End of discussion."

She shrugged. "Well, it isn't 'end of discussion' until I remind you how important it is that I be able to reach you. What's with you letting her take over like that anyway?" she asked. We sat down at the kitchen table. "That's not your style, or is everything in that book of yours total bullshit?"

"Listen. I didn't expect this outcome from the procedure, and it knocked me for a loop. I needed to rest, and as much as I hate to admit it, she did the right thing by cutting me off for a few days."

"It was more than a few days, Bradford."

She pulled her laptop out of her leather bag and placed it on the table. Above our heads, we heard the sound of my vacuum cleaner starting up. I pictured Josie in the bedroom pushing the thing with added force so she couldn't overhear our conversation; an obvious attempt to ward off her protective temper since she'd just vacuumed the day before.

"I'm fine to put all of this behind us, but promise me we're over the hump. I can't make you famous if I can't reach you."

"I promise."

"Okay, let's get down to business then. I've been keeping in close contact with all the heavy hitters, like your publisher and your producer at the station. I just told them that you're really focused right now, and that I'm working to relieve some of your stressors. I said you needed a middle man, and that that's part of my service. They bought it, so I'm the only one who requires explanations for now."

"Thank God. You're amazing."

"Well, regardless," she added with a prideful smirk. "News from the front is that your book sales are on a steady climb, but it's essential that we get out there and work this thing. Now, tell me again. When can you travel?" she asked, running her wireless mouse across the surface of the table.

"Not for another four weeks. He says he'll have to give me the okay at that point, but I know I'll be ready. I say start rebooking dates."

"You're sure? No unforeseen issues I should know about? No life-altering changes on the horizon?"

The tone of the vacuum cleaner changed as it ran across tile in the master bath.

"No. No life-altering anything," I said. Sweat trickled down the small of my back. "Smooth sailing from here on out."

I knew I could fix the situation with Ross before the tour. I had to.

"Good. Glad to hear it." She pulled up a spreadsheet of original tour dates. "I'm not sure yet, but I'm hoping that we can just move this whole thing ahead a month and start from scratch. In the meantime, I'd like you to do a few more phone interviews." She turned the laptop toward me so that I could see where she'd tentatively slotted them in.

"I can make these work. Email this to me?"

Geri nodded in agreement. Fatigue snuck in the room and joined us at the table.

"And your clients?" she asked.

"Let me worry about them. They're my business."

The vacuum cleaner shut off in the distance, and the condo went quiet.

"Fine," she said. "I've got enough to worry about anyway."

"Y'all okay down there?" hollered Aunt Josie from upstairs. Geri caught my eye and raised an eyebrow.

"I'm okay," I replied.

"Well, don't push yourself. Ya need your strength."

"I'm making her do jumping jacks," bellowed Geri.

Josie's ire became palpable in the pause that followed.

*   *   *

I made my way to the sofa to lie down after Geri left. Whether I had time for rest or not meant little to my physical being. How could I lose so much energy in so short a time? I stayed perfectly still and took breaths only when necessary. The sound of knocking on the front door gave me a jolt.

"Aunt Josie, can you get that please?"

Josie tromped down the stairs and opened the door. Fiona glided into the living room and tossed two newspapers onto the cherry wood coffee table.

"The *Trib* and the *New York Times*. Your book is mentioned in both so I picked them up." She smiled. "And this is for you," she said, handing Josie a homemade pie. "Blueberry. Candy won't eat any I'm sure, but knock yourself out."

"Oh, I will. Right this minute, in fact. Anybody else want some?" asked Josie. Fiona and I shook our heads. "Suit yourselves." She left the room.

"Seamus let you past the buzzer again?" I asked.

"Listen. We have to talk." Her tone sounded serious. She sat down on the end of the coffee table in front of me.

"About?"

"Two local news vans are parked out front, and they're asking questions—about you." I propped myself up on my elbows.

Shit. "What do you mean? What questions?"

"Hush." She lowered her voice and nodded toward the kitchen. "I teased Seamus on the way by and asked if he'd won the lottery or something. He walked me to the elevator and said they'd arrived about 20 minutes ago. They're asking him questions about you and Ross."

"What? Me and Ross, but how—" I sat up.

"I don't know, but something's up." Fiona's cell phone beeped with a text message. She ignored it.

"Shit. Geri just left here. Did you pass her?"

Fiona shook her head.

"God. If she saw them, she'll—"

Fiona placed her hand on my arm to stop me as Aunt Josie strolled into the room with a plate full of pie. "Mind if I peak through one of those papers?" she asked.

"Take them both." She grabbed the *New York Times* and headed back to the kitchen.

"What am I supposed to do?" I whispered to Fiona. "This is crazy. I was going to fix things before anyone found out. How could they know?"

The crashing sound of a plate breaking shot from the kitchen and startled us both. Aunt Josie walked back into the room holding a fork in one hand and a newspaper section in the other. She looked pale. Her mouth gaped open.

"You heard us, didn't you?" I asked.

She shook her head. "No."

"Then what's wrong?"

She walked over to the sofa and sat down beside me. "I started flippin' through the bullshit sections, you know? I just wanted somethin' mindless to have with pie. I never dreamed . . ."

"What is it, Josie?" asked Fiona. Her phone beeped again.

"It—it's Ross."

She tossed the society pages onto my lap. The fund-raiser had been featured in that day's edition of the *Times*. Ross smiled up at me from the center of the page with his arm around Cleavage Carrington.

CHAPTER 17

"When you're faced with unexpected challenges, you'll be grateful for a plan 'B'."

"Ms. Bradford. There're too many bloody reporters down here. I can't control who gets in and who gets out," said Seamus from the lobby phone. "I'm only one man."

"I don't know what to say. It's not fair to you, and I'm sorry."

My throat narrowed. My stomach threatened to give back breakfast. I never intended to cause this much trouble. I never intended to cause any trouble at all.

A knock came at the door. "Did some of them get past you to the elevator, Seamus?"

"One or two may have. I couldn't help it. It's bedlam down here I tell ya. Pure bloody bedlam." He paused. "Should I call the police, ya think?"

I put a hand over the receiver. "He wants to know if he should call the police," I said, looking from Josie to Fiona. My heart pounded against my ribcage.

Another knock echoed through the condo. A voice called out from the other side of the door. "Candace Bradford? WGN television. We'd like to ask you a few questions."

Our eyes darted back and forth between each other. Our mouths gaped open. Fiona shrugged and shook her head.

"Yep, tell him to call the police," said Josie. "We can't have them bangin' on the door all damned day. Don't see a whole big list of options here."

I gave instructions to Seamus and hung up the phone. Another bang on the door followed. Aunt Josie made a beeline for it.

"No, don't," I cried.

"Get her back out of view," Aunt Josie snapped at Fiona. I got pulled into the hallway as I heard the front door open. The flash of cameras reflected off the ceiling.

"Put those cameras away," said Aunt Josie. "Nobody wants to see my ugly mug, and I'm the only one here."

I could hear the rumblings of a small crowd.

Fiona's cell phone beeped with another text alert. She grimaced and pulled it from her pocket.

"Can we ask who you are?" asked a young man from the doorway.

"No, you can't ask me anything, but what you can do is shut the hell up and listen," she continued. "If I hear one more knock on this door—even a tap—there's gonna to be hell to pay." Silence followed, and I wondered how it could be that easy.

Fiona turned her back toward me and started texting.

"What do you know about Candace and her husband?" a young female voice called out.

"What did I just say?" screamed Aunt Josie. This time the silence stuck. She slammed the door and joined us in the kitchen with a face as red as summer. "Stupid sons-a-bitches," she snorted.

We all began lowering our voices.

"Did they leave?" asked Fiona.

"I highly doubt it, but I'd be shocked if they rap on the mahogany again. They'd damned well better not at any rate."

As a child I'd pictured my Aunt as a superhero. I'd forgotten the image until right that moment, but she'd somehow pulled her cape out of storage. It looked brand new.

"Jesus. The nerve of those people," said Fiona.

I sat down at the kitchen table. Every physical inch of me screamed for sleep. My incisions begged for medication. "Like this pain isn't enough to deal with," I whined, placing a hand on my abdomen. "Why is all of this happening?"

Fiona's phone beeped with another text message. She grinned when she read it.

"What's with the messages, Fiona?" I asked. "For Christ's sake."

"Oh, it's nothing," she replied. "It—it's no one. I'll shut it off." She tucked the phone into her pocket.

"I'll get ya some Tylenol," said Aunt Josie, heading toward the stairs.

"Tylenol? That's all they're giving you is Tylenol?" asked Fiona.

"At this stage, yes. A narcotics addiction is to be avoided at all costs. Then I'd really need a shrink."

"Shrink?"

"Oh, get this," I grew angry again at the thought of the suggestion. "Dr. J. thinks I should go and talk to someone." I slapped my hands down on the kitchen table and shook my head. Fiona didn't respond. I waited. "What? Don't tell me you think I'm crazy too?"

"No, you're not crazy. And what's with the stereotypes? I go to one." She floored me. My Fiona? There's no way.

"You? Go to a shrink?"

"Yes. I've been going for years, and she's wonderful. I highly recommend her," she said, grabbing her purse from the kitchen counter. She pulled a business card from one of the inside pockets. "Dr. Hedley. Her office is in the burbs, but she's—"

"Come on. You're shrink's name is Dr. Hedley? You're making this up."

Fiona giggled. "I know right? You should hear the name of my gynecologist," she teased. "Here," she said, handing me the card. "Honestly, you can't knock it 'til you've tried it."

Aunt Josie returned with the Tylenol. I looked at the card in my hand: *Dr. Leola Hedley Ph.D.*

"Tried what?" asked Josie.

"Nothing. I'm not going to see anybody," I snapped, tossing the card on the floor. Aunt Josie picked it up, looked at it, and tucked it into her back pocket.

My cell phone rang from the living room. My heart jumped into my throat. "Oh, God," I croaked. "You think he's heard about the reporters? You think that's finally him?"

"Only one way to find out," said Aunt Josie, leaving the kitchen in the direction of the ringing.

I rose from my chair to follow her. "Wait, I want to . . ."

"Y'ello?" Fiona looked at me and bit her lip. "No, she's not up to talkin' to anyone right now," said Josie.

"Who is it?" I feared superhero fallout.

"Ms. Jumpin' Jacks."

Geri. She'd heard.

"Bring me that phone," I barked.

Aunt Josie lumbered across the room wearing a scowl. She reluctantly handed it to me.

"Geri?"

"My receptionist just handed me a copy of the society pages, Bradford. Seems she likes to follow it for fashion tips," she snarked. I heard her take a long drag from a cigarette. "Wouldn't have happened to see a copy of it yourself by chance?"

"Yes, I saw it," I replied. "I saw it after you left."

"And any possibility that those vans outside your building pulled up because they saw it too?"

"It would seem so," I said, sitting back down at the kitchen table. She let out another long exhale.

"Okay, tell me that you gave him full consent to take that creature with him to that fund-raiser. Tell me that I somehow missed the entire chapter in your book about complete trust and how to let spouses hire balloon-breasted escorts during schedule conflicts. Tell me that those cutthroat bastards are going to report on how solid your relationship is, and what a glowing example you're setting since the release of your book." I dropped my head down onto the table. "Candace?"

"I can't."

"You can't what?"

"I can't tell you any of that."

"Well, what exactly can you tell me then?"

I lifted my head. Fiona and Josie moved toward me, and each stood with their hands on the back of a kitchen chair.

"That Ross left me when he found out about the hysterectomy," I confessed. "That I haven't seen him since the day I got home from the hospital." I wiped away a tear. "That I've been going through hell here trying to keep a lid on all of this. That I'm completely messed up, and I don't know which way to turn."

I heard her light another cigarette. The soft echo of my mother's ticking clock haunted me from a cupboard nearby.

"So bear with me for a minute while I recap all of this," said Geri. I stood again and walked toward the living room. Fiona and Josie followed at a safe distance.

"Your physical wellbeing isn't well at all, your relationship is on the outs, your husband has suddenly become a breast man, and you have nothing in your personal life to back up the book that I've gone out on my own to promote. Would that be an accurate summation, Bradford?" I flopped down on the sofa. "Would it?"

"I can't talk to you right now," I snapped. "I just can't." With no thought whatsoever, I hung up.

Fiona gasped. I looked from her face to Aunt Josie's half grin. "Oh my God. What have I done?" I asked, frantically touching the screen of my phone. "I have to call her back. I didn't mean to . . . Shit." My hands started shaking. "What will I say? How will I explain? What am I . . ."

"Stop it," snapped Aunt Josie, snatching the phone from me.

"Give that back," I yelped. "I have to apologize. She'll—"

"She'll what. Berate you and make you feel more like crap?"

"You don't understand. She's my publicist. I need her."

Fiona chimed in. "Candy, you hired her. You don't need her, she needs you. Why do you take this shit?"

I looked at my best friend in desperation. "She went out on her own because of me. She risked everything."

My stomach churned and I broke down into deep, heaving sobs. I grabbed the sofa cushion and held it against my abdomen. I wanted my life back.

"How could he take her to that fund-raiser?" I begged.

Aunt Josie sat down beside me. "Hush now, and keep your voice down." She began rubbing my back. She nodded toward the front door. "You don't want those press idiots to hear you. Y'all aren't supposed to be home, remember?"

"You're damned right I'm not supposed to be home. I'm supposed to be on the west coast signing books and giving interviews, that's where I'm supposed to be," I cried. My cell phone rang again. "Give me that damned thing," I growled.

"Oh, no you don't," said Aunt Josie. She looked at the caller ID on the phone and stuck it in her back pocket with the business card. "Y'all aren't in any shape to have a rational discussion. I'm puttin' my foot down. You can talk to her later."

"But I—"

"She's right, Candy," said Fiona, putting a hand on my shoulder. "You know she is."

"I don't know what's right anymore," I conceded.

The phone stopped ringing. My eyes drifted to the society page that now sat on the coffee table. I picked it up and tore the fund-raiser coverage into long, thin strips. Then I ripped Eunice's boobs into tiny little pieces. "That bastard."

"Yeah, he's a bastard, but he may just be in full-fledged retaliation mode," said Aunt Josie. "You no doubt hurt him pretty bad at the outset."

"I don't want to hear that," I sniffled.

"Regardless, the fact is, we have to figure out what to do next. Damage control, that's what we need," she continued.

"I can't think," I said. "Me, Ms. Total Mastery; *I* can't think. What's happened to me?"

"Then I'll think for you," said Aunt Josie, standing to her feet with purpose. "Fiona, I need you to scout out the immediate surroundings. Check the hallway, elevator, and stairwell. Talk to Seamus somehow and get an update. Do whatever it takes to get the scoop on those scoopers. Make sure they're away from this door, and see if the back entrance is clear."

Fiona nodded and stood from the sofa.

"Candace, come upstairs with me. We're gonna pack a suitcase or two," added Aunt Josie. She grabbed my hand and helped me to my feet. I allowed my entire world to slip from my hand into hers.

"Why? What's happening? Where are we going?"

"We've got to get away from here until things die down. You're comin' with me back to Rockford."

CHAPTER 18

*"Mentors come in all shapes and sizes.
Remain open to the advice of others."*

"We're gonna get out of here today, Kiddles. Get some fresh air," said Aunt Josie. It had been two weeks since we'd snuck out of the condo—and to Rockford of all places. The black hole that had become my life just continued to grow deeper.

"I don't want to go anywhere," I huffed from the living room.

"Well, I know you don't, and I really don't care. We're goin' for a drive regardless."

"Make me."

"What are you? Twelve? Now, get off your ass and get dressed." She wandered into the kitchen muttering under her breath.

I'd spent most of my days on the sofa with the curtains pulled since we'd arrived. The majority of that time I just stared at the wallpaper border that I'd helped to hang 20 years prior. Yellow roses with golden ribbon running through them outlined the room. She'd picked the color to go with the brown leather sofa that she'd bought secondhand. We'd filled the room with furniture from Goodwill back then, and it all still remained except the television I eventually replaced. She said she liked the way the room looked, and she resisted any suggestions for change.

While staring at the border, I repeated my new mantra: *I have to make a move; I have to make things right.* I whispered it over and over again until the words lost all meaning. Somehow though, the rhythm of them soothed me so I kept it up.

Could I decide on a course of action to make things right? No, I couldn't. I couldn't do anything. I stared blankly at walls and out through windows. I ignored the dogs when they tried to engage me with their stupid toys. I paid little attention to anything Aunt Josie said or did. I didn't care that she still had my phone, that I remained cut off from the world. For the first time in my life I truly wanted to be.

"Candace," she snapped.

"What?" I whined, still flopped out on the sofa.

"Get up and get dressed."

"Whatever."

I stomped up the stairs to change out of my flannels—blue jeans, sweater, ponytail, coat, hat, mittens, boots. All put together in a matter of minutes and without looking in a single mirror. I preferred not to see my reflection. I couldn't stand myself.

"Where are we going exactly?" I asked, climbing into the truck. She'd been in it with the engine purring for several minutes. Late November hung over us like an icepack in a cooler.

"For a drive like I said. Now buckle up." She headed down the road and merged onto I-90 South.

"Surely you're not taking me back to Chicago? You're the one who dragged me out of there, remember?"

She fidgeted behind the wheel. "No. Same direction, but not Chicago."

I rolled my eyes and let out a long sigh. My body slumped down in the passenger seat, and I stared out the window at the barrenness of an approaching winter. My own barrenness ached inside me. I shook my head to free myself of the thought of it.

I have to make a move; I have to make things right.

The sound of the engine lulled me for some distance. I actually nodded off until the sun aimed a sharp ray of light directly at me through the passenger side window.

"Nice out, don't you think?" said Josie when she saw me stir. "Well, cold but the sun's gotta feel good after bein' cooped up indoors for weeks."

I craned my neck and looked at my aunt long and hard. She glanced my way and grinned every few seconds. I shimmied my butt back to sit tall and straight in the passenger seat then turned my body directly toward her.

"Can I ask you a question?" I said in a firm tone.

"Depends on what it is."

"When, in all the years I've known you, have you taken me out for a drive with the sole purpose of talking about the weather?" I asked, "especially when the weather is shit?" She didn't reply. "Okay, well unless I've gone completely mad, which I admittedly may have done, you're up to something, and I don't like it." Again, no answer. "And we're getting far too close to the city if you ask me, so you'd better not be planning some kind of get-together with friends to cheer me up. I don't want to see anyone right now," I snapped. "Not a living soul."

"It ain't a get-together," she said, taking the exit onto Highway 31 south. I saw the sign to Elgin.

"Elgin? What's in Elgin? Where are you taking me?" I demanded. She sighed and checked her mirrors to change lanes.

"Okay, you're gonna kill me, but I know what's best for ya."

My barrenness transformed into a simmering pot of rage. "What . . . have . . . you . . . done?"

She turned a corner, drove half a block, and pulled into the parking lot of a small office building. I could see Fiona standing just inside the front door. She ran out to meet us when she saw the truck.

"Why is Fiona here? What's going on?"

A trap; I'd been trapped. My heart pounded. My eyes darted up and down the street looking for a way out. A bus route, anything.

"Let me out of this truck," I screamed, grabbing at the handle. Fiona opened the door from the outside.

"Oh God. I'm so glad you agreed to come here, Candy. Honestly. I know it's a big step, but—"

The simmer began to boil. "Agreed to come where? I didn't agree to come anywhere. What's going on here?" My eyes burned. Fiona stepped back from me. I wanted to kill somebody.

"Jesus, Josie," said Fiona, turning toward my aunt. "You brought her here without telling her?"

"Well, don't make it sound so damned dramatic. You think she would have come if I'd told her? Do you?"

The cold air made them both shiver, or maybe I did.

"Could we just step inside and discuss this for two minutes, please?" asked Fiona. "We'll freeze our asses off out here. Either that or we can all get in the truck."

Aunt Josie grabbed my arm to lead me in, and I pulled back. Fiona touched my shoulder and looked me in the eye. I trusted her. I wanted to kill her, but I trusted her. I walked ahead of them toward the door.

"Just for a minute, you understand me?" I balked. They nodded.

I could sense the non-verbal cues going on behind me. I contemplated turning around to bang their heads together. I opened the front door and stared down a long, gray hallway. Nondescript doors went from one end to the other. No pictures on the walls, nothing.

"What is this place?" I asked. "Tell me why I'm here." They stood speechless.

A door opened halfway down the hall, and a middle-aged blonde woman walked out. Tall, thin, and professionally dressed, she looked our way and began walking toward us. As she drew closer, I could sense a certain calm behind her steel-blue eyes. Aunt Josie wiped her forehead with the back of her hand.

"Fiona," said the woman. "Good of you to come as a show of support. You can't come in with us, of course," she winked, "but I'm glad you're here."

"I don't understand," I said.

She turned to me and held out her hand. "And you must be Candace," she said, smiling. I stood stunned. I couldn't move.

When I didn't take her hand, she grabbed mine and shook it. "Dr. Leola Hedley. I'm so pleased to meet you."

It all made sense: the deceit, the lies, the cover-up. They think I'm crazy.

"Oh, no you don't," I said, pulling my hand back. "Not on your life. If you think I'm going to . . ." I stepped back from them all. "How dare you bring me here like this."

"I don't understand," said Dr. Hedley, looking at each of us in turn. "Fiona? Can you explain what's happening here?"

"I swear to God, I thought she knew. Josie here was going to explain it all . . ." she said, glancing at my aunt. "That's how we left it. I gave her your number, and she called back to see if I'd come."

Everyone turned to look at my aunt.

"So, you're Josie Whithers?" asked the doctor. "We spoke on the phone?"

"Yes," she replied, staring down at the floor.

"Ms. Whithers. I'm sorry, but I thought I made it perfectly clear that the patient had to give full consent prior to counseling. Did I not specify that?" she asked. My rage shifted from all three women to Josie who now appeared to stand alone.

"Y—Yeah. Well ya did, but you don't know Candace like I do."

"Oh, that's rich," I spat. Dr. Hedley held a palm up to stop my outburst. She focused again on Josie.

"Did you bring her here against her will?" she asked her directly.

"I brought her here," she swallowed, "'cause she needs help." Her bottom lip started to quiver. We all stood silent.

"I don't doubt your concern for your niece, Ms. Whithers, but people have to be ready for counseling. They have to want it," she added.

Josie turned and looked at me. Big tears welled up in her eyes. Her entire body shook. "You do want help, don't you Kiddles?" she cried. "Surely you don't want to stay like this?" She sniffled and wiped her nose on the sleeve of her shirt. "Please, baby girl. I can't stand seeing you give up. I just can't. It's too much." She began sobbing. Fiona walked over to her and took her in her arms.

"I—I . . ." I tried to speak but couldn't.

"Please, Kiddles," continued Josie, crying into Fiona's hair. "Don't be like Lynn. Please," she begged.

Lynn? My mother? Dear God. I'm acting like my mother? Memories flooded my mind of her sprawled out on the sofa. She'd be there day and night not talking to anyone but herself. Christ. My eyes widened. Fiona shot me a pleading glance.

"I'm not crazy," I screamed out in defiance.

"No one's insinuating that you're anything of the sort," said Dr. Hedley. "From what I understand you're just going through an extremely difficult time right now, that's all."

"Look, I've been coming here for years. You don't think I'm crazy, do you?" asked Fiona.

"Maybe," I replied.

Fiona burst out laughing. "Well then, you're in good company, Candy girl. That's all I can say."

We reached a standoff and all stood in the hallway facing each other. Aunt Josie continued to cling to Fiona as though a lifetime's worth of tears had been waiting for that one embrace.

Dr. Hedley finally spoke. "Well, here's the situation as I see it." She looked in my direction. "You have a couple of women here who love you a great deal and are concerned about your recent turn of events, am I right?"

"What I have is a couple of meddlesome pains-in-the-ass that can't mind their own business," I snapped.

"Well, lucky you," she shrugged. "Regardless . . ." she raised her wrist to eye level, "I do have another," and checked her watch, "forty-five minutes or so on my schedule with your name on it. If you like, we can take all of that time or five minutes of it, and have a discussion to see if we're interested in working together. If you decide it's not for you, or if you don't want to talk at all, that's entirely up to you."

I had to admit I liked her. I would rather have had a fork stuck in my eye than be standing there at that minute, but I did like her.

"Kiddles," sniffed Aunt Josie, letting go of Fiona. "Please? For me?"

"Jesus Christ." My nerves twisted and gnarled together under my skin. "Who's paying for this anyway?"

"Ross," joked Fiona. "It's less than an hour, Candy. Talk to the woman."

"Ten minutes," I decided. "I'll give you ten minutes and not a second more," I crossed my arms across my chest. Fiona and Aunt Josie gave each other a hopeful glance. I could have smacked them both.

"That's fine," said Dr. Hedley, "but you're not giving me anything. Either you see some value in us developing a relationship or you don't. If you think you can decide in ten minutes, that's fine."

She turned and headed down the hall toward the door from which she'd come. I dragged my feet and followed, frowning at my conspirators on my way by.

CHAPTER 19

"Hold your cards close to your chest. Be confident but cautious when meeting others for the first time."

Dr. Hedley's office looked completely different from the stark hallway we'd just left. She had a reception area that housed four chairs and a desk with no one at it.

"That desk is here for show. I prefer to do my own scheduling," she acknowledged. I respected that.

The walls had been painted an earthy taupe, and from them hung original works of art in various styles. A red and gold abstract oil painting caught my eye. One of Fiona's perhaps.

"If you do decide to come back, this will be the area where you'll wait until I call you." We crossed the small space where she opened another door that led to a private room. I hesitated and peeked through the doorway like a child afraid that a monster might step out to greet me. A black and white lab-mix dog did instead. His tail wagged like he'd known me for years.

"This is Skinner," said Dr. Hedley, stepping into the office. "Please," she continued. "Come in and shut the door."

That world. I didn't know if I could enter it. The pounding in my chest pulsed up into my ears.

Skinner rubbed against my leg. He licked my hand and headed inside, but not before pausing to glance over his shoulder at me. I sighed and crossed the threshold.

Dr. Hedley directed me to a loveseat against the wall. The entire room looked like the corner nook in a trendy bookstore. Shelves stuffed full of books and various trinkets, braided throw rugs on the floor, and a small table in the corner that held a collection of unused incense holders. Not a monster's lair by all appearances, but I remained wary.

"Now, just before we get started, I want to apologize for any of my part in this misunderstanding. I should have booked this appointment with you directly, but I was reassured that you were aware and since you all knew Fiona . . . Well, it doesn't matter what I thought. It was a huge mistake, and I'm sorry."

She crossed the room and made herself comfortable in a big leather armchair facing me. We sat silent for a moment. She continued, "so, I would usually ask what brought you here, but that answer would appear to be your aunt." She grinned and looked me over from head to toe.

I crossed my arms in front of my chest. Should I do that? Will she think that means something? I put them back down at my sides and crossed my legs instead.

"Would you say you're close?" she asked, "your aunt and you?"

"Well, we were until today."

She nodded. "I understand."

"Do you?"

She shrugged. "Maybe. Can you tell me why she wanted you to come?"

"I don't know. Because she thinks I'm a raving lunatic perhaps?"

Skinner came over and leaned against the loveseat. I reached down to pat him. "A lot's been happening lately. I suppose she's worried," I added.

"Worried in what way?"

I stared at her for a moment not sure of how it all worked. "I'm not myself. Apparently I'm behaving like someone else."

"Yes, she mentioned someone named Lynn."

"My mother and I'm not going there." I stopped patting the dog. "We're not talking about my mother."

She shrugged again and tucked her feet up under her. Skinner curled up at my feet. "Well, would you like to tell me what, specifically, has been happening lately?"

"No, I would not," I said, "other than the fact that my entire life has gone to shit."

She nodded her head again. "I see."

I realized the futility of my lack of input into the conversation, but I couldn't help it. It all felt so alien, opening up to someone I'd just met—alien and absurd.

"Okay, what about your aunt? Can we talk about her?"

I shrugged back.

"Is she from your mother's side or your father's?"

"Neither. She's a friend of the family. More a friend of Mom's, I guess."

"Ah," she said. "I thought I saw a hint of resemblance, but obviously not."

"No. More like a dog and the owner. The more time we spend together, the more we look alike."

Dr. Hedley smiled, and Skinner perked up his ears. I reached a hand over the arm of the loveseat and began rearranging the incense holders like pawns in a game of chess.

"Is there an uncle?" she asked.

"No, no uncle. She's lesbian. She lived with a woman for a few years after I moved out, but they're no longer together."

"After you moved out? Then you stayed with her at some point?"

"She raised me after Mom . . ." The chess moves stopped. "I'm not talking about my mother."

"Ah, yes. Thanks for the reminder," she said. "And your aunt's sexuality. Does that bother you?"

"No," I snapped. "Why would it?"

"Just asking."

I picked up an incense holder from the table—one shaped like a butterfly. I began turning it over and over again in my hands.

"Are your parents still living? Can I ask that?"

"Mom, no—dad, yes. He lives in Rockford." I could picture him—right at that moment—flopped out on his sofa pouring a beer into his blank expression. "No more talk about family."

"Okay. Got it."

She put both feet back on the floor and leaned forward with her elbows on her knees. "How about we talk about today then?"

I uncrossed my legs and straightened my back.

"You didn't know you were coming here. How are you feeling about all of this?"

"I'm livid, if you want to know the truth."

Dr. Hedley didn't speak. She just sat in her chair staring at me as though I'd said nothing at all. The dog let out a long, bored sigh, and my every nerve began to twitch. Slow at first, the sensation grew into an overwhelming urge to bolt from the room. I set the butterfly back where it belonged.

"Let me just make it clear that I don't believe in therapy, I never have. I've known people who've tried it and it didn't work. It's all about inner strength and tapping into that on your own, not about being weak and spilling your guts to perfect strangers."

"So, is that what you've been doing?"

I fidgeted on the loveseat. "What?"

"Taking control of your life? Finding inner strength? Is that why she brought you here?"

The dog lifted his head and turned to look at me. His tail wagged, and my lip began to quiver. Don't cry here—Jesus, not here.

"Candace?"

I swallowed once—twice. "No," I whispered.

"No what?"

"No, I'm not handling it. Not any of it." Skinner stood on all fours and rested his head on my knee. "I'm a complete screw-up. Satisfied?"

Dr. Hedley passed me a box of tissues. "I highly doubt that you're a complete screw-up, Candace. In fact, I get the impression that you're anything but. Your aunt told me about your long list of successes over the phone."

"That's all gone now, don't you see?" I grabbed several tissues from the box and held them against my face.

"No, I don't see because I don't know the details, but I did a little research after your aunt's bragging. You've apparently written a book to help others acquire the necessary tools for a successful life. Isn't that correct?"

"Yes," I sniffled.

"And how does that differ from what I do?"

The walls of that trendy little nook began to close in on me. Words like *Psychotherapy*, *Anger*, and *Pathological* jumped off the spines of her books to taunt me. I took a long, deep breath and struggled to compose myself. I'd reached my limit.

"Look, I think I've had enough, do you mind? You said I could take as much time as I wanted, and I don't want anymore."

"Your call entirely." She rose and handed me a business card from her desk. "I'd be happy to work with you if you decide to come back."

I blew my nose with the tissues and wiped the tears from my face. As I stood to leave, the room gave a slight spin to the right. I reached for the arm of the loveseat to steady myself.

"You okay?"

"Fine. I'm fine. I do this on occasion since surgery." I pushed through the dizziness to stand tall.

"And surgery's one of those things we can't talk about?"

"Precisely."

I headed back out into the reception area.

"Candace?"

"Yes?" I said turning back to face her.

"I don't know your aunt, and I definitely don't agree with her bringing you here unprepared, but don't be too hard on her, okay? It's obvious that she loves you very much, and that she doesn't know where to turn."

"Well then, maybe she should be coming in here instead of me."

"Maybe. But just so you know, I don't offer family rates." She grinned and closed the door behind her.

*   *   *

Aunt Josie and Fiona sat on the floor in the lobby. They rose when they saw me coming out of Dr. Hedley's office. I walked toward them without eye contact. I passed by and out the door without a word. I could hear them flustering behind me. I proceeded to the truck and waited for it to be unlocked. Fiona spoke first.

"You okay?" she asked, trying to catch my eye.

"I want to go back to the house." I flared my nostrils and stared off into the distance. "Now."

"Listen, don't be mad, okay? We did this out of love, nothing else," she continued. "And granted, Josie should have told you."

Aunt Josie jumped to her own defense. "She never would have come, and—"

"I said I want to go back to the house—now."

A bitter cold wind whipped around us, and I pulled my coat collar up around my neck. Aunt Josie unlocked the truck and I got in slamming the door. Fiona held up her cell phone and mouthed the words "*Call me,*" through the passenger's side window. I turned away from her.

Out of the corner of my eye, I could see the two meddlers embracing. They exchanged a few whispers before Aunt Josie climbed into the truck beside me.

I didn't say a word for the first twenty miles or so. I'd let my anger fall away, but I didn't tell her that. She'd needed to pay for what she'd done and I knew my silence would serve as sufficient punishment. I didn't have the energy to stay mad. I just wanted to get back to the sofa; back to the numbing mindlessness of television and wallpaper borders.

A light snow began to fall, and I passed the time by following individual flakes as they met their demise on the windshield. Aunt Josie sniffled at one point, and I turned to see a tear in her eye. I decided that the silence had gone on long enough.

"You afraid I inherited Mom's suicide gene or something?"

She turned, startled. "Ah, n—no. Not that you inherited anything, but you've had that same look on your face the last couple of weeks. A distance like she had. I ignored hers. I ain't makin' that mistake again, so help me—least of all with you."

She wiped the tear away. I turned and looked back out of the window. Field after field of lifeless cornfields blanketed in snow came and went from view. A genuine detest for winter made me shiver.

"So, you're not mad then?" she asked.

"I don't know what I am," I said, "or who for that matter." Exhaustion and confusion had become my only consistent reality; that and a gray fog of sadness that stayed draped over me like a cloak.

"Did you like her, though? Dr. Hedley, I mean?"

I shot her a glare. "She was fine, but if I ever see her again it will be nobody's business but my own. You understand me?" Josie nodded. "I still maintain that therapy's pointless."

She opened her mouth to reply and thought better of it.

The snow picked up some, and following the path of the flakes proved to be too challenging. I looked at Josie and pondered how she'd felt at the time of my mother's death. Could going to Elgin that day have been more about her guilt than my stability? I didn't dare ask—or insinuate.

"You think Dad ever feels guilty about Mom?" We had an unspoken rule about discussing her death; at least I did. We could only take the conversation so far.

"More than any of us, I suppose," she replied. "He left her, remember? Probably the hardest thing he's ever done in his life. I ain't never seen a man love a woman more than he did."

How did that make any sense? I tried to remember what life had been like when he'd lived with us. I couldn't.

"Well, I don't believe that for one minute."

"Believe what you want, Kiddles. Sometimes the sufferin' of folks we love is too damned hard to watch. Helplessness can eat a person up inside, especially someone like your Daddy."

"Meaning?"

"Well, come now. We both know that God shorted him on emotional strength. What little he does have goes to dealin' with how much he ain't. Make sense?" It didn't. I loathed weakness, and none more than the recent display of my own.

She hit the blinker on the truck and took the first exit for Rockford.

"Well, why did he have to leave me there to watch her suffer?"

"You came out of the womb stronger than him, Candace, and he knew I was keepin' an eye on ya."

The same way she'd kept an eye on Mom?

We drove a few blocks and reached a stop light. A crow swooped in and perched itself on the light post.

"She loved those damned things, you know," she said, nodding in the bird's direction.

"Crows?" I remembered the one that had flown beside my car weeks earlier.

"Yep. Thought they had secret powers or something. Said they could read her thoughts."

A memory of my mother returned for the first time: her throwing bits of every meal into the backyard for the birds. She'd talked to them too, I think.

Aunt Josie reached over and patted my knee. "He wants to see you, by the way."

"Who?"

"Your Daddy, that's who."

"God knows why. He just sits there with nothing to say when he does see me."

"Hell, Bill Bradford ain't got nothin' to say to anybody, not unless it's hardware related, but layin' eyes on you would do him a world of good. It would you too. He calls every few days to see how you're doin', you know."

"You didn't tell me that," I said. The light turned green and we made our way closer to home.

"You ain't exactly been receptive to me tellin' you much of anything now, have ya?" I shrugged and slumped down in the seat. "I'll have him for dinner this week if you're okay with it."

"Whatever."

We rounded the corner and the house came into view. Hallelujah.

"Has anybody else been calling to see how I'm doing?" I asked. "Like a wayward husband by chance?"

"No. Houdini ain't reappeared, but I'm not exactly sure why you'd want him to anyway. I never did like that boy."

I turned to her in surprise. "We made a commitment to each other, Josie. This is a marriage we're talking about." She didn't reply. "And besides, failure is never an option for me. You know that."

Not an option, and yet I'd done nothing lately but swim in it.

"Honey, all relationships fail on some level, whether they make it or don't. You need to let go of that crap. Besides, is it just me or did the word *love* somehow get skipped in that explanation?"

CHAPTER 20

*"Stay focused on task lists, and never fall
behind on correspondence."*

"Your Daddy will be here around five o'clock, Candace. I'm fixin' to run to the store for some odds and sods. You want anything?" asked Josie, entering the living room.

"Wine maybe?"

"Gotcha covered. I'd ask you to come with me, but every gossipmonger in town will be whisperin' behind me as it is."

"Ah . . . that's okay. I'll be just fine here with the dogs."

Patches, an off-white spotted beagle mix, and Toby, an aging Lhasa Apso, stood staring up at Josie hoping to tag along. She threw on her black parka and patted their heads.

"Go on, lil' bits. Your big sister's gonna stay with ya today." The dogs hung their heads and walked in my direction.

"Actually," I said, "there is something you can get for me, but you're not going to like it."

"What's that?"

"Grab me some entertainment rags from the newsstand? If I'm going to get my life back, I need to know what I'm up against."

Josie shook her head. "Candace, I'm thrilled that you're feelin' better, but—"

"But nothing. You can't protect me from all of this forever."

"Well, I wish I could," she said, grabbing her keys from her pocket. "Speaking of which, you think you're gonna be okay here alone when I have my night shifts comin' up?"

"Sure. I'll be fine," I said. "I would like to get my own wheels back at some point though. I hate the thought of being stuck here without a ride. Even if I don't go anywhere, I like to know I can."

"Well, we'll figure somethin' out, but I could get a ride to work and leave you the truck. That fancy box on wheels of yours will draw more attention to you being here than a rented billboard. Especially with old Nosey Natterson across the street."

Josie pulled the sheers back from the small window on the front door and peeked outside.

"Well, shit. Speak of the devil. Here she comes, and with food no less."

"Mrs. Daw?"

"Yep. That damned woman never misses a trick. She's snoopin', no doubt about it."

Josie shooed me into the kitchen. I called the dogs in after me.

"Why, Heloise Daw," she said, opening the door. "What have you gone and done? Cooked too many cabbage rolls for Jack?"

"It's not Jack. It's Norman and you know it. Honestly, Josie," said Mrs. Daw. "No, I saw you had your girl home and I wanted to make her something special. Let her know the folks of Rockford hold no ill will."

"No ill will for what, Heloise?" asked Josie, with the low grumblings of a mother bear.

"Well, honey. We've all read about her troubles in the magazines and papers. Why, Jenny Martin herself said she saw one or two clips on the television. People can say the nastiest of things. We just want her to know that we don't believe one word of it. I mean, a beautiful girl like that having a sex change operation. What on earth would possess someone to write a thing like that?"

I gasped. Did she just say—?

"Excuse me?" asked Aunt Josie.

"Well, I can understand a man leaving his wife if she did have that done, but I don't believe for one minute that Candace would . . ." Heloise paused. "She didn't, did she?"

"Jesus H. Murphy Frickin' Christ, Heloise. Have you lost your ever lovin' mind?"

"N—No, I—"

"No, you what?" hollered Aunt Josie.

"Well, no. I just thought I'd get the facts straight, is all. Stop all the rumors for her. Why, it's only a matter of time before they figure out where she is, and don't you want the community to be prepared?"

Aunt Josie let go like an F-5 tornado. "What I want is for all y'all to mind your own damned business."

"Well, what kind of thanks is that?" asked Mrs. Daw. "I worked all morning on this lasagna, and—"

"I don't care if you worked a week on it and flew the pasta in from goddamned Italy. We're not accepting it, so you and Jack Daw can eat it yourselves. Better yet, why don't you take turns stickin' it up each other's asses?"

Patches started barking. I held her collar to keep her back.

"Well!" screamed Mrs. Daw. "I never."

"And you never will again. You ever get the urge to do me or my girl any favors in the future you'll be one sorry woman if you follow through. Sex change operation—if that don't beat all."

The door slammed shut. The dogs and I jumped.

"You've probably had that operation yourself," Mrs. Daw hollered from the front stoop. "We know all about your kind."

"Oh, sweet mother of God. Give me strength," muttered Aunt Josie.

Josie stomped into the kitchen with her face as red as a chili pepper. We stood staring at each other in shock, then her eyes started sparkling and she burst into laughter. She put a hand on my shoulder and bent forward as loud guffaws escaped her.

I grabbed the back of one of the wooden kitchen chairs to steady myself. The more we laughed, the more the dogs barked and wagged their tails. Tears streamed down both our faces. I tried to catch my breath. Endorphins bounced off every inch of my insides. I'm alive.

"You catch all that?" she asked, wiping away tears.

"Oh my God; you told her to stick food up her ass. You said it—out loud."

The hero that keeps on giving. "Well, she's had it coming for a long time. And by damn, that look on her face was fantabulous. You shoulda seen it." She slapped her thigh and let out one last laugh. "God, I wish I'd got a picture of that."

"You were priceless."

The faint smell of lasagna still lingered in the air, as did small servings of Heloise's remarks. "You think they're really saying that about me? That I had a sex change operation?"

"Oh probably, but look at it this way. The truth will sound pretty insignificant if that's the case," she scoffed. "Honest to Pete. Just when you think people can't get any nuttier."

*   *   *

With Josie out of the house I could take a small step toward returning to the world, if only in a virtual sense. Fear walked with me to the tiny alcove where Josie's computer sat covered in dust. Knowing full well that she didn't have WiFi, I pulled the internet cable from the back of her PC and plugged it into my laptop.

Over 500 emails awaited me when I'd finally logged on to my account. I bowed my head and prayed for the strength to sift through even a portion of them.

Breathe, Candace. *Make a move.*

Just in case, I ran an email search on Ross's address: nothing. I then searched on Geri's. She'd sent over 30 messages, but none in the last five days. A gnawing ache began in the pit of my gut. I knew I'd have to call her.

Most of the emails came from clients; the first one from Sophie Blanchard. Her testimonials had been key to promoting the book. Now she'd had enough.

> *I'm sorry Candace. I have tried to reach you for weeks. Appointments have come and gone without a word, and your lack of professionalism has appalled me. I send my deepest regret for your current situation and wish you future successes in every sense, but your services will no longer be required. Please refund my down-payments at your earliest convenience.*

My shoulders slumped forward. The dogs came to me, one on each side, and began nudging for attention.

"Not now," I snapped, diving back into the emails with a new onset of tightness in my chest.

More of the same followed. Clients canceling services—none of them able to reach me. Some expressed panic; most said they felt deceived and cheated. One or two reached out to offer help, but so few.

What had I expected? I'd known all along this could happen but I'd been paralyzed to take action. Overwhelmed and paralyzed. Damned, stupid surgery and the money? Most of them had paid in advance.

Aunt Josie's phone began ringing. Maybe she'd forgotten something. I stumbled over Patches to answer it.

"Hello?"

"Well, she lives and breathes. Who knew?"

"Geri," I sighed. "Geri, I—I—"

"Nope. I don't want to hear it. I don't want to hear that your aunt has your phone, that you've been an emotional wreck, or that you're in a straight jacket. I don't want to hear any of it. My assistant has been doing cartwheels over here trying to find this stupid phone number, but now I've got it and we're talking. Period."

I moved to the kitchen and plopped down in a chair. "I'm listening."

"Have you seen or heard any of the press coverage of your little drama?"

"Very little."

"Oh, well. You wanted publicity? You got it. None that would sell a boat to a castaway, but you got it. Pictures floating all over the place of you collapsing at that damned interview."

My hand flopped down on the table. "What?"

"That's right. Not to mention that you've had everything from a mental breakdown to a sex-change operation. Rather impressive, don't you think?"

"Not really," I whimpered.

"Well, you're right considering that nothing they're saying adds up to mastery of crap. They're calling the book *Total BS*."

"Christ."

"And the worst part of all is that I can't defend you because I don't know what the hell's going on."

I wanted to tear through the back door and run screaming down the street. I wanted out of the conversation—out of everything. *Make things right.* I fought the urge to hang up on her again.

"And your radio station's been hounding me to see what's up. They said they've tried to reach you too. You're expected to start taping again in a few weeks and they want answers. What gives?"

"I'm sorry. I just didn't feel up to—"

"Did you ever want this, Bradford? Any of it? Or was this all just simply a game for you; a little pastime to screw everybody over?"

"Of course I wanted it. It's my life's work. It's m—my . . ."

I couldn't finish. My head dropped onto the kitchen table with a thud. Patches rested her chin on my lap and whimpered. Toby let out a baffled-sounding yelp.

"There's only one possibility of recovery, from what I can see. And you owe us trying to salvage this thing."

"Anything." I wiped my eyes with my shirt sleeve. "I'll do anything, I swear."

"You'd better. It's either this or you're through. I'll make sure of it."

"Okay, okay. I get it," I barked. "What do you want?"

"A press conference. I'll set it up and you'll be there. I'm going to figure out the right angle to take and script something beforehand that you're going to read word for word. And I swear to God, if you don't answer a phone—any phone—from now on . . ."

"I know, I know. I'm through."

"You'll be dropped like a chainless anchor in Lake Michigan. That's a promise."

*   *   *

Josie had returned from the store and started fussing in the kitchen to the soft sounds of her favorite country station. I'd left her a note saying I'd grown tired and gone for a nap. I hadn't slept. I'd spent the time staring at the ceiling and watching the shades of the room alter with the setting sun.

The spare room—my room—hadn't changed since I'd left for college in the mid-nineties. The antique twin bed still creaked when I rolled over in it; the same crocheted bedspread kept me warm at night, and the poster of Brad Pitt—that I'd thumbtacked to the pink floral wallpaper—still smiled down on me from across the room. Josie had kept it all just the same so that I'd feel at home when I visited. I did feel at home; small, defeated, and at home.

The room shifted into complete darkness. Winter had made the days short and the evenings painfully long. I rose and felt my way through the bedroom and out into the light of the hallway. As I wandered downstairs and into the warmth of Josie's big kitchen, a knock sounded at the back door.

"Bill Bradford," said Aunt Josie, opening the door for my father. "Always a pleasure."

"Josie," he nodded, handing her a six-pack of beer.

The dogs wagged and sniffed around Dad with pleasure. They knew him. I, on the other hand, stood at the other side of the room with my arms folded.

"Candace," he said, now nodding in my direction.

"Dad," I replied. "Good to see you."

I walked to the kitchen drawer and dug out a corkscrew.

"You're looking good," he said to me.

I turned wishing I could say the same. He'd always been too thin, but he seemed almost gaunt now, and his hairline had retreated since I'd last seen him. He'd aged. He'd always aged, but long absences made reality even harsher.

"Thanks," I muttered. "All things considered, I guess."

I popped the cork on a cheap Chardonnay and wondered when I could start working out again. 'Looking good' my ass.

"You want one of these?" I asked, pointing at the beer he'd brought. He nodded yet again.

"So," piped in Josie, "I hear old man Campbell's sellin' the hardware store."

"Yep," said Dad, taking a big gulp of his beer.

"That gonna affect you any?" she asked.

"Nope. Not as far as I can tell, anyway."

"Well, I guess they'd be hard pressed to find a replacement for you regardless of who owns it. Nobody's been there as long as y'all have."

He nodded.

Small talk. Damned, stupid small talk. My whole life—as long as I'd known that man—we'd blithered nothing but small talk when we'd blithered at all. I couldn't listen to it without wanting to throw up.

"You two mind if I just watch a little TV before dinner? I had a little run in with Piranha Perkins today, and I need to blank out for a bit."

Aunt Josie threw her shoulders back in defense mode. "So help me, if she—"

"It's fine," I said. "It'll be fine. I just don't want to discuss it right now."

I turned and walked toward the living room. I could hear Dad asking questions behind me.

"Who's this Perkins person then?"

Yeah, now he takes an interest. Like if this 'Perkins person' had turned out to be some kind of threat to me, he'd actually do something about it. Not dear old Dad. Not on your life.

I turned the volume up on the TV to drown out the content of the kitchen conversation. Just the faint sound of voices could be heard and the occasional laugh from Josie. She could pull words out of anybody, even Bill.

"Your phone's rockin' off the counter in here," she hollered.

I started getting up off the sofa. "Yeah, I turned it on again after strict instructions from . . ."

Aunt Josie walked into the living room holding my cell. She stared down at the caller ID with her mouth gaped open.

"What? Who is it?"

"Ross. It's that son-of-a-bitch of a Ross."

CHAPTER 21

*"No matter how important someone is to you,
you can always live without them."*

"Ross?" I gasped. "Is that you?" I grabbed the bottle of wine from the kitchen counter and hurried up the stairs for privacy.

"Yeah, it's me."

"Where . . . I—I mean, how . . . ?" I stopped at the top landing to catch my breath. Stay calm; make things right.

"I'm at Todd's."

I made my way to the bedroom. "But you can't stand Todd?"

"Seems we've worked a few things out over the last little while. Go figure."

"Well, it's good to know that you're working things out with somebody," I snapped. "I've been losing my mind here." Damn, why did I say that? Breathe. Don't screw this up.

"What do you want me to say, Candace?"

I held my breath wanting to hear him say he loved me, that he never wanted to leave, that'd he'd be there in a few minutes to pick me up.

I set the wine bottle down on the bedside table and held onto the glass. "I don't know. That you're sorry?" I heard him sigh. "I—I mean . . . I'm sorry."

"Look, I am sorry for some things but not others."

"Like?"

"Like I'm sorry that you got some shit press over our situation and that it ever had to come to this. And maybe I'm sorry that I haven't returned your calls, but it was the only way I could handle everything. I just had to step back from everybody, you know?"

I sat down on the crocheted bedspread. "No, I don't know." I did, however; I'd been doing the same thing to everyone else.

"Does that include Eunice Carrington? Is that what you were doing in New York? Stepping back?"

I looked down at the wine glass shaking in my hand.

"Hey, I told you I might take her to that fund-raiser, and you didn't appear to give a shit."

I set the glass down beside the bottle and put my hand between my knees to steady it.

"Ross, don't you see what that little exposé in the newspaper has done? It's ruined me. Who's going to take me seriously when I can't even control my own husband? I—I mean—"

"Aha," he bellowed. "And there it is."

"I didn't mean control you. I meant—"

"Oh, yes you did. You don't know who you really are, do you? Or what it's like living with someone who's always perfect. Do you have any idea what kind of pressure that puts on someone like me?"

"What do you mean—someone like you? What are you saying?"

I stood and paced at the end of the bed.

"Look, I didn't call to argue."

"Well, don't you think we should argue? We need to hash all this out if we're going to—"

"We're not going to, Candace."

I stopped pacing. I didn't hear him right. He didn't mean it. "Ross, what are you saying?"

"We're not going to hash anything out. I'm done."

He's done? After ten years of marriage, he's just done? My jaw dropped. My heart pounded in my chest.

"But what about *until death do us part*? What about our promise to each other?"

I moved toward the dresser and leaned on it for support. My reflection looked pale and ghastly. Nothing but silence came from the other end of the phone.

"Look, I just met a therapist," I continued. "I—I know I've always sworn against them, but maybe she can help, you know? Maybe she'd let us talk to her together. It's worth a shot, right? It has to be."

I wanted to reach through the phone and touch his face. I wanted to look into his eyes and show him my sincerity.

"It's not worth a shot to me," he said. "I'm sorry, but I haven't been happy for a very long time."

My knees weakened, and the floor tilted under me. I made my way across the room and sat back down on the bed.

"You haven't been happy?"

"Actually, I've been miserable. Not just with us, with everything. Don't you see? I was never cut out for this bullshit."

"What bullshit? What are you talking about?"

"Being married, being a lawyer. You name it."

A dull ache started behind my eyes. A slow burn rose in my throat. I topped up my wine and took a huge gulp.

"Call it a midlife crisis," he continued. "Call it whatever you want."

A vision of him arm-in-arm with Cleavage Carrington flashed before my eyes. "It's her isn't it? That's why this is happening. It's that slut," I screamed.

I heard the television turn off downstairs.

"Don't bring her into this. She was my date, that's all. This has nothing to do with anyone but me, you understand?"

Warm tears spilled out over my lashes. The walls spun in circles around me.

"Why are you telling me this over the phone? Can't we at least meet and discuss things? Please, Ross?"

I bent forward and gasped for breath. He didn't answer. "Ross?"

"Here's the deal," he began.

I sat up tall. "Deal? What deal?" This can't be happening.

"So there are a few major publications competing for me right now."

"Competing for you?"

I took another swig of wine and swallowed hard.

"They want to pay me for our story."

"Ross, you wouldn't," I begged. "Tell me you haven't talked to them. Please."

"Jesus, Candace. They think you've had a sex change operation. I mean, how fucked up is that?" he half giggled.

"Ross, I swear to God . . ." I bit my lip until it pained me.

"Don't worry. I haven't said a word to them." I sighed and ran my fingers through my hair.

"Thank you," I whispered. "Geri's planning a press conference, and I just don't need—"

"Back to the deal." I sat stunned.

"I need to get on with my life and start fresh. Now that I've made my decision, I don't want to waste any time. The deal is I won't talk to the press if you agree to list the condo."

The phone dropped from my fingers in seemingly slow motion. I reached down to pick up it back up, and my throat tightened. I stared at it in my hand for a few seconds before putting it back to my ear.

"Are you there?" he shouted.

"I'm here," I replied without moving my lips.

"I could use the money, Candace, and from the sounds of things you could too. I mean, your book isn't exactly a bestseller now, is it?"

I stared at a frayed edge of carpet by the bedroom door and couldn't speak.

"Sorry about the book thing, by the way," he continued. "I know it meant a lot to you, but let's be honest. *Total Mastery?* It's bullshit, Candace."

"Why is everyone calling my book bullshit?" I screamed into the phone. "And what the hell would you know? You can't wipe your own ass without your father standing over you with instructions."

The ache in my head turned to stabbing pains. Heat enveloped me.

"Whoa up. Jesus, listen to yourself," he taunted. "Losing *control* are we, sweetheart?"

"Don't call me 'sweetheart,'" I snapped. I put a hand to my forehead and began rocking back and forth. "Ross, please. Can't we please talk about this? It's only been a matter of weeks. It's too soon."

"I don't need time. I want to liquidate, and I want to get on with my life. End of story."

"But I—I . . ." Think of something to say—make things right.

"Listen to me. I've taken what I want out of the place, and I've had a real estate guy in, so—"

"You've done what?"

"He actually thinks we can make some hefty coin on the place. And thanks for waiting until I left to stash that goddamned clock of your mother's in a cupboard. I hated that thing. But I did wind it while I was there. Don't ask me why."

"Leave my mother out of this," I snapped.

"Whatever. All that's left is for you to sign the papers and book the movers."

I grabbed my wine glass by the bowl, and my wedding ring clinked against the side of it. "I don't want to sign anything, Ross. I don't want any of this. I want us to—"

"You sign, or I sing. It's your call."

I couldn't believe his callousness. Sing? He could distort things and make me look worse. But what could he possibly say? I tried to think of potential stories that could further damage myself or hurt my family. Nothing came to mind until—my mother. I still had an obligation to protect her. Shit.

"I'll sign."

I hung up the phone and stood in the middle of the room wanting to scream. Anger at both Ross and myself danced inside me making my stomach turn. It twirled faster and faster wanting to escape.

I grabbed my purse from the dresser in a rage and threw it across the room. It hit hard against the bedroom doorframe just missing my father's head. I stared at him wondering how long he'd been there, then I dropped to the floor in a heap by the bed.

Dad moved toward me like treading through land mines. He sat down on the mattress near me. I couldn't look up at him. He reached out, placed a trembling hand on my head, and stroked my hair with trepidation. I laid my head on his knee. How I had tears left in me at all I'll never know, but they flowed for disenchantment and for the first display of tenderness I'd ever seen from my father.

When I lifted my face I saw the wet stain of tears on the leg of Dad's blue jeans. I'd drained myself dry. I wiped my nose and gazed across the bedroom. My purse leaned against the wall by the door just inches from the frayed edge of carpet. Dr. Hedley's business card lay face-up beside it.

CHAPTER 22

"If you start feeling anxious, take a deep breath and reorganize!"

"Good to see you, Candace. I'm pleased that you decided to come back," said Dr. Hedley.

I gazed around the room. Her eyes followed mine. I saw that Skinner's bed lay empty in the corner. I wanted to crawl in it.

"I left him at home today," she said.

I gave a slight grin and gazed up at the bookshelf. All those words jumbled together inside hard, cold covers; all those theories about people needing therapy. I found it unnerving.

I crossed my legs and began tapping my foot. "So, how does this work exactly?" I asked.

"We talk. That's how it works."

"About?"

"Whatever you like."

A pit of anxiety bubbled in my stomach. I shouldn't have come.

"How about we start with why you decided to call?"

"I don't know. Desperation perhaps?" I sighed. "I feel like my mind's gone missing. Fiona tells me that shrinks are good at lost and found."

She smiled. My foot tapped a little faster. "I don't know. Maybe I'm crazy," I continued. "Crazy people never know they're crazy until it's too late, do they? Everyone's saying I am, so . . ." I shrugged.

"Not fond of the word 'crazy'," she said. "Let's try another angle." She tucked her legs up under her and relaxed back in her armchair.

I wanted to trust this woman, I really did.

"I heard from my husband," I said. "I guess that's what spurred me to call." I looked down at my tapping foot. It appeared to have a mind of its own.

"And you hadn't heard from him prior to this?"

My shoulders slumped forward. I glanced at the box of tissues beside me. "Not a word. He left me right after my surgery."

She tilted her head to one side and frowned. "Okay . . . We can discuss that if you like, but let's start with what surgery you had."

"A hysterectomy." My abdomen flinched. My heart ached.

"And he left because you needed one?" she asked, raising an eyebrow.

"He left me when I told him after-the-fact."

I grabbed a handful of tissues. Dr. Hedley cocked her head to the other side. "I don't understand."

"I didn't want to worry him. They were just going to go in and look around. There was a small chance of me having to have this, and I—I didn't . . ." I blinked back tears. "I was sure everything would be fine. I thought I could handle it."

"So . . . you didn't tell him."

"Right. I didn't tell him."

She nodded.

"Anyway, he left when I got home from the hospital, and I didn't hear from him until the day I called you."

"And?"

"And he doesn't want to reconcile." My blinking intensified, and my throat began to burn. I wiped my nose with a tissue.

"Candace, you've obviously suffered two major losses over a very short period of time: first your uterus and now your husband. Anyone would be challenged to cope effectively under those circumstances."

"Well, there are a lot of people out there who wouldn't consider my husband to be that much of a loss. I still loved him though, you know?" I whimpered.

"No doubt you did."

I sighed. "I read once that even the end of bad marriages can be devastating; that people can mourn the loss of a belief system as much as they do the other person."

"True."

"Well, I guess my belief was that I'd always be able to make it work, you know? The marriage for sure, but everything else too." I uncrossed my legs and pulled at the hem of my skirt. "My clients, my reputation, my home. Now I've lost everything."

"And how does that make you feel?"

"Don't you understand? I wrote a book called *Total Mastery.* It was on its way to being a bestseller. I teach people how to take responsibility for their lives and maintain control. Don't you see how serious this is?"

"So, you feel responsible for everything that's happened then. Is that what I'm hearing?"

"Of course I'm responsible. This is all my fault. Everything that happens in our lives is our own doing." I crossed my legs again and tapped my other foot against the small table in front of me. She looked down at the movement. I stopped.

"So, was it your fault that you had to have a hysterectomy?"

"Probably," I said, searching for an explanation. "I don't know. Maybe I didn't go to the hospital soon enough when my appendix burst years ago. That's what caused all of this mess, apparently. I must have screwed up back then and . . . oh, God."

I sniffled, wiping the tears from beneath my eyes. Dr. Hedley waited for me to continue. "There's an expectation, don't you see that?"

"From whom?"

"Everybody? Look at the media reaction alone. It's not all in my head. I've let people down."

"Explain how."

"I just said how," I snapped.

She sat in silence watching me. I moved my arms down toward my abdomen and started a slow rock forward and backward. My breaths became labored.

"I feel like I'm going to erupt sometimes," I cried.

"Like right now?"

"Yes." I puffed out a few short breaths. "Is there something wrong with me? Do you think I'm crazy?"

"Candace, we're not using that word, and I—"

"Whatever," I barked. "What's wrong with me?"

She untucked her legs and put both feet on the floor. "It would appear as though you may have bouts of anxiety, and quite frankly, I'm not surprised given what you've been through."

I looked her in the eye and kept rocking. Please don't let me down. Please.

"I want you to focus and try something with me." I nodded. "Slow your breathing down. Nice, slow, deep breaths. Can you do that for me?" I nodded again. Jesus. Make it stop. "In through your nose and out through your mouth." I did as instructed. "Now close your eyes and repeat after me: my mind is calm."

"My mind is calm," I said between breaths. "But it's not."

"Try again."

"My mind is calm." Focus, damn it.

"Keep going."

"I can't."

"Yes, you can. Concentrate on your breathing."

"My mind is calm." My lungs began letting more air in. "My mind is calm." I put a hand to my forehead and ceased rocking. She patted my arm again.

"Good, you're getting it."

"But I don't get anxiety. Why am I . . ."

"Candace—one step at a time."

*　　*　　*

Morning arrived wrapped in a cloud-filled sky. I rolled onto my back for a deep stretch and listened as Aunt Josie's truck pulled in the driveway. The sound of fresh snow crunching under her tires initiated the excited clicking of doggie toenails on hardwood. Toby and Patches ran to the door to greet her. I swung my feet over the side of the bed and smiled. I'd felt a bit better since my visit with Dr. Hedley. There may have even been the occasional glimmer of hope.

The back door squeaked open. "How are my whittle babies?" said Aunt Josie. A chorus of barks followed as she stepped inside. "Who's been good while Mama was away? Huh?" Playful panting gave the answer. "Did y'all take good care of our girl while Mama was workin'? Did ya?"

"Yes they did," I hollered down through the floor vent.

"Oh good, you're awake," she called out. "Now, get your ass down here and watch me wind down. I'll put some java on for ya."

I headed down the creaking staircase in full fuzzy-slipper mode.

Josie's kitchen had always been my favorite part of the house. That's where we'd stored our memories—in the sounds and smells of that room. Coming home from school to hot chocolate, chats at the big wooden table, baking cookies at Christmas, her helping me with homework. The decor did little to portray the magic of the space. Off-white walls in need of a fresh coat, blue-painted trim around the door and window, and curtains made from red-and white-checked dish towels. I felt grateful to walk into it that morning with it completely unchanged.

"Hey," I nodded in Aunt Josie's direction. Wet noses nudged up under my nightie and soaked my knees. "How was your night?"

"Oh, you know. Short staffed, a pain in the ass doctor, a cardiac arrest. Same old shit. How was yours?" she asked, pouring water into the coffeemaker. I marveled at what she dealt with in that job.

"Well, a hell of a lot better than yours apparently."

"Bah," she sputtered, waving it all off. "All in a day's work when you're savin' lives. You can't take it too seriously, or you'd never go back."

"But still . . ."

"But still nothing. You doin' okay?" No more talk about her.

"I'm doing okay. I sat in the living room with the dogs most of the night and read mindless babble. Happy to report that I wasn't obsessing as much."

"Good to know."

We sat down across from each other at the table waiting for the coffee to brew. Dark circles pooled under Josie's eyes. I thought of how my situation must only be adding to her burdens.

"So, Fiona's picking me up in a few hours," I reminded her.

"I told ya you could take the truck if you needed it."

"I know, but I really want to get my car while I'm there."

"Well, I understand that, and thank God Fiona's goin' to support ya. I just wanted to offer is all." She rubbed the top of her head. "I'd go myself if it weren't for this damned stupid schedule of mine."

"It's okay, really," I reassured her. "You've missed enough time because of me."

The coffeemaker beeped and Aunt Josie rose from the table. She poured me a cup and brought it to me. "Has that bitch-assed publicist told you what you're gonna have to say yet?"

"Apparently the statement hasn't been finalized, but she said I'd have time to review it in advance."

She shook her head.

"I'll be fine," I said, trying to reassure both of us.

"Uh-huh."

"I will. I promise. Fiona will help me pack up the condo this week, and she'll watch my back while I smooth things over with the press. Don't worry, okay?"

Aunt Josie nodded. "Hope all goes well, Kiddles. I mean . . . with everything."

"Me too. Trust me."

My mind is calm. My mind is calm.

She reached across the table and took my hand. "I was thinking I might put the Christmas tree up while you're gone, seein' as the holidays aren't far off."

I grimaced.

"Been a long time since we woke up on Christmas mornin' together, baby girl. You okay with it?"

I nodded. "Can't promise to be overly festive this year, but go for it."

"Fantabulous," she said, pulling her hand back and slapping the table. The dogs jumped to attention. "I've got one more shift to put in, but I'll have it up by the time you get back." She grabbed Patches by the ears and snuggled her face. "And no one's gonna pee on the tree. Isn't that right little one?"

Toby jumped up to get in on the action. I watched Aunt Josie's playful nature with the dogs and wished for the millionth time that I could be more like her. She could inspire wonder. She'd certainly inspired mine over the years, and always when I needed it most.

A deep yawn resonated from her chest. "I really am wiped out, sweet girl, so I'm gonna take these two out for a quick you-know-what and hit the hay."

The dogs ran in circles while she put her coat and boots back on. She grabbed the door handle and paused. "I'm worried about you goin' back into that city and up against those bastard reporters."

Her face grew more tired looking. I shared her concerns more than I cared to admit.

"I won't be alone, and I kind of miss it, you know? The city, I mean." Regardless of everything that had gone on, I longed for even a small taste of what I'd once had.

"Candace, I . . ." She looked down toward the floor as though the words she needed might be scurrying about with the dogs. I rose from my chair and embraced her.

"I love you, Aunt Josie. Have I told you that lately?" My heart flushed with warmth.

"Not for a long time, Kitten, but I've always known it."

She pulled back, took my face in her hands, and stared into my eyes as though searching my cellular composition. "You're the light in my life, little one. The light in my life." And with that, she kissed my forehead and headed out the door with wagging tails in tow.

"Come on you flea-bitten mongrels," she hollered.

The wind whipped a flurry of snowflakes up past the kitchen window, and all three of them disappeared.

*   *   *

Fiona arrived on schedule, and we headed off to brave the tasks at hand. We rode in silence for the most part, other than the soft sounds of a meditative CD that she'd brought along for my benefit. Always thinking, my Fiona: always putting me first.

Her old Jeep never seemed warm enough to me in the winter, which she insisted had everything to do with me being underweight. I, of course, disagreed and grabbed a blanket from her backseat to wrap around my legs. The sky looked gray and gloomy, save for a small patch of blue that appeared to sit right over Chicago.

Chicago, Chi-town, The Windy City: it had been home to me for so long, and as we hit the city limits the patch of blue extended, allowing the sun to reflect off the skyscrapers like a beacon. Every fiber of my being vibrated with the inherent beat of its pace.

"Holiday shoppers," said Fiona, nodding at passersby.

"Josie's putting up a tree," I scoffed.

"You okay with that?"

"What does it matter?" I asked, looking out the passenger side window.

"I don't know. It might be kind of nice."

I turned back to face her. "Your folks still going to Ireland for the holidays?"

"Uh-huh. They leave in a few days, actually. We celebrated last week. Notice the new scarf?" She flipped her multi-colored accessory in the air. "I got this and five tubes of cobalt blue oil paint. They still think I can't afford it," she giggled.

"Well, you're welcome to join us for Christmas if you don't mind watching me wallow in red and green self-pity."

We pulled up in front of the condo building that had once been home. A slight nausea rose in me, and I pondered how unchanged a place could look when nothing remained the same.

"Thanks for the invite, Candy, but I've actually kind of got plans."

"Kind of?"

I gazed at the Christmas lights on the front entrance. The traditional wreaths peeked out through the lobby windows, and old Seamus had donned his famous Santa hat embroidered with shamrocks. I wondered if Ross ever missed the place, if he ever missed us.

"Yeah well," Fiona continued.

"Yeah well, what?" I asked, turning to face her.

She let out a long sigh and cut the engine. "Well, you need to find out sooner or later. I'm in love."

CHAPTER 23

"Preparation thwarts disaster."

"In love?" I asked. "Since when?"

"Since the last few weeks or so."

"Fiona."

"I know, I know. It's fast," she added. "It's too fast, but my gut's just telling me. It just is."

"Telling you what?"

She smiled and placed a hand over her heart. "That he's the one."

She really means it. She's lost her mind.

"Come on. Let's get you inside," she said. "I brought wine, and I'll tell you everything."

I walked toward the condo building afraid of the memories it stored. As my feet stepped forward, my mind moved back through all the years I'd spent there with Ross. The dinner parties, the holidays, the tender moments. I'd believed in all of it. I gripped Fiona's arm to steady myself.

Seamus lifted his Santa hat and gave a slight bow as we approached.

"Sweet Mary and Joseph. 'Tis a fine thing to see your face here again, Ms. Bradford. And yours too, my Irish lovely," he added, beaming at Fiona.

Fiona acknowledged him with a flirty grin.

"It's good to see you again too, Seamus," I said. "Sadly, I'm here to do some packing." A tear escaped me unannounced.

"Aye, I figured as much. Sad for us all so it 'tis. Sad for us all." He shook his head. "You'll be missed."

"Thank you," I whispered.

Fiona whisked me toward the elevator.

"Jeez, I'm gonna miss old Seamus," I said as we rode up to the condo.

"You'll miss a lot of things, sweetheart, but you'll be okay."

She rubbed my back through my heavy winter coat. The elevator doors opened and I walked toward the condo door. Trepidation met me in the hallway. I stopped walking and leaned against the wall.

"You want me to go ahead and open the door for you?" asked Fiona.

"Please."

I handed her the keys and watched as she strutted off with confidence. She reached the door and disappeared from view.

My mind is calm. I practiced my breathing; in through my nose and out through my mouth. *My mind is calm.*

I reached the open door and peered inside. I stood for a moment surveying the entrance.

"All clear in here, hon. In fact, nothing's changed," she said from the living room.

I walked toward her voice. "Haven't been upstairs yet, though," she continued. "How you ever aced a two-storey condo in the heart of the city, I'll never know."

Connections, that's how. Some divorcee who'd hired Ross ten years earlier. She'd needed out and we'd needed in. I wondered if he'd lined someone up to buy from us as well. The whole place felt cold and somehow unfamiliar, but everything remained in place.

"He told me he'd taken his things," I said. "I don't understand."

Every piece of furniture had been left behind; every lamp, magazine, and book untouched.

I asked Fiona to check his bedroom closet for me. She headed up the stairs and I walked to the kitchen to check the cupboards: cups, saucers, mugs, glasses, plates—all there. I opened the cupboard that held the pots and pans. My mother's antique clock laid ticking atop the frying pan. It appeared to be losing time. I shut the door on it.

"His closet's empty," said Fiona, as she rumbled down the stairs. "And the Maya Eventov painting is gone from above the bed." A wedding gift from Ross's parents. "Of course, he didn't take any of the paintings *I* did for you," she scoffed. "No love lost there."

"I don't get it." I walked back into the living room and opened the entertainment bureau. "His CDs, his movies: Christ, even his photo albums are still here. None of it makes sense."

"Unless he just doesn't give a shit about any of that stuff."

"Ross?" I pondered. "Well, the Ross I knew gave a shit. Now I'm not so sure who that guy was."

My foundation shook at the thought of having lived with a stranger for ten years.

"Jesus, Fiona. It's like he's just given up on everything."

"Except Maya Eventov and the odd Armani suit." She shrugged. "I'm opening some wine. What do you say we put some jammies on and chill out? Getting here was a big enough deal. We can figure out a packing plan in the morning."

"Make mine a double," I joked. "Can you do that with wine?"

"In a big enough glass you can." She pulled two bottles of our favorite from her bag and held them high in the air.

I moved toward the staircase and glanced upward. "I don't want to go up there."

"So don't."

"No," I shook my head. "This is silly. I have to get a grip. It's not like I'm going to run into him or anything."

I started up the staircase knowing full well that I *would* run into him; the memory of him anyway. It weighed heavy with every step I took and the closer I got to the bedroom, the more the smell of his cologne taunted my senses. We'd spent so much time up there, on our laptops for the most part, but nonetheless.

I reached the doorway to our bedroom and hesitated. His words echoed through my brain. "*You* did this to us, Candace. Remember that."

The door creaked open and I tiptoed inside. Again, nothing looked different other than the lone hook over our bed where the painting had hung. The empty wall made me think of what my life had become, and I ached for my husband from my shins to my shoulder blades.

Had he ever loved me? Had any of it been real? And the passion we'd shared, had that all been an illusion as well? I couldn't bear the thought of it.

"Wine's ready, and believe it or not, I brought cheese," Fiona called out from downstairs. I put my hands on the dresser to support myself.

Pajamas, you came up here for pajamas. Focus. Push through this.

I opened a few drawers and found a cozy pair of flannels with pink piping: Ross's least favorite. I wanted to wear them for that reason—to reinforce what he no longer wanted. I repulsed myself. I put them on and stared into the dresser mirror. Nothing looked right, nothing at all.

"Who are you?" I whispered to my reflection. "And what have you done with Candace Bradford?"

"You okay up there?" Fiona hollered.

I dropped my head and squeezed my eyes shut. "Yes, I'm okay. I'm coming."

I made my way back downstairs to find Fiona in a snowman—patterned flannel nightie. I couldn't help but giggle as she grabbed the hem of it and curtsied.

"Perfect," I said, thankful for her antics.

She handed me a gargantuan glass of wine. "Cheese is on the coffee table in the living room."

I followed behind her to the sofa. We remained silent for a moment sipping our wine.

"You all right?" she asked.

"Honestly? No. I keep thinking it's all just a bad dream, you know, and I just want to wake up."

She nodded, and I noticed a definite glow about her.

"Okay," I said, taking a sip of wine. "I want to stop wallowing in self-pity." I set the glass down and braced myself to be supportive. "Tell me about this new love of yours."

"Candace, I've really been reluctant to mention him to you with everything that's going on. The last thing you need right now is a love story."

"That's where you're wrong. If there's anything I do need, it's to hear something positive." A lie if ever I told one. "Who is he?"

"His name is Étienne Aurandt," she said, with a girlish grin. "And he's beautiful."

I picked my glass up and raised it to hers. We clinked together and drank.

"And? Where did you meet?" My first meeting with Ross flashed through my mind. He'd smiled at me on campus, and I'd literally swooned. He had been beautiful too when we'd met: stunningly.

"Well," said Fiona, wiggling herself back into the cushions. "Remember when you called me after your surgery? When I was on that blind date?"

"That guy?"

"God no. Étienne was the sommelier at the wine bar that night," she tittered. Her cheeks glowed a crimson red.

"Seriously?"

"Uh-huh, and we had instant chemistry. Pretty awkward scenario considering I was there with someone else, but the sparks just flew. I went back there a few days later, and he asked for my number."

"A few days? You didn't waste any time, did you?" I teased.

"Well, when a girl finds electricity, she has to plug in for a charge, right?" We both laughed.

Wow, chemistry. Would I ever find that again? I felt around my left hip for my estrogen patch and found it still in place.

"Anyway, he's from France originally. Been over here about eight years and is a citizen now. His mother owns a vineyard near Mercury." She topped up our glasses.

I smiled at her. "Fiona, I'm genuinely happy for you."

She reached out and hugged me tight to her snowmen. I swam in them. When she let go, I swung my bare feet up on the coffee table and shut my eyes. I thought about life's passage of lovers and how heartbreaking it could all be.

"Well, one thing I know for sure is that I'm taking you for a pedicure when all of this packing and press conferencing is over with," said Fiona, nodding at my feet. "I don't care if we're in the dead of winter. You can't be running around with only one third of your toenails red."

"I can't," I whimpered.

"What do you mean, you can't?"

"I can't, because Ross painted them for me. That little bit of red is all I have left."

*   *   *

The morning of the press conference arrived and with it came a gripping tension at the base of my neck. For the first time in my life I dreaded speaking in public. Days before Geri emailed a copy of the statement she had prepared for me to read. I went over it umpteen times but still struggled to come to terms with the content.

Fiona did her best to try and talk me out of doing it at all, but I had obligations. I owed them all a shot at turning things around: Geri and her new company; my producer at the station; and ultimately myself.

"It might work," I said to Fiona.

She maneuvered her way through a maze of stacked boxes in the kitchen and took the statement from me. "And it might not. I'm telling you, you don't have to do this." Her eyes scanned the page and she shook her head.

"I know, I know. It's total bullshit. How am I going to pull this off?"

I fidgeted with the waistband of my navy blue Dolce & Gabbana skirt. The suit had grown loose on me since I'd worn it last. Even my high-heeled boots seemed bigger. The whole ensemble, in fact, felt strangely out of character.

"Just say the word," she said, lifting the statement over her head as though ready to rip it in half.

"Very funny," I replied, reaching up to take it back from her.

I glanced around the condo. Boxes sat lined against every wall. All the things Ross and I had shared ready to be shut away in a storage locker. Things I'd need easy access to would go to Fiona's where she had the room. I'd stuffed some suitcases to take to Josie's.

"You sure you're okay to handle the movers for me next week?" I asked. She'd offered and I'd accepted. I didn't have the strength to watch the place get emptied out by strangers.

"Sure thing. I told you, I have to come to town for a meeting anyway."

I ran my hand along the many edges of cardboard. "Amazing how much a person doesn't need when you really look at it."

Fiona shrugged. "Maybe that's what Ross thought when he left all his shit behind."

"Who knows what the hell he thought."

The entire condo was just one big box really, and I had to shut the lid on the whole thing. A slow and gentle *tick—tick* echoed off the empty walls. "Do you mind taking Mom's clock to your place for now? I can't stand the sound of it dying, and God knows which box the key ended up in."

"No problem," she said, picking it up with great care and wrapping it in her new colorful scarf. "And you're sure you don't want me to drive you?"

"No. I need my wheels, and I don't want to have to come back here again after the conference. It's too hard."

She placed a hand on my shoulder. "Well, I'll be right behind you."

"Thank God. I couldn't face Geri and Karen by myself, let alone a room full of reporters."

She grabbed me and held me tight. I looked over her shoulder at the remains of a life that I'd never intended to ruin. I began to sniffle.

"Now, now," said Fiona. "We mustn't ruin our make-up."

*   *   *

Geri and Karen stood at the front entrance to the hotel wrapped in their long winter coats. Geri threw her cigarette to the ground and stomped it into the slushy sidewalk when I came into view. Karen, who'd been standing far enough back to avoid Geri's smoke, walked up and grabbed me in a warm embrace.

Karen had always been supportive and kind. She looked maternal with her short, plump body and slightly graying bob. Her hazel eyes dominated her smile with deep laugh lines jutting out toward her temples. She'd hugged me every day that we'd spent together since we'd met, and she'd nurtured me through my growing pains at the radio station.

A handful of reporters rounded the corner and began snapping pictures. Fiona appeared out of nowhere and pulled me from Karen's arms. Geri ushered us inside the hotel. All four of us ducked into a guest room that Geri had booked for a pre-conference briefing. The room looked generic and bland, like a thousand other rooms in a thousand different cities. I yearned to be anywhere but there.

We peeled our coats and gloves off and threw them on the bed.

"That wasn't so bad. If there's only a few of them, she should be—" began Fiona.

"The conference room is packed. Those idiot stragglers couldn't get in," snapped Geri, as she reached up to fix the shirt collar under my jacket.

"I'll help her with that," barked Fiona, pushing Geri aside.

"Would you two stop it?" I waved them both away and looked in the dresser mirror to try and fix the collar myself. "I'm nervous enough without all this henpecking."

"She's right," said Karen, who walked up behind me to help with my wardrobe. "She needs calm right now not conflict." She smiled at me through the mirror. I reached back over my shoulder and squeezed her hand.

I turned to see Fiona and Geri scowling at each other. My jaw tightened. "Okay, that's enough. I need you both to step out of here. Either that or I will."

"Oh no you don't," said Geri. "We need to go over your statement again, and—"

"I've gone over it more times than I can count. I just have to read it, for Christ's sake. What is there to brief?"

"You sure you want us *all* to leave?" asked Fiona.

"Yes. Please. I just need a minute to calm my mind."

They reluctantly turned toward the door.

"Karen? You coming?" asked Geri.

"Just let me use the restroom," replied Karen.

"Karen can stay," I announced.

Fiona peered in from the hallway with her mouth gaped open. "Candy, what gives?" she asked. Karen continued into the restroom and shut the door.

"Please, Fiona. I want a chance to talk to her alone."

Geri began to close the door. "And no arguing in the hallway either. Go in opposite directions or something," I demanded.

The door slammed shut.

I stood alone in that moment and wore the stillness of the room. So much had happened in the last few months. So much that had been unexpected, unwanted. Now I had to face the music. It had been playing in the background since the surgery—endless refrains blasting through my brain when I'd begged for nothing but silence. Now it would be forefront, and the band would be holding cameras and microphones wanting me to dance.

I leaned on the dresser and stuck my face in the mirror. The dark circles around my eyes made me look hollow. I bowed my head and began to bargain.

"God, please. Get me through this day, please," I whispered, "just this day. I can take it from here, but this is too big for me to do alone. I promise I'll . . ."

Karen came out of the restroom and startled me.

"What? Did you forget I was in there?" she asked with a grin.

"Sorry. I got caught up in a little prayer," I said. She motioned for me to sit down beside her on the end of the bed.

My hands rested on my lap. She reached out and took them in hers.

"So, things have apparently been quite eventful for you since I saw you last," she said.

"That's an understatement, and I feel just horrible about how all of this has no doubt affected the show. I've been meaning to call you, Karen, I really have, but I just got completely overwhelmed. Me, of all people." I cast my eyes down toward the floor.

"Look at me," she said. I did and her eyes pierced right through to my soul. Her round face smiled and a calmness passed between us. "I know this may be hard to believe, but you're not the first person alive who's gotten overwhelmed and found themselves in crisis mode."

"I know, but I teach people how to avoid this very thing."

"And you do a great job of it, but sometimes life just gets the upper hand."

I shook my head. "It could have been avoided. I made mistakes. I should have known better."

"Well, it is what it is at this point, and now you're going to try and fix it. That's pretty much all that matters don't you think?"

"And the show?"

"I don't know about the show, Candace. What happens to it won't entirely be my decision, as you know. We'll have to see how things go today and what the public reaction will be. We'll gauge the risk and make a solid business decision that best supports the station overall."

"So, I may lose the contract entirely," I said, nodding.

"Not necessarily. Listen—regardless of what's gone on with you in the last little while, you've done a lot of people a lot of good through your advice. The messages in your book are all solid, and you're a damn fine example of how applying them can bring success."

"Yeah, right."

"No, I mean it. And now you've had a setback, and so maybe your next step is to help people who have setbacks."

A faint tap came to the door.

"Go away," I hollered.

"Now, don't give up your life's dream of helping people because of some bad press. Find a way to turn it around, Candace. That's the girl I know and love." Karen squeezed my hands and released them.

"You okay in there?" Fiona called out from the hallway. "Candy?"

"Damn it, Fiona," I barked.

"Come on, hon. Let me in."

I sighed and Karen put her arm around my shoulder. "I'll be right there in the room with you, and I'll stand behind you no matter what happens with the show. You know that, right? I'm a friend first."

"Thank you. And again . . . I'm sorry."

"Forget about it, sweetheart. Now let's put this behind us, shall we?"

I stood and straightened my suit jacket. Fiona looked wary in the hallway when I opened the door. I waved the statement in the air at her and smiled. "It's time."

"You're sure you're okay with doing this?" she asked.

"I have to be," I replied. "Hang on to these for me?" I handed her my coat and purse. "I'm going to want to duck out as soon as it's over."

I looked back at Karen, and she nodded. We walked out into the hallway and shut the door behind us.

"Where's Geri?" I asked.

"I'm right here," she called out as she rounded the corner at the far end of the hall. We paused to let her catch up. The smell of a freshly-smoked cigarette wafted along with her.

"Smoking in the girls' room?" asked Fiona.

"Never mind what I was doing. It's none of your business."

I shook my head and began walking in the direction of the conference room. Everyone followed. A ring of sweat began forming on the collar of my shirt. My palms moistened.

"Oh, I forgot to mention that I've planted a few familiar faces in the crowd for the question period," said Geri. "You'll know them when you see them."

"Question period? You didn't say anything about a question period," I balked.

Karen leaned in and whispered, "You'll be fine."

"Nice move, 'Perkins,'" said Fiona with sarcasm.

"Well, it's a press conference. You didn't think you'd get out of here without answering questions, did you?" said Geri.

The hallway began to narrow. I grabbed Karen's arm and continued walking.

"Who?" I asked, keeping my eyes forward. "Who did you plant?" Breathe, for Christ's sake. Breathe.

"Andrea, Lisa, Jason: all friends of mine. You met them at my business launch party."

"But what if I—?"

"You'll know them. Trust me. I told them to shoot you a few signals throughout your statement to make themselves obvious. They know to scream the loudest and wink or something. Just point at them specifically and you'll be fine."

"But what are they going to ask me?" It would never work.

"Generic shit . . . you know. If you're excited about your upcoming promo tour, what cities you can't wait to visit, advice for people who spread stupid rumors. Stuff you can handle that won't cause a stir."

Weakness threatened to buckle my knees.

Fiona put her arm around my waist. "I don't like this," she said.

"Well, who the hell does?" barked Geri.

"Let's just remain calm," added Karen.

I tightened my grip on her arm. "Let's just get this over with."

CHAPTER 24

"Remain calm, or at least appear to be."

"Okay, Karen and I are going in to do the intro," said Geri. "Just wait out here until I say your name. And don't let her talk you into leaving," she added, shooting a glance toward Fiona.

She straightened her back and left us in the hallway. Karen smiled at me before doing the same. Camera flashes shot off inside the door like fireworks.

"Jesus," I said. Fiona took my hand.

"I'm telling you, we can still run. The planet won't implode, and your heart won't stop beating."

I looked down toward the floor and took deep breath after deep breath after deep breath. "Christ, it's hot in here."

I could hear Geri in front of the reporters mumbling something about a chain of events; how I would explain everything, how it all got misconstrued. Then something about the important message of the book. "But I'll let her explain the details of everything herself," she added. "Ladies and gentlemen: Candace Bradford."

Fiona gave my hand one last squeeze.

My feet moved forward. My mind fought to stay put.

Cameras clicked from all directions as I entered the room. Flashes skewed my vision. I had to blink to focus on my path to the podium. Silhouettes of Geri and Karen blurred in the distance. One of them moved toward me and grabbed my hand. I stepped up and took my place.

"I'm right here," whispered Karen before leaving me to stand alone.

I approached the microphone and cleared my throat. The clicking of the cameras slowed to just the odd one, but my eyes still lived in flash mode. I couldn't recognize anyone. I couldn't see faces; just microphones—everywhere. My heart pounded in my ears like a jackhammer.

I took a deep breath and began. "Good afternoon."

I cleared my throat one more time and unfolded the piece of paper that held my pre-fabricated statement. The words danced on the page as my eyes fought to adjust back to normal.

"Thank you so much for coming out today and braving the cold Chicago weather." I grinned, but no one grinned back. Not that I could see anyway.

The paper started shaking in my hands. "As you all know, there have been numerous reports lately about my wellbeing and my personal life." Breathe. "These reports have all surfaced since the release of my book, *Total Mastery*, and they would indicate that I do not, and have not lived by the very advice that I give to others. This simply is not true."

A slight rumbling washed across the crowd. I continued. "As you can see, and unless I hired the absolute worst surgeon in the world, I did not have a sex change operation."

The crowd laughed out loud. Faces started to appear between the microphones. I thought I saw Geri's friend, Andrea. My shoulders relaxed slightly. I can do this.

"That is only one of the many rumors that have surfaced in the past several weeks. I will tell you that I did have a test recently under the care of a physician. I had a laparoscopy, which is essentially an exploratory procedure that my doctor performed due to an episode of abdominal pain. I'm happy to report that everything came out fine, and that I have not had any pain since." I paused and glanced toward Fiona. She stood in the doorway holding our coats in front of her. She didn't smile. I bowed my head down toward the podium.

"I would also like to address the issue of my relationship with my husband, Ross Simpson."

I glanced up at the audience. I could see them clearly now, and several had begun to whisper. Geri's friend Lisa winked at me from the far side of the room. This could work.

"Those of you from local media sources are familiar with Ross, and I believe several of you have attempted to obtain a statement from him regarding our current status."

Two linen carts collided in the hallway causing me to jump. Arguing ensued. Fiona reached back and shut the door.

"It would appear as though a great deal of concern arose when he was photographed with another woman at a recent fund-raiser in New York. That young woman was someone who works at Ross's office, and I gave my full permission for him to take her that event. I had originally planned to attend myself, but schedule changes made that impossible."

The gnawing ache of guilt wrenched at my insides. "They are not in a relationship as speculated. Ross and I are still a married couple."

My shoulders slumped. It's not a lie. We're still married. It's just bending the truth a little. Yes, that's what it is. I raised my head and looked back out at the crowd.

"Have I left Chicago? Yes, but only temporarily, and to be close to family. I spent a great deal of time writing this book. My heart and soul went into every page to make it as comprehensive and informative for the public as possible. During that period my opportunity to see loved ones became limited, so we're spending some quality time together now before I go on tour. None of this contradicts with the messages in my book. If anything, the apparent changes in my life are a culmination of my advice. Take care of your health, maintain trust in your relationships, and stay connected to family. I've written extensively about all of these issues at various points throughout *Total Mastery*."

The door opened again, and I looked up to see a shy young woman trying to roll in a beverage cart. Geri ran to stop her. Fiona stepped aside.

My fingers raced down the page to find where I'd left off. "I—I do, however, apologize to all of my fans and followers for my appearing elusive recently. I don't believe in rumors. I find them pointless, harmful, and childish, so it's been my choice to refrain from playing badminton with speculation."

Hands shot up in the crowd. People started hollering in my direction. I cut them off. "In conclusion, I want to say that the message of my book is one thing that has been substantiated through numerous testimonials. This has been my life's work, and I plan to continue to bring the essential message of maintaining control to those who need it. Thank you very much for your time."

I began folding the piece of paper. Cameras started flashing again, but I didn't care. I'd made it through. I'd survived the press conference.

I started moving away from the podium when Geri grabbed my arm and made an announcement. "Candace will now answer just a few questions."

Shit, the questions. I looked out into the crowd; nothing but lights everywhere. Flashing . . . flashing. Faces disappeared again. Where had Geri's friends gone? I couldn't see anyone.

Geri let go of my arm. I reached out for her in vain. I flailed in a sea of microphones and voices. The podium became my anchor.

A man's voice shot over the crowd from the left side of the room. "Candace, can you comment on the recent loss of some of your client base?"

"I—I—"

A woman's voice cut me off from the right. "Ms. Bradford. Is it true that Ross has left his father's law firm?"

Left the firm? What?

I shook my head. What is she talking about? "I—I'm not here to answer questions for Ross," I snapped. "I'm here to talk about my book."

The girl with the drink cart started rattling through the door again. Questions rang out from all directions.

"Did you also give Ross permission to take that woman to the Lookingglass Theatre last evening?"

"What? I—I . . ." The room spun and flashed like a strobe light.

"About the book, Candace," called a male voice from the center of the room.

"Yes, please. Anything about the book," I replied.

"It's been said that your obsession with control began after your mother's suicide. Is it true that she killed herself and was mentally ill?"

My mother? How do they know about my mother? Who's been . . . ?

A female voice called out from the same area of the room in which I'd seen Andrea. "Over here!" I pointed in desperation.

"Any comments on Eunice Carrington reportedly being pregnant?"

A collective gasp shot through the room and everyone went silent.

"Preg . . . what?" I threw a hand over my mouth.

A glass fell from the young girl's drink cart and smashed with an alarming echo. She shot me a look of terror. I mirrored one back.

"Ms. Bradford. Is she pregnant with Ross's child?" the woman repeated.

"P—Please, I . . ." Tears filled my eyes.

But he didn't love her. He said she had nothing to do with this. She couldn't be . . .

Cameras began flashing again. Pulsating shots of light attacked me like machine-gun fire. I started to put my head down on the podium when someone grabbed my arm.

"Come on," said Fiona. "We're getting out of here."

She pulled me toward the edge of the stage. Geri and Karen stood stunned in my periphery. I gulped sobbing breaths of air. Voices started screaming behind me. Cameras flashed at the back of my head.

"Fiona, what did they mean by . . . ?"

"Not now," she snapped, pulling me into the hallway.

"And why did they bring up my mother? Who would do that?" I begged.

We ran toward the fire exit. The hallway felt like a carnival funhouse with everything slanted and out of focus. My heel caught on the carpet and I fell in a heap.

"Get up," she ordered.

I stood and a wave of nausea hit me. Fiona pulled me through the exit and into the parking garage.

"Let's just get out of here, okay? There's no time for this. I knew you shouldn't have . . ."

A car whizzed past just missing us. We gasped and stared at each other, our breath visible in the cold winter air.

"Okay, you're coming with me," she said.

"No," I screamed shaking myself loose from her grip. "No! I need my car. I need my car." I stomped my feet like a spoiled child. "I need something of my own. I need" I bent forward and began sobbing uncontrollably.

"You need to get the hell out of here is what you need to do."

"No. Leave me alone. Everybody just leave me alone." I grabbed my purse from her arm and ran toward my BMW leaving my coat behind. My nose dripped like a fountain and tears blurred my vision. I dug for my keys as I ran and threw useless contents on the ground in the process. I wiped my face on my jacket sleeve and jumped in the car.

"Bastards," I screamed, shivering from the cold.

I turned the key and revved the engine. Throwing the car in reverse, I squealed the tires and drove past a handful of reporters who'd started running through the garage. Once on the street, I caught a glimpse of Geri standing in front of the hotel. Her face looked pasty white, and her shoulders slumped forward. She looked defeated. I'd ruined everything.

I rounded the first corner and raced down Michigan Avenue. A traffic light turned red at the last minute. I slammed on the brakes. My teeth chattered, and I held my breath. I turned the heater on full and began counting to ten and higher. "Eleven, twelve, thirteen . . . Christ, I can't take it anymore," I screamed. "Not one more thing!"

I pounded my fists on the dashboard. Pain shot through my hands and up my arms. I'd been pushed to the limit, and my own chapter ten came to mind: *Only you are responsible for your behavior.* "Damned stupid book," I screamed, slamming my fists on the dash again.

The light changed back to green, and I pulled into traffic. "My mind is calm. My mind is calm." She can't be pregnant. It's not fair.

I rounded the corner to head in the direction of the interstate. A Mercedes came out of nowhere and honked on the way past. I could see the driver spurting expletives in my direction. "You pulled out in front of *me*, asshole. Can't you see I'm calming my mind?!"

Snow began to fall from the bleak, dark sky. The traffic moved in fits and starts as I jerked my way toward the city limits. Every muscle in my body clenched. My head pounded with every heartbeat.

"It's the worst day of my life," I whispered. "I have no life. I've ruined everything."

My cell phone rang with persistence from my handbag. "Leave me alone," I cried.

Breathe. Just get me to the interstate. Breathe.

The sign for the I-90 exit came into view. A steady parade of fat snowflakes marched toward my headlights as though willing their own demise.

How had they found out about my mother? I'd never told anyone but . . .

My phone rang again. I wanted it to be Ross. I wanted it more than anything. I wanted my life back. "Oh God," I whimpered.

I checked my mirrors and pulled over on the side of the road. I put my head on the steering wheel and cried deep guttural sobs as the ache of defeat overcame me.

A truck honked as it sped past. I jumped. "Shit." Another car drove by lighting up the inside of my vehicle with its headlights. I caught a glimpse of my reflection in the rearview mirror. I'd become a ghost of my former self.

My eye followed a red silk ribbon down from the mirror to my crystal globe: the gift that Geri had given me when my future held promise. My world on a string.

"Damn book. I never want to hear a word out of it ever again!" I grabbed at the ribbon and yanked twice to free the crystal globe from the mirror. I threw it onto the passenger side floor, and the faint sound of breaking glass followed.

My phone rang again. I grabbed at my purse like an enemy's throat. I tore and ripped at it until I freed the phone from its clutches. I pressed on the screen to shut it off when I saw the caller ID: *Dr. Leola Hedley.* I answered.

"Hello?"

"Candace. I just saw your press conference on the news, and I wanted to make sure that you're—"

"I need to see you right away," I begged. "Please."

CHAPTER 25

Getting to Dr. Hedley's office in Elgin became my only focus—like seeking land in the midst of an ocean storm. The snow beat hard against my windshield, and the car's engine roared in defiance through the cold night air.

Dr. Hedley pulled into the parking lot just as I did, and we got out of our vehicles at the same time. The building stood in darkness.

"Come in," she said, turning the key in the front door and flipping on the fluorescent lights. No consoling hug. No fluff. Just a professional relationship and just what I needed.

I followed her down the long hallway to her office. She opened the door and turned on the floor lamp in the corner by the bookshelf. Various papers and books lay strewn across her desk. An opened bag of potato chips sat on the floor beside the leg of her armchair. She picked it up straight away and stuck it in the bottom drawer of her desk. I took my place on the loveseat.

"Aren't you cold?" she asked, removing her parka and rubbing her hands together for warmth.

I stared past her and through the window. "What was I thinking?"

"About going out without a coat on?"

"No. The press conference. How did I think that could work?"

She sat down in the chair. "Well, why don't you tell me?"

The floor lamp shot haunting shadows throughout the room. A tree branch swayed violently in the wind outside.

"It was my last chance to fix things."

"What things?"

"The book? My career? My life?" I said. "Everything."

Dr. Hedley didn't respond. We sat in silence while I thought of all the work that I'd put into writing that good-for-nothing book: hours, days—months on end. Had I really left Ross to fend for himself? Had he not been equally as busy?

My cell phone rang. "Damn thing. I'd like to throw it in a snow bank," I grumbled, pulling it out of my bag and turning it off.

"Well, you could."

The branch outside began scratching on the window pane behind her. She appeared not to notice.

"Could what?"

"Throw your phone away."

"You're kidding me, right?"

Again—no response.

What the . . . ? "Well, that would just be crazy, don't you think?" I asked. "Oh, sorry; I forgot . . . we're not using that word, but—for the record—it would be."

"Why is that?"

"Well first off, how would people get in touch with me?"

"I don't know that, but it appears to be a genuine source of stress for you."

I pondered which one of us needed more help. "But my whole life is . . ." I paused and looked down at the thing. "Is my whole life in this phone?"

"Is it?"

"I—I guess I thought so—sort of. My contacts, schedules, emails, texts: it's one of the things that keeps me . . ." I looked up at her.

"What?"

"In control." The branch slapped hard on the window causing me to jump.

I shook my head and threw the phone back in my bag. "This is ridiculous. I'm not throwing my phone away." I crossed my arms and legs. Body language be damned.

Dr. Hedley changed the subject. "Tell me about today."

The press conference played over in my mind from start to finish. "They said she's pregnant. Did they air that part?"

She nodded. "And how does that make you feel?"

"Overjoyed. What do you think?" I snapped.

Again, she sat perfectly quiet.

"Actually, I feel like God's punishing me if you want to know the truth," I whimpered.

"Punishing you?"

"Yes, punishing me." A slow burn rose in my throat and my eyes stung with the memory of flashing cameras.

"For?"

"I don't know. For not having kids myself when Ross wanted them? For not telling him about the surgery to begin with?"

I reached for her Kleenex box and pulled out a handful of tissues. "I've disappointed so many people."

"Candace, control can be—"

"You heard them. Apparently I'm obsessed with it because of my mother's suicide."

I stood and walked toward the window. The barren old tree bent and waved from the other side of the glass. I wrapped my arms around myself and shivered. A lump formed in the back of my throat.

Dr. Hedley stood and followed me. "So, it's true then? Your mother's suicide?" I nodded. "And how old were you?"

I held up seven fingers full of tissues.

"I'm so very sorry," she whispered.

I pressed my forehead against the cold pane of glass. My breath became visible on the surface of it. "That's exactly what Miss Weir said," I cried.

"Miss Weir?"

"My second grade teacher."

"Go on."

I turned back to face her. "She said it the day Aunt Josie came to remove me from class. I thought she'd come to take me to the fair or something, you know?"

Dr. Hedley directed me back to the loveseat and had me sit down.

"She used to take me out of school sometimes to do something fun and spontaneous. I just assumed . . . I—I didn't understand."

I closed my eyes tight and held the tissues to my face. Jesus, help me.

"But that's not why she was there, is it?" she asked.

I shook my head. Bile pushed upward into the back of my throat. I wanted to choke.

"Why did she do it?" I begged. "Why did she have to kill herself? Was I really that . . ." I swallowed hard. "Was it really all that bad?"

Dr. Hedley raised an eyebrow as she took her place in the armchair. The tree scratched repeatedly on the glass.

"And how did the press find out?" I cried. "Why would they ask such a thing?"

"That's their job, Candace—to dig up skeletons and hit raw nerves." She paused. "Who have you hurt specifically?"

"Everyone," I sniffled.

"Everyone?"

"Yes, everyone."

For the first time in my life, I caught a glimpse of my mother's incapacitating sense of failure. For a brief moment our burdens intertwined.

"Have you hurt Fiona?"

I shook my head.

"Josie?"

"No. Maybe . . . I don't know."

"So, not everyone then."

"No, I guess not." I started counting on my fingers. "But Ross, Geri, my producer, Dad, my clients—the world."

"The world? That's no small feat."

"You know what I mean. I'm a laughing stock."

"Well, I'd hazard a guess that the majority of the world has gone on about their business since your press conference and haven't given it a second thought."

I looked up at her wanting to believe.

"And how have you hurt your father exactly?"

"I should have kept a better eye on her for him," I said. "He loved her, you know. I really believe he did. I mean, I know he left us and everything, but Josie said . . ." The words stuck in my throat.

"Candace."

"What?" I cried.

"You couldn't have stopped her. You were a child. You know that from an adult perspective now, surely."

"Maybe, but . . ."

"And do you think your father blames you?"

"No. He probably blames himself." I put my hands back over my face. "I'm not comfortable with this. It's hard to talk about."

"I know it is, but I'm proud of you for trying. The deeper the issues, the harder they are to bring to the surface."

I took a deep breath and exhaled myself to the point of empty. I wiped the tears from my face. "So what now? How do I fix this?"

"Well, 'fix' is a big word, but I think it's important to explore why you want total mastery—why you feel such an intense burden to please people and not let them down."

I nodded.

"I know it doesn't seem like it now, but some of those tough questions they posed today may have helped unlock a few things for you."

"Like a filing cabinet?" I whimpered, wiping my nose.

"Excuse me?"

"Nothing. Just a place in my head where I keep things."

"Well, I get the sense that it's pretty jam packed in there. Maybe we can work on going through a few of those files and throwing some of the old stuff out—into a snow bank of sorts. What do you say?"

* * *

The wind died down on my drive back to Rockford. The snow continued to fall through the night sky, but it appeared less frantic. The driveway sat empty when I got to the house, and I remembered that Aunt Josie had been scheduled to work. I had the place to myself.

I walked in through the back door and Patches and Toby ran to greet me.

"Yes, I see you," I said bending down to pet them both. "You don't care that I'm an exhausted failure, do you?" They wagged a little quicker in response.

I rounded the corner to the living room and saw the Christmas tree. She'd put a lot of work into it. Every ornament I'd made as a child stared back at me. I didn't have the heart to plug it in. The thought of the holidays made me ill—physically and emotionally ill.

The phone began ringing. I ignored it and the answering machine kicked in. *You've reached Josie and you know what to do . . . beep.* "Kiddles? You there yet? Christ, if I don't get a hold of you soon, I'm gonna blow a . . ."

I ran back to the kitchen and grabbed the cordless receiver. "Josie?"

"Thank Christ. I've been worried half sick all day. I tried your cell phone and . . ."

"Yeah, sorry. I turned it off. I couldn't face talking to anybody." Patches barked up at me.

"Well, you probably don't feel like talkin' to me now either, so I won't keep ya. I just needed to hear your voice and know you made it home."

A short pause followed.

"Did you see any of it?" I asked, wandering into the living room.

"I saw it. Why do you think I've been half sick? Sons-a-bitches. If I'd been there I would have—"

"Yes, I know. And I love you for it."

"Well," she paused. "As long as you're okay."

"I'm here—safe and sound."

"See ya in the morning then?" she asked as though not thoroughly convinced.

"You will."

I peeked outside through the front curtains. Heloise Daw stared back at me through hers.

*   *   *

"Christ," I whispered, waking from a nightmare. Some kind of a celebration had been taking place in my dream. One where Ross danced with my mother and everyone wore black. Could I not get a moment's peace?

I sat up on the side of the bed and put my head in my hands. Both dogs came over to acknowledge my return to the real world. The sun hadn't joined us yet.

"Yeah, yeah, I know. You love me," I said to them as they nudged against my legs. "And you'd love me even more if I let you outside, wouldn't you?"

They began prancing, and I ushered them downstairs. Before opening the back door I peeked through the dish towel curtains. A car sat parked in the back alley with someone in it. I caught my breath and pulled the curtains shut again.

God. Surely the press didn't follow me?

When I looked back out the car had pulled away.

You're completely paranoid, Candace. Get a grip.

I swung the back door open and let the dogs out into the cold, dark morning. I looked at the clock on the stove: 6:00 a.m. Josie would be home in a couple of hours. I decided to run a bath and soak before she arrived.

I filled the tub with hot water and bubbles then let the dogs back in. They ran in circles around the kitchen table dropping little balls of snow with every step.

"Lovely."

I walked back upstairs to the bathroom. The dogs followed pushing past my legs. "Settle down now, okay? It's quiet time."

Toby looked up at my face and cocked his head. "Oh, I know. You're the cutest one. Yes you are." I removed my flannel pajamas and threw them on the floor for him to lie on. Then I stepped into the steaming bath.

I immersed my body as Patches curled up in the doorway as guardian. I turned on the hot water tap with my foot in hopes of scalding the chill from my bones.

Why did I have to have that dream? Bad enough to think about this shit when I'm awake without . . . I sat up to turn off the tap.

You've reached Josie, and you know what to do . . . beep. Both dogs perked up their ears. I sat perfectly still.

"Yes, Geri Perkins here . . . again. Candace, if you're there, wake up and pick up the damn phone." Patches turned to face me. "Candace?" I slumped back down in the water. "Fine. Be that way."

"It's 6:00 a.m. for Christ's sake," I hollered, my voice echoing off the peach-colored tile that surrounded me.

"I'm calling to inform you that our professional relationship is now severed. Yesterday's fiasco, and your reluctance to communicate, have left me no choice but to cancel our contract. I'll be visiting my lawyer this afternoon. And I will no longer be your go-between. Your publisher will be in touch with you directly, as will Karen. You're on your own, and thanks for nothing."

The click of her hanging up echoed throughout the house.

I put a wet washcloth over my face and breathed through it.

So, there it was: the final blow. I'd officially screwed up every aspect of my life.

I could just drown myself. I could slump down under the water and breathe in through my nose and not out through my mouth. It would be that simple. No more humiliation. No more failures. No more . . .

The dogs began barking in a frantic chorus and ran down the stairs. I let out a gasp and sat up. Something, or someone, had set them off. Shit.

The back door opened and Aunt Josie's voice rang out. "There's my babies."

I breathed a sigh of relief and relaxed back in the tub.

"What are all the lights doin' on? Candace?" she called out.

"Yep, in the bath. I woke up early."

"You okay?"

"I've been better. Why are you home so early?"

"We lost a patient last night," she called up from the bottom of the stairs. "They had me hang around in case of an admission, but I begged to come home early when one didn't happen. I'll put some coffee on for us."

I soaked while listening to her putz in the kitchen; so many memories of that sound as a kid. Me nodding off on the couch after school or doing homework in my room, and all the while she'd been a comforting presence in the background.

Before long she made her way up the stairs with two steaming cups of coffee. She set one on the side of the tub, closed the lid on the toilet, and sat down. I moved the bubbles around to cover me like I had as a child.

"Don't listen to your messages while I'm here, if you don't mind. Geri just left one. She's dropping my contract, and I'm sure there are more of the same on there."

"That self-righteous bitch. I swear I'd love to—"

"Well, you can't really blame her now, can you? Think about it. She invested in me, and I screwed up."

"I don't care. I don't like the way she talked to you. I'd still like to kick her ass." I had to grin. "And I'd like to kick the ass of every one of those reporters too, as far as that goes."

I held my nose and dipped my head under the water for a few seconds. When I popped back up, she'd pulled out a fresh towel for me.

"Dr. Hedley says it's their job to dig up skeletons and go for the jugular."

Her movement paused. "So, you saw her then?"

"I did," I replied, avoiding eye contact.

"And she said what now?"

"That they dig up dirt on people. Who knows, maybe there's a whole Candace Bradford team that runs around looking for crap on me. At least they've found out everything at this point. Not that it matters anymore anyway."

I waited for a response. When I looked up at her, she had both hands on the edge of the sink and her head hung forward. Her reflection in the mirror looked pale and weathered.

"What's the matter?" I asked.

She turned to face me. Tears sat in the corners of her eyes. I sat up in the tub with the facecloth over my chest. "What's wrong? What is it?"

She handed me the towel. "Dry yourself off, Kiddles, and meet me downstairs." She let out a long sigh. "It's time you and me had a serious talk."

CHAPTER 26

I walked down the stairs toward the glow of Christmas lights. Josie had plugged in the tree. I could hear her sniffling in the kitchen. I rounded the corner in my housecoat and found her sitting at the table. A cardboard box and a bottle of scotch sat in front of her. She filled a shot glass and motioned for me to sit down.

"A little early, don't you think?" I asked, taking the chair across from her.

"No. Not for me, it isn't. It's the end of my day, remember? Been up since yesterday afternoon."

She drank half the scotch in her glass and wiped her mouth on the back of her hand.

"What's going on?"

She rose from the table and grabbed some tissues from the counter.

"And what's in the cardboard box?" I asked, removing the towel from my wet hair and draping it across the chair beside me.

"We'll get to that," she replied.

"You're freaking me out here."

She sat back down and placed a handful of tissues on the table. "I don't mean to. This just isn't easy is all." She ran her fingers through her short graying hair and gave the ceiling a hard stare.

"So, the time has come that I tell you a story."

I shrugged. "Okay."

"One you need to hear from me." She drained the rest of her shot glass. "Not from some asshole reporter."

"Jesus. What now? Seriously, I—"

"Just . . ." she raised her hand like a traffic cop. "Hear me out. It's important."

I relaxed back.

"I know you don't know much about me, other than my bein' a friend of your mama's, and that I came from Texas."

"And that you raised me like your own," I added, trying to comfort her.

"Didn't I just," she said, shaking her head. "I've dreaded this day for a long, long time, Kiddles."

"What is it, for God's sake? Did you kill somebody or something?"

"Not intentionally," she whispered under her breath.

"Okay, what the hell? Tell me already." She poured another shot and drank the whole thing back.

"Here goes," she said, slapping her hand down on the table. "I grew up in Fate, Texas—if that don't beat all. We used to say that Fate is what sealed our fate, but then my family loved excuses. Daddy ran off when I was five years old and never came back. That left me, my mama, and my brother Bobby to fend for ourselves, and mama wasn't much of a fender."

She looked back up at the ceiling and shook her head. "Mama drank a lot, and she had a long string of boyfriends that she'd bring home to try and ease the pain of life. I *guess* that's why she brought them home, anyway. Who'd know for sure?

Some beat her, some abused me. None were worth the dirt they carried in on their boots."

"Jesus, I had no idea," I said, reaching across the table toward her. She pulled away.

"I'm not tellin' ya this for pity. It has bearing on the rest of the story," she snapped.

"Sorry."

She looked me in the eye and poured another drink.

"I ran away from home when I turned fifteen. Figured I'd be better off on my own than watchin' her kill herself. Bobby'd left a year before me." She paused.

"You still in touch with him?"

"Nah." She gave a half-hearted grin in my direction. "The only kin I've got is right here in this room."

Her eyes looked afraid, like a ghost lurked in the shadows. She grabbed the neck of the scotch bottle and held it tight.

"God, I thought I knew so much in those days; tough little street kid headin' out to see the world. Christ. I didn't know shit; hopped a train if you can believe that. Deep down I was as scared as hell, but no one was ever gonna find that out. No siree."

Her face grew more anguished. I fidgeted in my chair.

"Ended up in Chicago. Yep, sure did. The City of the Big Shoulders. I thought I'd died and gone to friggin' heaven. It was summer, mind you, and there were people everywhere—outdoor music, lots of homeless folks like myself, good parks to sleep in. Imagine me sleepin' in a park." She shook her head and released her grip on the bottle.

Patches came over and rested her head on Aunt Josie's knee. "Met a boy there. Ashamed to say I didn't even know his name." She looked down at her lap, closed her eyes, and then looked back up at me. "I knew him for a whole 24 hours, and he made me feel like somethin' special. Boy, he sure did. Talked to me direct like, told me I was pretty, and even bought me a hotdog," she chuckled. "Sounds pretty pathetic, doesn't it?"

I didn't answer. She'd become the story. I sat back to soak it all in.

"Well, one thing led to another, and we had sex that night in the park behind a hedge. It was all fast and furious like it often is with youngins. We fell asleep in the grass afterward, and when I woke up the next morning, he was gone and I was pregnant."

"Jesus. Josie, I . . ."

"Now, please. I've gotten this far." She sniffled and grabbed one of the tissues. "Where could I go? Sure as hell not back to Fate."

I watched as she blew her nose and tucked the tissue into the sleeve of her sweater.

"There was a gas station in Chicago where I'd buy my cigarettes, and I hung out there most nights. Got to know the lady who worked the night shift, and she talked the manager into hiring me."

She paused and twirled her shot glass around and around on the table. "That lady on night shift was Lynn."

"Mom?"

"Lynn," she nodded. "She befriended me; watched out for me kind of. She and Bill had this little place a few blocks from there, and she let me sleep on the sofa. Bill didn't care. Hell, if she'd brought home Charles Manson, Bill wouldn't of cared. Always was a quiet, pathetic sort, but he loved her like nobody's business. Would go along with any and every harebrained idea she came up with, and she came up with some doozies, believe you me."

"What happened next?" I leaned in toward her. For those few moments, my own ridiculous life left my consciousness. I wanted more.

"I didn't have any health insurance. I didn't have diddly-squat, least of all a future. I got real depressed and had nowhere to turn. I knew I couldn't raise a baby, I just knew I couldn't. I was 16 years old by that time, Candace. Remember that," she said, reaching into the box.

She pulled out an old faded scrapbook and slid it across the table toward me. I looked at her before opening it, her eyes full of tears; her bottom lip quivering.

I opened the scrapbook to the first page. A black and white photograph stared up at me. Browned scotch tape held down the corners. The young girl in the picture had to be Josie; God, so young. She looked to be in a hospital bed, and a tiny baby slept in her arms. The picture captured Josie's beautiful smile as she stared down at the infant. I read the handwritten caption underneath: *Candace Bradford—Born March 28, 1977—6 lbs. 7 oz.*

Shock hit me like a wrecking ball. "I—I don't understand," I said, looking up at her.

Her tears had spilled out and soaked her face. Her whole body shook.

"What does this . . . ?" I turned to the next page—Josie in the hospital bed holding a baby with Mom standing beside her smiling.

"But there's got to be some kind of a . . ." The next page—Mom standing with me in her arms, while Dad looked on.

My brain had misfired or something. This couldn't be happening. It didn't make sense.

I flipped frantically through the pages of the book. Pictures of me from every conceivable year as a kid: birthday parties, school shots, Christmases.

"What the hell is going on here?" I demanded. "What are you trying to tell me? Is this some kind of a joke?"

I pushed the chair back in a flurry and braced my back against the kitchen counter. Breaths rushed in and out of my lungs. My hands shook. I wanted to run and she sensed it.

"Please," she cried, standing at the table. "Please, just hear me out. Please." I froze in my stance. "Candace, I had nowhere to turn. Lynn suggested it—the adoption I mean. She said she'd raise you right—see to it that you were loved and got an education."

"But how?"

She sat back down.

"I put Bill down on the birth certificate and said we were married. We told everybody I was 19 and that my ID'd been stolen. Bill showed them the marriage certificate. Nobody paid any damned attention in those days."

"No," I said, shaking my head. "You're making this all up. You're twisting this around to mess with me. You couldn't have."

My heart sat in my throat, and I wanted to spit it out at her.

"I swear as sure as I'm sittin' here that I didn't know she was crazy. I'll swear it 'til the day I die."

I started pacing through the kitchen. Toby got underfoot.

"Get out of my way," I screamed. He ran into the other room with his tail between his legs. I put my hands over my face and whispered through them, "My mind is calm."

"I left. Yes I did, and it was wrong, but she'd convinced me I was doing the best thing for you. The toughest day of my life was gettin' on that bus. Toughest day of my life."

She poured more scotch. I flopped back down in the chair and examined her face as though meeting a perfect stranger.

"I ended up in Omaha. Followed a group of young kids there like myself. They were wanting to see some folk festival or something. I stayed at a hostel and ate at a mission nearby most days. That's where I met this woman who turned my life around. Betty," she nodded, "God love her, she saved my life

I'm sure of it. Without her, I'd never have gone to Creighton to get my nursing. Probably would have ended up like my mama."

Who is this woman? Bill's not my father? I'm not a Bradford? I—I . . .

"How did you get all of these pictures of me?" I demanded, slamming the scrapbook shut.

"Lynn sent them to me. She'd said she'd keep me in the loop, but right around the time I graduated from nursing school, the letters and pictures trailed off. I wrote more times than I can count, but she wouldn't answer me. I knew something was wrong, and I knew I had to come back. I'd made better of myself by then and I wanted you in my life. I'd always wanted you in my life."

I rose from the table again. "I'm sorry. I just don't understand? All this time, and you're telling me now? Why didn't you tell me before, you of all people? Have I not been through enough? Why?"

She hung her head. "I wanted to tell you from the start. I wanted you to know. Lynn didn't, and Bill—well," she shrugged. "I moved to Rockford to keep an eye on things, and I found her in bad shape. I didn't want you livin' with her anymore, and I started putting pressure on her to have you live with me. She wouldn't hear of it. In fact, the more I pushed the more she pulled back, until that day that she . . ."

"But—"

"I thought you'd blame me, don't you see?" she cried. She pulled the tissue from her sweater sleeve. "It was my fault. I wouldn't let up on her." She shook her head and pounded her fist down on the table. The dogs jumped up from the floor.

"And how in hell could I tell you about all of this when you'd just lost your lifeline? You were seven years old, baby girl. Bill and I talked it over, and we—"

"Oh, so you and Bill decided, did you? Who else knows about this?" I demanded.

"Nobody, but I couldn't risk you finding out from the press."

"Nobody? Surely someone else knows." Anger churned in the pit of my stomach.

"Lynn and Bill moved here to Rockford right after you were born. Their parents lived elsewhere, and they hadn't seen any of them in years. They just sent pictures on. They'd have no way to know she hadn't been pregnant. Nobody knew." She hung her head.

The floor fell out from under me. It fell out and left me hanging in mid air. I'd lost so much in the last few months, and now my identity had been ripped away as well; everything that I thought to be true—gone.

Josie became smaller and smaller at the kitchen table. My head swam. My knees buckled and I started to fall. Josie leapt from her chair and moved toward me to keep me from hitting the floor.

"Don't come near me," I screamed, grabbing the kitchen counter. Tears flooded my eyes. I steadied myself. "I trusted you. You were my rock." I gulped for air.

"I still am, baby girl."

"Don't call me that."

"I'm still here. You can still trust me. You're my life's blood."

She grabbed my arm, but I removed her hand. "Don't touch me, and don't ever talk to me again. I can't stay here," I blurted, heading for the stairs. "I have to pack. I have to get out of here. I have to—"

"But I'm your mother!"

CHAPTER 27

I gripped the steering wheel with both hands after calling Fiona. I had nowhere else to turn. The two most important women in my life had now betrayed me. No reason to stay in Rockford existed. No reason for much of anything did. As the car rolled toward the interstate, my phone rang from the front pocket of my purse. I ignored it.

Field after field of white snow swam in and out of view as I made my way south down I-90. Tall, skinny trees reached toward the sky begging for sunshine and the chance to bear leaves again. I'd always hated winter but none more than this one. Without Fiona, I think I'd . . .

I shook my head to clear my thoughts. I tried to concentrate on the sound of my snow tires gripping the road beneath me.

I could drive off into one of those fields—or maybe into an oncoming transport. Then I wouldn't have to deal with . . . I shook my head again, harder. Stop it. Breathe. Just get there. Get to Fiona.

I rounded the grove of fir trees near her farmhouse, and my phone rang again. "Shut up," I hollered. It stopped. Tire tracks led my way through the snow and down Fiona's laneway. As I got closer, I saw an unfamiliar Lexus SUV parked out front.

I second guessed my decision to go in when Fiona opened the front door. I cut the engine and sat staring at her for a moment. How beautiful she looked in the morning light. How I wanted her life. How I wanted anyone's life but my own.

"Candy, for Pete's sake. You'll catch your death," she called out.

I climbed out of the car and lumbered up to her front porch. She embraced me. The smell of bacon wafted past my nose. Christmas decorations stared at me from over her shoulder.

"Is someone here, Fiona, because I can . . ."

He entered the doorway wrapped in a blue terrycloth robe. "You must be Candace." The beauty of his smile matched the warmth of his thick French accent. With curly brown hair, a five o'clock shadow, and a tall, thin frame, he dripped sexuality like honey from a heated spoon.

"Candace—Étienne Aurandt," Fiona said, holding her hand out toward him as though presenting a piece of art. Her hand waved back toward me. "Étienne—Candace Bradford."

"Pleased to meet you," I said, suddenly aware of my ghastly appearance.

"Enchanté." He smiled and tipped his head forward in the slightest of bows.

"Fiona," I said, attempting to fix my hair. "I really think I should . . ." I looked in the direction of the car.

"You really should get your ass in this house is what you really should do," she said, grabbing my elbow and pulling me inside. "Étienne, could you pour our friend a cup of coffee please?"

He raised his cup in the air as though to toast us and headed toward the kitchen.

"Where are your bags?" she asked.

"Well, there's only one and it's in the car. I saw the SUV, and I wasn't sure if I should stay."

"Nonsense. You need to find some solace somewhere, and this place has plenty of room. We'll grab the bag later," she said, smiling her warmest smile. She shut the door behind us, and I prayed that she never join the list of disappointing people in my life.

Fiona's success as an artist emanated through every drywall pore in her home, and the holidays only added to the magic. She'd gone all out this time, probably for Étienne. I felt like I'd stepped into the Christmas layout of a quirky design magazine; that, and a very personal moment that didn't deserve my intrusion.

She took my coat and ushered me into the living room where the fireplace crackled and blazed full of flames. A huge Scotch Pine stood in the corner of the room laden with handcrafted ornaments of every conceivable size, shape, and color. Tiny sparkles of light danced throughout its limbs. A paper maché star crowned the picturesque creation, and the entire tree seemed to reach out wanting to embrace me.

"Your tree's amazing, Fiona."

I envisioned my own box of decorations stacked in a dark storage unit; all of them the same color. Silver on silver. A total lack of imagination.

"Thanks, hon. I'll admit that I got a little carried away this year." She winked.

I looked over every inch of the room, and my eyes came to rest on the mantel where Lynn's clock sat in silence.

"It quit ticking as predicted," said Fiona, following my gaze. "But I still think it looks lovely there. You okay with that?"

I nodded and fell back onto her patchwork sofa. Fiona sat down beside me and took my hand.

Étienne entered the room and handed me a cup of coffee. "I am not sure how you take it, but there is some cream in the fridge, and . . ."

Fiona gave him a gentle wave to leave the room. "Well, I'm sure that you have been here before, so I will leave you two beautiful women to talk." He grinned at Fiona. "Voilà. I'm just going to talk to my brother on Skype, okay?"

"Sure, no problem," she said, and he left the room. "His mother's in France, and she's had a small stroke. They think she's going to be fine, but she's in the hospital for observation. His brother took the train from Paris to be with her, but it's eating Étienne up being so far away, I can tell."

"Bad week for mothers."

Fiona squeezed my hand. My phone beeped with a message.

"So, tell me. I don't understand. Josie's your mother? Is that what you were saying on the phone?" I nodded and set my coffee down on her diamond-shaped coffee table. "Jesus. I'm shocked." She shook her head then shrugged. "Well. I am, and I'm not."

"What do you mean?"

"I could never figure out how you weren't related to be honest with you. I mean, I know you're as different as night and day in so many ways, but Candy come on. You look so much like her."

"You think?" I asked. It had honestly never crossed my mind. Why would it?

"Ah, yeah. I think."

I shrugged, and stared up at the silent clock. "I stormed out," I said. "I left her sobbing at the back door. She should have told me."

Fiona blew out a long breath. "Tough situation to judge if you've not been in it. I would think so, anyway."

"Whose side are you on here?"

"Oh, no you don't. I don't play sides. I love Josie and I love you. And quite frankly, she loves you too. Almost like . . ." She cocked her head to the side and shrugged.

"Like what?"

"Well, I was going to say 'like a mother,' but apparently we've covered that."

My phone started ringing again. "Jesus. That godforsaken thing," I said. "There's never anything good on the other end of it anymore. I've given up answering it." It rang a few more times and stopped. "Besides, I know it's Josie and I don't want to talk to her."

"Or that crazy bitch, Geri," said Fiona.

"Oh no, it won't be Geri. She left a message on Josie's machine this morning. We're through. She's canceling our contract. I'll no doubt lose the book too *and* the radio gig." I rubbed my thighs with my hands. "See? It only gets better."

I stood and walked over to the fireplace for warmth. I ran a finger over the edge of the mantel clock and found the old spot on the side where a small piece of wood had chipped off. Lynn had tried to hide it with brown marker. Guess she'd tried to hide plenty of things. It's funny how cover-ups always looked worse than the original imperfection.

"Candy, I'm so—"

"Don't be sorry. I brought this all on myself. You were right from the start."

My cell phone beeped again. I turned in the direction of it with a mounting rage.

"Candace, it's been a horrible chain of events. You can't be blaming yourself for all of it, surely."

Fiona's landline rang.

"Hang on," she said, heading toward the kitchen.

"Don't answer it. It's her."

"And? I'm still talking to 'her,' and it's my phone."

I followed her as far as the entrance to the kitchen.

"Hello?" she said. "Oh, hey Josie. Yeah, she's here." I began pacing. "Yeah, she told me the whole story."

Whole story my ass. How about how betrayed I feel? How deceived and humiliated? "No, I realize that, but she's not in any mood to talk to you right now." Fiona turned toward me. "At least, I don't think she—"

"No, I most certainly am not," I hollered.

"Yeah, well. You heard her. But she's okay."

Not in my opinion, I'm not.

"No, she can stay here as long as she likes. Not to worry."

How can I stay here with Mr. Terrycloth Bathrobe?

"Yes, I'll tell her. I promise. You okay?"

I walked closer and gave Fiona a warning glare. She turned her back on me. "I can't imagine, Josie. I just can't."

"Excuse me," I called out, like a spoiled child.

"Yeah, I will. Love you too." And with that, she hung up.

"What did she want?" I demanded.

"To know that you're okay. To tell you that she loves you. To say she's sorry . . . for everything."

"Whatever," I snapped, heading back into the living room. My cell phone rang again. "Jesus, does she ever give up?" I darted toward my phone and pulled it from my purse prepared to yell at Josie. My jaw dropped open when I saw the caller ID.

"What is it now?" asked Fiona.

"Ross," I said, hitting the button. "Hello?"

"Candace?" said Ross from the other end.

"Good guess." Silence followed and I regretted my tone.

"I'm sorry," I said. "Are you still there?"

"I'm here," he replied.

I shrugged my shoulders at Fiona and she shrugged hers back. She left the room but pointed to let me know that she'd be nearby.

"Saw your press conference," he continued.

I sat down on the floor cross-legged. "Quite the show wasn't it?"

"They're bastards. They're hounding us like crazy too. It's too much."

I began rocking back and forth on the floor. "Us? So it's true about you and Eunice, then?"

"Yeah. It's true."

My insides twisted and knotted pulling me forward. My head bent toward my knees. "So, she's pregnant?" Please say no.

"Only a couple of weeks." My head swam. "One of her goddamned friends must have leaked it. You shouldn't have found out that way. Seriously."

All hope left me. Nothing remained. "And the firm? You're leaving the firm?"

"Yeah. Already left, actually. Eunice and I are—"

"Ross. You have no idea what the last few days have been like for me." My ribs tightened around my lungs. "You and me—and all that mess—that was bad enough, but things have gotten worse since then. I don't think I can bear to hear any more bad news."

I put my hand over my mouth and fought to keep from crying.

"Hey, listen. I'm sorry. Really, I am. For everything, you know? But that life we had? The one I had? It was never me. I was miserable in it."

"You think that one was bad? Try this one on for size," I snapped.

"I just want to write, Candace. It's all I've ever wanted to do, but Dad and his goddamned expectations . . ."

"But I tried to support that. I tried to encourage you, didn't I?"

"I'm sorry."

All the concessions I'd made over the years, and all of the career/relationship balancing I'd done for him slammed together in one big angry collision. "Why are you calling me? What do you want?"

The Christmas tree now glowered down at me from the corner. The whole room looked more menacing than festive. I tried to take a deep breath but coughed instead.

"We're—ah—moving in a few weeks. San Diego."

I rose from the floor. "What? But you're a Chicago boy. You said you'd never leave here."

"I know what I said, but I need to get away from this godforsaken Simpson yoke around my neck. Eunice's family is out there, and she'll need help with—"

"Don't say it. Don't you say it out loud, so help me."

I began pacing through the living room. I wanted my uterus back. I wanted it all back.

Ross sighed. "I'll email you all of our forwarding info, but I wanted you to know in person that I'm filing for divorce."

I stopped pacing and grabbed the fireplace mantel. "In person? This is what you call in person?" I screamed.

Fiona came rushing toward me from nowhere to calm me down. "Whoa, sunshine," she whispered, putting an arm around my shoulder.

I took the phone from my ear and shook it in my hands. "You no good, rotten piece of shit."

Intense heat rose up my neck and into my head. Pressure built up behind my eyes. I pressed my thumb hard onto the phone with shaking hands. I hung up wanting to push right through the thing.

"How dare he." I looked around the room like it had burst into flames. I had to get out.

"Candy? Calm down. Come here and—"

"No." I pulled away. "No!"

My arms possessed an exaggerated strength that I wanted to use to ring his neck. I shook free from Fiona and ran to the front door. I needed out.

Shoeless, I trudged out onto the snow-covered porch. Every insult, every injury, every betrayal, and every mistake culminated in a whirl of energy that swung my arm in a pitch-like motion while my body rotated in circles: once, twice around with my arm over my head. Then my feet stopped in place and my hand opened sending my cell phone through the air and into a huge pile of snow.

"Jesus," whispered Fiona from behind.

I turned to see a half grin on her face. I stood in front of her hyperventilating like a steam train on an uphill climb, each breath visible in the cold winter air. My feet began to feel the wet snow against them when Étienne appeared in the doorway.

"Sorry, honey," said Fiona. "Candace was just having a . . ."

She looked at him like part of his face had gone missing. "What's wrong, baby?"

She reached up to touch his cheek.

"It's my mother," he said. "She has had another stroke."

CHAPTER 28

Christmas morning arrived at Fiona's with everything wrapped in dread. I woke up before anyone else, donned my housecoat over my flannel pajamas, and made my way downstairs to make coffee. Fiona's Christmas tree looked asleep without its lights on, and I found myself tip-toeing past the living room entrance as though afraid it might wake up. Vincent lay curled in a ball on one of the kitchen chairs. He lifted his head and yawned when he saw me. His lack of enthusiasm for the day matched my own.

I got the coffee started then moved to the kitchen window to look outside at the backyard. A fresh blanket of snow had fallen during the night and only one set of tracks could be seen on the surface of it. A rabbit perhaps; no reindeer prints at any rate. No magic. The rising sun gave the morning a peaceful sheen. Had it been a Christmas I wanted to remember, I may have even found it spectacular.

Fiona joined me in the kitchen as the coffeepot sputtered and completed its chore. She came to me without a word and gave me a compassionate embrace. I succumbed to it with little emotion. I just wanted the day to be over. She pulled the cream from the fridge as I poured two large cups of coffee. I announced that I would be leaving her alone with Étienne to open their gifts.

"Don't be silly. Besides, there's something under the tree for you as well."

"But we promised not to exchange, Fiona."

"It's not from me. It's from Josie. The box arrived yesterday."

A sense of longing caught me by surprise. I pushed it aside. "Not interested."

"Candace," she said, sitting down beside the cat. "It's been a few weeks now. Don't you think you've tortured her enough at this point?"

"Me? Tortured her? That's rich." I put the cream back in the fridge and shut the door harder than intended.

"Come on. It's Christmas."

"It's a bitterly cold day in December. That's all it is to me." I turned to leave the room.

"Where are you going?"

I looked back at her. "Upstairs to write in my journal. Dr. Hedley's been hounding me to express myself, and I figure today's as good a day as any to start."

She shot me a look of concern. "You're sure you don't want to join us?"

"I'm more than sure." I started toward the stairwell.

"Oh, and Candy?"

"Yeah?"

"About dinner."

"What about it?" I asked, turning again to face her.

"A friend of Étienne's is joining us. Marc Vallée. They knew each other in France, and he's all alone for the holidays, so we invited him."

Irritation made my jaw clench. "Fiona. Please tell me you're not trying to set me up."

"It's not a set up, Candy. Calm down. He literally has nowhere to go, and he's a great guy. Seriously, it will be fun."

Fun—what did she know?

I made my way back to the spare bedroom; a room that now provided solace. The beauty of the space soothed me somehow. Fiona had painted a grove of trees along each wall and had laden them with delicate, multi-colored flowers. The pale blue background extended up to the ceiling where billowing clouds looked real enough to float.

I settled onto the pale, rose-colored duvet and dug out the notebook Dr. Hedley had given me. Nothing fancy: no moleskin binding, no linen pages. "Just something to get you started," she'd said.

I opened the first page and stared down at the empty lines on it. I'd written an entire book and had no idea where to start with expressing my feelings. I let out a sigh and began writing. *Day one. Present under tree from aunt/mother. Don't care.*

I could hear Étienne stirring awake down the hall. Guilt rose in me for intruding on their holidays together. Gratitude wrestled it for first place. Where else would I have been if not with them?

I heard their bedroom door open, followed by the clomping of his weary feet on the steps.

"Joyeux Noël, ma cherie," he crooned when he'd reached the main floor.

"Oh Étienne. Our first Christmas," Fiona gushed.

"Gag me," I whispered under my breath.

I remembered my first Christmas with Ross. I'd gushed as well. Gushed until all the gushiness in me had spilled out over every monotone decoration in my apartment.

Fiona's laughter sliced through the morning stillness, and I resisted my heart's yearning to feel joy for her. I put my pen to paper: *Best friend in love. Gushing like an idiot downstairs. Shoot me.*

Fiona's phone rang. I cocked my head to listen.

"Hello," she lilted. "Oh hi, hon. Merry Christmas." I opened the bedroom door a crack to hear more clearly.

"Yep, it arrived yesterday."

Damn it—Josie. Of course she'd try and call. Why couldn't everyone leave me the hell alone?

"No, her cell phone has . . . well . . . taken a powder."

Very funny.

The cat appeared through the crack in the door and peered up at me.

"Well, I highly doubt it but let me try. Hang on." Her footsteps neared the bottom of the staircase. "Candy?"

I held my breath.

"Candace?"

"What?" I replied with a bothered tone.

"Josie's on the phone."

"And?"

She paused. I could visualize her and Étienne exchanging a glance.

"*And . . .*" she mimicked. "She'd like to speak to you."

I hesitated.

"Please?"

"No," I said. "I can't."

The cat rubbed his face against the door frame and began purring.

"Candy, I—"

"Fiona, not today."

I heard her sigh. "She won't, Josie. I'm so sorry."

I closed the door and retreated back to the bed. My reflection in the dresser mirror looked defiant, like a spoiled teen. Not flattering in the least.

Footsteps started up the stairs. I braced myself for a lecture from my well-intended friend when . . .

"Candace?" Étienne's voice spoke from the other side of the door.

"Yes?"

"May I . . . ?" he asked, turning the knob on the door and peeking in.

"Y—Yes," I said, sitting up straight and pulling my housecoat tight around me.

He flung the door open wide and stood within its frame. "Please, you must excuse me for being so forward, but I feel in my heart that I must speak to you."

"Okay?"

"Candace, we don't know each other well, and Fiona has told me only a small amount about your situation."

"Well, she shouldn't be telling you—"

"No, no. Please. Let me finish," he said, holding the palm of his hand up to stop me. "I know that you have suffered a great deal over the last few months, and I know that this Josie person has disappointed you a great deal."

I started to open my mouth. He put his palm up again.

"Candace. My mother is very ill in France. She may not survive. I have taken this woman for granted all my life and she loved me no matter what." He closed his eyes for a moment, and his Adam's apple rose and fell in a deep swallow. "If I could speak to her today on the phone—on Christmas—I would tell her how grateful I am, how much I love her."

A tear snuck its way into the corner of my left eye. "I'm not saying I'll never speak to her again," I said. "It's just . . ."

The tear tracked down my face and fell onto my journal with a splat. It landed right on *aunt/mother,* and the two words bled together.

"Sometimes the world takes opportunities away from us that we thought would always be there. I just had to say." He raised both hands in the air with a shrug. "Bon. I have said my peace." And with that he left and closed the door.

I looked down at the open journal and picked up my pen.

I don't care about opportunities. I don't care about his mother. I don't care about Christmas, and I don't care about . . .

Frustration rose in me like a French soufflé. I threw my pen across the room hard against the bedroom door.

*   *   *

Marc Vallée arrived at 4:00 p.m. as expected. I watched from the upstairs window as he got out of his blue Volkswagen Jetta and pulled the collar of his coat tight around his neck. The wind whipped snow up around him as he pulled a large box from the trunk. He appeared tall, blonde, and handsome from a distance and I wanted nothing to do with him.

I made my way down the stairs as the sound of knocking announced his arrival.

"Hey, bonjour mon ami," Étienne called out, opening the door.

"Bonjour, et Joyeux Noël, eh?" the stranger responded.

I stepped into the hallway with a view of the door. Marc stomped his snowy boots on the porch and stepped inside. He set the box down on the floor and grabbed Étienne in a huge embrace. Fiona came from behind and walked past me toward the two men.

"Marc," she said, with arms open. "Welcome."

He brushed the snow from his hair. "Ah, merci beaucoup. You look beautiful," he said, reaching into the box. "And this is for you."

He handed her a bottle of Beaujolais, then he caught my eye. "And this must be your friend?" he asked, reaching a hand out in my direction.

"Yes," she smiled. "Yes, it is. Marc, meet Candace. Candace, this is Marc."

I moved toward him and put my hand in his.

"Enchanté," he said. He turned my hand over and kissed the back of it.

My face flushed red. How dare he.

Marc reached inside the large box again and brought out a small gift wrapped in gold paper. He handed it to me. "And this, Mademoiselle, is for you"

"Well, I . . ." Now what?

"Oh, Marc; how sweet," chimed Fiona.

"Ah, oui. It is sweet, actually. They are chocolates from France."

I hated chocolate. "Well, thank you," I said, for lack of a better response.

"Come in," said Fiona. "I'll open the wine."

"It smells fantastic in here," said Marc.

"The girls have been cooking all day," added Étienne. "We are in for a great American dinner, my friend." He slapped Marc on the back.

"Oh, and speaking of dinner," Marc said, reaching back into the box. He pulled out a pumpkin pie and handed it to the hostess.

"Oh my God, I may have fallen in love with the wrong man," joked Fiona. She winked in my direction and headed into the kitchen. I followed her.

"What the hell was that?" I asked in a whisper.

"What the hell was what?"

"That wink, that's what. You said this wasn't a set up."

"It's not a set up. Would you relax?" She set the pie on the counter.

"And he brought me a box of French chocolates, because . . ."

"Because he's a nice guy, Candy. For Pete's sake."

Étienne peeked in the kitchen. "You okay with Marc and me having a glass of wine by the fire before dinner?"

"Absolument," said Fiona with a grin. "But it's only a matter of minutes before this is ready. Don't get too comfortable."

He smiled and walked over to kiss her on the cheek. I announced that I'd set the table and slunk out of the room.

The dining room had been partially prepared. A red crocheted tablecloth lay draped across Fiona's antique table. Seven white candles sat in a variety of holders waiting for flames. I dug through Fiona's grandmother's sideboard and pulled out various pieces of mismatched china. None of the silverware matched either, but everything worked in the most elegant way. How did people get comfortable with being mismatched? I wanted more than anything to know.

Instrumental Christmas music began playing from the stereo in the other room. Male voices bantered back and forth in French. Pots and pans rattled in the kitchen. The aroma of holiday traditions wafted throughout the house. Handcrafted ornaments smiled at me from every corner. Big flakes of snow drifted in silence past the window as moonlight replaced the sun. I couldn't have been more miserable if I tried.

"Étienne? Can you carve the turkey, please?" Fiona called out.

"I would be proud," he said, strolling past the dining room with his wine glass held high.

* * *

Dinner went surprisingly well, and I shocked myself at feeling almost happy for the first time in ages. Maybe it was the distraction of our chatter, or maybe the wine, but I did notice that Fiona's mood seemed to worsen as mine improved.

The music continued to play in the background, and I enjoyed listening to Marc and Étienne switching back and forth from French to English. All seven candles had burned down to almost nothing, and several empty wine bottles now littered the table.

A pause came in the conversation, and Marc stared in my direction. "So, Candace," he began. "Tell me about yourself. What do you do for a living?"

"Seriously?" I scoffed.

"Oui," he said, looking at the others with a confused expression. "Seriously."

"So, you don't know who I am?"

Again, he looked around the table. He shrugged and leaned back causing the two front legs of his chair to lift off the floor. "Ah, no. Should I?"

His smile began to appear seductive. My cheeks flushed warm and I had to look away.

"Marc is a French professor, and he teaches yoga on the side, Candace," said Étienne. "Not a lot of interest in celebrity gossip."

He and Fiona giggled. I found nothing remotely funny about the comment.

Marc leaned forward and rested his arms on the table. "So, I am having Christmas dinner with a celebrity?" The light from the candles glistened in his sea blue eyes.

"Candace was quite . . ." began Fiona. "Oh sorry, I mean *is* quite famous."

She looked at me with genuine regret.

"No, no. It's okay. I was somewhat famous—or on the verge of it anyway—but not so much anymore. Well, famous for no longer being famous maybe." I raised my glass in a half-hearted toast and took a sip of wine.

"Well, I must have my picture with you for my family in France."

He raised his glass as well and drank while staring deep into my eyes. My body quivered and an old familiar tingle sent a warm flush through me.

"Speaking of family," said Étienne, tapping his wine glass with his fork.

"Mais oui," said Marc, with a solemn tone. He raised his glass toward his friend. "To your mother, Étienne."

We clinked our glasses together and drank. A spinning sensation warned me that I'd had enough.

"Yes, my mother. As you all know, my brother has been taking care of things since she has been ill, but there is news."

But I didn't want to get serious. I wanted to tingle more. I wanted to dance.

I glanced at Fiona. Her head drooped forward and she stared at her lap. Étienne reached over and grabbed her hand.

"But she's still alive, no?" asked Marc.

"She is, but she will not get better."

"I'm so sorry, Étienne," I said.

"Fiona and I have talked about this until we can talk no more," Étienne continued. "I have no choice but to move back to France to run the vineyard. When I leave tomorrow, I will not be returning."

Marc and I looked at each other with mirrored shock. A cry escaped Fiona, and she ran from the room.

CHAPTER 29

I heard the front door shut the next morning as Fiona and Étienne left for Chicago. She'd insisted on following him back to the city so that she could say goodbye at the airport. My heart broke for her while my head pounded out the rhythm of a hangover.

I swung my legs over the side of the bed and rubbed my eyes. Vincent pawed at my bedroom door wanting in. I opened it, scratched behind his ear, and made my way down the stairs expecting a mess. Everything looked spotless. She must have woken up early or been unable to sleep. I turned and jumped at the site of Marc strolling into the kitchen with a handful of glasses and a dish towel thrown over his shoulder.

"Well good morning, gorgeous," he said with a sly grin. His hair stood on end in spots. A slight new growth of beard shadowed his chin.

"Oh, I didn't know . . ." I grabbed the neck of my housecoat and patted down my hair. "What are you doing here?"

"Too much wine. Étienne insisted that I sleep on the sofa."
He shrugged. "Good idea from him, so I stayed to clean up for
them."

He put the glasses in the sink. My head pounded even
harder.

"Well, I wouldn't have . . ." I stammered, feeling like an
idiot. I looked around the room like some magic wand might
appear out of nowhere to zap me into a fully awake, fully
functioning woman.

"Listen," he said. "I am about to leave now. I don't want to
make you feel uncomfortable."

"You're not making me uncomfortable," I said, fidgeting in
place.

"Ah, yes I am," he said. "Fiona said that you would not like
finding me here, and I was going to leave before you woke up.
Mais voilà. I moved too slow."

How dare she tell him that. He grinned again then walked
toward the front door to put on his coat and boots.

"Thank you for cleaning up, Marc. And thank you for the
chocolates."

"No, no. The thanks are all mine. It was a great Christmas
for me, with my family so far away. I shared it with an old
friend and some beautiful new ones."

He winked and heat rose in my cheeks. When he grabbed
the door handle, he hesitated and turned back to face me.

"Do you think sometime that you might like to have dinner
with me or see a show or something?" he asked. "I—I mean, we
are both alone, and I would love your company."

In that moment I yearned for Ross and the life we'd shared.
Even after all we'd been through, and how much pain there'd
been, it was too soon to just move on. I wasn't ready. Not even
close. "Marc. I'm sorry, I really am," I said. "It's only been a few

months since my marriage ended, and I just don't have it in me to get emotionally involved."

"Who said anything about emotionally?"

"I beg your pardon?"

He threw his head back and laughed. "No, seriously; I understand," he said. "Really, but if you change your mind . . ." He reached into his wallet. "Please don't hesitate to call."

He handed me his card. *Marc Vallée—Kundalini Yoga Instructor.* I held it in my hand and stared at it. Someone had asked me out. A hot French yoga instructor, no less, had asked me out. I looked up again and smiled.

"I will," I said. "Thank you for that."

"For what?"

"For—well—this," I replied, holding up the card.

He grabbed the door handle again and grinned.

"You are a beautiful woman, Candace. I would be a fool not to try, no?"

He shrugged and walked out the door. I ran to the living room window and peered around the curtain to watch him drive away.

"Wow," I whispered to myself.

Vincent rubbed up against my leg meowing. "What's up buddy? You want to ask me out too?" He meowed again. "And where were you last night? Hiding under the tree?"

Ah yes—the tree. There it sat looking pathetic now that Christmas had come and gone. A brown cardboard box sat alone and unopened beneath it. I sat down on the floor and pulled it toward me, seeing my name on it. Yanking a corner of tape, the lid flipped open. Inside it sat a smaller box about four inches thick and 14 inches wide. It had been wrapped in green and red paper and a tag had been taped across the front. *To my Kiddles, I'll always love you. Josie xo.* A greeting card in an envelope lay loose beside it.

Vincent put his feet up on the edge of the box and looked inside.

"Nothing for you, old man."

I first took the card out of the box and opened it. Puppies in a basket decorated the cover along with the words, "*Merry Christmas.*" On the inside? "*And a Happy New Year.*" Really original. I looked at the signature. *You'll always be my daughter in my heart. Dad.*

I put a hand over my mouth, and my eyes filled with tears. Bill. He'd never sent me a card before in his life. Not one. It wasn't his thing. Maybe Josie had put him up to it, but either way . . .

"It's not going to happen," I announced. Vincent looked up at me and blinked. I tossed the card back in the box and shut the lid. "I can't deal with this right now. I just can't."

*　　*　　*

Fiona spent the next week moping, and she didn't enter her studio once. She said that she didn't have the heart to paint and spent most of her time either in bed or on Skype chatting with Étienne. I gave her all the space she needed but when New Year's Eve approached, I insisted she join me—in celebration for the end of a horrendous year. I'd burn the calendar at midnight. I needed something symbolic to push me forward, and I believed that she did too.

I heard Fiona stirring in her bedroom in the early evening, and I tapped on her door. "Hey, the wine's breathing. Are you?" I asked. "And I have prime rib ready for the oven." I waited but she didn't reply. "No arguing, Fiona. We're ringing in the new year together."

She opened the door. "I'm fine with that," she said with a soft grin on her face. She looked a bit better somehow. Softened and resigned maybe, but better.

"Super. I'm going to start cooking. Want to help?" I asked. "We could have a cocktail to get us started."

"No. I'm going to call Étienne again. It's almost midnight there. You okay with that?"

"Absolutely." I held out my arms and she walked into them. "I'm sorry that you're spending the evening with me instead of him."

"Well, you know I love you, but I am too." I released my hug, and she smiled before making her way to the office.

I enjoyed cooking, but I hadn't done it in ages, not with the schedule I'd kept for the last few years. Ross and I had memorized the take-out menus in our neighborhood, and the local maître d's knew us by name. Now I couldn't remember the last time I'd eaten out; maybe my lunch meeting with Geri. I shuddered at the thought of letting her down.

I poured myself a vodka with cranberry juice and put an oldies station on the radio. I wanted to move my body. I wanted to move forward more than anything; forward and away from my mistakes. The further I got into the meal preparation (and the vodka), the further away the whole mess of my life seemed to get.

"Wow, it smells great in here," said Fiona when she emerged from her long chat with Étienne.

"Why, thank you Ms. Fitzpatrick." I raised my drink in the air and smirked. "I've been slaving, and I appreciate your appreciation."

"So, where's this wine of yours?"

"On the table," I said, pointing toward the dining room. "It's our fave."

"Châteauneuf-du-Pape?"

273

"You betcha," I replied. "And there's more than one bottle of it. We've earned it."

"Cheers to us," she replied. "Let's get this year over with."

*   *   *

Laughter filled the house during our meal, and we sat at the table for hours talking about nothing that mattered. Nothing emotionally charged anyway. Just talk for the sake of sharing. It's what our friendship had always been based on, and I swam in the warmth of it.

"A beautiful meal, my dear friend," said Fiona, raising her glass. "I couldn't have done better if I'd stayed up all week."

"What the hell does that mean?" I snorted, feeling slushy from the wine.

"I don't have a flipping clue, but my Dad says it all the time." She laughed and then her face grew serious. "Shit."

"What?"

"I was supposed to call them in Ireland and I totally forgot." She rose from the table in a rush.

"Well, it's too late now, Fiona. It's the middle of the night there."

"You don't understand. If they don't hear from me they'll be sick with worry. Let me just pop them an email to explain myself, and I'll be right back," she said. "Christ, you'd think I was 16 years old, wouldn't you?" She laughed again and stumbled out of the room.

The Temptations started singing "My Girl," on the radio, and I jumped to my feet.

When it's cold outside . . . I've got the month of May.

I sang along and danced my way back and forth from the dining room to the kitchen with dirty dishes in hand. I'd just filled the sink with soapy water when Fiona tangoed past me to fill her glass.

"Email sent and the fireplace is begging for a fire. What time is it?"

I glanced at my watch. "About half an hour from a fresh start."

"Cheers again," she yelled, dancing a circle around the cat and sashaying into the other room.

Well, I—guess—you'll—say. What can make me feel this way? My girl—my girl—my girl. Talkin' 'bout my girl. My girl.

My girl, Fiona, had cheered up immensely, and I couldn't have been happier. I attributed it to the wine and said a silent prayer in appreciation of grapes. I couldn't stand seeing her sad and she felt the same about me. But now—together with food, wine, and music—we were on top of the world.

The Temptations stopped singing and the radio station went dead.

"Hey," I called out.

"Hang on," Fiona replied. A few seconds later Edith Piaf broke into "La Vie En Rose." I smiled and began swaying and staggering to the music.

"Oops," I giggled, losing my balance. "Ah, to hell with it." I threw the last of the food in the fridge and waved a hand over the sink. "I'll clean up later."

"What did you say?"

"I said we need a waiter," I replied, making myself giggle.

"You coming in here or what?"

I grabbed my wine and waltzed into the living room. The early warmth of a fire greeted me with Fiona seated in front of it. She'd plugged in the tree, and I caught a glimpse of the cardboard box beneath it. I turned away and kept on dancing. Sadness tried to cut in but I brushed it off.

"You opened it, I see," said Fiona.

"Not really. I started to."

"And?"

"And nothing; this is a happy night. I don't want to talk about boxes, or mothers, or books, or boyfriends." Fiona looked away. "I'm sorry. I didn't mean that, really. If you want to talk about Étienne, I'm all ears." How I hoped she didn't.

I sat down on the sofa to give her my full attention.

She grinned and took another drink. "I'm tipsy," she confessed.

I reached my glass out toward hers. "To the end of an eventful year." We toasted. "And don't let me forget to burn my calendar."

"You definitely take the cake for one of the worst years ever, Candy. I mean, seriously."

"It's true, isn't it?" I emptied my glass and rose to get our champagne for midnight.

"Jesus. Think about it," she hollered after me. I grabbed the bottle from the kitchen counter. "And now that your contract's been dropped—"

"What?" I returned to the room and stood staring at her. "My contract?"

"Ah shit. I'm sorry." She rose to her feet. "Stupid wine. I've been meaning to tell you, but with the holidays and Étienne leaving, I . . ."

"Which contract?"

She put her hands on my shoulders. "Josie told me that your publisher's been calling. They've canceled the contract for your second book. She thought we should know."

My body relaxed under her touch. Edith began another song. "Well, it's not like I wasn't expecting it. I suppose Karen's been trying to reach me too?"

"Apparently yes," she said. "I'm really sorry, Candy. I didn't mean to blurt it out like that. We're having such a good time, and—"

"Ah, forget it. Seriously, I'm not even remotely surprised. And who can blame them?"

Fiona gave me a gentle hug and sat back down on the floor by the fire. I unscrewed the wire from the cork on the champagne bottle.

"Well, Josie's been protecting you as usual, for what it's worth. She won't say where you are, and she's threatened them within an inch of their lives if they try and track you down." She shook her head. "You've got to admit that the woman has a way about her. I mean, how she dealt with Geri alone was hilarious."

"They really rubbed each other the wrong way, didn't they?" I grinned and took my place on the sofa. An unexpected sense of relief sat down with me. No more contracts. No more obligations. No more chance of disappointing people.

"I personally would like to see the two of them in a mud-wrestling match."

I burst out laughing at the thought of it. "Or roller derby," I cried. Fiona slapped her leg sending the cat out of the room in a blur.

The CD stuck in the player. *Je repars à zéro . . . Je repars à zéro . . . Je repars à zéro . . .*

"Oh, God, it's too funny. Make it stop," I cried, falling back on the sofa in a fit of giggles.

Fiona rose and staggered toward the sound. I fought to gain composure. She turned the music off and put the TV on instead.

"She's a hell of a woman, that Josie. I wouldn't want to run up against her."

I sighed and sat up remembering Heloise Daw and all the other evils she'd defended me against over the years. A hell of a woman, for sure, but I didn't want to think about her anymore that night. I shook my head and my thoughts scrambled.

"I wouldn't want to run into Geri either, for that matter," Fiona continued, flipping through television channels. She stopped on the live New Year's Eve broadcast from Times Square.

I aimed the champagne bottle at the Christmas tree and gave the cork a gentle push. "Hey, Geri's not so bad, Fiona. She's intense, but she's not so bad." The cork popped and shot through the branches.

"Are you kidding me?"

"No actually, I'm not. In fact, I'd like you to recommend her to some of your high-profile friends if they're looking for a publicist."

"Jesus, Candy. You're not serious."

I poured champagne into our empty wine glasses. "I am serious. I owe her, and nothing bad can be said about the work she did. She's amazing, and she deserves a break."

Fiona looked at me like I'd lost my mind. "You're a better woman than I, Candace Bradford."

"Oh yeah, right," I scoffed. "Okay, enough about Geri, and enough about me," I said, desperate to change the subject. "How are you anyway?" I took a sip of champagne and my head seemed to fill with bubbles. The lights on the tree gave a slight blur.

"You mean with Étienne?"

I nodded as the crowd in Times Square began counting down. *Ten—nine—*

"Well, I've been meaning to talk to you about that actually."
Six—five—

"I'm all ears," I said, staring at the TV.

Two—one—

She reached up and turned my face toward hers. "How would you feel if I moved to France?"

Auld Lang Syne began playing in the background.

CHAPTER 30

I had very little to say to Fiona after New Year's Eve, and our being in the house together had become awkward. We'd begun to resemble magnets with like poles; her trying to draw me in—me pulling away. The very thought of her dropping her entire life for someone she'd just met made me furious. I wanted to fly to France and slap Étienne for brainwashing her into it.

Fiona had started packing almost immediately. She'd stuffed belongings into boxes and carried them down to the basement for storage. All of her art supplies got labeled and put away. She'd asked me to stay on, rent free, to take care of things for a while, and she'd wanted to leave enough room for me to make the place my own; like that could even happen without a concrete identity to work with.

Now the day of her departure had arrived. I'd spent the morning shuffling from room to room like a confused senior. Fiona stayed busy filling suitcases upstairs. She came down with one of them and set it by the front door. I turned my back to her.

"Candy?" she said. I ignored her. "Listen, I just wanted you to know that your staying here is a godsend."

Vincent sauntered up to me and rubbed his head on my shin. "And the cat; I don't know what I would have done otherwise. Not gone, I guess."

"Well, piss on the cat then. I'm not looking after him," I snapped.

"Candy, please."

I turned to face her. She seemed pale and her eyes looked reddened.

"Fiona, why are you doing this?" I asked. "It's crazy, don't you see that? Your whole life's here."

"I love him, Candy. I'm miserable without him, and what the hell? It's France, right? I can paint anywhere, and if it doesn't work out, my place, my cat, and my best friend are all right here waiting for me." She forced a grin.

"I can't guarantee I'll be here if you come back."

"Candy, come on," she begged. "I don't want to leave with us like this."

"Then don't." Every inch of me shuddered at the thought of life without her.

Fiona sighed and looked at her watch. "Look, I'm sorry, okay?"

"Whatever." I turned away from her again.

"Okay, seriously. I'm not sure when the whole world started revolving around just you, but I have a life too you know. I've wanted a relationship like this for as long as I can remember, and I'm not letting it go. Period."

I couldn't answer. I just stood staring at the wall in defiance. Why couldn't she have her own life here? Why did everyone have to leave me?

"Fine," she said. "Don't say anything if that's what you want. My brother's going to be here in an hour to take me to the airport, so I have to finish getting my shit together. I've made a list of things you need to know about the house, and it's on the kitchen counter with the keys to the Jeep. Use it as long as you need to. I don't care."

She turned and left the room. I wanted to run after her but didn't. Instead, I turned to stare out the window at her old yellow Jeep that sat nose-to-nose with my BMW. They say that choices in vehicles say a lot about a person. Fiona's said *down-to-earth*. Mine used to say *success*, but it now hollered *fraud* in bold red paint. Looking at it filled my gut with anger. Driving it now embarrassed me to no end. Regardless, the time had come to sell it.

The sound of suitcase zippers echoed from upstairs drawing me out of my thoughts. Why did she have to meet him anyway? Why now?

I needed air. I grabbed an empty grocery bag from the kitchen, donned my coat and boots, and headed outdoors. Might as well get rid of everything familiar all at once. I'd clean the stupid car out and list it right away, then everything that defined me could go to hell.

A January thaw had hit. I could hear the constant drip of water splatting on the porch as I stepped out onto it. I wished it had snowed enough to cancel flights. Maybe she'd have changed her mind with enough time.

I stomped through wet slush to the car and opened the driver's side door. I hadn't had the thing long enough to accumulate much in it, but a few gum wrappers had been tucked in one of the compartments, and some loose change decorated the cup holder. A handful of old CDs I'd once loved sat in the center console. I tossed them in the bag along with no desire to ever listen to them again.

I reached over and opened the glove box. There sat the blue Tiffany box on top of my owner's manual. I opened it and found it empty. But the globe? I remembered that I'd tossed it after the press conference. Memories of that horrific day made me cringe. I reached down to check under the passenger seat.

"Ouch," I cried, pulling my hand back. A small trickle of blood popped up on the thumb of my left hand. I put it in my mouth and sucked. My irritation grew with the taste of injury. I reached in again and pulled out half of a crystal globe. Two other smaller pieces followed, and I could feel a collection of tiny shards dispersed throughout the carpeted floor.

"Some world on a string," I whispered. I tucked the three broken pieces back into the Tiffany box and placed it in the bag. When I returned to the house, I placed the bag in a cardboard box that sat on Fiona's office floor; the same box that housed my still unopened Christmas gift from Josie.

I turned to see Fiona standing in the office doorway. She'd carried another suitcase down the stairs with her.

"Feel free to take over this whole room," she said. "Do whatever you want with it."

I eyed the suitcase and walked past her toward the kitchen.

A knock came to the door.

"Surely he's not here already," she said, walking toward it. I heard the front door creak open. "Can I help you?"

I moved into the front hallway and hid well behind Fiona to sneak a peek at the intruder. A young girl, not more than 20, stood on the porch wearing stiletto boots and a miniskirt; her ears glowed beat red under her cropped blonde hair.

"Uh . . . is Candace Bradford here?" the girl asked, wiping the hair from her eyes. Her foot slipped a little on the slush and she caught her balance.

"Who's asking?"

"Amy. Amy Sparling. Publishing Assistant," she said, reaching a hand out toward Fiona. Her enthusiasm told me she hadn't been assisting for long. Just what I needed: an overzealous snoop from the publishing community.

"Well, I'm not sure what to tell you, Amy Sparling, Publishing Assistant, but I—"

I stepped forward moving Fiona out of the way. "I'll handle this."

"Be my guest," she replied, turning to head back upstairs.

"Ms. Bradford?" The young woman gushed. "Oh my God, you have no idea how much it means to finally meet you." The girl danced a little on the porch; I assumed because of the cold.

"From Illinois originally, are you?" I asked, amusing myself.

"No, Florida, but it's nice here." Her teeth chattered and she peered past me into the warm house. I pulled the door up against my back to block her view.

"And what exactly is it you want, Miss Sparling?"

"Well . . ." She reached in her oversized leather bag and pulled out a business card. I looked it over. She worked for one of the largest publishing companies in Chicago. I raised an eyebrow. "We're interested in your story." She hopped up and down a few times. "Boy, it's really cold, isn't it?"

"No, it isn't actually." The *drip, drip* from the eavestrough echoed in the background.

"Oh, well. Guess I'm still getting used to it." She rubbed her hands on her thighs. "So, like I said, we're really interested in—"

"My story; I heard you."

"Yeah, you know? Your side of it; what really happened."

She's got to be kidding me. "So, you basically want to exploit all the shit I've been through, is that it?"

"No, no," she said, waving her hands in front of her. "Nothing like that. You don't understand. We love you. I—I love you," she stammered. "Well . . . not like that," she shook her head. "I'm making an idiot of myself. I'm such a loser."

She hung her head. I could see her knees shaking. My conscience kicked in.

"Step inside the door," I motioned to her, rolling my eyes.

"Oh, thank you. Thank you so much." She jumped past me in a flash.

I pulled the door shut. "You were saying?"

"Well, this was all my idea, actually." Go figure. "I wouldn't be where I am today if it wasn't for *Total Mastery*. Honest to God, I wouldn't. I mean . . . it's brilliant."

I crossed my arms in front of me and stared at her. She continued. "So, I presented the idea, and they liked it. To have you write a book for us. I mean, to tell your side of the story. What really happened and all." She cupped her hands to her mouth and blew into them.

"This must be some kind of joke," I scoffed.

"No, not at all, and we know there'd be a market for it. Look at all the media attention you got over this. Everybody knows you at this point." Not everybody. I flushed at the memory of Marc Vallée.

"Look, you have no idea how many people think you got a bad deal out of all of this, and it could be a great story. Maybe it's your chance to set the record straight and get back on track, you know? Maybe re-release the book and start fresh."

Re-release? Would anyone really want it?

"What do you think?"

I looked at the young face of enthusiasm standing before me. "How exactly did you find me anyway?"

"Oh, I had to do some serious investigative work," she grinned with pride. "First, I found out where your aunt lived. She hollered at me by the way."

I had to smile.

"Then I asked around the neighborhood, and this nice lady across the street suggested I try your friend, Fiona. She told me what she looked like and everything."

Damn that Heloise Daw.

"Then I did some Googling, you know, and I found Fiona's website. I saw that she lived near Huntley, IL, so I drove there and started asking around. That's how I got here." She beamed.

"Hmm, well, I'm sorry you had to waste all that time," I said, reaching for the door handle.

"N—No, please," she called out. "Please say you'll think about it."

She reminded me of how I'd been at that age; all full of possibility and excitement. Hell, I'd been that way only six months prior. Amazing how so much can change in so little time.

"Okay," I said. "I'll think about it. But don't come around here harassing me. If I want to talk to you I'll call you, okay?"

"Okay, deal . . ." she said. "And promise you won't sign with anyone else without talking to me first?"

She thinks there'll be others? "I promise."

"Great," she said, leaning forward like she wanted to hug me. I stepped back. "Well . . . okay then. I'll go." She walked out onto the porch and turned to face me. "You can't know how much it means to me to have actually met you. You just can't."

She stumbled through the snow in her heels and I closed the door. I walked back into the office and tossed her card into the box with the bag from the car and the unopened Christmas gift.

*   *   *

Three overstuffed suitcases now sat at the front door. Vincent sniffed at each one of them, and his one ear flattened out. He knew that suitcases meant nothing but trouble, and he didn't like goodbyes any more than I.

"He's been a nervous Nelly for days," said Fiona, as she came down the stairs for the last time. She picked up the cat, held him tight against her chest and began crying. A sinking sensation ran from my throat to the pit of my stomach.

"Fiona, you don't have to do this if you're having second thoughts. Just don't show up for the flight; easy as that."

Vincent jumped free from Fiona's arms and flipped his tail in her direction.

"Remember what you said to me once?" I continued. "If you change your mind, the planet won't implode, and your heart won't stop beating? Well, it won't, and how I wish I'd listened to you that day. Please listen to me."

Fiona wiped tears from her eyes. I saw a glimmer of hope, so I continued, "We'll put everything back where it was, and Vincent and I will do a happy dance. We can set your studio back up, and—"

"Candy, stop it. I'm not having second thoughts. I'm going."

I turned and walked into the living room then flopped onto the sofa. The whole house sagged around me; every inch of it weighed down by her leaving.

I put my hands over my face. The distance would be too great. She'd never been to France without me. It's where *we* went; *our* place. Nothing would ever be the same again.

Vincent jumped up on my lap. He purred once and then stopped.

The sound of a car horn rang from outside.

"He's here," said Fiona.

I began rocking back and forth, and the cat jumped down to the floor.

She won't be here anymore. She won't be tangible. People far away seldom are. They turn into ghosts or something, like they never existed at all. I rose from the sofa and walked toward her in desperation. "I hate this," I cried. "I hate everything about this. You have no business leaving me all alone like this."

"You're not alone, Candy."

A car door slammed outside.

"What do you mean I'm not alone?"

Vincent rubbed against Fiona's leg and meowed again. A new tear came to her eye and she reached down to scratch his worried little head.

"You mean the cat?" I asked. "Give me a break."

"No, I don't mean the cat." She looked me in the eye. "I mean Josie."

"Oh, no you don't." I paced around the suitcases. "How dare you bring her up to me."

"Get your head out of your ass and call your mother, Candace. This has gone on long enough. You're being childish."

I stopped pacing. "Oh, nice move: playing the guilt card on me just before *you* get on a fucking plane to France?"

Fiona's shoulders slumped. She closed her eyes and shook her head.

"Did she put you up to this?" I demanded.

"No, she didn't put me up to anything, and I'll be damned if I can figure out what your problem is with her anyway. She's done nothing but love you wholeheartedly your entire life. Who cares if she kept a stupid secret?"

Footsteps thumped onto the front porch, and a knock came to the door.

Fiona reached for the doorknob. "You're killing her, Candy, and she doesn't deserve it."

My teeth clenched. "She let me down, don't you see that? And now you're doing the same."

"I'm not discussing this with you any further. Your reaction to her is unwarranted, and you know what needs to be done."

She opened the door, and her brother stood like a centurion within its frame.

"Ready, Sis?" he asked.

"Ready."

Fiona turned in my direction and a flood of emotions overcame me. I wanted to grab her neck and strangle her. I wanted to grab her neck and keep her from leaving. I wanted to grab her neck and tell her I loved her.

"Candy, I love you, and I'll always love you," she sniffled. "And whether you believe it or not, I'm always here for you even if we're not in the same country."

"You don't love me. If you loved me, you wouldn't go."

"I'll wait in the car," said Fiona's brother.

"No," she said, turning toward him. "I'm coming. Help me with these bags."

He grabbed two of the suitcases. Fiona picked up the third.

"Candy, I'm sorry," she cried. "Don't try and make me feel bad for leaving. I've been there for you at every turn, and now it's time for you to do something for me."

"What?" I whimpered.

"Give me your blessing. I need you to be happy for me."

"I can't."

She swallowed hard and closed the door behind her. I dropped to my knees.

CHAPTER 31

Weeks passed at the farmhouse in unsettling silence. The rooms had become larger since Fiona left. Everything she'd touched—everything she'd handpicked to express herself with—now meant no more than paint, stucco, and fabric. The vibrancy had faded, even in Vincent. He stuck to me like Velcro and watched my every move; nothing but a pair of lost souls.

Wet, fat snowflakes fell outside the window. Something about being stuck between winter and spring irked me. Nothing beautiful to define the season; nothing but slush and dirty snow to look at.

I made a pot of coffee and sat down at the dining room table with a fresh cup. I opened my journal to the first blank page and picked up my pen. Vincent jumped up and began batting at it.

"Go ahead. Write something," I said. "I'm sure you'd make more sense than I do." He meowed and curled up in front of me on the table.

I began to write: *Day 5,093,875 in this house alone. Do I exaggerate? Won't be long now. They'll find our bodies—Vincent's and mine—balled up on the sofa with a hole in the drywall where I stared myself into submission.*

Stupidity, pure stupidity. I drew a line through my words and stared at the page. Dr. Hedley and her bright ideas. I stretched my arms over my head and pulled at my ponytail.

I have got to wash this hair.

I considered going back to bed. What had my life become? From burgeoning celebrity to mindless babble with a one eared cat and periodic naps: pathetic.

A car door slammed outside. Vincent's head turned.

"Who the . . ." I got up and started across the room. I opened the front door to peek out.

"Dad?" I said, opening it all the way. Bill Bradford in the flesh. He nodded.

"Ah . . . come in." I stood back to allow him entry. He took off his boots then tipped his ball cap before removing it. With his coat still on, he stood staring at me. My nerves jangled.

"You want to . . . sit down or something?" I asked, holding a hand out toward the living room. He nodded and moved past me toward the patchwork sofa. He sat down and stared at the floor, turning the brim of his hat over and over in his hand.

"Coffee?"

He looked down at his watch.

"Coffee's fine."

I walked to the kitchen and tried to formulate a plan for conversation.

"Nice place you've got here," he called out.

"Well, it's all Fiona's doing. All I did was walk into it."

Small talk. Back to the godforsaken small talk.

"Heard she's run off with some Frenchman."

I shook my head and poured two cups of coffee from the pot. "France, Dad. She moved to France."

"Wouldn't catch me over there. Not for love 'er money."

"No shit," I muttered under my breath.

"What's that?"

"Nothing."

I added two spoonfuls of sugar to his coffee the way he liked it, then I walked back into the living room. He took his cup and nodded in thanks. Vincent jumped up on the sofa and rubbed his head on Dad's right thigh.

"I'm not much for cats," he said, nudging him to the floor.

"That's why he wants to sit there."

Vincent shot me a look of annoyance. I shrugged.

"So? You drove all the way here. What's up?"

"Nothing. Nothing really." He set his coffee down on the diamond-shaped table and began pulling at his shirt collar.

"You're not sick or anything, are you?"

"Nope. Not sick."

I took another sip of coffee and peered out of the front window. I let out a long sigh and figured we'd sit like that forever.

"Just wanted to talk to you, is all," he said. I turned to face him. Talk to me? Bill Bradford wants to talk me?

"About?" I set my cup down and tried not to spook him into changing his mind.

"You and Josie." He started playing again with the brim of his hat.

My face and ears flushed warm. "Did she send you here?"

"Nope. No she didn't. She doesn't know I'm here, and don't tell her either."

I looked down at his hat. His hands shook.

"I saw her a week or so ago," he added, without looking at me. "She's all tore up about you not speaking to her; says she told you all about Lynn and the adoption."

My lips pressed tight together as the muscles in my neck tensed to the point of painful. I didn't respond.

"You get my Christmas card?" His voice broke, and he wiped his nose on the back of his hand.

"I did."

He nodded, sniffled, and got up to walk to the fireplace. He stood at the mantel with his back to me, running his fingers along the edge of Lynn's silent clock.

"We never meant to hurt you, Candace. Not one single one of us," he whimpered.

I'd never seen him cry.

"Well, I don't see how you—"

"Please," he said, holding a shaking hand out behind him. He didn't turn to face me. "I've been trying to come here for weeks. Just . . . hear me out."

My breathing became slow and shallow. I sat frozen in the chair.

"It's a hell of a thing to watch someone you love turn into a stranger." He checked his watch and turned the hands on the mantel clock to reflect the correct time. "All the while you sit there and feel your insides eating away at yourself, gnawing like you'd starve to death otherwise. Knowing that if you say something—anything—it will only make matters worse."

He lowered his head and rubbed his eyes.

"She told me to leave so many times." He bent forward and shook his head. "I couldn't stay any longer. I just couldn't do it."

He put his head down on the mantel. I sat stunned as his shoulders shook with the spilling of emotion. My heart squeezed tight in my chest. I bit my lip. I wanted to go to him, say something to make him stop.

"I should have taken you with me. I should have," he said, lifting his head. He slammed his fist down on the mantel. I jumped. "Weak, stupid son-of-a-bitch that I am. I was so damned afraid she'd kill herself with you gone. You were everything to her. Then she went and did it anyway," he said. "I failed you and everyone else."

"I—I . . ." He put his hand out again.

"Please." He moved the minute hand forward another two minutes. "Josie knew you needed out of there. She was smart enough to know you were the priority. I was too in love with the woman. I couldn't think straight. She meant more to me than . . ." He wiped his nose on the sleeve of his jacket. "Well . . . more than anything or anybody. You included, I'm afraid."

He bowed his head again then raised it and turned to face me. His eyes had turned red and puffy; his expression now looked pained.

"We should have never agreed to taking you from that kid. I knew it was a stupid idea, but she was hell bent." He looked back at the mantel clock. He moved it forward another three minutes, and it annoyed me. "You got the key for this thing?"

"Somewhere." I wanted him to leave it alone. I wanted everything to go away; the hurt, the lies, everything.

"Doesn't matter," he said, sitting back down on the sofa.

A ray of sunlight shone through the window and onto Fiona's Tiffany floor lamp. A cascade of colors reflected from it to the wall behind Bill's head, then disappeared again.

He looked up at the clock and down at his watch. His foot began tapping.

"I don't stake any claims on you, Candace. The fact that you even called me 'Dad' at the door is more than I'll ever deserve, but Josie?" He shook his head. "That woman loves you with a fierceness I've never seen before or since. She came back to do right by you." He looked me straight in the eye. "She sure as hell did. And she did do right by you, too. You tell me she didn't raise you well."

I couldn't. I couldn't say anything. Not a word.

"It's not right; you not speaking to her."

I stood and walked to the window. Vincent rubbed against my leg. I picked him up and held him tight. "I—I don't know what to say. I'm just so damned mad; all three of you and your goddamned secrets. Why?" I turned back toward him.

"Why?" he scoffed. "Why the hell does anybody do anything? They think it's the right thing at the time? They're too stupid to know any better? I don't know. All I know is that folks screw up, bad sometimes. Bottom line."

"That's it? My whole life has been a lie, and all you can say is 'folks screw up sometimes?'"

"Pretty much." He glanced back at the mantel clock, and my annoyance hit a breaking point. I put the cat down and stomped over to the mantel. I spun the minute hand forward on the clock by half an hour.

"There," I barked. He dropped his eyes to the floor.

I walked back to the chair and sat down.

He waited a moment then lifted his gaze and stared hard into my eyes. "You can't run away from this thing with Josie, Candace."

"Who are you to tell me I can't run?"

"I'm the one that's learned you can't, that's who I am. It doesn't work." He reached out for his coffee but changed his mind. "I've been running all my life. I've been running in my armchair with a cold one in my hand. Running as fast as I can, but you know what happens when you do that? One day you wake up and find that you've run so far there's nobody there that knows you, nobody that gives a shit."

I put my hands over my face and absorbed the truth of it. I was alone now; all my friends, family, clients—all gone.

My hands dripped with tears, and he let me cry.

"It's so hard, Daddy," I whimpered.

"There's not much that isn't, Candace."

I looked up at him and saw that the shake in his hands had worsened.

I wiped my eyes. "You need a drink?"

He put his hands between his knees. "No . . . no thanks. I've overstayed my welcome as is."

I thought of what it must have taken for him to come that day and say what he'd said; maybe not much for the average man, but a lot for Bill Bradford.

"Look, I can't promise anything with Josie, okay?" I said. "I'm having trouble putting all of this together. Fine that all of you get to clear your conscience and wipe the slate clean, but I have to make sense of it all, you know? Nothing about my life is what I believed it to be."

"I understand," he said. "Believe it or not, I do. But there's one more reason I came to see you."

"What?"

He reached into the breast pocket of his jacket and pulled out a business-sized envelope. He held it flat against his leg with his right hand and tapped his left foot at a frantic pace. I waited.

"This here is the note Lynn left behind," he said, patting the envelope a few times.

My heart jolted. "A note? You mean a—"

"Suicide note," he said, nodding.

Sweet Jesus. I stared at it from across the room. A piece of her—her goodbye.

"To you," he continued.

"To me?" My body went limp. My insides ached for her.

"She didn't write to anybody else," he said, dropping his head. "Just you."

I walked over to the sofa and sat beside him. A tear ran down his face and dripped from his chin onto his jacket. I put my hand out and he passed me the envelope. I ran my fingers over the surface of it.

"But it's sealed. How do you know it's for me? There's no name on it, or . . ."

"I read it and sealed it up myself," he said. "She sent it to my place just before she . . . well, you know. She probably thought Josie'd hide it from you if she got it, but we talked about it at the time and decided it would be best to—"

I rose from the sofa. "What? Best to do what?" I turned and paced toward the window and back. "Jesus, Dad. You kept her letter from me?"

He bowed his head again. "You were seven years old, Candace. You'd already been through so much, and—"

"Oh my God, I can't believe this. No. No, I can believe this," I said, nodding. "Just another case of folks screwing up, isn't that right Dad? Huh?"

I stood over him and he shrunk down to nothing. "And why now, after all I've been through?"

"I thought it might help in some way, with you and Josie I mean."

I threw my head back. "Is that why you kept it for the last 29 years; some kind of emergency patch kit? Is that what this is?"

He shook his head. "I was supposed to burn it at the time, but . . ." His whole body began to shake.

"Then why? Why did you keep it?"

"Because . . ." He swallowed hard "She wrote it, don't you see? It may be the last thing she ever touched. My Lynnie; it's all I had left."

CHAPTER 32

I couldn't face the letter right away, I just couldn't. Part of me wished he'd never delivered it. All of me wished the truth had stayed hidden.

I had tucked the letter in behind the mantel clock after Dad left, and while the clock continued to sit in silence, the letter whispered my name incessantly. Vincent slept in a ball on the floor beneath it as though guarding the thing. I tried to distract myself by unpacking boxes that I'd had delivered from storage. Maybe I'd hoped to find courage in one of them. I don't know.

Early one morning I poured a cup of coffee and prepared to finish emptying the last few boxes. Fiona had packed the one I'd chosen to start with that day. I could tell by the creative tape job. I sat cross-legged on the floor of the office and opened it. Inside sat a stack of old pictures and a small collection of souvenirs.

Vincent strutted into the room wide-eyed. "Nothing in here for you, Vinny," I said, grabbing a handful of photos. Some of my favorites from college were in there including many of Fiona and me. We'd been such an unlikely pair; her an art major with a style all her own, and me, Miss Business, dressed like everyone else on campus. Somehow we'd become instant friends regardless.

The cat rubbed his face against the corner of the box and purred. "Yes, I miss her too, and I'm an idiot for being so angry. You're absolutely right."

A young Ross jumped out at me in the next picture; big man on campus. Every girl had wanted him, and he'd picked me. Huh. He'd *picked* me, and I'd gone along for the ride; somehow feeling honored to be his chosen one. I wondered if Eunice felt the same way now.

I turned the box over to empty the remaining contents onto the floor. An old manila envelope landed on the top of the heap. As a kid I'd scribbled "Mama" on the outside of it in red crayon. I'd taped the flap shut when I reached my teens to lock her away from me. As the years passed I grew more and more afraid to let her out. I closed my eyes to focus my thoughts, then I tore the piece of tape from the envelope and reached inside. Not a lot of pictures existed, because she hated having them taken. And she rarely smiled, but when she did my heart would dance like a marionette.

I picked up the first photo and held it to the light; her and Dad. My God, they'd been so young. I marveled at Bill in the picture and what he'd become. He looked at my mother with such adoration then, like he wanted to protect her from everything.

Then there was the one of the three of us seated at the picnic table and laughing. I wondered if Dad ever laughed anymore. I couldn't remember the last time I'd heard him do it. In fact, if not for the photo, I'd be hard pressed to believe he ever had.

Then I found it; the picture that showed up in my mind every time I allowed myself to think of her. The black and white Lynn and Candace shot. She looked so beautiful; her seated on a sofa in a gorgeous fitted dress; me about two years old standing on her knee and pulling at her beads. Both of us smiled for the camera that day. Both of us seemed happy. As I stared at the picture the memory of her perfume came to me and brought the moment to life.

Vincent started batting at something that poked out from under the stack of pictures.

"What are you into now, little one?"

I reached down to investigate his newfound toy and discovered the key to the mantel clock.

"Wow," I whispered.

I sat there with the key in one hand and the pictures of Lynn in the other. "It's time, isn't it?"

Vincent meowed.

"Okay," I sighed. "But not here." I looked at Lynn's face in the photo and spoke to her. "We're doing this together."

I rose to my feet and made a mental note of what I'd need. I grabbed an old backpack of Fiona's from the front closet and began filling it. I took a picture frame from the bookshelf and replaced its photo of the cat with the black and white shot of Lynn and me. I then placed it in the backpack along with a bottle of Shiraz, a crystal glass, and a corkscrew. I took the key to the clock into the living room and placed it on the mantel. The letter I just held for a moment, its contents weighing heavy in my hands. Shaking off my hesitation, I stuffed the envelope in with the photo and turned to leave.

Dressed in Fiona's woolen cap and down parka, I walked outside to meet an early March wind. I jumped into the old Jeep and tossed the backpack on the seat beside me. When I turned the key in the ignition it started without complaint, so I headed out with the engine still cold.

It had been years, but I knew how to get there. Instinct, like a goose heading south, only my south put a knot in my gut the size of a melon. Clouds filled the sky above me and large patches of snow still littered the fields. Winter wouldn't go away any time soon. I could tell.

When I reached the cemetery, I drove through the wrought iron gate, and the sky became increasingly gray. A light sprinkle of rain mixed with snow began hitting the windshield. Plastic flowers and headstones decorated the landscape, and barren trees drooped and sagged as though in mourning. Two fresh graves had been dug from my vantage point, and I prayed that no small children had been left behind. My throat tightened, and I held onto the steering wheel like a life preserver.

"God, give me strength," I whispered.

The Jeep bounced over rocks and through potholes until I stopped the truck at the end of the drive. I grabbed the backpack, along with an old beige blanket and an umbrella from the backseat, and started my walk to her resting place. My heart beat faster with every step as I half expected to find her standing there, waiting for me.

I held my breath and rounded her headstone to face it full on. Plain black, no angels, no crosses: LYNN ELIZABETH BRADFORD (née GALLAGHER) November 24, 1956—June 23, 1983. I lingered on the words, "Loving mother," beneath her name. A burning sensation rose in my throat, and I fought back tears.

My hands shook as I laid the blanket out at the foot of her plot. I sat down on it, then I pulled out the wine and popped the cork. Pouring some into the crystal glass, I let out a loud sigh that got carried away by the wind.

Opening the umbrella, I tilted it on the ground to block the rain. Then I removed the photograph and the letter from the backpack and placed them both beneath it. I held the envelope in my hands for a brief moment then tore it open and removed her words.

The rain and snow became steady. The melon in my gut had grown tentacles. The wind tried to steal the umbrella. I gripped it with one hand and held the letter open beneath it with the other. Then I paused.

No one else could be seen in the cemetery that day, but I could sense eyes watching me from every gravestone. Not Lynn's, but the eyes of others who seemed to judge me somehow for disturbing her, for bringing up the past.

What was I thinking? Why did I come here? Why couldn't I have just . . .

The wind flapped the letter against my wrist.

"Okay," I whispered. "Fine."

I anchored the umbrella tight between my knees and took a long drink of wine. "Here we go, Lynn Elizabeth Gallagher Bradford," I said, raising my glass to her headstone. "Please help me through this."

I began to read.

My Dearest Peanut:

My God, she'd called me Peanut. I hadn't thought of that in years. The sound of her whispering it seemed to come from behind me. I turned to see no one there.

> *I can't leave without saying goodbye to the only thing good in this world. I know this won't make any sense to you now, but someday i pray that you understand and forgive me. That you'll know that this was the best thing for everybody. The best thing for you.*

"Jesus. I'm not sure I can do this," I said aloud. The wind tugged harder at the umbrella. I set the wine glass down and held the letter with both hands.

By now Josie will have told you the truth. She wasn't supposed to come back like this. That wasn't the deal. Now she says she can't stay away, and that you shouldn't be with me. She's right.

The wine glass tipped over and painted the fibers of the blanket red. I grabbed the bottle and took a drink from it.

Peanut, she's better for you than i am. I'll ruin everything if i stay. You don't deserve to see that happen.

Did she really believe that? "How could you believe that?" I asked, looking down at the picture of us. Tiny raindrops slid down the glass of the picture frame. The faint caw of a crow echoed in the distance.

I shouldn't have taken you as my own. She didn't want me to, but I convinced her. I just wanted something to love, and you came to me like an angel.

"Some *thing?*" I asked, looking down at the image of her face again. The rain and snow turned fat and heavy in the sky and began pelting my face.

Please remember that none of this was your fault. You'll be much happier without me here. You have to trust me on this.

i love you with all my heart xoxo

"I—I can't . . ."
My knees let go of the umbrella, and I rose to my feet disoriented. I put a hand on my head and turned to look

around the cemetery. Surely someone could make sense of this for me. The melon reached up through my torso and started strangling my throat. I stared down at the letter getting wet in my left hand. I picked up the wine bottle in my right.

A fueled rage burst inside me as I stared at her headstone. "You talked her into it? But I didn't believe her. I didn't want to believe her!"

Rain soaked through my woolen cap and parka. I wanted to lash out. I wanted to break something.

"You wanted some*'thing'* to love?" I asked. "That wasn't part of the *'deal?'*"

I looked at the wine bottle in my hand. I swung my arm back and threw it as hard as I could. The bottle hit at the top of her headstone breaking into chunks. Wine dripped down the face of it and into the crevices of our last name.

"Why did you let me love you so much? Why?" I cried.

The wind snagged the umbrella and carried it across the cemetery. It caught on a neighboring headstone. The picture frame toppled over fully exposing our mother/daughter moment to the elements. I dropped to my knees and swung my fist down hard onto it; once, twice. The glass in the frame shattered under my bare hand. Blood and rain crept through the cracks of the glass and onto the black and white.

I stood again and held the letter upward with both hands to catch the rain. Blood from my cut seeped in with the water to stain and weaken the paper. I gave a tug and ripped it in half. I folded the two halves together and ripped at them again; then again and again until red wet pieces of paper dropped in tiny clumps at my feet.

"You shouldn't have left. I could have helped you. I could have . . ."

Tears and raindrops washed down my face. A huge gust of wind picked up and carried the pieces of paper across the cemetery. I threw myself back down on the blanket and sobbed into its wet surface. I sobbed until my body melted into the earth that covered her.

"Why, Mama. Why?"

A whisper tickled at my right ear. *Get up.* It came from a place about which Lynn knew nothing; a place faintly familiar to me and yet completely unknown. The roots of my family; Josie's family.

Get up. Now.

CHAPTER 33

"So, you survived the holidays all right, I see. Other than your hand, maybe?" asked Dr. Hedley, nodding down at my bandage.

"A little run in with the past."

I started picking at a corner of tape that held the gauze in place. She appeared unfazed by my comment.

"I wasn't sure you'd be back after canceling your last few appointments. I tried to reach you, but—"

"Yeah, sorry. I threw my phone in a snow bank."

"Uh-huh."

"No, really. I actually did."

"Well, well." She tucked her legs up under her and gave an almost undetectable grin.

That's it?

Her dog, Skinner, stood in the middle of the room wagging his tail.

"You know, I've read that book of yours since we last spoke," she continued.

"Oh, great. Well, you're probably the last person who ever will. They're saying it's a load of crap."

"Well, for the record it's not, and none of what's happened to you takes away from the solid advice in it. Really."

"Maybe."

I thought about all of the people I'd disappointed and wondered if any of them would agree.

"So you canceled your appointments, because . . ."

"I just had a lot going on, that's all."

"Well, I have very few clients who don't have a lot going on, Candace. Therapy is a commitment, something you need to decide whether or not you take seriously."

Great. A lecture.

"I do take it seriously. I just needed to try and deal with a few things on my own first."

She didn't reply. Skinner headed for his bed in the corner.

"Some things you just have to handle alone," I added, crossing my legs.

"Like?"

"Like family secrets and messages from the dead." I folded my arms across my chest.

"Okay, but why?"

Did she hear what I just said? "Why what?" I began rocking my right foot at the speed of impatience.

"Why do they have to be dealt with alone?"

"Oh, I don't know," I said, "maybe because that stuff is nobody else's business?"

She shrugged her shoulders, and I wondered why I'd bothered coming back.

"Fine. Because it's just easier that way," I added. "At least it is for me."

"A lot of people would say that coping without support is more difficult."

"Well, I guess that would depend on where the support's coming from—or not coming from. I did call Fiona when I had my surgery, didn't I?"

She nodded.

"So, I do reach out sometimes."

"Okay. So we're getting somewhere."

"Like, where?" The pulse of impatience moved up my leg and into my spine.

Dr. Hedley placed both feet on the floor and leaned forward with her elbows on her knees. "Did Fiona help you with this family secret of yours as well?"

"Yes. Well . . . sort of." I looked over at Skinner. He'd curled himself into a protective ball. "She's moved to France, you know."

She nodded again. "And are you happy for her?"

"Of course, I'm happy for her," I snapped. "Why wouldn't I be?"

She sat back in her chair. Guilt tapped at the door for only me to hear.

"I didn't come to talk about Fiona," I added, looking back at the dog.

"Okay. We'll move on to something else, then. You mentioned a family secret."

I stared at her for a moment. She possessed a warmth and depth that drew me in despite how uncomfortable her questions made me. I let out a long sigh.

"Josie," I said, lowering my eyes. "She was afraid the press might dig up information on our family that could hurt me."

Dr. Hedley leaned forward again. My eyes filled with tears as they met hers. "Take your time," she said.

I thought about all of the events I'd been through lately. How everything had fallen apart. How much I missed Fiona, and yes . . . Josie.

"She's my mother," I whimpered.

Dr. Hedley handed me her box of Kleenex. "I see."

"You see?" I took a handful of tissues from the box and wiped my nose with them. "That's all you have to say?"

"Well, it certainly explains the resemblance, and her dogged over-protectiveness, but she must have been extremely young."

"Sixteen." Pressure built up in my skull and pressed on the backs of my eyes.

Dr. Hedley shook her head. "A difficult time for a young girl. It must have been horrible for her to give you up, especially when she obviously loves you so fiercely."

"Well, this isn't about her, is it?" I snapped.

"No. No it isn't."

A fire began deep in my chest. I took a deep breath and exhaled half expecting to see smoke.

"And, the message from the dead? Does that have anything to do with the woman you lost?"

I nodded. "Her suicide note."

"Jesus, Candace."

"I know, right?" I replied, feeling some much needed validation. "My father—who's not my father, by the way—hung onto it for years. And for his own selfish reasons I might add." The familiar claws of anger scratched at my insides. "They decided not to share it with me at the time, he and Josie."

"But he felt now was a good time?"

My shoulders dropped. "It was written to me."

"She wrote it to you specifically?"

"That's what I just said, isn't it?" I barked.

"Do you still have it?"

I shook my head.

"And how did she die? Do you mind me asking?"

"She jumped head first from a hotel balcony."

Memories of the newspaper coverage sent a shiver through me that rattled my earrings. I bent forward with my chest to my knees. All the shame and guilt came back like it had never left.

"Candace. Obviously the woman—"

"Don't you see?" I sat forward and looked her in the eye. "It's not just her. It's all of them. One damned mistake after another: everybody lying, keeping secrets, leaving me."

"And, why do you think they kept this secret from you, Candace?"

I put a hand to my forehead and began rocking back and forth. "I don't know."

"Any theories at all?"

I leaned my head back onto the loveseat and flopped my arms down at my sides. I gazed up at the ceiling in search of answers.

"I suppose, in some sick way, they were trying to protect me?"

"What was that?" she asked, cupping a hand to her ear.

I jolted forward. "I said: to protect me!"

Wait a minute. I caught myself and held my breath. My eyes searched hers.

"Jesus."

"Jesus, what?" she asked.

"That's exactly what I did." The top of my head lightened like the lid had been opened on a pressure cooker.

"Explain, Candace."

"Ross. I did the same thing to Ross. I kept the surgery a secret to protect him, didn't I?" I leaned back again on the loveseat. "And Josie. I didn't tell her at the time either."

I put a hand on top of my head. My mouth gaped open.

"What are you thinking?" asked Dr. Hedley.

"That I've been judging them all on my own behavior."

"And what was Josie's reaction when you didn't forewarn her about the surgery?"

I remembered Josie's embrace when she'd shown up at the condo. She'd been disappointed in my not telling her, angry even, but she'd let it pass, and I'd fully expected her to do so.

"I'm just as bad as the rest of them, aren't I? Worse maybe."

"As bad as, or as human as?"

I fidgeted on the loveseat.

"Candace. People make mistakes, and sometimes for perfectly innocent reasons. Some are made in the name of love, protection, or even maintaining control. You have to realize that people are generally just doing the best they can at the time."

"That's what Bill said, but I . . ."

"Did you intend to hurt Ross or drive him away?"

"Of course not."

"Did you think at the time that you were doing the right thing?"

"Yes, but . . ."

"Your family is hardly perfect, but nobody's is. And here's a news flash for you: you're not perfect either." She leaned back in her chair. "And neither am I, but you're not to share that outside of this office," she added, grinning.

My God. I sat for a few moments feeling completely drained of strength. Images danced through my mind of Josie taking care of me as a child: all the comfort, all the love, all the support. And Bill, even. Hardly father-of-the-year material, but he'd come to me. He'd brought me that letter, and none of it had been easy for him.

"I always thought Josie was perfect, you know? My superhero. I couldn't bear that she'd lied to me. And all this time I thought I was battling genetics."

"How so?"

"I don't know. I think I was trying to be as perfect as Josie so that I wouldn't end up like Lynn. Ironic, isn't it?"

"Being perfect is a grand expectation, Candace."

"Tell me about it." I wiped my nose with the tissues. "Maybe being disappointed in Josie distracted me from being disappointed in myself. I don't know anymore."

"Maybe, but let me ask you this . . ."

"What?"

"You've been through an awful lot since last fall, and you've reminded me on several occasions of how everything in your life has changed."

"Yes?"

"Well, I'd like you to think about what hasn't changed."

"What do you mean, nothing? Everything's changed."

"Has it?" she asked, crossing her legs. "Think about it."

Skinner got up and wandered over to my side. He leaned against my leg and stared straight ahead at Dr. Hedley. I sat forward and reached down to pat his head. I thought of how much he reminded me of Patches in his disposition. Patches reminded me of home.

My hand stopped. I looked up wide-eyed at Dr. Hedley. She raised an eyebrow.

"What is it?" she asked.

"Home," I whispered.

"What about it?"

"It hasn't changed." I put a hand over my mouth and began to cry. Skinner looked up at me and wagged his tail.

"She's always been there for you, hasn't she?"

I nodded and convulsed to the point of sobbing. The dog rose to all fours.

"It's okay, old boy," said Dr. Hedley. He let out a whimper and sat back down.

"She has; her and Fiona. God, even Bill in his own useless, pathetic way," I cried. "Regardless of my busy schedule, regardless of what's been happening in my life, regardless of my . . ."

"Mistakes?" she asked.

"Exactly."

*　　*　　*

The sun shone bright on my drive home that afternoon—not a cloud in the sky—still, one hung over my heart like a weighted balloon. I had to make things right for sure this time; right with Josie and right with Fiona. I pulled in the drive and stared at Fiona's old farmhouse. They *had* always been there for me—all of them.

Vincent greeted me at the door. I picked him up and hugged him with gratitude.

"You're my little man, aren't you?" He purred and jumped out of my arms. Then he turned to look at me, flipped his tail, and ran into the office.

"Hey, what's the hurry?" I ran after him afraid that he'd killed something in my absence.

I rounded the entrance to the office and found him sitting on my Christmas box from Josie.

"You're creeping me out," I said. He flipped his tail again. "Okay, fine."

Vincent moved to the top of the desk and stared down at the box. "What's with you, anyway?"

He gave a soft meow.

I scratched the top of his head and sat down in the desk chair. I pulled the box across the floor toward me and opened the lid. The card from Bill still sat open on top of Josie's gift. I read it again and grinned. Puppies in a basket, but at least he'd tried.

I set the card aside and pulled out the gift wrapped in red and green paper. I re-read the tag. *To my Kiddles, I'll always love you. Josie xo.*

"You will, won't you?" I whispered.

I grabbed a corner of the paper and ripped it off in one piece.

Another scrapbook. This one bound in red leather. It looked thicker than the first one, and my eighth grade picture smiled up from the cover—the one of me holding my junior achievement award.

Vincent started batting the crumpled gift wrap with his paw. I picked up the scrapbook and carried it to the dining-room table for better lighting. I took a deep breath and opened the cover.

"My God," I whispered.

I turned each and every page at a slow, steady pace as my eyes scanned the contents. Everything I'd ever accomplished stared up at me: a full-fledged history of my endeavors—every award, every newspaper article, every business card, every certificate. An entire lifetime of successes—even things I'd forgotten.

Girl Scout badges, report cards, blue ribbons, pictures I'd drawn, stickers I'd collected, homemade Christmas cards. Jesus—and the pictures. The day my braces came off, day-camp, gymnastics, school shots, my broken arm, my swim meets. Even pictures of my many haircuts with locks of hair taped beside them. Everything: page after page of my life through her eyes.

I reached the inside back cover where she'd pasted a copy of my interview from the Rock River Times. In it I talked about my new book release and upcoming visit to the Rockford Social

Club. In that article I'd raved about my Aunt Josie and how I could never have succeeded without her.

I rested my elbows on the table and put my hands over my mouth. She'd saved all of these things, every last one of them. And I *couldn't* have done it without her, none of it.

I moved the scrapbook off to the side and laid my head on the table. A ray of sunlight crept around the edge of the curtain and hit me square in the eye. What would my accomplishments have been without her there to cheer me on?

I sat up and closed the scrapbook. How had I not even known she'd made them? I wondered what else I didn't know about her, that I hadn't taken the time to find out.

I have to make a move. I have to make things right.

I stood from the table and Vincent meowed at my feet.

"Yes, I know," I said, crossing the room. "You've been right all along. I admit it, already."

I grabbed the phone from its base and dialed Josie's number. It began ringing right away. My heart pounded in my ears, and an intense longing kept rhythm with it.

"Y'ello."

"Aunt Josie?"

"Kiddles?" she yelped. "Is—is that you, baby girl? For real?"

Tears spilled out onto my cheeks.

"Yes, it's me," I cried. "Can you come? Now? Please?"

CHAPTER 34

Early March in Illinois. A time of year that inspired confusion. Robins sat between patches of snow listening to frozen dirt. Tiny buds peeked their heads up through the ground and out from the ends of branches. Canada geese soared overhead on their way back home. All of nature wondering if the time for spring had come at last; some parts of it maybe forcing the issue.

I sat on the front porch step wrapped in an old sweater while the sun fought hard to break through low lying clouds. Fiona crossed my mind, and I wondered how her move had gone. I needed to call her. I would call her—soon.

A cold breeze stirred through the old maple tree out front and rustled a few of its stubborn leaves that had hung on all winter. I watched and waited until Aunt Josie's truck roared up the laneway.

"God, help me," I whispered. I leaned fully forward to gather strength, then grabbed the railing and stood like an unsteady child.

The truck came to a dramatic stop sending dirt and slush out from behind its tires. Josie jumped from the vehicle looking tired and stressed. She paused beside the driver's side door to gauge my response. I threw a hand over my mouth and began to cry. She ran to me and pulled me into her arms.

"Kiddles," she said, squeezing me with months' worth of pent up hugs. I went limp in her embrace and soaked in every ounce of her. "Oh, my girl." We cried on each other like sprinklers.

Another cold wind whipped up and blew my hair into both our faces. She let go and wiped my tears with her fingers.

"You want to come in?" I asked.

"You shittin' me?"

I grinned and led her inside.

"Something to drink?" I asked, as we strode toward the kitchen.

"Hot tea if you've got it. I'd ask for something stronger, but I've gotta work tonight." She leaned on the back of one of the kitchen chairs. Nervousness danced through the empty space between us as I plugged in the kettle.

"What happened to your hand?" she asked.

"It's nothing, really. Please . . . sit." She did, and I sat down in the chair closest to her. Neither one of us spoke for a moment, but words hung in the air waiting to be shared.

Vincent wandered in and arched his back against one of the table legs.

"Who we got here?" asked Josie, leaning down to pet him.

"Vincent—Fiona's cat. He feels it's his duty to stick his nose into every aspect of my life," I grumbled.

"He lose the ear in a scrap?"

"She assumes so. He showed up like that."

"Poor little bastard."

The kettle whistled. I got up and poured hot water into two cups. I set them on the table with a box of tea bags.

"You okay, Candace? I mean, you been okay?" she asked, reaching out for my hand. I pulled back.

"I've been better," I muttered. "It's been really tough, you know?" If I'd closed my eyes I could have easily been back in high school seeking her comfort.

"I know it's been tough, and I'm sorry. Sorry for every damned thing," she said, lowering her eyes to her lap.

"It's just so much to absorb."

She nodded.

"Then the note and everything . . ."

"What note?" she asked, looking back up at me.

"The suicide note. Bill brought it by here, and I—"

"He what?" she hollered and got up from her chair. "Jesus H. If anyone was born on the day God'd run outta brains, it was that man." She paced to the sink and back.

"Okay, okay," I called out. "Settle down. He thought he was doing the right thing."

"And what in the hell was he doin' with it in the first place? I thought he'd burned that son-of-a-bitch of a thing years ago."

"He couldn't—or at least that's what he said. He couldn't let it go because she'd touched it or something." I rolled my eyes, and felt a deep yearning to be loved half that much.

"Oh, sweet mother of God," Josie said, sitting back down. She rapped her fingers on the table a few times and took a deep breath. Her face softened and her bottom lip stuck out a little. She began tracing the outline of the painted paw prints on Fiona's table. "So, you seen Bill, then?"

"He showed up here unannounced, Josie. I didn't invite him, if that's what you're asking."

"Nope," she threw her hands up. "None of my business. You can see whoever the hell you want."

"Why, gee. Thanks."

"Just sayin' is all." She rapped her fingers twice more.

"Well anyway, he thought it would help if I read it."

"Help with what, for God's sake? Have you not been through enough?"

"Help with us," I said, pointing back and forth between the two of us.

"Hmm," she said, nodding. She pulled her tea bag up by the string and let it drip into her cup. "And? Did it?"

"Maybe—a little."

She set the bag on her saucer, and we sat staring at each other for a bit. Her eyes may have looked like mine, her nose definitely. Weird how I'd not noticed it before.

"Do I look anything like him? My real Dad, I mean?"

"Oh, he was a looker, there's no denyin' that. When you were small you'd smile like him from time to time, but then—after a while—I couldn't picture him at all anymore. Didn't care to really."

"He hurt you, didn't he?"

"Hell no, he didn't hurt me. Plenty of folks did before—and have since—but that boy?" She shook her head. "Only knew him long enough to get pregnant. No love lost there, and I couldn't hate him if I tried. If anything, I'm grateful to him."

"Grateful?" She had to be kidding.

"Gave me you didn't he?" She slapped the table and grinned. Her eyes moistened.

"Still, your life could have been a lot different if you hadn't had to come back here and pick up the pieces."

"Hey now," she said, reaching across the table again. This time I let her take my hand. "My life could have been a lot different if I'd not had a reason to improve it. I was headin' for pure hell before you pulled at my heart strings. You saved me,

Candace. Don't feel like you took me away from anything, got it?"

She meant it, every word of it. She'd turned her life around for me.

"Oh, Josie," I said, wiping tears from my eyes. "I've missed you so much."

"Not half as much as I've missed you; not even close to half." She squeezed my hand to breaking point. "It's been hell," she said, her voice breaking. "Shit."

She took her hand back. I rose from the table and grabbed a roll of paper towels from the kitchen counter.

"Do you see why I couldn't tell you any of this before?"

I set the roll down on the table. She grabbed a square from it and wiped both eyes.

"Tell me again."

"Because you needed someone to trust, and I'd already lost you once."

"But I . . ."

"You were devastated when Lynn died; flat out devastated. If I'd told you she wasn't your mother, how would you have coped?"

"I don't know how I would have coped, but maybe I would have. Don't you think I should have been given the opportunity to try?"

"At seven years old? Shit," she said, shaking her head.

She tucked her paper towel into the sleeve of her denim shirt. My knee started jumping under the table. An ache gnawed under my breastbone.

"Ah hell, maybe it was me who couldn't face it. I don't know anymore," she added.

"Yeah maybe," I said, accusingly. "Maybe you couldn't face it, Bill couldn't face it, and Lynn couldn't face anything; some fucking legacy."

"Hey. Watch your . . ." she'd begun to scold. "Ah, forget it. And maybe you're right, but I really and truly wanted to protect you, Candace. From all of it, don't you see? I mean, I never thought she'd do what she did. I felt responsible for the whole damned mess."

Her shoulders slumped forward. I caught a glimpse of what she'd look like as an old woman.

"Well, I guess nobody really expected her to—"

"Goddamn her, anyway," said Josie.

The muscles in her jaw flexed. She pushed her chair back from the table and stood, placing her hands in the front pockets of her jeans. "I'll never be sorry I had ya kid, but why I had to run into that woman when I didn't know which end was up?" She shook her head.

"Well, maybe—"

"Ah, maybe nothin," she said. "I've gotta tell you something else too."

"Jesus, now what?"

"No, no—nothing like that. Just that I'm glad the whole damned mess is out in the open, that's all. I've been carrying that secret around so long it's worn a hole through the lining of my gut. Guilt and shame tuck me in at night, young lady" she said, pointing at herself. "And I'm tired of the both of them."

"They've been coming around here for the last several months too," I confessed.

"Well, to hell with them."

She sat back down and shimmied her chair in closer to the table. She took a sip of tea and her eyes roamed around the kitchen as though in search of something. They settled hard on me.

"So, you think ya can find it in your heart to forgive me?" She held her right hand over her heart and raised her left in the air. "I swear I'll tell you the truth every second of every day from this point forward."

"I'm willing to try, if . . ." I swallowed hard. " . . . you'll forgive me too."

She blew out a long, slow breath and I watched as tears ran down her face and onto the front of her shirt. "There's nothing to forgive you for, baby girl. Not a thing."

She raised her teacup in a toast. "To no more secrets."

"No more secrets," I echoed, standing to embrace her. She stood as well and grabbed me like a lifeline. Comfort and calm encircled us both.

Time seemed to stand still while we held each other. Neither one of us wanted to let go. Lynn's mantel clock chimed four times from the living room. With hesitation we loosened our grip.

"You still got that old clock?" she sniffled, pulling the hidden paper towel from her sleeve.

"Sure do. Wasn't working for a while, but the cat found the key."

She nodded. "Lynn would be glad you have it."

I smiled, wondering if Lynn had ever been glad of anything.

"She loved you, ya know. She really did."

"I'd like to hear more about her sometime, what she was really like."

"Jesus. I'm not so sure you would."

I shrugged my shoulders.

"Sorry, Kiddles. I don't mean to sound callous, but that woman had some major issues. Either she hid it real well when you were born, or I was just too young and stupid to see it. Anyone's guess, but she got worse over time. Boy did she."

"I remember some of that. At least, I think I do."

"Well, I'm not really being fair to her. It was a different time then. Folks didn't know much about mental illness, and God love her, if she'd had a proper diagnosis and had gotten some medication, things might have turned out a lot different. Either way, I didn't have any choice but to take you from her. I couldn't leave ya with her the way she was. I just wish she hadn't . . ."

"Yeah, I know. Me too."

Josie picked up her tea cup from the table and walked it to the sink. "Well. Wish I had more time, but I'd better get my hiney back down the road and get ready for that 12-hour shift."

"Did you sleep today?" I asked.

She walked toward me. "Nah, my girl called," she said, putting a hand up to cradle my cheek. "Who needs sleep? Besides, I'll sleep better tomorrow than I have in years."

Vincent meowed up at us.

"Come on," she said. "Walk me out."

We made our way through the front door and locked arms on the way to the truck. A soft breeze picked up carrying a bit of southern warmth with it. Nature may not have been confused after all.

"So, can I call you now? When I feel like it, I mean?" she asked.

"Sure. Why not." I smiled at her as we reached the truck.

"Oh, I almost forgot," she said, opening the door and pulling out two manila envelopes. "These damned things came to the house. Had to sign for them both. Looks like legal business. I didn't know if I should bring them today, if you'd need them, or . . ."

I took them from her and sighed.

"Probably divorce papers, or any number of dissolving contracts."

"Kiddles, I'm sorry."

"Nope, don't be sorry. It's time to let go of all of this anyway."

I looked down at the envelopes and turned them over in my hands. She put a finger to my chin and lifted my eyes up toward hers.

"You okay, little one? Really?"

"I'll be okay, Josie. Now that you're back . . . I'll be okay."

I watched as the old truck rattled down the laneway. Josie's arm reached out through the driver's side window and waved with abundant enthusiasm. I grinned to myself and turned back toward the house.

It looked different to me somehow, more inviting or something. Vincent stared out through the dining room window at me and pawed at the pane of glass between us. I headed inside.

I pulled the front door shut behind me and walked into the office. Tossing the envelopes on the desk, I sat down in the chair in front of them. One big mess, that's what everything had been. One big mess stirred up in a pot full of secrets. I'd stick to my end of the bargain; honesty moving forward.

Vincent sauntered into the room and rubbed against the box on the floor beside me.

"That's right, buddy. No more secrets." I scratched under his chin. "Everybody's going to come clean, isn't that right?"

He got up on his hind legs and pawed at the lid of the box.

"You confessing something now too? Did you hide a mouse in there, or something?"

I opened the lid, and the Tiffany box stared up at me. I reached in to remove it and caught my finger on the edge of a business card. I pulled it out and read it: *Amy Sparling—Publishing Assistant.*

Vincent meowed.

"You know, you freak me out sometimes, cat. You really do."

His ear flattened out, and he left the room.

I opened the Tiffany box and set it beside Amy's card on the desk. I ran my finger over the three chunks of crystal that remained of my globe. I could hear the mantel clock ticking from the other room.

"Yep, time to tell the truth," I whispered. I put the lid back on the Tiffany box then picked up the desk phone and dialed. It rang twice.

"Amy speaking," chirped the voice on the other end of the phone.

"Amy Sparling?"

"Yes, this is she."

"Candace Bradford."

I heard her gasp.

"Candace? Really? It's really you?"

I had to chuckle. "Yes, one and the same."

"Oh my God, I can't believe it," she gushed. "Please tell me you're calling, because you want to tell your story."

"That would be why."

"Oh my God," she screamed.

I pulled the receiver away from my ear until she finished. "Well, you said to call, and I—"

"Yes, yes. I—I know. Oh my God. You have no idea what this means. I mean, I haven't been doing this that long, and I'm such a huge fan, and . . ."

"Okay, calm down and hear me out."

"Okay, okay," she said, letting out a sigh. "Go ahead."

"First off, if I'm going to do this book for you, I have a few stipulations."

"Fire away." Her excitement shot through the phone line.

"I want to do it my way. Tell my story the way I want to tell it. I want to be brutally honest, and I want to have full say in everything from title to dust jacket."

"Well, I . . ."

I waited.

"I'd have to get approval," she continued, "but I know I can talk them into just about anything. I just know I can. I mean, it's you, and they loved the idea, and . . . Oh my God!"

I thought how even God himself must get tired of hearing her say that.

"When can you get final approval?" I asked.

"We have a meeting tomorrow morning and I could run it past the powers that be. I could probably get an estimate on an advance for you too. I'll bet I could." She paused for a moment, and I could hear the clicking sound of fingernails on a keyboard. "Okay, I've added your name to the agenda, and I can call right after the meeting and let you know. Would that work?"

"That'll be fine."

I stared down at the envelopes on the desk. Sign one off; sign one on.

"Oh my God," she squealed. "I can't believe this. Candace Bradford. I'm so excited!"

I shook my head. I had to admit to enjoying some limelight again. One shining little limelight called Amy Sparling.

"Any thoughts on what you'd want to call it? The book I mean?" she continued.

"I've got a couple of ideas."

CHAPTER 35

Vincent rubbed his head under my chin to wake me. His low purr vibrated through my chest.

"What's up buddy?" I looked over at the bedside clock. "Ten? You never let me sleep that late. Mr. Generous this morning, are we? A birthday present *purr*haps?"

I stroked behind his one little ear. We both gave a hearty stretch and put our feet on the floor. I caught my reflection in the bedroom mirror. Thirty-six years old on that day, amazing. And I didn't look a day over, well, thirty-six years old.

I stood and changed into jeans and a long sleeved T-shirt, then I lumbered down the stairs to start my day. I had just hit the button on the coffeemaker when the phone rang.

"Hello?"

"Candy girl."

"Fiona? Oh, my God—a voice for sore ears. I've been so wanting to—"

"Yeah, me too; now hang up and get on Skype."

"Skype?" I said, fussing with my hair. "But I look like shit."

"Oh, who cares; I want to see your face. I'm hanging up," she said, and the phone went dead.

I stood staring at the receiver in my hand. She'd called. I should have been the one to call her. I should have made the first move. I pulled the pot from the coffeemaker and poured a cup before it had completely finished brewing. Excitement rose in me like champagne bubbles as I made my way to the office and turned on the computer. The phone rang again, and I answered it assuming she'd grown impatient.

"It's okay, girlfriend. I'm logging on now."

"Ah, Candace?" a male voice replied.

"Dad?"

"Yeah. Did I catch ya' at a bad time?"

"Oh no sorry, I thought you were someone else. Fiona wants me to . . . oh, it doesn't matter. She can wait. How are you? Everything okay?"

"Yep, fine. Just wanted to wish ya' happy birthday, is all."

He'd remembered. He'd sent a card at Christmas, and he now remembered my birthday. I sat down at the desk and my jaw went slack.

"You still there, kid?"

"Dad, I . . ." I loved him as much at that moment as I'd ever loved anyone.

"Listen, Josie's invited me over there for your birthday dinner tonight. You okay with me coming? I know I haven't always been around for these kinds of things, but if you'll have me . . ."

"I'd love it, Dad. Really I would."

Vincent meowed up at me.

"Great," he said. "So, I'll see ya' tonight then."

"Okay, sounds good. And thanks."

"You're the one that needs the thanking. Oh, and I meant to tell you . . . if you ever need any help around that old house you're in, you call on me, okay? I know a thing or two about fixin' troubles."

"Yes, you do." I grinned and took a sip of coffee.

"Know one or two things about causing them too, come to think of it." We both laughed.

"Okay, I'll let you go, kid."

"Before you do, Dad . . ."

"Yeah?"

"I love you. You know that, right?"

The phone went silent on the other end. I got up from the desk and wandered toward the window. A robin stood yanking a fat worm out of the grass.

"You know I'm not much good at . . ." His voice broke.

"You don't have to be. Just wanted you to hear it, okay? I'll see you tonight." I hung up and sat back down at the desk.

Vincent meowed at me, and I remembered Fiona. "Oh yes, your mama. Let's see her face, okay?" I clicked on the Skype icon.

"Well about time, hon. Did you go and primp first?" she laughed. The wall behind her had been painted a deep purple, and I could see a bouquet of poppies and cornflowers in the left-hand corner of the computer screen.

"Do I look like I primped first?"

I grabbed an elastic band from the top drawer of the desk, threw my hair into a ponytail, and rubbed the mascara from beneath my eyes.

"No, but you look as gorgeous as always, regardless."

"Jesus, you do too Fiona." Her face appeared a slight bit plumper to me, and she glowed even more than usual.

She opened her mouth to speak. "Nope . . ." I said, raising a hand toward the camera. "I'm talking first."

She closed her mouth again then stuck her tongue out at me.

"Fiona, I was an idiot. I behaved like a spoiled brat when you left here, and it's been eating at me ever since. I'm sorry."

She put her right hand over her heart and tilted her head with a grin. "Candy, you don't have to apologize."

"Oh, yes I do. I was entirely self-absorbed like you said, and I should have given you my blessing. Étienne's wonderful, and he's perfect for you. I could see that right away. I was so wrapped up in being miserable that I wanted everyone around me to be miserable too. It's just sick."

"Listen, I get it. Really, I do. And I knew you'd pull yourself out of it. I just had to come here, you know? I had to be with him."

"I do know, and—again, I'm sorry. Really sorry."

I pulled my feet up and sat cross-legged in the office chair.

"Well, you do seem better. I've been worried about you all along, but I figured some time to yourself would do you good. That old farmhouse can be a great friend to share secrets with."

"Well, I've sworn off secrets, for what it's worth," I said, giving her my best Girl Scout salute.

"Really? How cool is that?"

"Yep. Part of the new Candace Bradford."

"So, can I tell people, or are you hiding this from everyone?"

"Very funny, Fiona."

I missed her sense of humor. I missed everything about her.

"Well, I wish you were here, but France is obviously agreeing with you."

"It certainly is," she said, flashing an exaggerated grin. "Oh, and Happy Birthday best-friend. Twenty-nine again?"

"You know it."

She giggled. "How's it feel? The second half of your thirties, I mean?"

"I don't know. Weird, I guess. In some ways I don't feel any different than I did at twenty. In others, I'm in no way the same."

"Like how?"

"Hmm . . ." I furrowed my brow and thought about it for a few seconds. "More empowered, maybe? Less obsessive?"

"I like that. 'Empowered'," she repeated, nodding her head.

"And . . ."

"And what?"

"I'm going to start writing again." I sat up tall and threw my shoulders back, "today in fact."

"Candy, that's wonderful," she said, putting her hand back to her heart. "Oh, hon. I'm so glad."

"Yeah. Remember that Amy Sparling chick that came by here before you left? The one in the mini-skirt who didn't know how to dodge a snowflake?"

"How could I forget that little gem? I was ready to shoo her away when you stopped me. Guess it's a good thing I didn't?"

"Well, she left me her card and I called her a few weeks ago. They want me to write my side of the story, and they've agreed to let me say what I want without restrictions. I'm expecting a nice hefty advance too."

"Jesus, Candy. You're going tell all in a *tell-all*? You?"

"I know," I laughed. "Sounds crazy, doesn't it? But I don't care anymore."

"Honestly?"

I nodded.

"Oh, thank God. It's a good place to get to, and I couldn't be happier for you if I tried."

"Yeah, it's time. I need to start a new chapter and close an old one. Make sense?"

"Sure does. Speaking of which . . . we talked to Marc a few days ago," she said, in a lyrical tone. "Remember that gorgeous hunk of French pastry that spent Christmas with us?"

"Ah, no," I said, putting my index finger to my chin. "Whoever could you mean?"

"Oh, stop it," she said, waving a hand at the camera to dismiss my antics. "You remember him. Anyway, he asked for you."

"Did he now?" I raised an eyebrow.

"He did, and I gave him the number to the farmhouse."

"You what?" I leaned in toward the camera.

She held both arms out wide. "Go ahead, shoot me."

Marc Vallée; my heart rate increased at the thought of him. "He was gorgeous, wasn't he?" I said, leaning back in the chair.

"Honey, if you don't go out with him, I'll personally fly back there and kick your ass."

"Well, if it means you flying back here, I'll definitely not go," I teased.

"Hey. Speaking of flying back," she continued.

A glimmer of hope. "You're coming home for a visit."

"No, not for a while; in fact, it looks like I'll be staying here for good, actually." She cringed as though expecting fall-out from the statement. I just gave her my best pouty expression and kept quiet. "You wouldn't be interested in buying that old farmhouse, would you?"

"The house, Fiona?"

"Well, if the book does well, and all. There's no rush. I mean, you can stay there as long as you want and think about it, but . . ."

"You're selling? But you love this place."

"Well I do, but it seems as though I have more incentive to stay here now." She gave a coy glance toward the ceiling to elicit a response.

"You're getting married."

"No, God no. I want a relationship, not an institution. You of all people know that. Pieces of paper don't mean a thing," she scoffed. "Jesus, Mary, and Joseph; my parents are going to have a fit."

"Why? What's going on?"

She blew out a long breath. "I'm pregnant, Candy," she said in a soft whisper.

"She sure is," hollered Étienne from the background. His face made a brief appearance on the computer screen as he wrapped his arms around her waist and nuzzled into her neck.

"Oh, go away," she teased, waving him off. He kissed her cheek and disappeared again.

"You're pregnant? You're really pregnant?"

The empty space inside me ached from lost possibility.

"Six weeks," she said, grinning.

"Fiona. Oh sweetie, I'm so happy for you."

Vincent meowed from the floor. "And speaking of babies, say hello to this one," I said, picking him up and putting his face in view of the camera.

"Oh, Vinny," cried Fiona. "Oh, he looks so good. Miss you my little kitty pants." Vincent gave an annoyed yowl and jumped down in a flash.

"Fickle little bastard, our Vincent," I joked. We giggled a little and then sat absorbing each other's images.

"You will come and see me, right?" she asked, then she really began to cry. Her face crinkled up, and big tears spilled across it. Her shoulders shook between sobs.

"I will, Fiona. You know I will."

"And the farmhouse?" She blew her nose.

I nodded and smiled, "Definitely interested."

"Oh good," she sighed, reaching for more tissues.

I ached to have her in the same room with me. "You okay, Fiona? I mean, are you truly happy there? Everything's okay?"

"I am, Candy. I've honestly never been happier in my life. It's the bloody hormones." She burst out laughing. "I'm a flipping roller-coaster of emotion."

"God, how's Étienne handling all this," I teased.

"Like a trooper." She blew her nose one last time. "His Mom's in a facility here now, so it's been an emotional time for him too, but he loves running the vineyard. Says he'd forgotten how much he loved it here. I do believe we're in our element."

"And you're painting?"

"Like a fiend," she said. "And Josie? Do I dare ask?"

"She's good. And yes . . . we're speaking." I grinned.

"Thank the Lord," she said, casting her gaze toward the heavens.

"Yeah, she's having a birthday dinner for me tonight, and get this: Bill's coming. A regular, old-fashioned family meal." I rolled my eyes at the camera to fake how lame it all seemed. She saw right through me.

"That's super. Give them both my love, will you?"

"Sure will."

"And email me the minute you talk to Marc. I want to hear every juicy detail."

"That's my Fiona; always the romantic."

"You betcha." She puckered up her lips and kissed her computer camera. "I love you, hon. Have some wine for me tonight, will you? I'm on the wagon for a few months," she said, patting her belly.

"Done."

I kissed the computer camera back at her, and we signed off.

The world felt right again. How could I have been so stupid when she left? And now she was pregnant. Everything she'd always wanted, and she deserved every bit of it.

I threw on my old sweater and headed through the house toward the front door. The sun shot rays of light through every room and made the place look magical. I pondered buying it. Why not? It exuded perfect in every way, and with Bill willing to help . . .

I opened the front door and walked out onto the porch. A warm breeze wrapped itself around the house and embraced me to it. Finally, some legitimate warm weather. I stretched my arms out at my sides to feel the full effect of a long-awaited spring.

Maybe I'd write outside. What the hell.

I opened the door to get my laptop when a white delivery van turned into the laneway. I shut the door again and walked down the steps to greet it. A handsome young man with jet black hair pulled up and cut the engine.

"Delivery for a Miss . . ." He checked a clipboard from the passenger seat. "Candace Bradford?"

"I'm Candace Bradford."

"Super," he said, jumping out of the van. He grinned at me, and his eyes flashed a pale and sparkling green. I followed him around to the back door where he opened it and reached deep inside. The view of his Levi's from behind made me raise an eyebrow and smile. I grabbed the ends of my ponytail and twirled them. When his torso emerged from the van, he held a large bouquet of white chrysanthemums in a clear vase.

"Wow," I said. "They're huge."

"Lady at the shop says they symbolize truth. What do I know?" He shrugged and winked at me.

My face flushed warm. "I have some cash in the house. If you want to wait here, I can run in and grab a tip for you, and . . ."

"Nah, don't worry about it," he grinned. "Your smile's enough of a tip for me." He jumped back in the van, winked again, and drove off. I put a hand to my cheek and smiled.

I carried the flowers inside and looked for a card. One peeked out from the center of the bouquet. I opened it.

> *Happy Birthday, Kiddles—From the biggest fan of all of your endeavors. I love you, Josie. xo*

I closed my eyes and held the card against my heart. He'd said they symbolized truth, and she'd no doubt known that. I bowed my head and swooned in gratitude. I stuck the card in the center of the bouquet and placed it in the middle of the dining room table. The sun jumped onto the petals at first opportunity. Beautiful.

I walked straight to the phone and dialed her number.

"Y'ello."

"You're an angel, you know that?" I said.

"Kiddles? Aw shucks. The flowers ya' mean? Twas nothin'."

"Nothin' my ass."

"Ha! You're soundin' like me now," she laughed.

"Suppose I am." I walked toward the hallway mirror and stared at my reflection. A little bit of Josie stared back.

"Bill's comin' tonight. You okay with that?"

"Yeah. He called actually; wanted to say happy birthday."

"Well good for him, that old snake-in-the-grass. Guess, ya' just never know about folks, do ya'?"

"No, I guess you don't."

I began walking through each downstairs room of the house with phone in hand. My eyes took in every inch of the place, and I knew I wouldn't change a thing if I owned it.

"You hear from any other birthday wishers?"

"Oh, yeah I did, Fiona, as a matter-of-fact."

"Well, fantabulous. Man, am I glad to hear that."

"I know. We had a little chat, and I'm thrilled," I said. "Oh, and she's pregnant."

"Well, isn't that nice. Good for her and what's-his-name."

"Étienne, Josie. His name's Étienne."

"Yeah—what you said."

I grinned. "What time do you want me there?"

"We'll eat around seven, but you can come any time. You can come now as far as that goes."

"Well, I'm going to write for a few hours, but I'll shoot for around five. I have to drop those papers off at the courier before they close, too."

"Were they divorce papers like you thought?"

"Yeah, and documents from my publisher." I ran my finger along the bookshelf and brought up a tip full of dust.

"Can't be easy for ya', Candace. I'm sorry."

"Don't be. I feel okay about it all, I think. Those envelopes have been sitting here for weeks gnawing at me, and now it's time. It's all good."

"You're sure?"

"I'm sure."

"Well, I'm glad you're fixin' to write again."

"Remember, it's a tell-all. You sure you're okay with that?"

"With you tellin' the truth? Hell yeah. And you can tell any old thing you want when it comes to this girl. I'm done with secrets. In fact, I'll give ya' a few extra juicy details and pre-order a copy for Old Lady Daw across the street. She'd love it."

We both laughed.

"Oh, you're a scream. No doubt about it," I said.

"Yep, certainly been known to do some screamin' in my day. Some *at* Old Lady Daw, as you well remember."

"How could I forget?" The dogs barked in the background as though they remembered too. "Oh and hey. Can I bring anything tonight? Lasagna maybe?"

"Very funny. No, just your ever lovin' self, baby girl."

"Super. I can do that," I said. "Oh, and one more thing." I shuffled into the dining room to sit by my bouquet.

"What's that?"

"Just wanted to add how much I love you . . . Mom."

The sun shone through the window just a hint brighter. Stillness filled the receiver.

"Jesus, Kiddles," she said in a half whisper. "It's your birthday, and I'm gettin' the present? Doesn't hardly seem fair."

"Oh, it's fair," I replied, "more than."

We hung up, and I stared into my flowers. I marveled at the beauty of them in the sunlight: truth illuminated. Somewhere in the distance a crow cawed at the day, and I thought of Lynn.

"Yes, it's time to write the truth, little man," I said to the cat. He made a playful jump out of the room as I rose from the table. I peeked out again at the day. Outside would be perfect.

I walked into the living room and grabbed a cushion from the sofa. I carried it outside and stuffed it into the old rattan chair that graced the farmhouse porch. The big curved arms, sloping back, and its matching side table would make for an inspiring outdoor office. I positioned the chair to look out at the old maple tree in the front, then I went inside for supplies.

I walked to the office to retrieve my laptop. I opened the desk drawer and found a pad of paper for making notes along the way. Then I looked for my favorite pen and found it on the floor by the boxes.

"You playing with my pens again, Mr. Vinny?"

He blinked, arched his back, and rubbed against the leg of the desk chair.

I thought of what else I might need, when the blue Tiffany box caught my eye on the desk. I grabbed it and made my way toward the door.

I walked outside and sat down in the big chair. I arranged my supplies on the little table and opened my laptop. I hit the power button and tilted my face upward. I let the warm breeze massage my face and thought of how the last few patches of snow would soon be gone.

All powered up, I opened a new document on the computer screen. A new start: endless possibilities at my fingertips. It hadn't been long since I'd thought possibilities had come to an end, but not now. Now I had hope.

The Tiffany box beckoned from the table beside me. I opened the lid and reached inside to pull out the three remaining chunks of crystal that had once been my globe. I shook out the box and banished all remaining chards to the wind. They danced in slow motion over the porch railing just as the sun peeked through the branches of the big maple. With the light hitting them just right, they looked like particles of stardust floating their way to the earth below. I smiled.

The cursor blinked on my computer screen. I stared at it while ideas for a title swam through my head.

Do I dare? They said I could call the book whatever I wanted and the first one got called that anyway. Ah, what the hell.

I turned the Tiffany box upside down on the side table and set the pieces of crystal on top of it to catch any blessings of light. Then I placed my fingers in position on the keyboard and began to type:

Total Bullshit
By: Candace Bradford

out loud. I liked it. It worked.

e grabbed my ponytail and tickled the back of my neck with it. I took a long, deep breath and stared down at the crystal chunks as a ray of sunshine found them through the swaying branches of the tree. Only one place to start:

Chapter One

"When your world shatters to pieces, you'll discover what's solid and worth hanging onto."

ACKNOWLEDGEMENTS

People think of writing as a solitary act, and it is for the most part, but creating an actual book is another story (pun intended). For that you need support, and I've had lots of it.

First and foremost, I wouldn't be a writer had it not been for my dear friend, Jenesse Aurandt. Everything I write honors her memory.

I did it, Nessy. I went and wrote it.

I also have to mention the phenomenal Creative Writing Program at Southern Methodist University (SMU) in Dallas, TX. My facilitators, in particular Suzanne Frank and Misa Ramirez, mentored me along my journey and remain a constant source of inspiration.

Thanks also to fellow classmates and writers Claudia Petrocchi, Sarah Lunzer, Joe Strong, Robert Stahl, and Cynthia Stock for their insightful critiques. You have each brought out the best in me, and I admire your work.

For proofreading my manuscript at various stages, and providing valuable feedback, I thank Lois McGuire, Sheila

n Foster McLean, and Elizabeth McGinley. The
ies from a good polish.

As for the cover, I had a vision of what I wanted from the outset. Thanks to the talented Lauren Honcoop for her initial sketch of my idea. And heartfelt gratitude to Rebecca Timmons for far surpassing expectations on the final design. I just love it, and I'm thrilled to have you in my corner.

It would take pages to list the many friends who have cheered me on over the last couple of years. You all know how you are, and please know that I'm grateful. Special thanks, however, go out to Regan Gorman for supporting the project and calling me "Author," to my dog, Toby, for listening to me read my entire manuscript out loud, to Dave Barber for a lifetime of, "You've got to write this shit down," and to Jason Broz for—well—absolutely everything. I'm so blessed.

Sincere thanks to iUniverse for offering an option to writers who want to be independent in their creativity.

And endless gratitude to my parents for a safe place from which to venture. You're my constant, and your love is the foundation of all things that I believe to be possible.